THE BEST OF
JEANI RECTOR

Editor of The Horror Zine

FICTION COLLECTION

"Jeani Rector's stories are fast-paced and clever. They grab you quickly, pull you into the deep end of the story telling pool and drown you with delight. You need this." – Joe R. Lansdale, nine-time Bram Stoker award-winner

THE
HORROR ZINE

Published by The Horror Zine Books

Since 2009, The Horror Zine has published exceptional horror fiction by emerging talent and today's leading authors. The Editor is Jeani Rector, whose own short stories are now collected for this book.

The Horror Zine's mission is to provide a venue in which writers, poets, and artists can exhibit their work. The Horror Zine is an e-zine, spotlighting the works of talented people, and displaying their deliciously dark delights for the world to enjoy.

The Horror Zine is accepting submissions of fiction, poetry and art from morbidly creative people.

Visit The Horror Zine at
www.thehorrorzine.com

For this book:
Edited by Dean Wild
Bat art by Riaan Marias
Kindle and cover design by Bruce Memblatt

The Best of
Jeani Rector

A Fiction Collection written by
the editor of The Horror Zine

Published by The Horror Zine Books
Copyright 2015

TABLE OF CONTENTS

Maggots
The Bus Station
Reanimated
Flytrap
The Golem
The Janitor
Love Story
Cold Spot
Apartment 17
Flight 529
The Dead Man
The Famous Film Star
Horrorscope
The Boogeyman
Urban Legend
Under the House
A Case of Lycanthropy
The Freegans
Ghoul
The Hole
Spiders
A Teenage Ghost Story

MAGGOTS

"I'm here to tell you about maggots."

The man behind the podium never seemed to stand still. He shifted his weight from foot to foot and sometimes he took a step or two, moving forward and back. His hands waved through the air to give his story emphasis. His manner was animated, alive; which was ironic since this man's profession was the analysis of insect activity after death.

He looked into the auditorium at the university students that comprised his audience. The Forensic Entomologist was a guest speaker and the subject was forensic science.

"Since our topic today is the very important task of establishing time of death of a crime victim," the man began, "I want to give you an overview of the cadaver as an ecological system. For this talk, I will outline the details of an actual case upon which I recently worked."

He started the story. "The flies were the first to find the body."

He noticed with satisfaction that many students leaned forward in their seats. Always grab them right from the start, the Forensic Entomologist thought to himself.

"Picture this in your minds," the man continued. "Just minutes ago, the body had been dumped in the forest."

Now she lay, still and silent, on top of brown, decaying leaves. The summer sun was just beginning to rise, but its light did not yet penetrate the forest canopy overhead. The dead woman was hidden in the shadows.

His eyes traveled over the students who were watching him intently in return. "No one had discovered the body yet. No one knew she was dead, except for the killer. But the flies knew."

The Forensic Entomologist heard a collective gasp from the audience, and he paused for effect. Taking a leisurely step or two away from the podium then back, he faced the students once again.

"They were blow flies," he told his audience, "and these insects located the dead woman within ten minutes after the body was discarded."

Landing upon natural openings on the body, the flies immediately began laying eggs in the nose, mouth, and eyes. In another hour, the flesh flies arrived.

"Now, flesh flies," he told them, "bear live maggots."

Within eight hours, the body was stiffening with rigor mortis. Within thirteen hours, the entire corpse was rigid. The dead woman lay on her back, facing the sun, which now shined overhead. Half-open eyes revealed clouded corneas that stared without sight through the bushes.

The blood, no longer circulated by the heart, began to settle on the underside of the body, which created a purpling of the skin called livor mortis. The result from livor mortis was that the back, buttocks, and the back of the legs became permanently darkened once the blood clotted in the tissues. The temperature of the body lowered, cooling at a rate of one and one-half degrees Fahrenheit per hour.

Within twenty hours, the blow fly eggs began to hatch. The blow fly maggots, in the first larval life stage called instar, began to consume the moist, soft tissues of the body. These maggots in turn attracted ants, beetles, and small wasps that preyed upon the maggots, not the flesh of the victim.

The Forensic Entomologist stopped speaking because there was movement in the audience. He watched with interest as a few students, ashen-faced, made their way towards the exits. When those students left, the man faced those who remained.

"Within twenty-four hours," he continued without acknowledging that anyone had left, "the body became bloated with gas as bacteria became active."

Within thirty-six hours, the body was once again limp and pliable as rigor mortis reversed and the stiffening of the limbs disappeared. The gasses escaped and the bloating withdrew. The fly maggots molted into the second instar stage at fifty hours. The body stopped cooling because the frenzied activity of the insects heated up the corpse once again.

The fluids from the victim were seeping into the soil beneath, and there would be no re-growth of vegetation in that spot for over a year. The body began to dry out and hide beetles and millipedes began to arrive.

Within one hundred and fifty hours, the third instar maggots ceased to feed on the flesh of the victim. They began leaving the body, crawling in squirming white masses across the leaves on the forest floor. They would find a secluded, dry spot away from the body to pupate.

By the seventh day that the body was lying on the ground in the summer heat, the dead woman was decomposed and appeared unidentifiable.

"When this woman was found, nobody could determine the time of her death. But the insects could."

A hand rose from the audience. "Dr. Mason," a young student said, "I'm Sheila Watts, and I've read your book. You've explained that insects are very predictable in their behavior. Could you talk about that?"

"I could, if we weren't out of time," Dr. Mason said. "Don't worry, I've been invited back to speak here next week. I'll finish up then. See you all next week, and now, I'll turn the class back to your professor."

Mason packed up his paperwork and walked out of the classroom. But he hadn't gotten very far down the hallway when he heard his name called. Turning around, Mason saw the person calling his name was the same student that had asked about insect predictability.

"Class is dismissed," Mason said with a smile.

"I know," Sheila said. "But I really want to know more. Is there any way I could come and see your lab?"

"My time is limited," he told her.

"Here, take my number and call me when you have time. Any time. I'll come to your lab."

Mason took the card, but made no promises. "We'll see," he said. But he was thinking, *There is no way I am going to invite a woman to be alone with me in my lab. That could be suicide.*

And so he left the college, and made his way home alone.

On the drive back to his house, Mason remembered things he had done in his past. And that night he had a nightmare, the same one he had been having a lot, as of late.

He dreamed of maggots; squirming through dead flesh, and they were eating their way into a bloated state and then molting. After the molting, the maggots were larger, and able to consume even more of the putrid flesh of the cadaver. The remaining flesh of the body sank into the skeleton and even those remains began to disappear into the digestive system of the white worms.

Always at this point Mason would awaken, the sweat streaming down his forehead and soaking his underarms. He didn't know why he had the same dream over and over again; and understood even less why he should feel a sense of dread when he woke from it. Insects, in all of their stages, were creatures that he respected and even admired. Why should he dream nightmares about them?

Flies and their offspring were the recyclers of the world. Without flies, the world would be overcome with rotting corpses and animal excrement. Flies were a necessary mechanism of the world's ecosystem. Simply put, flies cleaned up messes in every stage of their development, but especially when they were maggots.

He stopped thinking about the dream. Instead, he lay in bed, alone, wishing for a partner. He felt horny, and was restless in his bed until he gave in and got himself off. He didn't like doing that; masturbation was messy. But he had made a vow to stay away from women and on this morning he needed some sort of relief.

So Mason spent his day writing research papers and keeping his mind on his work; but by the time the next morning arrived, he felt the same urges as he had felt the morning before.

What was the answer?

His thought drifted to the pretty young college student whose business card he knew he still had in his wallet. Should he call her?

Against his better judgment, Mason's barrier broke. He knew it was crazy to have an attraction for a college student half his age because it could land him in big trouble.

And then he thought, *I may be a PhD., but I'm also a man. A very human man. Lord help me, because I am about to commit professional suicide. I am going to call Sheila Watts and invite her into my lab.*

He decided he would keep it on the up-and-up.

No you won't, a voice whispered in his head.

Yes I will, he stubbornly told the voice.

And so he rifled through his wallet until he found Sheila Watts' phone number, and called her. As Mason expected, she was happy to hear from him and delighted to come to his lab. Today.

16

He would keep it professional; they would discuss insects, and he would have a woman's company, no sex involved. To hear a feminine voice, to be able to see her youthful face, and to appreciate a curvy figure would have to be enough.

Mason knew that the last time he had invited a young woman into his lab, things had become complicated, and he had almost gotten in trouble. But he also believed that he had learned from his mistake, and would not repeat it ever again.

He opened the door to his lab and greeted the young college student inside. He felt buoyant; confident.

"Would you like to sit down?" he asked, drawing them both a chair. "What exactly is it you want to know about insects?"

When she sat, Sheila said, "I'm doing a college paper on insect behavior. I am particularly interested in maggots."

"Wonderful!"

She looked at him oddly. "You're the first person that I've ever known to call fly larvae wonderful."

"They are valuable creatures in so many ways," Mason said. "Unfortunately their reputation does not live up to their usefulness in the world."

He lifted a small, wide-mouth screw-top glass bottle from the bench and handed it to Sheila. It looked like it could hold about a pint, and inside were ten hard cocoons that resembled small footballs.

"I found these near a dead body that was discarded in the woods. I figured that these flies took at least six days to go through the entire larval development stages upon the body itself, then from one more day in this pupae state away from the body," Mason said. "So from the fly evidence, I knew that the corpse had been lying on the ground for seven days."

"That's unbelievable," Sheila appeared amazed.

"Not unbelievable. That's predictable," he said. "You'd be surprised at how accurate forensic entomology can be."

"But what about before maggots pupate?" Sheila asked. "What do maggots do to a dead body?"

"I'll tell you," Mason said. He wanted to get some sort of reaction out of Sheila, so he continued, "The cone shaped fly larva uses its specialized mouth parts, including hooks, to pierce the skin. Then it uses saliva to digest flesh and to suck up the liquid, just as

17

adult flies do. When the skin decays and ruptures and body fluids permeate the surrounding area, maggots will finally move off the body. The end result to a dead body left outside is not much."

"How do you know all of this?" she asked.

"I'm an expert," he told her. "I've seen it happen."

While he was talking to her, Mason watched her expression carefully. He could tell she was impressed by his knowledge, and obviously admired him. Was she sexually attracted to him as well?

Don't find out, the inner voice whispered. *Leave her alone.*

I can't leave her alone, Mason's mind answered the voice. *I have to have her.*

"I'll bet you're a quick study," he said. "I could mentor you."

"You would do that?"

He studied her, deciding. He was encouraged to see that she appeared eager and hopeful. Her eyes were big and her expression was wistful, wanting…wanting what? Wanting him?

But suddenly Sheila changed the subject. "What's behind that door over there, next to the insect cabinet?"

He felt irritated. It had been going so well. "Just one of my experiments."

"Oh!" she exclaimed. "Can I see?"

"No," he said bluntly.

She looked deflated. "Oh."

Now Mason felt angry. Obviously she wasn't what he had hoped for. He decided he had no time for her. "I think you should leave now."

She looked at him in surprise. "Just like that? Wait, I thought you said you wanted to mentor me."

"I've decided you aren't worthy. Now please leave my lab."

Suddenly Sheila looked just as angry as he was. "How dare you call me not worthy? Who the hell do you think you are?"

And she jumped up from her chair, and ran to the door by the cabinet. Before Mason could react, Sheila grabbed the door handle and pulled it open. Mason finally rose from his chair, but too late to stop her. She swung the door wide and looked past the door into the next room.

And just as suddenly, she turned back around to face Mason with a look of horror on her face.

"You should have left when you had the chance," Mason told her.

"I can leave now. Please," Sheila said. "I won't tell anybody, I swear. Please, just let me leave. I won't tell a soul."

"I already explained that you had your chance. Now you have no chance."

Sheila made a run for the front door, a burst for escape, but Mason caught her as she went by. She struggled in his grasp, fighting and kicking. She started to scream and he shoved his hand roughly over her mouth to silence her. She bit his hand and he cursed with pain, removing his hand. She started to scream again and he started to punch her face to shut her up.

But she was a wildcat, and Mason became aware of the difference in their years. Sheila was young and strong, and he was middle aged and winded from cigarette abuse. He couldn't seem to keep his grip on her; she was almost elastic, and kept slipping out of his grasp.

Suddenly she pulled away from him. In desperation, Mason tried to grab her once again. He only managed to get a handful of her shirt, and he could hear the material rip as she escaped.

He lunged after her, but she was quick, so quick…she reached the front door just out of his reach. He knew when she pulled it open, he had lost her.

And so he stopped, standing in place; watching her run down the walkway outside to her freedom.

He was resigned to his fate. He knew she would go to the police and now it would be all over for him.

But he wanted one more look at his maggots first.

Mason walked across the floor to the door next to the cabinet that Sheila had left wide open. He stood there, gazing fondly into the next room.

He loved flies, in all of their stages. But he especially favored the maggots. Maggots did such good for the world. He had been working with them for a long time, and had become very fond of them. It was almost as if they had become pets to him.

And so he stood in the inside doorway, watching the white worms squirm in and out of the body of the last woman he had let into his lab. She, too, had been alone with him in the lab, and now she resided in a bathtub, being devoured; being recycled. She was food for his maggots.

His maggots had to eat, didn't they?

But now it was all over. He knew what he had to do next.

And so Mason went to one of the drawers in the cabinet, the only drawer that was not labeled with an insect genus. Inside that drawer was a pistol.

He carefully tucked the pistol into a coat pocket, then carried the coat out to his car. He would drive out to the country, hide his car, then walk as far into the woods as he could.

Then, when he found an elusive area where he knew he wouldn't be discovered for a long, long time, he would shoot himself.

And he would become food for his beloved maggots.

THE BUS STATION

I'm not going to tell you who I am.

At least, not until you read my story first.

Because if I tell you who I am up front, you will put this paper down and walk away in disgust. You won't give me a chance to tell my side of the story at all.

But bear with me, because I promise: if you read this account, all of it, then I will tell you who I am at the end.

And maybe by the time I am done telling you my side of the story, you will believe me.

I woke up because I felt a gun poking into my ribs. Confused with sleep, I was bewildered as to where I was. Then I remembered: I had been hitchhiking and this was my ride, and now the driver of the old Pontiac was sticking a gun into my ribs.

"What're you doing?" I asked.

"Whaddya think," he said, "gimme your money."

I looked at him. The original unease that I had felt getting into this car was proving to be right. The driver seemed hyped up; his dirty hair was matted with sweat and his eyes almost glowed from either drugs or insanity.

And I instinctively knew: the minute I handed over my money, he would kill me.

Without thinking, I took advantage of the driver's attention to the road and pushed open the passenger door. "Hey!" the driver cried, but the surprise caused his reactions to slow.

I didn't know how fast we were going, but I judged it couldn't have been too bad since it was a country road. I had no other option. I curled into a ball and launched myself out the car door.

The flight through the air seemed endless, but I knew it was probably just seconds. The ground came up at me hard, and I rolled, jarring and scraping until I finally came to a stop. The old Pontiac gunned it and barreled away into the night, leaving nothing behind except me and the smell of exhaust.

I lay on the old country road in the dark, groaning, and moved slowly to check if anything was broken or otherwise badly injured. I gave thanks that I was a young man, sturdy and strong, and realized that I would survive this without more than a few scrapes and bruises.

But all of my belongings were now headed off into the night inside the crazy-man's Pontiac. My backpack held all my clothes, and that was long gone in a cloud of exhaust fumes. Fortunately, my money and ID were in my wallet, safely tucked into my back pocket.

And then there was the other issue. It was the middle of the night and I had no idea where I was.

I picked myself off the ground and dusted off my jeans. Then I took in my surroundings. Apparently the crazy driver had taken a detour while I was asleep in his car. Which made sense to me: if you plan to murder someone, you want to do it in a secluded location. I ought to know. Wait, I don't want to give you any clues as to my identity yet.

Anyway, I knew I was lost, but there was nothing else to do but walk. And so I did; I walked down the lonely country road in the night.

The full moon vanished and reappeared as clouds crept across its surface, creating shadows that danced in the night. The dampness in the misty air caused dew to sparkle on the roadside weeds, and the trees overhanging the road seemed to be ever so slightly moving and rustling in the cool, soft breeze. Crickets chirped merrily away, and a screech owl shrilled as it hunted in the darkness. The sounds of toads and frogs calling from either side of the road created a musical opus, and every so often I could hear rustling sounds within the roadside bushes, as though creatures of the night were stealthily traveling through them.

I kept walking, putting one foot in front of the other, not sure if I was going in the right direction; I wasn't even positive that there *was* any right direction. It was unnerving to be so incredibly lost. And what if the crazy Pontiac man came back?

Relax, I told myself. *This is America, and sooner or later there will be a town. This isn't some Australian outback wilderness where I'd starve to death before anyone found me.*

But in the meantime, my surroundings looked like something out of a horror movie. The mist swirled up from the ground, the moon

22

was full, and it was easy to imagine Bela Lugosi creeping through the vapor with his cape half covering his face. Long, twisted tree limbs seemed everywhere, and the full moon's light shined upon those trees, creating shadows that were stripes across the road in front of me.

Suddenly I felt a hand grasp my shoulder from behind.

I screamed and dropped to my knees in fright, shutting my eyes. My heart was pounding against my ribcage and I just knew it was the crazy Pontiac man, back to kill me.

"Don't yell!" a woman's voice said. "I'm not going to hurt you."

I opened my eyes and looked up to see an attractive, slender girl who was dressed like a hippie; she was very retro from the 1970s. She looked to be in her early twenties.

I got off the ground, but I could barely speak, because I was still trembling so violently from the scare. I managed to get out, "You surprised me. What the hell are you doing out here in the middle of nowhere?"

"Well," said the girl, "I could be asking you the same thing."

Despite myself, I grinned. It was true. It wasn't normal for *anybody* to be in the middle of nowhere at night. "I'm lost," I told her.

"Me too," she said.

Amazed that two people could be lost on the same country road, I asked her, "How come you're lost? I was hitchhiking and this is where I got let out." I didn't want to go into details. I figured telling her about the crazy Pontiac man would frighten her.

"I'm lost because I haven't been found yet," she said.

"What?"

"My body. I'm over there." She jerked a thumb to the side of the road. "In the bushes. But you know about women like me, don't you? Want to see what we look like after we've been discarded?"

I couldn't have heard her right. My jaw was open because I was so dumbfounded. Was she another crazy person?

Crazy! Everyone was crazy. What was it about this particular night that brought out the insane?

And then suddenly the young woman began to shake and tremble violently, and then her eyes rolled upwards until they appeared completely white. The skin on her face began to slide, falling off her face towards her chin. Her hair began to fall out as her scalp

23

disintegrated into patches, allowing the calcified skull to shine through in the moonlight. The orbs of her eyes shriveled, dried up and fell back into her head, and her nose began to crumble. Her teeth gleamed as the surrounding lips disappeared.

The hideous transformation continued, and spread to the body. She fell to the ground, and from out of the bushes leaped a coyote, who grabbed the young woman's arm in his mouth. The coyote yanked the arm free and instantly disappeared with it, once again swallowed by the foliage next to the road.

The outdated clothes on the body began to seem too large as the flesh shrunk away to leave only the structure of the skeleton. The heap of bones lay upon the road, and the clothes upon them began to visibly fray and tear. A strong breeze suddenly blew, picking up the lighter, smaller bones of the remaining hand and the feet and scattering them into the bushes.

The whole thing took only seconds, almost too fast for me to react. I threw my hands up to cover my eyes. "No!" I screamed to the night. "This isn't happening! Please, make it go away!"

I took my hands away from my face and looked.

Nothing.

There was no dead girl decaying in front of me, or decaying anywhere else. There was no girl. There never had been.

For the second time that night I sank to my knees on the road. I was horrified and exhausted. Why had I imagined such a terrible thing? Could it be my conscience haunting me?

But if it had been only my conscience, then why had it seemed so real? It had seemed so horribly real. I was baffled and still terrified.

I stayed on my knees for a while, trying to collect my wits. And when I finally stopped trembling, and my legs stopped feeling rubbery, I decided to deny the incident.

It wasn't real, I thought. *I'm tired and lost and my mind played tricks on me. Maybe I was even sleepwalking. Yeah, that's it. I hear that people sleepwalk all the time.*

And so I stood back up and started walking again.

Eventually the dirt road opened into one that was paved; it was no less lonely, but at least it appeared more civilized.

After walking for about an hour, I came upon a sign that read *Greyhound Station, Quarter Mile Ahead.* I was never so glad to see anything in my life as I was to see that sign.

24

Reaching the Greyhound Station, I saw what a small building it was. But of course it would be; this was the country where no one seemed to live, and frankly I was surprised that there would be any bus station at all, way out here in the sticks.

Pushing the front door open, I walked inside. It was a very small station, the smallest I had ever seen. Blue plastic chairs were bolted to a horizontal metal bar. The linoleum floor was faded, scratched, and dirty. The walls were painted a dull gray-green, and one wall held a rack of travel brochures.

I stepped up to the clerk's cage to buy a bus ticket, only to find it empty. A paper sign said *Be Back At* and underneath it showed a clock saying *Ten O'Clock*. I looked at my watch. It was already quarter after ten.

Turning around, I saw a young woman sitting on one of the plastic chairs. At first I was startled, thinking she was the dead girl on the country road, but then I shook my head. I would not think about the other girl; it had been a hallucination caused by exhaustion and fear. I was not going crazy, no, I was not crazy. This girl in the bus station was real.

I figured her to be a traveler just like me, because she had a dirty backpack on the floor in front of her. She had long dark hair and wore a fuzzy-looking jacket, but I knew from the tight jeans showing off her long legs that the jacket was hiding a magnificent figure underneath.

Was she all alone? There seemed to be no one else in the entire station.

Oh hell, after all that had already happened, what was one more risk?

I strode over to her and asked her if I could sit next to her. She looked around at all the empty chairs in the Greyhound station, then looked back to me. "Why?" she asked.

I sighed. "I'm tired, and I could sure use the company."

She giggled. "Yeah, look at this dump. It's not exactly hopping. What a way to spend Halloween, huh?"

I took that as an invitation and sat next to her. And then what she said hit me. Maybe that could explain the weird events of this evening. "It's Halloween?"

"It sure is. You didn't know? Where've you been all month?"

25

I didn't want to tell her where I'd been, so I changed the subject. "Where're you headed?"

"Chester Depot," she said. "Population seven hundred. My name's Mandy, by the way."

"I'm Floyd," I told her, and shook her hand. It felt so soft and inviting.

"Floyd? That's kind of an old fashioned name, ain't it? I mean, even for Vermont's standards."

"Tell it to my Ma."

"So, where're *you* headed?"

"Wherever the next bus is going."

"Well, ain't you the mysterious one? The next bus means you'll be riding with me to Chester Depot," she said. "Happy Halloween on a Greyhound. Hey, have you heard the Halloween ghost story about this bus station?"

"Nope. Remember, I'm the one who didn't even know it was Halloween," I reminded her.

She used a hand to brush the hair from her face, and I was stimulated. Her face was almost pretty, with unusual gray-green eyes. I'd let Mandy talk about anything she wanted if it would give me a chance to get close to her.

"Well," she began, "a few years ago, there was this girl waiting for a bus, just like me. Then *wham!* Some stranger walks in and blows her away with a shotgun. Now the dead girl haunts this bus station once a year, every Halloween night."

"Imagine spending an eternity out in the sticks, stuck here in this Greyhound bus station," I said.

"You don't believe me," Mandy accused.

"Well," I said, "Tonight is Halloween, and I don't see any ghosts, do you? Besides, I've heard scarier stories than that one."

"So tell me a scarier story."

"How about a guy that travels around the country killing people?"

She scoffed. "You ain't real original, are ya? I can read that kind of stuff in any newspaper."

Ignoring that, I looked around the empty bus station. "I have to admit, it's kind of spooky here. Good thing you have me to protect you from the so-called Halloween ghost."

"Yeah, but who's gonna protect me from *you?*"

I swung my gaze away from the room to study her face. Did she know? Of course not. This was a very trusting girl. My kind of girl.

She started laughing at her own joke, and I relaxed. "I'm harmless," I told her, hoping she would believe me.

Her gaze drifted, and then she turned around to look at the clerk's cage, still empty. "I wonder when that clerk is supposed to come back so I can buy my bus ticket."

"It does seem like a pretty long break, doesn't it?" I agreed.

We became quiet as an uncomfortable silence settled between us. Then Mandy said, "Did you hear that?"

I looked at her. "What?"

"I don't know," she said, "it sounded like something outside the station. Maybe the clerk is coming back."

The front door burst open, and Mandy screamed with surprise. A man stepped inside, carrying a shotgun. Raising the gun, he shouted "Trick or treat!"

I had an eerie feeling of being caught in slow motion, like someone had slowed down some sort of recording device. Seconds seemed to stretch like rubber bands. I had an out-of-body sensation like I was a third party watching from afar. It seemed so unreal.

I knew who he was.

And I knew I was about to die.

The man with the shotgun seemed hyped up; his dirty hair was matted with sweat and his eyes almost glowed from either drugs or insanity. I recognized him to be the crazy driver of the Pontiac.

He had tried to kill me once, and I had gotten away. Now he was back to finish the job.

The crazy man advanced, aiming the shotgun.

"Why are you doing this?" Mandy screamed at him, but I held my tongue. I knew there was no reasoning with a madman.

"It's Halloween and you're supposed to give me candy," the man said as he continued to approach us. "That's my treat. Got no candy, and I'll give you a trick. Now gimme your wallets. Throw 'em down on the floor."

"The Greyhound clerk is coming back," Mandy tried.

"No he ain't," the crazy Pontiac man with the shotgun said. I didn't ask how he knew no one was coming. Instead I thought to myself, *So that's why the clerk never came back.*

Mandy dug into her purse for her wallet and I retrieved mine. We both threw the wallets on the floor. I was watching the crazy man's eyes, and I understood that he would hurt us after all; yes indeed, wallets or no wallets.

You need a lonely spot to murder people, I thought. *With the clerk dead, there is no spot lonelier than a tiny bus station in the middle of nowhere.*

The man cocked the shotgun.

It was now or never. My mind screamed *NOW!*

I rushed at the crazy man, throwing myself, aiming for his legs, wanting to knock him down. Fear gave me power and adrenaline gave me strength. The crazy man's utter surprise made him hesitate and that provided me with an advantage.

I wrestled him to the floor. He still grasped the shotgun and I knew my only hope was to take it from him. Sweat poured into my eyes and I tried to blink it away. I couldn't let my vision blur. This was life or death.

I tried to hold the man down with one hand while at the same time, I reached for the gun with the other hand. He writhed, twisted and lurched underneath me like a bucking bronco. I couldn't get the gun; he kept jerking it away. I couldn't reach it…wait, where was Mandy?

"Mandy!" I yelled. "Help me! Get his gun!"

I could hear her coming. I couldn't look at her because I was still fighting the crazy man on the floor. But my heart leapt with hope…with Mandy, it would be two against one!

And then the shotgun went off. BLAM!

The sound was deafening and my ears were ringing. *Thank god,* I thought, *it wasn't me. I wasn't shot!*

An extra burst of energy seemed to come from nowhere. Perhaps it was the gun going off; perhaps it was the idea that I had come so close to dying that I had nothing left to lose.

I don't know where my strength came from, but it did. I shoved the crazy man against the floor, and wrenched his gun arm so hard that I could feel something inside it snap. The man roared with pain and I used that to my advantage.

I grabbed the shotgun.

Jumping to my feet, I swung the gun around and cocked it. I didn't think twice; didn't hesitate for even a moment. Aiming the gun at the crazy man's face, I pulled the trigger. Both barrels blasted and the man's face exploded into fragments, splattering everywhere.

I stood above the desecrated man for a moment, studying the damage, morbidly fascinated at the after effects of a shotgun blast to the face.

"Trick or treat," I said to the dead man. "It's your trick and my treat."

And then I remembered Mandy.

I turned around. She was lying on the floor, her arms and legs crossed in an unnatural position. Her face was unrecognizable. Blood poured from her head, creating maroon puddles upon the floor.

So the crazy man's shot had been an accurate one.

I sighed sadly. Now there would be two ghosts to haunt this bus station every Halloween night. Three, if Mandy's ghost story was correct.

Then I picked up my wallet from the floor of the bus station, and put it back into my pocket. Stepping over the two bodies, I headed for the door. Maybe I would have better luck with hitchhiking than I did trying to catch a Greyhound bus in the middle of nowhere on a Halloween night.

For a moment I questioned myself. Shouldn't I be feeling more emotion after everything that had happened inside that bus station? Instead I felt numb. Maybe I was in shock.

Or maybe I was just glad that the crazy Pontiac man was dead and unable to threaten me anymore.

The girl out there on the country road was dead too, a voice spoke in my mind, *and she came back. Hadn't she looked familiar?*

"No!" I shouted out loud. "There was no girl on any road! The only dead girl is Mandy! And she's real! And the crazy Pontiac guy is real too! And he's just as dead as Mandy is! And none of it is my fault!"

With that, I started walking back to the road, feeling glad it was paved. If the road was paved, that meant civilization was close by.

I wondered about the time. Checking my watch, I saw it was quarter to twelve. I felt a wave of superstition pass through me; it couldn't be a good thing to be lost at midnight on Halloween night.

I began walking quickly in the direction away from the Greyhound Station. The darkness had become dense because clouds were covering the full moon. The wind was mild, but an occasional gust suggested a pending storm. The air was unseasonably warm for October, a drastic change from the previous week, but it was humid and thick with moisture.

A rumbling sounded in the distance, reverberating softly across the land. I could smell rain, and I hoped it wouldn't arrive until I got to wherever I was going.

I noticed something in the road ahead. It looked like a dead deer on the road. *Somebody must have hit it with a car,* I thought. *Maybe the crazy Pontiac guy hit the deer. No, he's dead.*

Well, whatever it was, I would be seeing it up close soon. I rapidly approached the thing, and a feeling of apprehension crept up on me. The hairs on my arms stood up in their follicles, and I felt a tingling in my fingers.

And then I was close enough to see what it really was. This was no deer.

A man was lying in the middle of the road, wearing a Greyhound uniform. Suddenly he sat up and said, "You want to buy a bus ticket to Chester Depot? That'll be forty dollars one way."

I could feel my eyes bulging. I threw my hands over my face and screamed. *No!* This was *not* happening! The crazy Pontiac man had killed the clerk! The clerk was somewhere back at the station! No one was here on the road but me; no one had *ever* been here on the road but me!

Reluctantly I took my hands away from my eyes. The road was empty. There was no Greyhound clerk lying there, and there never had been. Was I going crazy? Of course not. I was just feeling overwhelmed. I had just witnessed shotgun killings back at the bus station. That would be enough to shake anyone up. And I was feeling irrationally superstitious on a Halloween night. I just needed a good night's sleep.

Probably Mandy's Halloween ghost story set my imagination off, I thought. *Soon, if I keep walking, I'll find a town and then all of this will be over.*

And when I finally found a town, I checked myself into the cheapest motel I could find. I used my real ID. And I slept a deep, dreamless sleep.

Until the next morning when the cops banged on my motel door.

So now you see what went down on that Halloween night. I didn't kill anyone. At least, not that night.

The prison psychiatrist is telling me otherwise. He is telling me that there was no crazy man driving a Pontiac. He is telling me that I manifested the phantom "crazy man" as a delusion because I was unable to accept that it was me who murdered the clerk and the girl in the bus station. He is telling me that I invented a scapegoat to take the blame because I could not face my own wrongdoings.

When I went to court, they had all this evidence against me for Mandy's death. The clerk's death too. It was truly baffling. I just cannot figure out why they never found the crazy Pontiac man's body there in the bus station.

Okay. Now I am ready to tell you who I am.

I wanted to tell my story first, because I want you to understand it all.

You see, I cannot believe that I would have felt any guilt over killing a clerk or a girl at a Greyhound bus station. Let me tell you why.

My name is Floyd Tapson. Yes, *that* Floyd Tapson. I've murdered three girls in three different states, before I ever met Mandy. I was a traveler, and sometimes the urge would become so overwhelming…it would build and build until I felt compelled to act it out.

So, shouldn't I know who I killed and who I didn't? God, it's so confusing. The cops say it was my shotgun that Halloween night. What's so ironic is that I'm in prison for two people I *didn't* kill, and nobody knows about the three that I *did* kill.

Either way, I'll bet there is a ghost or two haunting a little, out-of-the-way Greyhound Bus station in Vermont. If you ever find yourself there on a Halloween night, can you write me a letter and let me know if one of the ghosts is the Pontiac man? Then finally they'll believe me that there really *was* a crazy Pontiac man.

REANIMATED

Zombies had been a mainstay in popular fiction for years, even decades, before they became a reality.

And when the zombies actually appeared, it was discovered that all the books and films had gotten it wrong.

A college student raised his hand. "How did this happen?"

"That's for the scientists to figure out," the professor answered as he strolled back and forth in front of the class.

"Do you think it was something that the military did?" another student asked.

The professor stopped pacing and faced the class. "Look, this is not a science class and we are not a military school. This is a sociology class. That means we are having a discussion about how to fit these reanimated people back into society. There are millions of them."

The professor paused, then continued, "Let's look at the socio-economic impact. How will the governments around the world find jobs for these reanimated people? Jobs are hard to find even for those who have never died. Will the undead require financial assistance until they are situated? And who will pay for that? What about all the elderly, whose pensions stopped when their death certificates were filed?"

He waited for his words to sink in. Then he added, "Where will all these undead be housed, and are they technically refugees? And if they are refugees, from what? Not from dangerous dictators, but from death itself. For that, there is no precedent to give us information about the best way to proceed. But these are people nonetheless, and they have rights as citizens…of a sort."

A third student raised her hand. "Can't most be taken in by their families?"

The professor answered, "One would think so. But emotionally…well, a lot of taxpayer dollars will have to go towards psychologists. After all, the shock of a dead family member suddenly showing up on the doorstep can be a deeply traumatizing event for the living."

The first student raised his hand once again. "What if a zombie, uh, well—"

"We don't call them zombies," the professor interrupted.

The student continued, "What if a *reanimated* person comes home to find her husband had remarried? Or what if another had been in a nursing home with Alzheimer's before death and that person's children thought they were finally getting out of debt from paying for it?"

"Ah," the professor said. "Now you are finally sounding like a sociology class."

Janet was watching CNN when the story broke.

At first it didn't register; it was too incredible. Too impossible.

And then her thoughts rushed to Jeffrey, and her hand went to her heart. Could CNN be talking about Jeffrey? Was it indeed possible?

She rushed for her cell phone. But for the first time ever, a recorded message came on saying that "all circuits were busy."

So she sat back down on the couch, stunned and bewildered. What did this mean?

She thought of Jeffrey. They had been married less than a year when he suddenly became sick. Trips to the doctor and eventually to the emergency room left them without a diagnosis. How could doctors not know what killed him in this day and age of medical advancements?

The funeral had been a heartbreaking affair. Jeffrey's wealthy father wouldn't acknowledge her. His mother had a few choice words for her before she too turned her back. They hadn't wanted their promising son to marry a nobody.

She was indeed a nobody. Janet had come from the poverty of the Ozarks. But she was pretty, even beautiful, and she knew it. When she was old enough for boys to notice her, and notice her they did, she decided she would marry up to someone who looked like a prince and had money like one, too.

And that prince was Jeffrey Hall. Janet had been so happy when he proposed. It was a dream come true. Everything about the marriage was just as she had hoped.

Now she was a widow, a very young widow, and Jeffrey was gone. Or was he?

She needed to find out. She reached for her cell phone again.

The local high school gymnasium was temporarily converted into a Reanimated Center. Police were stationed everywhere to control the milling and anxious people in the crowd who were desperate to see their loved ones.

Janet attempted to push her way through the masses, but a policeman ordered her to go to the back of the line. Intimidated, she complied.

And there she found Jeffrey's parents.

"Janet," Mrs. Hall said, "how nice to see you."

Janet was dumbfounded. "Nice?" she echoed. "Since when did you think it was ever nice to see me?"

"Now listen," Mr. Hall came straight to the point. "You have legal precedent over us in this situation. As Jeffrey's wife, you have more say about what becomes of him than his mere parents, the ones who brought him into the world, and the ones who had him for twenty-four years compared to your one."

So that's it, Janet thought. *For once, they need me.*

"Look," Mr. Hall continued, "We can stop our legal proceedings against your taking Jeffrey's estate. All we ask is that you let us take him home instead of you. Do that and we'll leave you alone."

Janet realized she could finally stand up for herself against these two. "Estate? There is no estate for a person who is not deceased. I am Jeffrey's wife and everything is community property once again. And as his wife, I am taking him to my home. Because my home is Jeffrey's home."

"Let me see my son, please," the mother pleaded. Janet tried not to notice Mrs. Hall's tears, because it was disconcerting to see them in a woman so hard.

Janet told her, "I'm not completely heartless. But I don't know what to expect. If Jeffrey is still himself and seems okay, then let me get him settled first and then decide what to do."

They stepped aside, seeming to accept her decision, and Janet began to slowly inch her way in the line toward the gymnasium door. She left the Halls behind, moving steadily towards her husband.

When she finally entered the large gym, she found it just as crowded inside as outside. More police were sorting people and taking identification. When it was her turn, the police officer was young, dark skinned and dark haired. He took her ID, peered at it, and then looked at her strangely.

"You're Janet Hall?" he asked. "You're not what I imagined."

She was used to that. After all, the death of a wealthy person usually made the news when it happened. Jeffrey's death had been displayed on television and in the newspapers. It made sense that the public would wonder what his wife was like.

"Is there a problem?" she asked.

"No," he said, still looking at her oddly. "Proceed to the left."

A social worker met her in front of a curtained section of the gym.

"Did you receive the preparation package? You did? Good. Proceed inside."

The curtain was held open and Janet entered. The light was dimmer inside, but her eyes adjusted immediately and she saw Jeffrey.

He was seated in a metal folding chair. He looked pale and his hair seemed longer. He wasn't wearing his burial suit and tie but instead was dressed in casual clothes which had probably been provided by the social workers. It seemed so odd to see Jeffrey in jeans, because he never wore them.

She ran to his side, and crouched on the ground to be at eye level with him. "Jeffrey! How are you?"

She didn't know if it was proper to ask a dead person how he was, but then she told herself that he was not dead. He was reanimated.

"I want to go home," he said.

"That's fine, Jeffrey, we can do that."

<< — >>

She held his hand as she led him up the steps to their very large home. At over four thousand square feet, it was luxurious and was surrounded by two acres of beautifully maintained gardens. The upkeep was quite costly, and Janet had been stressed over the legal battles for the inheritance.

But now that Jeffrey was back, everything would be all right once again. Now, life could be reset and rebooted.

She sat him down on the same couch where she had been sitting when she first heard the news on CNN. It was surreal; just a few days earlier all of this had seemed so impossible. Now that it was actually happening, she was amazed at how easily she accepted it all. One could get used to anything, she decided, even this, once the initial shock passed.

Except that Jeffrey seemed different; distracted. He wouldn't hold her gaze, but she felt confident that with enough attention and gentle care, she could bring him back to what he used to be.

"What do you remember?" she asked him.

He shifted on the couch, his hair falling into his eyes. He looked away, vacantly brushing the unruly hair from his face. "Most things, but not all," he finally answered.

"Not all about things in general, or not all about us? Do you know who I am?"

For the first time, he met her eyes. "I ought to know my wife."

She wasn't sure she understood his tone. "So you know I am your wife, and that we were married almost a year. We had an anniversary, but you were unable to celebrate it with me because you were sick. Would you like to do that? Have a belated celebration?"

He looked away again. "Whatever you want."

"What about you? What do *you* want?"

"I want to be left alone until I figure things out."

Shocked, she stepped back. "Well," she said, "I see some things never change."

Janet was dismayed as she stepped into the bedroom, leaving Jeffrey alone as he wished. She felt hurt and worse, afraid. What did the future hold for him? For her? For them both?

But by dinnertime, she had gotten over it. After all, Jeffrey's behavior could be understood. He had been through unimaginable trauma.

She wanted to ask him what death was like but felt afraid of the answer. Wasn't death the universal mystery? Perhaps now that millions experienced it and came back to tell about it, the mystery would finally be solved.

She was distracted by the ringing of her cell phone. She answered it to hear a strange voice. "This is Malcolm Harrison, attorney at law."

"I'm rather busy now, what can I do for you? Can you make it quick?"

"I'll try," Harrison said. "I wanted to notify you that Mr. and Mrs. Hall have filed a wrongful death lawsuit against you concerning their son, Jeffrey Hall."

"He's not dead!" she cried.

"We are determining the legality of whether Jeffrey Halls is dead or not," he said. "You will receive court documents in the mail."

She hung up on him.

Jeffrey came up from behind and startled her. "Is everything all right?" he asked.

He reached for her and pulled her close. She rested her head on his chest and took in his scent. He still smelled clean like fresh wood shavings.

"I think things will be better now that you're back," she told him.

He took her chin in his hand and pointed her face upwards. She could see his golden-brown eyes, his finely chiseled nose, and his masculine jawline. He looked like the prince he was when he rescued her from out of the Ozarks.

"Let's have our anniversary celebration," he whispered, and led her into the bedroom.

She didn't know what caused the change in him from earlier in the day. Perhaps he had come to grips with his situation and decided to begin living instead of dying. Perhaps he remembered the fire he had always felt towards her, the passion that clouded his judgment as to who made a proper wife, and who didn't.

Janet had always loved the power she had over his emotions. If that power transcended death, then she felt more powerful than anything else on earth.

He guided her towards the king-sized bed and shut the door behind him. "Take off those blue jeans," she told him as she lay on the bed.

Jeffrey complied, standing near the door, and the pants fell to the floor. She admired his strong, muscular legs. Then he unbuttoned his shirt and dropped it to the floor, where it landed in a heap on top of the jeans.

She gasped.

A huge, purple gash ran from his pubic area to above his nipples, where the single ripped and jagged laceration then branched out into two directions, each side tearing up to almost the shoulders where the y-incisions finally ended. Thick black stitches held the gaping wounds together, and when he moved to come towards her, the stitches stretched and the flesh seemed to pull apart, and Janet was afraid they wouldn't hold, and his insides would be disgorged onto the floor.

She screamed and tried to use her legs to propel herself backwards on the bed, but her dead husband kept coming.

He reached behind his head with a naked arm and yanked at his hair.

With one move, he pulled his scalp forward until it flipped over onto his face, completely obscuring his features like an inside-out pelt. The skull gleamed brightly in the lamplight, glistening with wet red tint. She could see that the bone had been sawed and the top of the skull sat like a morbid hat, unattached but not falling from its perch.

"Stop it, please!" she cried in fright. "Whatever happened to you, please don't do this!"

He stopped walking. He took his scalp and gently placed it back on his head, covering his skull. His face was smeared with blood and it seemed pronounced against his unnaturally pale skin.

She thought the macabre performance was over. But then Jeffrey began pulling at the crude black stitches that covered his stomach and chest.

"The pathologist didn't put my organs in the same places that they were before the autopsy," he said. "He just sort of threw them back in afterwards and stitched me up. My heart and my pancreas are in my stomach."

Janet screamed, "Please! Why are you doing this?"

"Of course, the pathologist thought that was fine since I would just be going into the ground. How about your organs, Janet? Is your heart in the right place?"

"Please stop, please."

"Not yet. I gave you my heart in life. Now I will give it to you in death."

He tugged at the stitches and pulled them. They unthreaded in one long string, the cord like a ribbon, going into one hole and coming out another like a long black worm. The chasm that was his chest began to open, the skin rubbery and the yellow fat beneath becoming visible. Intestines began to tumble out of his stomach area, and from out of the mess a red, veined, globular heart fell to the floor, its ventricles cut and waving.

She vomited on the bed, and felt dizzy and faint.

"You asked me before how much I remembered."

Unable to look at him, she spoke into her hand that she held to her mouth. "How much?"

"You gave me Ricin. It's so rare, the doctors couldn't find out why I was sick. And the pathologist didn't find it in the autopsy. For a country girl from the Ozarks, you came a long way in life."

"Jeffrey, now I know it's better to have you alive. I had to learn the hard way. I want you back; it's too hard without you. Everyone hates me because they suspect me even though no one has proof."

"But now there's proof. The pathologist who did the sloppy autopsy didn't expect me to come back to tell about it. Neither did you."

She wiped the vomit from her mouth, and turned to face him. She gave him the look she had always given him. She unbuttoned her shirt to show him her charms. It had always worked before. She had power over his emotions. She was more powerful than anything on earth.

When he sat on the bed and reached for her, she knew her power worked. She still held him under her spell.

But suddenly he grabbed her neck and began to choke her. She clawed at his face, shredding ragged sheets of pale skin under her sharp fingernails. He squeezed his large hands tighter. She bucked like a bronco to try to knock him off, but he held on, pressing against her larynx until her hyoid bone broke.

He stood up, letting his wife's dead body tumble from the bed to the floor. He walked out of the bedroom and out of the house without looking back.

Three hours later, Janet reanimated.

FLYTRAP

Aaron saw it, and asked the storekeeper, "What's a plant doing in a pet shop?"

The storekeeper looked like someone from a past century, with a handlebar moustache and a stained apron. "That's a Venus flytrap. Technically a plant, but it sure seems like an animal to me."

Aaron peered at the plant closely. It was in a small, red clay pot and had a rosette of five leaves that arose from a bulb-like stem. The leaves were green, and looked like they had small claws with red interiors on their tips.

The storekeeper spoke again. "Fascinating little thing, isn't it? Did you know that the trapping mechanism is so specialized that it can distinguish between living prey and raindrops? It won't close its claws on raindrops. But an insect…well now…"

Aaron interrupted. "How much?"

The storekeeper smiled. "Last one left. You can have this baby for only twelve ninety-five."

"I'll take it."

<< — >>

He brought the plant home and placed it on the mantle in the living room. Then he realized he forgot to ask the storekeeper about how to take care of it. Did it need sunlight like other plants? Was he supposed to catch flies for it, and if so, would it eat dead flies or be so picky that it only wanted those insects when alive?

He stood beside the fireplace, staring at the plant. Impulsively he stuck his finger into one of the red claws. It immediately closed, but the plant's grip was too slight to matter. He removed his finger and figured that flies weren't as strong as he was and therefore couldn't escape so easily.

He decided to find out more about the Venus flytrap from the internet. He sat at his computer and googled it.

He read:

The Venus flytrap is found in nitrogen- and phosphorus-poor environments, such as bogs and wet savannahs. It survives in wet sandy and peaty soils. Venus flytraps are popular as cultivated plants, but have a reputation for being difficult to grow. Place your plant in a sunny window that faces south. As long as the Venus flytrap receives four or more hours of direct sunlight in the window, it should do well.

So obviously the dark fireplace mantle was an inappropriate spot. Aaron picked up the little plant and moved it to a windowsill. He felt the dirt inside the red clay pot with his finger and decided it needed water.

Next he went to his back porch where he had a flypaper strip hanging from the awning. He felt revulsion at the sight of so many dead insects, but decided that he was now responsible for the plant, so he reached for the sticky yellow strip and plucked a dead fly from it.

Holding the dead insect by its wings, Aaron thought, *How disgusting*.

He entered his house once again and went to the window. With the fly held delicately by his fingertips, he wondered how to serve it to the plant.

He left the dead fly on the windowsill and went to retrieve a toothpick. Impaling the dead insect upon the tip, he nervously aimed it into one of the claws. He was relieved when the claw clamped shut.

Over time, touching flies no longer disgusted him. As the weeks went by, the Venus flytrap seemed to be happily growing. *So much for the internet's claim that they are difficult plants*, he thought.

Then came the day when Aaron went to his porch and saw that there were no flies left on the dangling, sticky yellow strip. He felt panicked. How would he feed his plant? By now it had become a pet to him.

What would draw flies? The answer came to him: Animal waste, particularly that of dogs. But he couldn't go to his neighbor's yard with a shovel. Instead, he took a plastic baggie to the park down the street and was rewarded in his quest there.

He placed a paper towel on his back porch and dumped some dog feces upon it. The smell was overpowering. The sunlight glistened on the mess, and Aaron imagined he could see it steam with the heat.

He watched it for a few minutes, trying to breathe through his mouth, then realized that the flies would alight on the dog shit all right, but how would he actually catch them in mid-flight? Unlike a sticky flypaper strip, here the flies could come and go as they pleased.

He went to the store and bought a butterfly net. Bringing it home, he went back to the porch and was surprised to see what looked like dozens of flies buzzing on and off the dog shit. It was a home run! He swung the net around like a crazy person, and felt jubilant that he captured so many flies with his swings.

He brought his prizes inside, and impaled one of the flies with a toothpick. Fascinated by its struggles, Aaron decided that the fly did not have enough intelligence to realize its situation. It floundered and didn't seem to realize that it was now unable to fly.

He found himself staring at the fly, alive and squirming on his toothpick. It must be nutritious for his plant to be growing so well. He watched it move. He wondered if his Venus flytrap could taste its food. What would a fly taste like?

Although he lived alone in his small house, Aaron glanced furtively over his shoulder. He was possessed with a compulsion so strong that it was impossible to resist.

Slowly he brought the toothpick to his mouth, and stuck out his tongue to taste the fly.

He was startled at the fly's movement; he had never put his tongue on anything in motion before. It was an interesting sensation; it seemed to awaken some primal instinct within himself. The fly tasted metallic, but overall, it was not revolting.

Suddenly ashamed at his own weird behavior, he quickly removed the fly from his tongue and took it to his flytrap plant. He felt happy that the plant accepted the fly. Aaron imagined that the Venus flytrap was grateful to him for the treat of a living insect.

<< — >>

Aaron was unable to go to work. He couldn't motivate himself to leave the house. He was not surprised when his boss left a voicemail stating he was fired.

By now he was used to the stench. It started when he left the back door to the porch open. The warm summer breeze wafted the smell from the dog feces inside. Eventually Aaron realized that flies also liked garbage, so he got into the habit of never emptying the trash can in the kitchen. It was beginning to overflow, the garbage spilling onto the floor.

And now in the kitchen, he swooped upon his prey with the net. He saw with satisfaction that he had captured probably twenty flies. He held the end of the mesh with his hand, blocking any escape.

He loved the green ones. Not only were they beautiful to look at in all their iridescence, but he savored the buzzing activity the live flies could create inside his mouth. He liked to allow them to crawl on his tongue; the sensation was stimulating. And when he bit into them, they had a slight crunch on the outside and were wet on the inside, so he always ate the green ones first.

THE GOLEM

It was the time of the Blood Libel.

Rabbi Loew felt uneasy as he peered out his window. Tensions between the gentiles and the Jews were rapidly increasing. What made this particular night so much more significant than the other stressful evenings was the fact that Passover had begun, and part of observance included the baking of unleavened bread.

Judah Loew heard the rumors. Despite the ridiculousness of the content, the rumors persisted and were believed by the gentiles on the other side of the gate. *Of course the Christians believe the rumors*, Loew thought, *because they are the ones who started them.*

On his side of the gate, Rabbi Loew was afraid for his people. The Jews in the ghetto of Prague were increasingly becoming the object of Christian persecution. Why, only that very afternoon, a gentile had stood at the ghetto gate and shouted, "You Jews murdered Christ! We ought to crucify all of you!"

And what could the Jews do? By law, they were not allowed to leave the gates of the ghetto. Nor would they want to, because to leave the security of the ghetto community would be to risk one's life at the wrath of the gentiles.

And now there was this new rumor. The Christians were accusing the Jews of baking the unleavened Passover bread with an additional ingredient other than the water of *matzoh* and flour. The additional ingredient was supposed to be the blood of murdered Christian children.

Rabbi Loew shook his head sadly. No matter what went wrong in the Christian community, it was always the fault of the Jews. Christians blamed Jews for everything. If a child went missing, a Jew had snuck out of the ghetto in the middle of the night and committed murder. If that same child turned up floating face down in the Vltava River, well then, the Jews had committed murder by drowning the victim. If a disease spread through the Christian community, then the Jews were poisoning all the wells. If the weather turned bad, then the Jews were incurring the wrath of God.

Loew wondered, *How can anyone believe that Jews are murdering Christian children to use blood in bread? This is the year 1580, and in these modern times, people should be more tolerant of others. It is not like a hundred years ago when superstitions abounded. In God's glory, Jewish people do not murder children to bake bread.*

Rabbi Judah Loew was an aging man; his beard was gray and his posture stooped. He had lived a long time and had been devoted to his people during his entire life. He could not forsake the Jews living in the Prague ghetto now.

But what could he do to help his people? Instinctively Loew understood that very soon, all the tensions would come to a head and the gentiles would burst through the gates of Prague to destroy the Jews.

Somehow he would save his people.

He sat in a chair in his front room, watching the fire that warmed the cottage. Deep in thought, Loew almost didn't hear the faint knocking at his front door. When he did hear the knocking, Loew's first thought was that his wife would answer the door. But then he realized that his wife was fast asleep in the other room.

So he stood, stretched, and walked to the door. "Who's there?" he softly asked without making any moves to open the door. These days, one couldn't be too careful.

"It's Itzak," came the voice of Loew's son-in-law. "Open up, Father, I have news."

Loew let Itzak inside. "Warm yourself up by the fire," Loew invited.

But Itzak only stood inside the door, closing it behind him. "There's no time. A child has been found dead. Father, the child was found inside the ghetto gate. And the child is a gentile."

"What!" Loew sputtered. "That's impossible. It's only another rumor, Itzak."

"No," the son-in-law said, "I saw the dead child myself."

There was silence for a moment.

"Then it begins," Loew finally said.

"Yes, the slaughtering of the Jewish people of Prague begins," agreed Itzak. "I think the Christians put the dead child within our gates."

"We don't know that," Loew said.

"It is a set-up!" cried Itzak.

"That is not the problem," Loew said.

"What are you talking about?"

"The problem is to figure out what we can do to protect our people."

The words sunk in. Itzak asked, "What can we do? The gentiles will be storming the gates by morning to kill us all."

"I will pray," Loew said.

Itzak's face grew scarlet. "You will pray! You will pray! And all of our people will be slaughtered like cattle."

"God will protect us."

"Father, you are a Cabalist."

"Cabalism is a mystical interpretation of the Scriptures that is communicated only in an appropriate setting and in discreet ways," Loew said.

"No Father, you know what I mean."

"I seek religious and mystical experiences through Cabala. I seek truth through the divine interpretation of Cabalism."

"Cabalism has two sides. Two interpretations."

"Itzak, what are you saying?"

"You know what I'm saying." Itzak was grim. "The *Sephir Yetzirah* is the Book of Creation. Only a righteous man, a pure and just man, can use Cabala to achieve the power of Genesis."

"It would be an abomination!" Loew cried. "It would be a monster!"

"Father, you must create a monster to save your people."

Loew rubbed his eyes with shaking hands. He and his son-in-law remained standing in front of the door, neither of them speaking. Loew gazed into the fire, deep in thought. He felt apprehension and dread. But most of all, he felt resignation.

His son-in-law was right. The Jewish people of Prague could only be saved by a monster.

"It may be just legend," Loew whispered.

"No, it is not legend," Itzak said. "It is Cabala. It is the other side of Cabala, the dark side. It is dark magic. It is no legend."

"We will need three people," Loew said.

"Does that mean you'll do it?"

"Do I have a choice?" Loew felt a hot tear trickle down his withered cheek. "Can I in good conscience allow my people to be

46

slaughtered? But on the other hand, can I in good conscience be so arrogant as to pretend I am God?"

"No," said Itzak as he opened the front door, "you don't have a choice. I'll fetch Yakov, and then we'll be three."

Loew shut the door as his son-in-law walked into the night. He knew that in order to prepare to use the power of the Cabala, he must be ready. He must be pure. He must be cleansed.

He began to heat water on the cookfire, then got his nail clippers. The primordial protection that Adam had in the Garden was the shields of the finger and toenails. The cleansing and paring of the nails was vital in order to be open to Cabala's power. Carefully Loew clipped his fingernails and his toenails, and then threw them into the fire to be burned.

When the water on the cookfire was warm, Loew poured it into a glass. With his right hand symbolizing Hesed, he poured the water on his left, and then reversed the process. The left hand symbolized Din. Now his hands were clean.

He undressed and then carefully chose his ritual garments. He put on clean clothes that had been purified from washing. Finally Loew was ready, and he sat in a chair, patiently waiting for his son-in-law's return.

He didn't have to wait long. He heard a knocking on the front door. Again Loew questioned who it was before he opened the door. He let Itzak inside, and then softly greeted his favorite student, Yakov. Young Yakov desired to become a Rabbi, and Loew felt that the youth had the qualities to achieve his dream.

"I know why I'm here," Yakov said before Loew had a chance to explain.

"Good, then we are all of the same mind," Loew said. "We must go to the river immediately."

All were aware of the risks involved to travel to the river. All understood that it was against the law to go beyond the walls of the Jewish ghetto. But Itzak knew of a secret crevice in the wall where rocks could be removed. It was a way out; an escape into the world beyond.

It was late, very late. By the position of the moon, Loew judged the time to be about one in the morning. He took a deep breath when he walked out his front door, sniffing the air. The air smelled fresh and there was no scent of rain.

Loew and his followers stepped quickly through a deserted, narrow lane of the ghetto. The sky was incredibly clear, and the moon was a tiny crescent. Millions of stars sparkled and shimmered, and the night sounds were beautiful as crickets sang in their search for mates. Loew took another deep breath of the fragrant night air, and felt how wonderful it was to be alive in such a world. God had created beauty, but mankind created hate and prejudice. It was up to Loew to join God and mankind together to achieve peace.

Silently the three traveled through the dark streets of the ghetto. They had no candles and the moon's light was dim. Loew knew when they had reached the right place at the wall because Itzak signaled with his hand to come forward.

All three quickly removed rocks from the wall. The opening was small and it was fortunate that none in the trio were overly large. When all three men squeezed through the space, they reached inside to pull the rocks back into place. It would not do to leave the hole exposed in the wall for any guards to see. If the hole was discovered, then none of the three could ever return home.

It was exhilarating to experience such an adventure, and Loew chastised himself for permitting such an emotion. He saw it as pride, and to be prideful was to sin. Rabbi Loew understood that in order for Cabala to work, he needed to be righteous and pure in thought.

So he focused on the purpose of this dangerous trip. He was doing this for the salvation of his people.

Once outside the wall, the three men were careful as they walked the streets of the gentile city. They crouched and stayed within the dark shadows of the buildings. They walked quickly and with purpose. Loew's eyes darted back and forth as he traveled, searching for anything amiss. His senses were heightened and adrenalin coursed through his veins.

The buildings became sparse as Loew and his followers reached the edge of the city. He smelled water and knew he was close to the river. Soon he heard the water, and felt the slippery mud beneath his shoes. Moving underneath the trees and through the underbrush, Loew found a location that seemed to fit his needs.

The dusky, earthy scent of damp mud filled his nostrils. Mud was what Loew had been seeking. And there was a lot of it here.

"Let's begin our work," Loew instructed.

In the dark of the night, the three men got to their knees. They used their hands as shovels, their fingers as molds. They scooped the rich, fertile mud and began to push it into a mound. They worked together as a unit, shaping the wet earth until it began to resemble something. It resembled a silhouette lying flat on its back.

It resembled a man.

Loew stood erect. His arms and his knees were slick with wet mud. His hands were caked with earth and he held them out in front of him.

"I can create a man, but I cannot create a soul," he said. "That is for God alone."

"What do you mean, Rabbi?" asked Yakov.

"This earthen man shall be mute and without will," Loew explained.

"But you are his will," Itzak said. "This man shall do your bidding, am I right?"

"Absolute power corrupts absolutely," Loew said softly. "I hope you are right and that this abomination will awaken to do my bidding. If he awakens at all. That has yet to be seen."

"What is this thing we are creating?" asked Yakov.

"This is a golem," Loew answered. "I will name the golem Josef, after Josef Sheda of the Talmud. Josef Sheda was half human and half spirit, and saved the Jews from conflict. It is a fitting name for this golem, who is to save the Jews of Prague."

Then Loew said, "We have three people here. Each of us represents the elements of the Cabala. I am air. You, Itzak, are fire. And you, Yakov, are water."

"The earth is the fourth element. Who represents the earth?" asked Yakov.

"Why, the golem, of course," Loew said. "In Genesis it says, *And the Lord God formed a man of the dust of the ground, and breathed into his nostrils the breath of life.*"

Rabbi Loew began to chant, "*Shanti, shanti, dahat, dahat.*"

The surrounding countryside darkened even more as clouds quickly covered the moon. Sudden gusts of wind yanked the leaves from the bushes, and their limbs became horizontal as they yielded to the heavy flow of the strong breezes. Night creatures scurried to the safety of their burrows. The sound of the rushing Vltava River rose to a roar.

Loew raised his voice to be heard, and shouted the Hebrew words of Cabala, "*Ato bra Golem devuk hakhomer v'tigzar zedim chevel torfe yisroel.* Life to the clay man!"

The wind began to howl through the trees at an accelerated rate. Small whirlpools of leaves and debris swirled around the man of mud, who was still supine on the ground.

Once again, Loew got to his knees. He leaned forward, bending over the golem's head. He had a thin stick in his right hand. On the forehead of the clay monster, Loew used the stick to draw the Hebrew word *EMET*.

"*EMET* means truth," Loew shouted above the wind as he rose to his feet. "The truth is to be told."

A large tree branch, close by, came crashing down. The wind was relentless in its fury. Nothing was spared. The clothes of the three men were flattened against their bodies as the wind pressed against them. They leaned forward as to retain their balance, unconsciously pushing back at the wind that pushed them forward.

And then the thing made of mud moved.

The golem's huge hand closed into a fist. His knee rose as he tucked his massive foot closer to his body. The monster's elbow bent to prop himself into a sitting position.

The wind suddenly ceased. There was no sound, except the river, and even that became almost quiet. The stillness of the forest was eerie. No owl shrieked and no mouse squeaked. No crickets chirped. There was total and absolute stillness.

"Josef," Loew spoke, surprised at the steadiness of his own voice as it broke the silence of the forest. "You must awaken now. You must arise and follow me."

It was frightening to witness the golem rise to his feet. The man made of clay seemed to extend nearly into the sky as he stood erect. He was almost seven feet tall and his arms and shoulders were massive. His head was almost square and his eyebrows protruded like that of a Neanderthal. The features on his face were vague because he was smooth and appeared almost unfinished.

The golem looked like what he was: a monster made of mud.

"Rabbi," said Yakov and his voice shook, "how can we sneak such a being back into the ghetto?"

"He is dark like the night," Loew answered.

"But he is so large," Yakov said.

"He is dark like the night," Loew repeated. "He will not be easily seen. And God will protect us during our journey back."

"Have faith," Itzak told Yakov.

"Josef," Loew commanded, "you will follow me."

The lumbering hulk started to walk, his huge feet shuffling. Yet the golem made no noise as he lurched forward. Appearing clumsy and oafish, he nonetheless walked silently and steadily.

This creation will be very efficient at what I will set him to do, Loew thought. *And I am afraid. Deathly afraid.*

Loew was not afraid of the trip back to the ghetto. He was afraid of what he would be forced to do once he got there.

Silently and carefully, they made their way back through the city of gentiles.

Three men had come out of the ghetto.

Four men were returning.

When they reached the secret hole in the ghetto wall, the men had a problem. There was no way that a huge creature like the golem could possibly squeeze through the tiny opening.

"He will climb," said Loew. And the golem mounted the stone wall and then scaled it.

Rays of dawn light were beginning to streak the sky with colors in the east. The men could see themselves more clearly now as they pushed the rocks back into the wall to disguise the escape route. They knew that time was running out for them, and also running out for the Jews of Prague.

The morning sun was rising quickly now, and its light was reflecting off of the slick mud surface that was Josef. The monster could be viewed in all his massive proportions, a hideous caricature of a man. To view the creature was to experience awe mixed with fear. It was very obvious that Josef could be strong and threatening.

Just as they began to head back to the Rabbi's cottage, the three men stopped in their tracks to listen. Josef mimicked the men, making no sound of his own. But then there *were* sounds. Loew could hear a large crowd of people somewhere outside of the wall and they were approaching the gate of the ghetto.

"They've come!" cried Itzak in a panic. "The gentiles have come to kill the Jews of Prague!"

"Rabbi," pleaded Yakov, "send the golem."

Loew hesitated. To send Josef would be fury unleashed. At the last minute when it really mattered, Loew found himself uncertain.

"I can't," he said meekly.

"Send the golem or we die!" cried Itzak. "We will all be slaughtered, every one of us! Think of your family!"

"I don't know what to do," said Loew.

"It is no sin to defend oneself!" shouted Itzak.

"Please Rabbi, send the golem," begged Yakov.

Grimly Loew stood there, his feet planted on the ground as though he were a tree. He could hear the gentiles getting closer, and he could tell that there were many in number, probably hundreds of angry people, all coming to kill.

He needed to decide. Perhaps the golem was an evil being. But nothing was more effective to fight evil than another evil. The gentiles were coming for a spree of mass murder. That was the worst evil of all.

He, Rabbi Judah Loew, would send the golem. He would burn in Hell for this act so that his people could live.

"Josef." Loew spoke to his monster as though the golem were a child. "You must protect the Jews from the gentiles. The Christians are storming the gates of the ghetto. You must stop them." Loew hesitated, and then added, "Josef. Stop them any way you can. Do whatever is necessary so that the gentiles do not enter the ghetto."

"Thank you, Rabbi," breathed Itzak.

Yakov said nothing. He just watched and waited.

The golem turned his square head towards the gate. He straightened his massive shoulders and then began to lurch forward. The monster walked with huge strides, and the earth shook beneath his feet. The immense hands were clenched in anger. The protruding forehead and brow were knitted with rage.

Loew watched with dread. Yes, it was fury unleashed. Because the golem was simply a reflection of Loew's own inner hatred, the hatred that he always denied existed. But the hatred for the gentiles was there, and now the golem would mirror that hate.

A righteous man could possibly create a righteous golem. But a man who secretly hated would create an atrocity.

It was too late. Josef was going to have his way with the gentiles.

And Rabbi Loew was horrified at himself, because he found he had no desire to stop his monster. He had set his evil creation free to do the destruction that he himself secretly wished to do.

The golem ripped the gate off its hinges as though it were a toy. He stomped out of the ghetto, pounding the ground with his feet. His massive arms outstretched, the golem began grabbing the gentiles, one right after another. He ripped them apart, tearing off arms and legs and throwing pieces of people by the wayside. The gentiles tried to run, but Josef also ran in his lumbering but fast gait.

Loew shut his eyes, but the screams of the gentiles could not be ignored. It was horrible, horrible, but the Rabbi was rejoicing in his heart.

Yakov began to panic. "Rabbi, call him off."

Loew just stood where he was, his eyes closed.

"Rabbi, the golem is killing people," Yakov tried again.

"He's right," Itzak agreed. "Stop the golem. The golem has done enough."

Loew did not move. *Absolute power corrupts absolutely.*

"Rabbi!" Yakov began to shout to be heard above the screams of the gentiles, "Stop the golem!"

"No," Loew said.

Yakov stared at Loew in disbelief. The young Yakov hadn't wanted anyone killed. That was not supposed to be part of this. The golem was created to threaten, not to maim and murder. Why was the Rabbi allowing the golem to commit the same mortal sins that the monster was created to prevent?

"Stop the golem or I will," Yakov said.

Loew laughed. "And what could a mouse like you do to stop a powerful monster like Josef?"

"I don't know, but I intend to do something."

With that, Yakov ran to follow the golem.

Passing the ruined gate, Yakov picked up speed. The sun had risen fully now, so he could see the huge monster in the distance. It sickened him to view all of the blood and body parts that were littered on the countryside. Yakov tried to run without seeing what lay everywhere on the ground. He shut his ears to the screams and the moans of the maimed and wounded gentiles.

And finally Yakov reached the golem.

Josef loomed directly in front of Yakov. Without thinking, Yakov leaped and landed on the golem's back. His arms around the golem's neck, Yakov hung on to the monster's back.

Josef stopped moving. Then he reached behind himself and pulled Yakov over his head. The monster literally threw Yakov over his head and the young man landed hard on the ground.

Yakov couldn't breathe for a moment. He lay on the ground, gasping for air. The moment was too long.

Josef approached, and the massive clay man loomed above Yakov.

Yakov was doomed.

Suddenly he heard a voice. It was Rabbi Loew!

"Josef," Loew said, "don't hurt him. Don't touch Yakov."

Yakov turned his head to see Loew standing behind the monster. Loew was breathing very hard. The Rabbi had run after both he and the golem and now he had caught them.

"Rabbi," Yakov said, as he still lay on the ground, "put an end to this."

Loew stood without speaking, his breathing beginning to calm. The monster didn't move. It was waiting.

"Do the right thing," Yakov tried again.

Loew looked around as though seeing the gruesome scene before him for the first time.

"These people have families too," said Yakov. "Let's be the first ones to end the hate. Let's lead by example."

Still Loew did not move. The golem waited for his master's decision.

"You have accomplished what you wanted to do," Yakov added. "It's over."

"Yes, it's over," Loew finally agreed. "Josef, come to me. Bend down. Let me whisper into your ear."

But instead of speaking into Josef's ear, Loew quickly rubbed a letter of the word *EMET* off from the monster's forehead.

The letter was *E*, and once removed, the word *EMET* was then changed to *MET*.

While *EMET* was the Hebrew word for truth, *MET* was the Hebrew word for death.

The golem crumbled, turning to earth once again, and it left a huge mound of mud upon the ground. Dust to dust.

Author's note: All of the characters in "The Golem" were real people who lived in the 16th century. It is a fact that in 1580, Rabbi Loew single-handedly saved the Jews of Prague from slaughter by the gentiles. It is legend about how he managed to do that.

The Jewish stories about the golem may have been the inspirations for Mary Shelley's *Frankenstein*.

THE JANITOR

Craig parked in the empty lot and got out of the car, his windshield reflecting the glare of the brightly lit school sign. He was tired. Somehow his Monday night shift had come too soon.

He studied the school as he walked toward it. High school kids had to be the messiest people on the planet. He knew if he had paid attention and worked harder during his own high school days, he'd have a better job than this by now. But he hadn't so this was the result.

"Make the best of things," his mother always said. "Being a janitor is an honest living." Yeah, and all good dogs go to heaven.

Craig took the large yellow cleaning can out of the closet, and began to lug it towards the first classroom. It was about the size of an urban garbage can, made of hard plastic, and it was on wheels. It contained all the supplies he needed to do his job.

He cleaned the brightly lit classrooms first. They were the easiest; the teachers always watched the students and made sure they didn't disrupt the rooms too badly. He moved on to the gymnasium, another fairly easy clean.

After he did all he could in the gym, he knew it was time for the rest of his job. He stepped out into the night air, locked the gym door behind him, and started walking across the grassy quad towards the bathrooms, still lugging his cleaning supplies behind him.

He hated cleaning the bathrooms the most. They were in their own small building, boys on one side and girls on the other. Who knew what he would find there; sometimes things he didn't even want to look at, much less touch, so he always left the bathrooms for last.

Everything was locked at night, even the bathrooms. He started fumbling with his key ring as he walked, not seeming to find the right key, when suddenly he understood why he was having so much trouble. He couldn't see the keys very clearly.

Craig hesitated and glanced around. Why was it so dark? He looked ahead and noticed all the poles containing fluorescent lights that surrounded the freshman bathrooms were black. None of the lights were working.

Everything seemed quiet—too quiet. The sense of stillness was overpowering. There was simply no sound, no motion, as if all the night creatures were silently hiding; watching and waiting. No crickets chirped; no owls screeched.

The intense stillness was finally broken, and movement began again, as though the world was releasing the breath it held. A slight wind picked up. A creaking noise sounded as two twisted limbs of an old, gnarled tree rubbed together in the soft breeze. The seed heads of ornamental grasses fluttered with a sighing sound. Clipped boxwood shrubs rustled as branches shuddered in the wind.

Craig felt spooked. He wished he had a flashlight, more for cold comfort than for the visuals it would give him. Everything seemed threatening in the dark; everyday things seemed to take a sinister undertone. It was more of a mood than a lack of sight.

He wanted to turn around and go home but knew he couldn't. He needed this job, as lousy as it was. He couldn't afford to lose it.

You're not a little kid, afraid of your own shadow, he told himself. *Buck up and be a man.*

So he started walking towards the bathrooms once again, resolving to clean them and then move on. It was what he did five nights a week. This night would be no different. So what if none of the lights were working?

When he reached the overhang of the building, it seemed even darker under there. The roof shaded what little light the moon delivered. The bathroom building was brick, and felt cold to his touch as he leaned against it, fumbling with his keys. God, why couldn't he find the right key?

Finally he felt it, the small one with the knob on the tip. Next he had to feel the door to find the keyhole. As his fingertips glided over the metal doorjamb, he noticed how cold it was, colder than the brick. Maybe he had never noticed the temperature before since he could normally see it and didn't have to feel it.

The key connected with the lock, and Craig pushed the door open. He reached to the wall for the light switch. He found it and flipped it up.

Nothing happened. The bathroom remained dark.

No way was he going into that pitch black bathroom. He would have to call the school office in the morning and explain the situation, that he didn't feel safe because none of the lights were working. They couldn't fire him for that, could they?

Craig began to turn around when he dropped his key-ring. He cursed as he heard it bouncing into the bathroom, jangling as it tumbled and rolled the keys end over end.

Oh my God, I can't go in there!

But his car keys were on that ring. Unless he retrieved them, he had to spend the night in these dark school grounds. Which fate was worse?

He needed the keys. He knelt on the cement floor of the bathroom, feeling the coldness of the stone on his knees all the way through his pants. He held the door open with his foot as he leaned over and began feeling around the cement floor, his fingers doing what his eyes could not, searching for the key ring.

He realized that the keys must have fallen further into the room than he initially thought. He crawled forward, and his foot slipped from the door and it slammed shut with a *bang*. Craig could not suppress a small scream before he realized that the door only locked from the outside. From the inside, it could be opened. He was not locked in.

He noticed he was panting. Trying to slow his breathing, he gathered his wits about him and once again began feeling over the cement floor for the key ring.

I can do this. I am not afraid of the dark.

His fingers groped the cement and he felt something on the floor that gave a little at his touch. Craig hesitated, then touched the thing again. It felt wet and…did he feel it move?

A sour scent of musty brine assaulted his nostrils. Craig jerked his fingers back and decided to get the hell out of the bathroom, keys or no keys. He tried to rise to his feet but his legs were like rubber beneath him. He staggered; his body rocked with fear, and made an attempt at reaching the door.

He heard the thing slam against him more than he felt the blow, and understood that whatever was with him in this bathroom was big. He could hear someone sobbing and realized it was he who was doing the crying.

Please God, get me out of here! Please God please God…

The creature dragged him down to the floor with its weight. He tried to push it off, but he couldn't seem to grasp it. Its surface was slimy and his hands slipped off.

He tried again to shove the wet, cold bulk with all his might and finally made contact. His hands seemed to sink into rubbery flesh that enveloped his fingers and didn't slow the assault. Stench of rotted seaweed and polluted ocean filled his nose and his panic rose to desperation.

He pulled back his arm and landed a punch on what he hoped was the face area. The thing grunted and then made a growling sound.

Craig tried to shove his forearm backwards, because he knew that a sharp elbow could be an effective weapon, but he was disoriented in the dark and didn't know where to aim. He was aware of intense, searing pain. It felt like the creature was attacking him for an eternity, although what was left of his rational thoughts assured him it had only been for a few seconds.

He managed to roll out from the creature's grasp. He hoped with all his might that he was rolling in the right direction, towards the door. He honestly didn't know.

And suddenly he felt the door, and he cried out loud with relief and renewed hope. He shoved the door open and the cool outside air slapped his face. He staggered to his feet and began to run across the grassy quad; a loping, lopsided gait because his left leg wasn't functioning properly.

He felt an adrenaline surge as he realized he was going to make it. He was going to escape whatever beast had been in the bathroom. He was going to survive!

And then behind him, he heard the bathroom door open again as the thing came out.

LOVE STORY

"I find the odor of death very erotic. There are death odors and there are death odors. Now you get your body that's been floating in the bay for two weeks, or a burn victim, that doesn't attract me much, but a freshly embalmed corpse is something else. The cold, the aura of death, the smell of death, the funereal surroundings, it all contributes."

An interview with Karen Greenlee by Jim Morton
You can see the interview at
http://www.nokilli.com/sacto/karen-greenlee.htm

John Mercado lay on the steel table in the embalming room of Tranquility Mortuary.

Wearing her white surgeon's gown, Kathy Gables hesitated for a moment. She gazed into the young man's half-open eyes, noting that his corneas were cloudy. She would not close his eyes until later. In the meantime, his milky irises peeked from the half-closed lids as though he were watching her, as if he was trying to make eye contact to express, *Please be gentle with me.*

Because he was lying nude on his back, Kathy gently placed a clean towel over the young man's genitals to cover them from view. This was common funeral home practice—respect for the dead—but it was even more personal now, because Kathy found John attractive. She didn't want the distraction.

The embalming table was made of steel so that there would be no absorption of any body fluids. Kathy had gently placed the twenty-eight-year-old man's head upon a hard rubber block, raising it above chest level.

She began washing him with a soap that contained disinfectant, and when she was finished, sprayed him with yet another disinfectant, this one from a bottle. She towel-dried John Mercado, and then carefully shaved his face. She didn't want any nicks because although there would be no blood circulating and therefore no bleeding, a cut could turn brown, and she wanted to preserve his beauty. Gently she massaged hand cream into his face and neck, and on his hands.

Now it was time to embalm.

She decided to use the carotid artery located in the neck, the one that followed a line midway between the earlobe and the collarbone, and that ran along the jawline. She made an incision that was a little over two inches long into the sheath that enclosed both the artery and the vein.

To pump in the embalming fluid, Kathy inserted an arterial tube. But as the fluid was injected, the body's blood needed to be removed simultaneously, so the corresponding vein was inserted with a "push-pull" rod that would suction out the blood. A machine hooked with tubes would accomplish both the purposes of injection and removal.

She mused that today's world was a mechanized world, containing machines and computers for both the living and the dead. Efficiency was everywhere, even in traditional mortuaries.

Kathy reached for the young man's hand. She hesitated, holding his cold hand in her own latex glove-covered hand. She studied his fingers; appreciating the well-manicured nails, and then gazed at the wrist and forearm…she was pleased at the masculine appearance of the hair on his arm.

Then she chastised herself. She couldn't allow herself to personalize this. She was here to embalm a body. She wanted to do it well, and most of all, she wanted to do it right. Now was not the time to feel aroused.

Kathy checked the body's rigidity. She knew that rigor mortis began setting in just hours after death, and a body could be completely stiff within thirteen hours after death. Rigor mortis always began in the face, around the jawline, before it continued down the body, ending in the stiffening of the arms and legs.

She knew that rigor mortis was caused by a chemical reaction within the body when oxygen was deprived from cells and tissue. Without oxygen, contractions were caused by adenosine triphosphate, otherwise known as ATP. This led to a complex reaction where actin and myosin fused to form a gel. The gel was responsible for the stiffness felt in the body.

What most people didn't realize was that after approximately thirteen hours, rigor mortis would begin to reverse until the body eventually became soft and pliable once again. Rigor mortis ended in the same sequence as it began: the face and the jawline first becoming slack, and then the softening of the tissues would continue down the body and into the extremities until the entire body was again yielding and flexible.

She held the young man's right hand and began to massage his arm, pushing the fluids into the system and assisting in the reversal of rigor mortis. When finished with that arm, she started massaging the left.

The embalming solution contained formaldehyde and glycerin, but also a dye to add color to the skin. When the embalming procedure was finally finished, Kathy was ready for the cosmetics.

She inserted a barbed wire hook into the roof of the mouth and another into the base, and the two wires were joined together at the lips and pulled shut. That would not only close the mouth but also keep it closed. Eyecups with small protrusions were inserted to grab the eyelids so that they too would remain closed. Then she carefully applied makeup to the young man's face and hands to further add lifelike color.

Once finished with the embalming process, Kathy stopped and gazed closely at John Mercado as he lay in repose. Now she could afford to let herself drift in thought. She noted with satisfaction that she had managed to achieve the peaceful expression that all morticians sought from their efforts.

She was glad she hadn't known John while he was alive; it would have ruined her burgeoning fantasies. Since she had no idea of the kind of person John Mercado had been before, now he could be anything she wanted. Certainly he could not do anything to disappoint her. He could not emotionally abuse her, could not reject her, and best of all, he could not criticize or humiliate her. He was perfect; quiet and submissive. He was someone who could give himself and ask nothing in return.

Kathy looked furtively over her shoulder. No one was expected to enter the basement embalming room. Embalming was a private act; it was generally a one-person assignment. She knew that she had at least an hour before anyone would expect her to bring John up to the main floor.

She removed the latex gloves with a snap, and tossed them to the floor. She'd pick them up later. Kathy gazed fondly at John, her John; her kind and silent lover. She imagined him holding his breath in expectation, his eyes closed in anticipation; waiting for her to make her move. He would never arouse anyone else, only her, and she loved him for his loyalty.

She caressed him, feeling the coolness of his supple skin, smelling the over-sweet chemical smell of formaldehyde, and relishing the underlying, musky scent of death.

Slowly Kathy removed the towel covering the genitals. She climbed up onto the table to lay with the dead body.

She wanted to be with the man she loved.

Afterwards, she felt a sense of dread.

It was getting past the time to put John into his casket for his viewing upstairs. She should already have done that by now.

Could she be so disloyal as to give John away to others? She had cemented an emotional bond with him; he was hers. Others shouldn't view her John; it was an intimacy that only the two of them shared.

What should she do?

She would keep him. She would take him away.

Pushing him off the table onto a gurney, Kathy wheeled John through the exit. She took the keys to one of the hearses from the peg and pushed John outside into the daylight. Carefully she moved him into the hearse. It took some effort on her part, because usually she would have the help of an attendant. But today she needed complete privacy to abscond with a dead body.

She tried to make John as comfortable as possible as he lay on the floor in the back of the hearse, considering that she did not have him placed inside a casket. Then she climbed into the driver's seat and put the hearse in gear. She drove away.

Panic engulfed her. What was she doing?

She would most certainly be caught, sooner or later.

Depression hit her and she felt powerless over her emotions. On a rational level, Kathy understood that what she was doing was unacceptable and was probably even a form of mental illness. She was filled with remorse over her sexual desires. She considered herself nothing better than a morgue rat.

But it was too late to turn back. Surely John Mercado would be missed by now. She should have already put him onto the upper floor for viewing. By now, people would be realizing he was gone, and that she was gone as well.

She didn't know what to do, how to undo what she had done; so all that Kathy could think to do was to drive. She had nowhere to go but her own house. She drove down back roads, hiding, until she reached her home. Once there, she was relieved to see that none of her neighbors were outside in their yards.

And so she wheeled the gurney inside her house. She laid John on her bed, hoping she would be able to spend some more time with him before the authorities came. She caressed his strong, unmoving jaw. He would never testify against her when she was caught.

Author's note: This is based upon a true story. A woman named Karen Greenlee went to trial in 1993. Karen had written a four-page letter of confession, calling herself a "morgue rat."

However, in 1993, California did not have laws against the molestation of a corpse. Karen Greenlee was only charged with illegally driving a hearse and interfering with the burial. For stealing the body and the hearse, she got eleven days in jail, a $255 fine, and was placed on two years of probation with medical treatment recommended. Meanwhile, the mother of the dead man sued, claiming the incident scarred her psyche. She asked for $1 million, but settled for $117, 000 in general and punitive damages.

Since this case, a California law has been enacted to make it illegal to defile a corpse.

All arrests in California are public information.

COLD SPOT
(A tribute to Joe R. Lansdale)

Troop hung upside down on the tire swing. He loved the way the world appeared when he looked at it this way. Sometimes it made more sense, being senseless, because today he couldn't understand things right side up.

He was turning ten next week, and everyone around him seemed to be forgetting that very important birthday. He would finally get to be double digits; didn't they understand that? Why, he'd waited all his life to have two numbers in his age. What else did he go to school for anyway, if not to be able to count?

It was always "Not now, Troop."

If not now, then when? For crissakes, his birthday next week was coming up fast. At least, as fast as anything could, being that it was summer once again. Everyone knew how time slows down in summer.

It didn't used to be like that, the way everyone ignored him now. Why, just a year ago everything was still normal. Of course, that was before his three year old sister drowned in the fish pond the summer prior to this one. Troop knew that was a terrible thing. He was truly sad to lose Deanna. But she wasn't the only child in this family. Didn't his ma know that? Did his ma forget about him? Or was she sorry it was Deanna and not him who drowned? Because that was how his ma was acting.

And then Troop pulled himself rightside up on the tire swing. Folks didn't nickname him Trooper—Troop for short—for nothing. They called him that because he always came through like a trooper. And now he had come through with an idea.

Suddenly, he knew how to get everyone's attention.

Everyone missed Deanna because she was gone. Well, what if *he* were gone too? Wouldn't everyone want him back then, the same way they wanted Deanna back?

He hopped down from the tire swing, his bare feet landing in the dirt, sending puffs of dust drifting up into the air. This summer was drier than most, and the southern heat made his upper lip sweat. The heat was a good thing; it meant he could leave without taking any other clothes except what he already had on his back. In fact, Troop figured all he really needed to do was to pack a lunch. Peanut butter and jelly would be right fine.

Troop went inside to the kitchen, letting the screen door slam behind him. He knew that no one would notice as he grabbed his backpack and rooted through the fridge. His ma was too busy with her misery, as she always seemed to be any more.

Oh, and he wanted to bring one more thing. Troop had read the book *Hatchet* by Gary Paulsen and it was about a boy who took care of himself without any grownup's help, and that was because the boy in the book had a hatchet.

So, the next thing Troop did was to go back outside and sneak into his pa's tool shed. Sure enough, there was a hatchet. Well, it was his now, and he stuffed it into his backpack along with the sandwich. Troop figured that by the time his pa found out, there would be no one to punish, because Troop would be gone. You don't get spanked if you don't hang around long enough to get caught.

And now, his provisions complete, Troop started his adventure. He'd sure show them!

As he walked down the dirt road, backpack in tow, Troop imagined how sorry his ma and pa would be when they realized he was gone. How they would wish they had treated him better! How they would wish they had made a fuss over his birthday while they still could have done that. Well, his birthday was yet a week away. Maybe he'd come home a day or two before it, so they'd still have time to shop for a present. By then, they'd be so happy to see him again…probably happy enough that his pa would forgive him for stealing the hatchet.

Troop had no intention of staying gone forever. He didn't see this as running away; he just saw it as getting his parents' attention.

As he walked away from the only home he had ever known, Old Man Carson's beat-up pickup truck passed by, choking the road with dust. Old Man Carson slowed to a stop, hung out the window, and called, "Where you goin', boy? Needa ride?"

Troop ran to catch up. He hopped into the passenger side, settling into the cracked seat that showed most of the stuffing. "Going to the creek for a swim."

"Your pa know you're goin'?" Old Man Carson asked.

"Yup, he does that," Troop lied. "I asked permission."

Old Man Carson hesitated. "You seem a mite young to be goin' into the holler all by yourself."

"Be ten next week. I'm old."

Old Man Carson laughed. "Reckon you are, then. I used to swim in the creek when I was half your age. And look how old I grew to be."

"Yup, you're a lot older than ten," Troop agreed. Old Man Carson guffawed, then put the truck into gear and started to drive.

After a mile or two, the scenery changed. The right side of the road became green with blackberry bushes, parsley hawthorn, and black gum. That meant there was water nearby.

"You want out here?" Old Man Carson asked.

"Yup, this'd be good," Troop said. The truck door creaked with rust as he pushed it open. Troop hopped out, and the dust on the road up here was more settled, and not stirring into the air. That was another sign there was water close by.

"I'll tell your pa where I left you," Old Man Carson yelled as he drove off.

Troop's heart sank at that, but what could he expect from grownups? They were all tattletales.

I'll just hide real good, Troop thought. He stepped into the holler and was instantly swallowed by foliage.

Once inside, Troop blinked. He had been here before, but never alone. He was used to the dry, flat yard at his house. In the holler, the denseness of the trees and shrubs blocked the sunlight, creating a surreal, twilight effect. With the darkness of the holler came a noticeable decrease in temperature.

The woods seemed to close in around Troop and he could no longer see the road behind him. He felt uneasy, and he hesitated. It seemed almost spooky. Could someone get lost in here?

And then the thought hit him, *Of course! I have a hatchet! I can mark the trees and leave a trail! Just like Hansel and Gretel, except I'm not dumb enough to leave breadcrumbs for the birds to eat.*

So he got the hatchet out of his backpack and began marking the tree trunks as he made his way deeper into the holler. It gave him confidence. He was smart. After all, he was almost ten.

Troop continued onward, further into the holler. There were rotted branches lying on the ground; old, moldy leaves left over from the previous autumn, and what appeared to be squirrel holes in the earth every once in a while. The ground was lush with short, wild plants that had such big leaves they appeared tropical. Trees of all ages were growing, some tall and wide, and some that were young and whip-like.

He was faithful about marking every third three with a hard swipe of his hatchet. Soon he heard the bubbling of the creek water up ahead. Following the sound, he came upon a muddy bank. Sliding down to the water, he reached to cup it with his hands, and took a drink. It was very clean and cold, and tasted wonderful. He hadn't realized until now that having an adventure could be such thirsty business.

His thirst quenched, his stomach growled with hunger. He sat on the bank and unwrapped his sandwich. He wolfed it down, and then immediately wished he had brought something for dessert. He was still hungry.

Well, he thought, *maybe I won't stay in this here holler overnight after all.*

But Troop decided to wait at least another hour or two before heading home. He had to be sure his parents had enough time to miss him, or else they'd be mad instead of sad that he was gone. And he sure didn't want that.

Shrugging, he took off his shirt and pants. *Might as well have a good time while I'm here,* he thought. He placed his clothes on top of the backpack on the bank, and then wearing only his undershorts, he jumped into the creek.

The cold water hit him like a rush, but his body quickly adjusted and then it seemed fine. It washed off the dust and dirt that he had carried from his yard. He felt good as he splashed around in the creek.

And then he heard laughter. Turning, Troop looked to see what was happening on the creek bank. Two teenage boys were standing there, and one of them was holding his clothes, laughing hard.

"Hey!" Troop yelled. "Put those back! They're mine!"

"Whatcha gonna do to make us, pipsqueak?" one of the boys yelled back.

Troop started wading towards the bank, but it was too late. The other teenager had hold of his backpack. *Oh no! Pa's hatchet!*

"Put it down!" cried Troop.

In response, the teenager threw the backpack at him. Troop tried to catch it but missed. The backpack floated on the current, moving quickly down the creek and away from him. He lunged for it, but it was already well on its way downstream.

Suddenly Troop didn't feel ten years old anymore. Suddenly he felt only nine. He burst out in tears.

"Hey, wouldya lookit that? We made the baby cry!" And the teenager laughed even louder.

The other teenage boy said, "Oh stop crying, you big baby. Here're your stupid clothes."

And he dropped them on the bank. And then he stepped on them, grinding them into the mud. Both teenage boys laughed, turned around, and then disappeared into the woods. It was as though they had never even been there at all, except the muddy clothes were proof they had. That and the missing backpack.

Resigned, Troop stopped his tears. It was time to act ten again. He needed his wits about him if he were to find his backpack. No matter what, he knew he couldn't lose his father's hatchet.

He reached the bank, and put on the muddy shirt and pants that the big boys had ground into the dirt. It was a shame to be all cleaned up by the water and then to have to get back into such dirty clothes again. He straightened up, and started walking downstream. He had no hatchet to mark his path, but he figured the creek would do as a trail marker. Birds sure couldn't eat a creek.

He followed the creek, which wasn't as easy as he had thought it would be, because a lot of trees had roots hanging down, trying to drink at the water. He had to step over the roots without slipping in the mud, and too often brambles grabbed at him with their thorns.

Just when Troop was getting scared that the backpack, and the hatchet inside, were lost for good, he saw it upstream, snagged on the roots of a swamp red maple. Sighing with relief, he leaned over, freed it, and inspected it closely. It seemed no worse for wear. He opened the flap and peered inside. The hatchet was still there.

The blackberry bushes had formed a little cave at that point in the bank. He sat there for a moment, trying to think. Was it his imagination, or was it getting dark already? He wished he had taken his father's watch along with the hatchet.

What would he do if he were caught in the holler after dark?

There was no need to remind himself that his original plans had included spending a few days and nights here. Now that it was getting dark, his original plans were out of the question. What had he been thinking earlier today, when he had left home?

He had to go back. Now.

Before it became full night.

Troop stood up, swinging the backpack onto his back. He strapped it into place. He tried to make his way carefully along the bank of the creek as he headed the way he had come, because he didn't want to slip on the mud and fall into the water.

But it was becoming very hard to see. It was getting dark. And in the holler, darkness came quickly because the sun was blocked by the dense foliage. The dim light of sunsets never found its way inside here.

A slight breeze rustled the leaves on the trees, making a sighing sound. The trail on the bank was narrow and difficult to navigate. Wild blackberry ran rampant through other wild plants and everything appeared intertwined.

And then suddenly the temperature dropped. Troop realized he had entered a cold spot.

He cried out in fear. All the neighborhood kids knew what cold spots meant. Every so often, you'd walk into a cold spot hanging in the air; they were small patches of temperature changes that just seemed to randomly appear in the otherwise hot, muggy summer nights.

And all the kids knew the cold spots were lost souls that wandered the earth endlessly, looking for children's breath to suck. Cold spots were haints!

Troop recited the incantation that all the neighborhood children knew was the only thing that could save them: *You're not in life, you belong in death, go away haint, don't suck my breath.*

He closed his eyes in fear and he wanted his ma.

Then the temperature rose, and Troop was relieved, thinking, *That was a close one.* He didn't realize he had been holding his breath, not wanting it to be sucked. He forced himself to calm down and to continue his journey home.

But it was fully dark now. And Troop was fully afraid. If there was one haint, would there be more? Haints came out in the dark of night.

Suddenly he heard a noise. The bushes deep in the holler were being broken and cracked. Something was stepping on them, pushing them aside, as it moved through the underbrush.

Something was coming!

The haint! He could hear it! It was coming to get him!

Suppressing a cry, Troop took off running. He left the creek bed because there was no traction available on the muddy banks. He twisted and turned to flee into the holler, running in the opposite direction from the sound, away from the haint in the woods.

The dense forest of the holler grabbed at him and tripped him. He couldn't see to duck the tree branches or to maneuver through the sticker-bushes. His only option was to hide in the bushes, shadowed by the darkness of the night.

Instinctively Troop knew that his small stature would be a benefit for hiding. He ducked into the dense underbrush, looking for cover, doing his best to draw himself in and somehow become even smaller than he already was.

He crouched under the rough bark of a fallen tree, and tried to weld himself into a large hole in the ground that some animal had dug. Troop tried to calm his rapid breathing and also to slow his racing heartbeat.

He held the hatchet firmly in his hand, but would a hatchet be any defense against a supernatural being?

He could hear branches snapping and the limbs of bushes being shoved aside. But the sounds seemed random. Maybe the haint couldn't tell where he was hiding after all.

Could it be that the haint was not all-seeing and all-knowing?

Was that too much to hope for?

Hot tears streamed down his cheeks, and as he curled into a tiny ball underneath the rotted log, Troop whispered, *You're not in life, you belong in death, go away haint, don't suck my breath.*

A sudden chill told him the haint was closing in. He could hear the thing in the holler moving again, and he understood that it was only a matter of time before he would be enveloped by a cold spot. He would die here, his breath sucked from his lungs, and no one would ever find his body. They would put his picture on milk cartons and people would look for him everywhere, but they would never find him deep in the holler. Not in this hiding spot, anyway.

He had to come out from under the fallen tree. He didn't want to die where he would never be found. He took his backpack off and rooted in it until he found his pa's hatchet. Holding the weapon in his hand made him feel braver.

As he peered out from his hiding spot, trying to decide what to do, Troop heard the haint move again through the thickets. Birds, nesting for the night in the trees, awoke and took flight together, as though they were a single entity. It seemed so dark in the woods, and his skin began to tingle. He had trouble breathing because his heart was beating so fast. He had a sense that something bad was about to happen so he gripped the hatchet tighter in his hand.

Troop's eyes searched the dark woods of the holler, looking for the source of the noise. And then he saw movement from behind the thick leaves of a shrub. Something was crouched in-between two trees, bending the limbs back with its presence. In the folds of shadow, Troop couldn't make out its shape or appearance.

And then there was a roar, and suddenly whatever had been hiding burst out of the trees. Troop screamed with fright, and his heart tried to jump out of his chest. He fell over backwards, tumbling back into the thicket. He lost his grip on the hatchet and it fell uselessly onto the ground. He continued screaming as the cougar soared through the air in a flying leap, coming closer at every second with the intention of tearing Troop apart with its claws and teeth.

And then a BOOM reverberated through the trees, echoing through the holler and the cougar fell onto Troop, and he screamed again. He pushed at it with all his might but the large cat lay on top of him, its body covering him and bleeding the warm, coppery life's fluid all over his face and hands. He couldn't get the cougar off; it weighed so very much. He kept pushing at the heavy animal's body and crying at the same time, when suddenly, like a miracle, the cougar was lifted and Troop could crawl away from it. He shut his eyes for a moment and he could hear the animal being tossed into the bushes.

Troop looked up to see who was standing there in the holler, holding the rifle that had killed the cougar. It was no haint, and Troop instinctively understood that he would never be afraid of cold spots again.

His pa put down the rifle and grabbed him in a wolf hug. He continued to hold Troop close against his chest that felt rough from the flannel shirt. Troop realized that his pa was shaking. Was he crying? Troop thought that only kids cried.

His pa buried his face in Troop's hair. From there, his pa's muffled voice said, "Your ma and I couldn't bear losing another child. We thought we'd lost you, you being all alone in this holler at night."

"How'd you find me?" Troop asked. But he was glad to be found. He wanted to go home.

"Old Man Carson told me where you went," his pa answered, his face still buried in Troop's hair.

That figures, Troop thought. *Grownups are such tattletales.*

APARTMENT 17

Blake

"Eighty percent of all of the species on earth are insects," John said, "so you might as well get used to them."

"I shouldn't have to get used to them inside my apartment," Blake said. He was sitting on a bench next to his friend, glad he was out in the fresh air, and not in the confines of his home.

"Call an exterminator," John offered.

"Gee thanks, I didn't think of that."

"Just trying to help."

"It's just that cockroaches are creepy, you know?" Blake said. "Dirty things. Kinda stresses me out and all."

"How bad are they?" John asked. "I mean, did you see a couple, or a lot?"

"Just one."

"One?"

"Well," Blake said, "one so far that I've seen, anyway."

"Don't you think you're over-reacting over one roach?"

"No!" Blake almost shouted. "I hate those things, you know? I hate 'em! They're filthy! And when there's one out in the open, there's probably a million others hiding."

"Okay, okay," John said. "I get your point. So call an exterminator. Your apartment complex should pay for it."

"I need to talk to Jarred," Blake said. "They're his roaches too. In fact, he's probably the one who brought them in the first place."

"Oh come on," John said. "It's an apartment complex. You're just one unit out of a lot of units. Anyone in the complex could have brought the roaches. They go through the walls to any apartment they want. You don't like your roommate much, do you?"

"It's not that I don't like him, it's just that Jarred is a slob," Blake said.

"You didn't know that before he moved in?"

"No, I sure didn't. And now that I know, I can't afford to tell him to move. I need his portion of the rent."

"Yeah, well," John said, "I gotta get to class. Good luck with your roach problem. See ya around."

Blake got up and walked down the campus drive area on the east end of the University, past the bookstore, and past the building that housed the Theater for Playwrights. He found his car in the parking lot, threw his book bag into the back seat, and reluctantly headed for home.

Driving, his thoughts turned towards his roommate. If he threw Jarred out, who could Blake replace him with? Finally he pulled into the apartment parking lot. He got out of his car and walked to his apartment.

It was number 17, located on the first floor of a two-story complex. Blake stood outside for a moment, considering it. Could roaches have really traveled from another unit, or was Jarred to blame?

He put the key in the lock and opened the door. The entrance opened directly into the living room, which was defiled by two socks and a dirty shirt on the floor.

"Jarred!" Blake yelled.

No answer. No one was home.

Well, I'll be damned if I am going to pick up his crap one more time, Blake thought.

Instead, he stepped over the clothes. Making his way into the dining area that was connected to the living room, Blake sat at the table and opened the laptop that was sitting there.

He googled cockroaches and read:

> *Cockroaches leave chemical trails in their feces. Other cockroaches will follow these trails to discover where more cockroaches are hiding. Thus, cockroaches can exhibit emergent behavior, in which group (or swarm) actions materialize from individual interactions.*

Oh my god, Blake thought. *Roaches shit all over the place, and then they swarm.*

The idea made him nauseous.

75

Suddenly he felt a tickling on his bare forearm. He jumped from his seat with a scream , knocking the chair to the floor. He brushed his arm frantically, and screamed again. He heard a knock on the apartment wall from the uptight neighbor next door who didn't like noise.

Grimacing but silent now, Blake scanned the floor, scrutinizing the tattered rug for any movement. He didn't see anything; perhaps it had been his imagination and nothing had crawled on his arm.

But that didn't mean there weren't roaches. Cockroaches were nocturnal; they were all hiding until dark. And then they would come out for real. And swarm.

Time to get an exterminator.

Blake pulled his cell phone from his pocket. He had the apartment manager's number programmed because he felt there was always a lot of complaining to do about this place. A cockroach infestation was just one more thing.

"Riverwood Apartments," the voice said.

"You need to send an exterminator to Apartment 17," Blake said.

"What's the need?"

"Roaches. Lots of them, all over. You people never take care of these apartments."

"I'm sorry you feel that way. Okay, well, it starts with an inspection before we call the exterminator."

"Send the inspector right away, then."

"We can have one over within the hour."

"See that you do," Blake insisted before he hung up.

He tried to settle down to wait for the inspector, but found himself nervously pacing around the living room, still stepping over Jarred's clothes. Finally he heard a knock on the door.

Expecting someone in protective clothing, Blake was surprised to find a casually dressed, middle-aged man on the stoop who was wearing only a shirt and jeans.

"I'm Larry, the apartment inspector," the man said. He reached his hand to shake, but Blake backed away. He didn't want to touch anyone who dealt with roaches and other vermin. Instead he held the door open and invited Larry inside.

After shutting the door behind him, Blake fidgeted nervously and asked, "So, how do you inspect?"

"I'm just going to take a look around," Larry said. "You know, poke around in your cupboards, look under the refrigerator, peck behind the stove. I'm going to be checking dark places in your kitchen. I'll be looking for the bugs, but also I'll be trying to find any egg cases— they're oval and brown-colored. And I'll see if I can find feces. They look like grains of black pepper. Any of these things are sure signs of a cockroach infestation."

Blake blanched. He remembered the google article. The thought of chemically-laden feces made him shudder. If there was roach shit, then there could be swarms on the way.

Larry entered the kitchen. "Pretty clean," he commented.

Blake was right behind him. "It's important to me to keep everything really clean. My roommate is a slob. All of this is probably his fault."

Larry turned to look at Blake. "Listen, before you go blaming your roommate, you ought to know that roaches can arrive in the grocery bags that you bring home from the store. And sometimes they live in sewers underneath the road. When that happens, they can come up through the drains in the kitchen or bathroom."

Blake didn't want to hear it. "Or they can come from my roommate's filthy things that he brought with him from his last filthy residence."

"Perhaps," Larry said, giving Blake an odd look. "Well, either way, I'll start looking around now. Why don't you wait in the living room? I won't be long."

"Don't you think I should help you here in the kitchen?"

Again, the odd look. "No," Larry said. "It's better if you wait in the living room, like I said. Frankly, you make me nervous."

"Whatever," Blake said, then stormed off. He was so angry, that when he once again saw Jarred's clothes on the living room floor, he picked them up and flung them into a corner. The roaches were Jarred's fault!

Finally he settled in a chair and waited.

About fifteen minutes later, Larry materialized out of the kitchen. "Well, I don't see signs of a cockroach infestation."

Blake jumped from his chair. "What! I saw them!"

"How many did you see?" Larry asked.

"Ummmm..." Blake said, "a few. Well, maybe less. But if there's one, there's sure to be more!"

77

"Well, I'm sorry," Larry said, "but I cannot justify calling an exterminator. I don't see any evidence of an infestation. Are you sure it was a cockroach you saw and not a cricket?"

"I'm positive!" Blake shouted. "I want an exterminator and I want one now!"

Larry was quiet a moment, then he said, "Listen. I'm aware of you, in Apartment 17. You call the manager's office a lot. I'm sorry, but when a guy cries wolf and all…you know?"

Realization dawned on Blake. "You think I'm lying. Get out. Get out!"

"I was just leaving anyway," Larry said as he opened the front door. "If you see more roaches, call the manager and I'll come back for another look. Good luck."

Blake slammed the door. Infuriated, he began to pace the living room once again. Then he bent down and grabbed Jarred's clothes, picked them up, and walked down the hallway to the hamper. He threw the clothes inside it.

Taking off his own clothes, Blake hopped into the shower. He rubbed and rubbed himself with soap, but he didn't feel clean. He just couldn't wash off the idea that cockroaches were in his apartment, leaving filthy trails of feces.

After the shower, he dressed and went into the kitchen, where he scrubbed down every surface with Lysol. When he was finally done in the kitchen, he went into the bathroom for another shower.

When Jarred had still not returned later that night, Blake felt frustrated because he had wanted someone to yell at, and someone to blame. Finally he said to hell with it and went to bed.

He climbed in the soft double bed, and pulled the quilt up to his nose. He had trouble drifting off, because he still felt angry. He boiled with anger at Jarred and the apartment complex. And of course he was still furious at that incompetent inspector, Larry.

Eventually he did drift off to sleep, and began to dream. He dreamed that he walked into his kitchen with a can of Raid and found a cockroach on the counter next to the sink; a huge, brown, greasy-looking thing. It began waving its feelers at him as a threatening gesture of malice.

Blake sprayed the roach, but then suddenly the sink right next to it looked like it contained a boiling black liquid. He realized it wasn't liquid at all, but roaches. Millions of cockroaches swarmed up from the drain to rush at him. No amount of Raid could hold them off, and they just kept coming and coming…gushing out of the sink drain…more and more and more….swarming up the walls, over the counter, and coming for him.

Blake started screaming as pain filled his head. He woke himself up with his screams, and while the visions of the roach-filled sink disappeared, his pain did not. His ear…it felt like a jackhammer was going off deep inside his ear canal.

Suddenly Blake realized that it was no jackhammer. Something was in his inner ear; something alive, and it was bouncing in a frantic effort to escape. With a dawning horror, Blake realized that a cockroach had crawled into his ear while he had been sleeping.

Terrified, his stomach lurched into his throat, and Blake leaned over the side of his bed to vomit right on the bedroom floor. No ideas of cleanliness obsessed him now; his only thought was to rid himself of the vermin that now crawled in his head.

Blake jumped out of bed. One foot hit the pool of vomit and he slid, almost falling. Flailing his arms, he righted himself and grabbed the cell phone that sat at the side of his bed. Dialing 911, he couldn't believe it when he realized that his battery was dead.

He rushed to his closet and pulled out some clothes. He felt his stomach lurch again as the roach in his ear continued to bounce about in its frenzied search for escape. Cursing, Blake wondered how the damn insect could get itself into his ear if it couldn't get itself out. Why couldn't it take the same route to exit as it had taken to enter?

He stopped for a moment, his stomach cramping with dry heaves. Then he threw on his clothes. Neglecting shoes, Blake grabbed his car keys and proceeded to drive himself to the nearest hospital emergency room.

Reaching the hospital, he double parked and jumped out. Racing inside the emergency room to the receptionist, he blurted, "A roach crawled into my ear!"

The rest of the people in the waiting room stared at him, mouths agape. But Blake had never been one to care about what others thought of him, and he wasn't going to start now.

"Calm down," the hospital receptionist said.

"You don't understand!" Blake shouted. "There's a cockroach in my ear! I'm not making this up! For god's sakes, get it out!"

A nurse entered the waiting room to see what the fuss was all about. She told Blake, "I'm Kathy. Please come with me."

She led him into a cubicle.

"Why aren't you taking me into the hospital?" Blake asked.

"Please sit down. Relax; I'll take care of it. Roaches entering human orifices happens more often than you'd think," she said.

"What!"

"First we must kill the insect," she told Blake. "That will stop your pain."

Kathy reached over to a medicine chest and pulled out a bottle. "Mineral oil," she said. "Here, let me pour some in your ear. It will smother the insect."

She had Blake tilt his head and poured a few drops of the mineral oil into his ear. Blake felt the hideous intruder in his ear struggle, and then slowly he felt the movement stop. The pain ceased as well.

"Now let me get the tweezers," Kathy said. She reached into Blake's ear. "Stay still. Very still. Let me get the thing. Oops, it seems to be falling apart. I'll have to take it out in pieces. Stay still."

When the ordeal was finally over, Blake felt exhausted. He knew he would never be able to enter Apartment 17 ever, ever again.

Blake stepped out of the hospital emergency room, picked up his cell phone, and called his roommate.

Jarred

Jarred had his key in the front door lock when his cell phone rang.

"Gotta answer this," he told Jessica. "It must be important for someone to call this late."

She shrugged.

He pressed the phone between his shoulder and his ear. "Hello?" he said as he unlocked the front door to let himself and his girlfriend into Apartment 17.

"Jarred!" he heard Blake shout.

"What's wrong, Dude?" Jarred asked. But then the phone slipped away from his ear.

Jarred entered the living room ahead of Jessica and shut the door behind them both. He put the phone back to his ear, and said, "What'd you say? I didn't hear you."

"They're in the apartment!" Blake was yelling into the phone. "Listen, I'm moving out. I'm not setting another foot inside that place."

Jarred felt stunned. He stood stock still in the middle of the living room and took the cell phone off his shoulder to hold in his hand to his ear. "What's in the apartment? What are you talking about, moving out? What about next month's rent?"

"You're on your own about the rent, Jarred," Blake said. "I'm going to send someone to get all my stuff. I'm not coming back. Not now, not ever."

And then he hung up.

"What was that all about?" Jessica asked.

"Christ, who knows? That guy is crazy," Jarred said. "He's a neat freak, you know? In fact, earlier today, I dropped some clothes on the floor just to annoy him. On purpose, of course." He looked around. "Ha. Looks like old Blake picked them up. He can't stand anything out of place. Like I said, neat freak."

"But you were talking about the rent."

"Yeah, it sounds like he's going to stick me."

"So," Jessica asked, "you need a roommate?"

"That depends." Jarred pulled her over to him, and nuzzled her neck. "I only want a roommate who'll sleep with me."

She pushed him away. "Oh big deal. I do that anyway."

"Hey, want some wine?" Jarred asked. "Why don't you have a seat on the couch and I'll get us some."

Once in the kitchen, Jarred noticed some grains of black pepper on an otherwise extremely clean counter. *How odd for Blake to spill something and not wipe it up,* Jarred thought. But it was just a fleeting thought, and he dismissed it almost as soon as it came.

Reaching for the refrigerator door, he yanked it open to browse its contents. There wasn't much food inside, but there was plenty of what really mattered: wine and beer. Jarred grabbed a three-quarters full bottle of red wine, and placed it on the counter.

He opened a cupboard door and reached for two wineglasses. Something seemed to move behind one of the glasses, but Jarred had other things on his mind. And besides, when he looked again, nothing was there but the glass.

He took the wine and the glasses out to the living room and set everything down on the coffee table, then joined Jessica on the couch. "Hey," he told her, "now that Blake is history, we can have parties here."

"What about your neighbor who hates noise?" Jessica asked.

"We could invite him. Why not? He can't complain on his side of the wall if he's over here on our side of the wall."

"Our side," Jessica pointed out. "You said *our side* of the wall. Does that mean I can live here now, too?"

"Uh…" Jarred said, "why don't we have some wine?"

"Nice try to change the subject."

"Yeah, well," Jarred said. "Anyway, Halloween is coming up in two weeks. We could have one hell of a party."

"Isn't the rent due in two weeks?" Jessica persisted. "You won't have it unless I move in. No rent, no apartment. And no Halloween party."

"Jesus, Jessica," Jarred said with exasperation. "You never give up, do you?"

"Nope. And I won't until *you* give up."

"Well then," he said, "I might as well give up right now, saving us both time. It beats being nagged. Okay, I guess you can move in. Congratulations, you are the proud half-owner of a real dump, which is what Apartment 17 is, in case you haven't noticed. Now you can decide whether you want to laugh or cry."

She did neither. She hugged him. "We can share a bedroom! That leaves Blake's old bedroom free. We can turn it into an office."

"Whatever. Here, have some wine. I need to get you drunk so I can stand you."

She hit his arm, but accepted the wine. They drank for over an hour, he more than she, and then both retired into Jarred's bedroom.

Meanwhile, when all the lights were turned out, other things besides Jessica moved into Apartment 17.

Jessica

It was late in the day on October thirty-first, and the apartment was decorated, if only loosely so. Mostly there were fake pumpkins on the counters and black cats made of paper taped to the walls. Jarred was making an extremely spiked punch that was to go inside a plastic witch's cauldron later on. The furniture was moved against the walls, making room for people who most likely would be standing once the Halloween party started.

"At least," Jarred told Jessica, "they'll be standing at the beginning of the party. If the party's any good, they'll be falling down drunk at the end."

They were in the kitchen, and Jarred noticed that Jessica was looking around. He stopped pouring vodka into the pink mixture that was supposed to be punch and asked, "What's wrong?"

"I was just noticing," Jessica said, "that this place sure seemed to get dirty in the two weeks I've been living here."

Jarred looked around, and then turned towards Jessica once again. "Dirty? What do you mean?"

"Well, look at it. Dirty dishes in the sink. No one's vacuumed in the living room, and there's just stuff lying around everywhere. And when's the last time you've looked into Blake's room? Did you know that there's dried vomit on the floor? I mean, how gross is that?"

They had been getting on each other's nerves since she moved in, and Jarred was finding himself continuously annoyed with her. "If it bothers you so much, then why don't you clean it all up?"

"Sometimes I do," she said. "But then the next thing I know, this place is dirty again. It takes two of us to keep it clean."

Jarred plunked the vodka bottle on the counter. "Listen," he said. "You're starting to sound like Blake, and I couldn't stand that guy. Clean this and clean that. I thought all of that crap was over when he left. Jessica, this apartment is not dirty; it's just lived in."

"Then you and I have different definitions of dirty."

Jarred sighed noisily. "Tell you what. There's no sense in cleaning this place up right now. We're having a party tonight, remember? You know as well as I do that a successful party trashes the place. So, if you just keep your yap shut now, I'll help you clean it all up tomorrow."

"My yap?" Jessica said. "Fuck you, Jarred."

And she left the kitchen.

Jarred was relieved when she was gone. He didn't feel like fighting. In fact, he was in a great mood. He took another taste of the punch. Then he poured himself a glass-full. *A little head start,* he told himself.

He heard someone knocking on the front door. He glanced out the kitchen window, trying to judge the time. It looked to be only around 6 PM, way too early for any party guests. He wondered who it could be.

"Hey, could you get that, Jessica?"

She didn't answer. He sighed again. She was getting to be just as annoying as Blake had been.

But if he asked her to leave, it would leave him with the question of who he could replace her with. He couldn't afford the rent by himself. And he sure couldn't afford to move. He wouldn't be able to come close to coming up with a 'first and last' for a new place. So, he was stuck here.

He started walking to the door. Apparently, he was supposed to be doing everything himself.

Opening the front door, Jarred saw two very young children standing in front of a protective adult, probably one of the children's mother.

Both children were girls around five years of age. One was dressed in a Princess costume and the other was dressed as a Ballerina.

Of course, Jarred thought, *trick-or-treaters.*

As if on cue, both little girls cried out, "Trick-or-treat!" and held up plastic pumpkins.

"Um," Jarred said, embarrassed, "we don't have any candy."

"Yes we do," Jessica said, suddenly materializing behind him. "I bought some. Because *one* of us has to take care of business."

She brought a large bowl filled with tiny, wrapped Milky Way bars. Instead of reaching into the bowl, she simply tilted the bowl and dumped some of its contents into each plastic pumpkin.

Both little girls' eyes went wide at the generosity. "Gee thanks, Lady," the Ballerina said.

"No problem," she told them. "Happy Halloween."

When the front door was shut, Jarred said, "I didn't realize that kids trick-or-treated at apartments."

"We won't get a lot," Jessica said. "That's why I just dumped the bowl instead of doling candy out one-by-one. We can afford to be generous since we won't get a lot of kids."

"Milky Ways, huh? Not my favorite, but I'll take one anyway."

She slapped his hand. "If you want a candy bar, buy your own."

"Whatever. I need a drink."

"Your famous last words are 'I need a drink,'" Jessica said, "except they're also your famous first words, middle words, and oh yeah, almost all your words."

"Jesus, Jessica," he said, "get off my back. Maybe you're the reason why I want a drink."

"Or maybe you're an alcoholic."

It took a lot of muster for Jarred not to answer back with an angry retort, but he decided it wasn't worth the fight. After all, it was Halloween. And he was excited about the party. So he went back into the kitchen to finish making the punch.

Despite himself, he started looking around the kitchen with a critical eye. She was right, it was a mess. Resigned, Jarred started removing dirty dishes from the sink and began loading the dishwasher. Reaching into the sink for yet another dish, he saw something move.

An insect quickly ran into the drain and disappeared. He felt his heart beat a bit harder, but then he realized that whatever bug it was, it couldn't be a roach. Roaches were much larger, weren't they?

Jarred had no idea of the roach's life cycle. He didn't know that they hatched as tiny nymphs, only to grow into the much larger, more recognizable cockroach later.

He finished loading the dishwasher, dumped in Cascade, and ran it. Then he grabbed a sponge and began wiping the counter. *Damn it,* he thought, *there's that spilled black pepper again.*

He knew that Jessica liked a spicy enchilada, but this was ridiculous. If she had to pour pepper on everything, why did she miss so much and get it everywhere?

He picked up the toaster to wipe underneath, and saw something unusual. Where the toaster had been sitting on the counter, there were these small, brownish, oval things. What the heck?

Jarred wiped up the odd things, and then placed the toaster back down upon the counter. He ran the faucet and rinsed the sponge. When he squeezed the sponge, its water ran dark. *Wow,* Jarred thought, *the counter was dirtier than I thought. I hate to admit that Jessica was right. This place is worse than just lived in.*

After he was finished in the kitchen, Jarred grabbed the vacuum cleaner and quickly ran it over the well-trodden living room rug. When he was done, he looked around with satisfaction.

Just then the doorbell rang again, and Jessica came back into the room to find another set of trick-or-treaters standing on the porch. Jessica dumped more candy for the kids from her bowl.

She shut the door, then looked around. "Been cleaning?"

"A little. Hey, want to have a drink with me and make up?"

She smiled mischievously. "There are better ways to make up." And she took his hand and led him into their bedroom.

The Ballerina

The Princess and the Ballerina were done for the night. As they were both only five years old, the Ballerina's mother figured they should finish trick-or-treating before the older kids came out. So even though it was only seven-thirty, the Ballerina's mother dropped the Princess off at her house, and then took her own daughter home.

The Ballerina couldn't wait to count her booty. But her mother insisted upon going through the loot first and checking the candy to make sure that no one hid razor blades and that all the items were in their original wrapping. The Ballerina's mother wasn't sure if the scare warnings were urban legends or not, as she had never personally known anyone to actually get a real razor blade, but she loved her Ballerina and therefore would never take any chances.

"Wait here in the living room while I go into the bedroom to take off my shoes," the mother instructed her Ballerina. "I'll be right back. Don't eat a single thing, you hear me?"

"Yes, Mommy."

The Ballerina figured that not eating was not the same as not dumping. So she emptied her plastic pumpkin onto the living room floor. Lots and lots of candy fell out of the pumpkin.

Along with the candy, two large, dark brown insects also fell out of the plastic pumpkin onto the living room floor. With lightning speed, they darted underneath the living room couch. Within seconds, the two insects had disappeared.

The mother came back into the living room.

"Mommy, I saw bugs."

"What?" the mother wasn't sure if she should be alarmed or not. "What are you talking about, Honey? What bugs?"

"Crickets," said the Ballerina. "Under the couch."

Smiling, the mother sat on the floor next to her Ballerina and began to sort the candy. "You know," the mother said, "the Chinese believe that a cricket in the house is good luck. It will probably sing you to sleep tonight."

The Party

People started arriving at Apartment 17 at around nine o'clock. Some wore costumes, but most did not. All seemed to be in their early twenties, except for one or two who looked to be younger. Rock music blared, and since Jarred didn't hear any banging on the wall, he figured that Jessica had remembered to invite the neighbor who hated noise.

The lights were on but dimmed, and people crowded the living room. Others were in the kitchen, helping themselves to the strong punch from the witches' cauldron. Still others brought their own, and it wasn't limited to alcohol.

The hours passed, and people got drunker. Some began coupling up. Blake's University friend John and a woman from the party named Claire were two of the guests who had the hots for each other.

John had a glass of punch in his hand. He put the drink to his mouth to gulp it down. Suddenly something from the drink stuck in his throat. He coughed. Claire, laughing, pounded him on the back.

John coughed something out; something big and dark. He peered downward, trying to see what it was, but the lighting in the apartment was too dim for him to make anything out on the floor. Besides, the rug was dirty, so everything was camouflaged.

"You okay?" Claire shouted above the music.

"I'm better than okay, because I got you, Baby." John forgot about the drink and backed Claire against the wall, tongue deep in her throat. Music pulsed around them.

"Hey," he shouted over the noise, "let's find a bedroom."

She said something he couldn't hear. "What?" he shouted.

"I said okay!" she shouted back.

"Let's go." He took her hand, and led her down the hallway.

He tried one bedroom door, but it was locked. He tried the other bedroom door, and it opened easily. John led Claire inside and shut the door behind him.

He didn't bother to turn the light on. He figured the bed would be by the window, and he guided Claire there. On the rug right next to the bed, he stepped on something stiff; something that felt like a dried spill of some sort.

He threw Claire on the unmade bed, and climbed on top of her. He was kissing her and removing her clothes simultaneously. He tasted her all over, and then unzipped his pants. He pulled his pants down but didn't bother to take them off.

Because they were both very drunk, they were frenzied in their lovemaking. Oblivious to their surroundings, they rutted in the dark, concentrating solely on each other.

When they were spent, they both lay on the bed, side-by-side in the darkness. They lay on their backs, facing the ceiling. They didn't speak; both just worked on calming their breathing.

"Hey, quit tickling me," Claire said.

"I'm not tickling you."

She hit him. "I said quit it."

"I'm not touching you!"

"Well, something is," she said. She swatted her arm. "Eeww, it felt like something was crawling on me."

They were quiet again for a moment, listening to the party still going on beyond the wall. "I hope there're no spiders in here," Claire said. "Maybe we should turn on the light."

"In a minute." He was finding it hard to stop from drifting off to sleep, and cursed the fact that he had gulped that last drink. It was knocking him out.

"John," Claire persisted, "I think there's something in this bed."

And then John felt something drop on him, like it had fallen from the ceiling. Suddenly he didn't feel so drunk anymore.

He sat up in bed, staring into the darkness.

More things were dropping on him. She was right, they were crawly things. He wiped his head with his hands, trying to brush bugs out of his hair.

He was conscious of Claire, next to him in the bed, also sitting up. He could hear her making strange sounds and she seemed to be frantically brushing herself off as well. Finally she yelled, "Something's crawling on me! Turn on the light!"

John pulled up his pants and jumped out of bed, dazed because he didn't know his way around this strange room. Then he remembered the way he had come in, so he headed towards the bedroom door.

"Hurry up!" Claire screamed. "There're bugs on me! Oh god, get them off of me! Get them off!"

John felt around the wall, and found the light switch. He flicked it on and turned to look at Claire, who was still on the bed.

He was horrified at what he saw.

Claire was sitting up, naked, with her hands on the bed. Hordes of huge, dark insects were amassed on the bed, on her hands, and swarming up her arms. More insects were crawling on her legs, traveling up her thighs toward her torso.

She screamed, lifted her hands, and tried to fling the roaches off. She thrashed her legs to dislodge the hordes of roaches clinging to them. Multitudes of other cockroaches were dropping on her from the ceiling. Dark masses of even more roaches were gathering on the ceiling, waiting their turn to fall onto Claire.

John yelled at her, "Get out of the bed!"

But he couldn't make himself move to help her. He couldn't overcome his fear and revulsion.

Claire was becoming overwhelmed with the thousands of milling, heaving, and crawling cockroaches. She was struggling but they were overpowering her. She sank back on the bed, lying down under the weight of the thousands of cockroaches, still struggling against them. She somehow managed to plead a final time, "Help me!"

John watched for another moment as she seemed to disappear underneath masses of frenzied insect activity. He felt frozen in place because he saw the insects flood into her mouth as she opened it to scream, and they swarmed into her ears and nose.

And then, finally, John was able to move. But he didn't help Claire. Instead, he opened the door and ran from the room.

He kept running. He pushed party-goers in the living room out of his way, and ran out the front door of Apartment 17. Like his buddy Blake had done, John told himself he would never be back.

The other guests didn't really notice John's frantic exit from Apartment 17. They continued to drink, and to smoke the joints that were being passed around. Everyone was having a really good time, one that most wouldn't remember come the next day.

Jarred was in the kitchen, finishing the last of the spiked punch. Jessica came in. "Hey," she said, "how come our bedroom door's locked?"

"I don't know about you," he said, "but I sure don't want any sloppy seconds. If anyone feels like getting frisky, let 'em use Blake's old bedroom, not ours."

He was swaying on his feet.

"Maybe you're the one who should use our bedroom," Jessica observed. "Maybe you should lie down on the bed before you fall down on the floor."

He leered at her drunkenly. "Couldn't get enough of me earlier, huh? You want to go into the bedroom and get some more?"

"You're drunk," she accused.

"Hello?" he said. "It's like, you know, a party?"

And he took another swallow of the punch.

The next thing Jessica knew, he was leaning forward. Then, sure enough, Jarred passed out and fell to the floor.

"Just great!" she said angrily. She bent over and tried to lift him off the floor, but he was out cold and too heavy for her.

Chad, a party-goer who was dressed as a Vampire, walked into the kitchen at that moment. "Wow, he's out, huh?"

"Yeah," Jessica said. "Hey Chad, can you help me lift him? I want to dump his ass into the bathtub. I'd put him in the shower, but you have to actually stand in the shower."

"I see what you mean," Chad said, laughing. "At least in the bathtub, old Jarred here can continue lying down."

Together they dragged him through the living room crowd and down the hall to the bathroom. Neither one looked into Blake's bedroom. Even though the bedroom door was half open, neither Chad nor Jessica noticed the dead woman on the bed inside.

"Put him in the tub, Chad," Jessica instructed. "Then go back to the party. "I'll undress Jarred and run the water. A cool bath should wake him up."

"Okay."

"Thanks, Chad," she told him as the Vampire left the bathroom, and she shut the door behind him.

She began undressing Jarred. It was not an easy task since she had to do it entirely without his cooperation. But eventually she accomplished it, and tossed Jarred's clothes onto the bathroom floor.

She reached for the stopper and plugged the rubber stopper into the drain hole of the tub. She grabbed the faucet and tried to turn it. It wouldn't budge.

Leaning forward, Jessica used both hands and strained to turn the faucet. It still wouldn't move. She wondered if someone had shut it off too tightly, or if something was blocking it.

Finally the faucet turned, but to Jessica's dismay, no water came out. Instead, the pipes seemed to groan, but remained dry.

Suddenly the faucet seemed to quiver and vibrate. *What the hell?* Jessica thought.

At the same time, she noticed that the tub's stopper was bouncing in the drain. It was jiggling and wobbling as thought something underneath it was trying to push it out.

And then suddenly the stopper popped out of the drain. Hundreds of dark brown cockroaches surged upwards from the drain into the bathtub. At the same time, more roaches started to stream out of the faucet, gushing in what seemed like millions into the bathtub, and enveloping the unconscious body of Jarred.

Jessica couldn't believe her eyes. She started screaming in horror. This couldn't be happening, it just couldn't!

Hysterically she started shrieking for help. None of the party-goers heard her over the music and other noise.

She tried to grab Jarred and lift him from the tub, but again his dead weight was too much for her and he kept slipping from her grasp. Next she tried to brush all the roaches off of him but it was a useless attempt, because they were like a fluid collective, and they almost behaved as though they were a single entity.

Together, as a unit, the thousands of roaches covered Jarred. They swarmed over his head, cutting off his air. Frantically Jessica tried to brush them off of his face, but there were so many roaches…just so many roaches…

Finally Jessica grabbed Jarred one final time. With a strength she didn't know she possessed, she pulled him out of the bathtub. He tumbled onto the floor, and the fall dislodged most of the insects. They dropped off of his face onto the floor, and Jessica began what felt like a strange sort of dance. She was trying to step on as many roaches as she could. She wanted to eliminate as many as possible.

She grabbed the bathroom towel and started snapping it at the insects. That made more of them drop off Jarred, and she continued her attempts to squash them.

Finally she tugged Jarred towards the bathroom door and managed to get it open. She screamed into the hallway, "Help! Somebody help me! Chad! Anyone! Oh god, please somebody help!"

She continued to drag Jarred over the floor, out of the bathroom and into the hallway. He began stirring.

"What the fuck? Hey, I'm naked," he slurred as he tried to look around. Then he screamed, "Bugs! Get 'em off of me!"

Party-goers started coming into the hallway. They grabbed Jarred and lifted him to his feet. The remaining cockroaches fell off of his naked body and landed on the hallway rug. Within seconds, the insects ran back into the bathroom and disappeared into the same drain from where they came.

Jessica raced back to their bedroom, grabbed an old suitcase, and yanked open a dresser drawer. She chose clothes randomly in her haste. She grabbed enough to get Jarred dressed right now, and also a few items to get them through a day or two somewhere else. Anywhere else but Apartment 17. She knew she would never step into Apartment 17 ever, ever again.

The Day After

Hung over and nursing one of the worst headaches of his life, Jarred lay in a bed. He reached to the nightstand and gulped a glass of water that had been sitting there. He was just so incredibly thirsty.

Suddenly his stomach revolted and he needed to vomit the water back out.

Jessica held the pan.

Finished, he laid weakly back on the bed. "It's awful nice of your mom to let us stay here at her house," he said.

"Yeah, we'll have to stay here until the police are finished with their investigation into Claire's death," Jessica said. "But I'm not going back to Apartment 17, no matter what the police decide. Not even if all the exterminators in the world go through the place. We're going to have to figure out somewhere else to live."

They were quiet for a moment, thinking about it.

"People will be talking about our party for decades," Jarred said. "I think we put cockroaches on the map. Maybe they'll be next year's hit Halloween costume. Either that or people will save the trouble of buying costumes at all and go to parties naked like I was."

"Not funny."

He was quiet again, then said, "You're right. Not funny."

They were quiet some more.

Finally Jarred said, "Thank you for saving my life. Claire wasn't so lucky."

Suddenly Jessica was angry. "Yeah, let's talk about that little matter of your life. Now that you didn't lose it, what are you going to do with it?"

Jarred looked at her. "Maybe I should stop drinking, for starters."

She studied him. "For real?"

Despite his terrible hangover, he smiled. "For real."

Jessica felt hope for their future together. Somehow they would get through this, and maybe even become better people because of it. She and Jarred wouldn't have anything to fight about any more if he would stop drinking. She had to believe there could be some good, somewhere, coming out of all that had been bad. She didn't want to think that Claire had died without anything good coming out if it.

It's all over, Jessica thought. *The nightmare has ended.*

As Jessica sat on the bed, talking to Jarred, she didn't pay attention to the suitcase that she had hastily packed just before escaping from Apartment 17.

She didn't notice that roaches were periodically squeezing out of the crack under the lid and dropping onto the carpeted floor, merely a few feet away.

FLIGHT 529

(a true story)

I'm startled awake by the sound.

I'm groggy with sleep, so I wonder for a second where I am. Then I become fully awake as I realize that I'm strapped into my seat on the charter jet heading out of Atlanta; destination Gulfport, Mississippi.

I hear passengers murmuring to themselves; questioning voices, expressing concern. To me, that means the sound is real and not a dream. I have a feeling of dread in my testicles. Yet we are still in flight, and no oxygen masks have deployed, so it couldn't be anything that bad, right?

My ears are popping, telling me we are descending. I tug at the plastic shade covering the window and open it. Sunlight streams in, and I am momentarily blinded by the sudden glare. I am blinking; my eyes are watering, so I am not sure what I am seeing...oh my god, it can't be!

What the...what? The engine; what happened to the engine?

I am finding it hard to get my breath. On the wing of the plane, outside the window, it looks as if some of the engine is gone. It's not entirely gone, but it looks mangled and really small. And oh Jesus, is that fire? Is the engine on fire? No, it is smoking, no fire, but lots of smoke.

I feel the plane making a turn, so I am reassured that the engine on the other side of the plane must still be working properly. I realize I am gripping the arm rests of my seat so tightly that my knuckles are white. Can an airplane fly on a single engine? I don't know.

I listen to the announcement that suddenly comes over the intercom: "Ladies and gentlemen, we have experienced a malfunction of the left engine, but this airplane is built to be fully capable of flying safely on the right engine. In the meantime, we are turning back to Atlanta. Please don't panic; everything will be fine. Please stay seated and keep your seat belts on."

The passengers had been completely silent during the announcement, but now the thirty-or-so people on this charter flight are talking amongst themselves, questioning the pilot's words.

"How can we fly on one engine?"

"Won't the plane be off-balance?"

"Does it seem to you that we are descending kind of fast? Are we nose diving downwards?"

"We're not going to crash, are we?"

I stop listening to the others.

I don't want to hear.

None of this seems real. This can't be happening; I don't want to die. Of course I won't die—the pilot seems to be calm, so why shouldn't I be just as calm? He must know what he is doing.

Oh please God, don't let me die. Stop it! Okay, I have a grip now, I won't let that thought come back.

The flight attendant gets up and starts explaining the emergency landing procedures. I listen carefully, because I figure anything I can do to help myself I will most certainly try to do.

And then when she is done and she disappears into her own seat, I force myself to look out the window again.

Descending; yes, we are definitely descending. I can see the ground looming closer by the minute. My heart sinks as I realize the terrain underneath us is not smooth and flat; instead, it looks like rugged, tree-covered wilderness.

Well, I am sure we will make it to the other side of the woods; just a few more minutes and we'll be in Atlanta.

But as I stare out the window, past the engineless wing, I no longer believe we will make it past the forest. It seems as though the tree tops are coming at us awfully fast. I can see the skyline telling me that our descent is indeed rapid. And suddenly I know the truth.

I know we will crash.

The calmness I experience at that knowledge is amazing to me. I am not screaming and I don't seem to be having a heart attack. I feel a serene acceptance; a matter-of-factness about my impending demise. I know I am about to die. Where is my panic? I don't know, but I am grateful that I am spending my final moments of life in peace.

So, it is true what I have heard about dying. My thoughts are not about myself, but about my loved ones. I hope my family will get past my death. I am grateful for the love they have shown me all these years. I feel they will look back on my life and know that I loved them just as much as they have loved me.

I realize that no one else in the plane is screaming either; no one is panicking. I suspect they are examining their own lives just as carefully as I am searching through mine. I hear some crying, but no one seems hysterical.

Did I do everything I wanted to do in my life? No. Did I do the best I could? I believe I can honestly answer yes. And I feel content that my best was good enough. At this point, it *has* to be enough.

And now I am looking back out the window, almost objectively watching the tree tops come up to meet the plane. The window seems engulfed in dark green. I am heartened to see that at least we are approaching land at an angle, and not with the nose aimed straight down.

Suddenly we are bumping, lurching and jerking, as the plane skirts the tops of the trees. The plane is being vaulted up and down as it hits and bounces off the tree tops. It is a bone-jarring, lunatic roller coaster ride.

And now the screaming starts; it is almost like the spell of serenity and acceptance has been shattered as the branches of the trees slam against us. The shrieks from the passengers are deafening; the crashing into the tree tops is jarring; and the bouncing of the plane snaps my teeth as my jaw slams shut with the impact, and I taste blood where I have inadvertently bitten my tongue.

And now I close my eyes as I feel the plane gouging the trees, shearing off the tops. I hear metal being ripped from the plane, and it is so earsplitting that it drowns out the screams of the passengers. I still have my eyes shut, and now I shove my hands over my ears as well.

I suddenly remember that the flight attendant had told us to bend forward and to brace ourselves into a crash position. I do it just in time, and I am crouched into a tiny ball as much as my seatbelt will allow…here it comes.

The final crash is tremendous, crushing everything; the overhead luggage compartments burst open and bags and suitcases fly throughout the cabin to become deadly missiles. The noise is deafening and I am tossed around violently, and the seatbelt tears into my stomach as the plane tries to dislodge me from my seat. I feel the plane lurch forcefully as it bounces and tumbles, and I am disoriented as to which way is up or down. The plane is shaking so intensely that I am sure it will rip apart at any second.

And then, just as quickly as the crash started, it winds down. The shaking subsides, and I cannot believe I am still alive; oh my god, I am alive. Irrationally I imagine the story I will be able to tell. Maybe I can get on the TV news; I can see it now: *Man Survives Airplane Crash*. I have no idea why I am thinking such idiotic thoughts; maybe I am stunned, maybe I am drunk with disbelief that I am really and truly alive.

But I am alive! I am alive!

And just as I am rejoicing that I have landed safely, still alive and intact, I smell an acrid scent. And before I can react, dark smoke comes billowing into the airplane cabin; where is it coming from? There must be a fire!

The smoke instantly becomes dense. I have difficulty seeing into the airplane because the black smoke is everywhere, engulfing everything into total darkness. I can't see! I can hear others talking excitedly; how many survived? No time to think about it, because I am fumbling with my seat belt. What did the flight attendant say? Yes, the escape route is across the aisle. Why did I have to sit on the wrong side of the plane?

There! My seat belt is off. I try to jump into the aisle, but people are already there. No pushing, please! I squeeze my way into the aisle, don't panic, don't panic. I find myself in the middle of a crowd inching towards the exit. I still can't see through the black smoke, so I am groping my way, and my fingers touch the person ahead of me. I hope he or she is going in the right direction because I have no choice except to follow.

I know that my seat had been fairly close to the emergency exit door and I don't envy the others seated further back. I can't tell who is behind me, but I know there are more people towards the back of the plane. I find myself hoping they are okay, but there is nothing I can do for them since I can't see anything through the dense smoke.

I am having trouble breathing, I hear people coughing, and now I am wondering if the smoke could be toxic. How ironic that would be to survive a plane crash only to die because of suffocation from smoke.

No, I won't think like that! I won't die. I have come this far, I can't stop now.

I can see a light from the emergency door through the black smoke; it must be open, yes, it is open. Thank god! I am there now. I reach the doorway and I am trying to pull in lungfuls of air; I need to breathe. I see the person in front of me disappear as he jumps from the doorway. I see an inflated slide, but it is not very long because the door is not very high off the ground.

As I jump onto the slide, I feel disembodied. I slide downwards, and hit the ground hard, tumbling. Trees are everywhere around me and the area is deep in shade because of them.

I am alive! I stand up, amazed that I can even do so.

I see a woman sliding down after me, and I reach for her hand to help her up. Then I start to run, but I feel pain in one leg, so my gait is a lopsided trot. I see the cone of the plane. It is smashed into the ground, crumpled, and oh my god, the cockpit is on fire. I can see the flames shooting out the window.

I hesitate. No one could survive that fire, could they?

Run! My inner voice cries. *Save yourself! Get away from the plane; what if it explodes?*

But I hesitate again. I hear something.

"Help me! Please god, someone help me! I'm stuck! I'm trapped!"

The voice is coming from the cockpit. What should I do?

I look closely at the cockpit. I see the co-pilot, with a hatchet in his hand. He is striking the window, but his efforts seem useless. Is it shatter-proof glass? Surely airplane glass must be incredibly thick. And yet, I hear the co-pilot calling for help, so he must have somehow put a hole in the glass.

I have to help him. I have to. I don't know why, but I just have to.

I rush to the nose of the plane. It is partially buried into the earth and so low that I can reach the co-pilot's window without stretching too badly. I am trembling with adrenaline and sweat is stinging my eyes. I look into the co-pilot's eyes, and I try to transmit an unspoken message: *I won't leave you.*

I reach in the hole he had made in window and take the hatchet from the co-pilot's hand. I hammer at the window furiously from the outside, hacking and hacking. The hole begins to widen, and I think I can now pull the co-pilot out.

I reach inside and grab the co-pilot's shoulders. I pull and pull, but his body is resistant. Suddenly it gives, and he tumbles with me to the ground, just as the flames are shooting out the window, seeming angry that their victim has escaped.

And then the plane explodes, and explodes again, but I am still alive. And so is the co-pilot.

OFFICIAL REPORT ON FLIGHT 529 IN WIKIPEDIA

Atlantic Southeast Airlines Flight 529 took flight on August 21, 1995. Flight 529 left the ramp area at Atlanta at 12:10, and took off at 12:23. At 12.52, it experienced engine failure and crashed in a wooded area near the farming community of Burwell, Georgia.

All of the passengers and crew aboard Flight 529 survived the initial impact; but there were nine fatalities caused by a post-crash fire.

The fire, which started about one minute after impact, killed the pilot named Gannaway, who had been knocked unconscious in the crash landing. The oxygen bottle behind the copilot seat later ignited, contributing to the strength of the fire. Warmerdam, the co-pilot, bearing a dislocated shoulder, sustained burns as he used his left hand to hold an axe and cut through the thick cockpit glass. David McCorkell, a surviving passenger, pulled the axe out of the cockpit through a hole and struck the glass in order to increase the size of the hole and help Warmerdam escape.

The probable cause of the accident was determined to be the failure of the propeller due to undiscovered metal fatigue resulting from corrosion. There had been at least two previous failures of the same propellers, but those aircraft had been able to land safely. The propellers had been recalled and serviced at a Hamilton Standard facility, but the inspection had been incomplete and the refurbishing work ineffective.

The National Transportation Safety Board (NTSB) criticized Hamilton Standard, who had maintained the props, for "inadequate and ineffective corporate inspection and repair techniques, training, documentation and communication," and both Hamilton and the FAA for "failure to require recurrent on-wing ultrasonic inspections for the affected propellers."

THE DEAD MAN

Tyler looked out the window. Lightning flashed, and where it had simply drizzled earlier, suddenly the sky opened to release torrents of water that slammed down upon the earth without mercy. The effect of the stormy weather was apocalyptic to his mood, and he had feelings of melancholy and paranoia.

This type of weather made it even creepier to handle a dead body. Reluctantly, he went back to finish the preparations for moving it.

The dead man was still lying on the bed, but the covers were on the floor, and the body was naked. Tyler had felt there was no sense in leaving perfectly wearable clothes on a dead man, so he took them. After all, why would a dead man need clothes?

But the nakedness revealed how pale a body could be in death. The blood, no longer circulated by the heart, began to settle on the underside of the body, which created a purpling of the skin. The back, buttocks, and the underside of the legs became darkened because the body was on its back, and gravity pulled all the internal fluids downwards.

He gazed into the dead man's half-open eyes, noting that the corneas were cloudy. The dead man's milky irises peered out from the half-closed lids as though he were watching every move. It made Tyler feel self-conscious and uneasy for a moment, but he tried to shrug it off.

He went back to the window. Looking up and down the street, he realized that the bad weather gave him privacy. Hardly anyone had ventured outside on this cold, rainy night, so perhaps the storm was a good omen after all; never mind that the thunder and lightning was making him feel superstitious.

Again, Tyler turned to the dead man on the bed. The body was hardening with rigor mortis, so it was difficult to maneuver. The process that had begun at the jawline was now moving down the body, stiffening the limbs and making them immobile.

Why hadn't Tyler anticipated this? He realized he should have curled the body into a fetal position while he still could. But now, the body was rigid and the arms and legs were outstretched, splayed woodenly across the bed, and resistant to Tyler's attempts to fold them.

But none of this had been premeditated, so Tyler was flying by the seat of his pants. He had thought he should wait until dark to dispose of the dead man, not realizing that time would mean the difference between a pliable body and a rigid one.

He needed the body to be small if it were to fit into the trunk of his car.

Should he cut it up? Maybe if the arms and legs wouldn't move, he should simply saw them off. As long as he didn't panic, he reasoned that he still had time to dismember the body. It was hours until daylight.

Tyler dragged the body off the bed. It slipped from his grip and fell to the floor with a solid thud upon the carpeting. He was surprised at how heavy the body was; so it must be true what people said about dead weight.

He tightened his grasp around the shoulders, through the armpits, and dragged the body towards the bathroom. The legs bumped across the carpeted floor; straight, not having any give. Tyler blinked at the bright light in the bathroom, and with one hand still gripping the body, he used his other hand to pull open the shower curtain, revealing a white, porcelain bathtub.

He strained to lift the body and to push it into the bathtub, face up. It tumbled stiffly but with the arms outspread; it wouldn't fit into the tub, so it lay over it, with one arm and one leg dangling over the edge.

Frustrated, Tyler lifted his foot and tried to stamp the body into the tub but the body resisted. Then he steadied his foot onto the dead man's stomach and put all his weight on it, one hand holding onto the curtain rod for balance.

There was a cracking noise as the dead body reluctantly gave up some of its unyielding posture; not enough, but it would have to do. The saw would take care of the rest. At least now the blood could be confined to the inside of the tub if Tyler was careful.

Tyler left the bathroom to retrieve the saw. He opened the inside door leading to the garage and flipped the light switch, and looked at the empty spot on the shelf where the saw had been.

How could he have been so stupid? How could he have forgotten that he had lent the saw to his brother-in-law the previous week?

Tyler felt sweat bead on his forehead. He was making mistakes.

This was a situation where even the tiniest error could bring the whole thing down. He knew he had to keep himself on a level plane; he needed to continue with a calm and calculating detachment from any emotions.

Don't make mistakes, he told himself. *You can handle this.*

So what to do now?

Think.

He would use a knife. It was not just any knife; he would use the Spyderco he had in his tool chest. Tyler knew that on the Spyderco knife, jimping was added to the blade's spine for slip-resistant cutting control. And it was sharp as a scalpel, with the added benefit that part of the blade was serrated, perfect for sawing through bone if that became necessary.

Clutching the knife, Tyler closed the garage door and headed back to the brightly lit bathroom. When he entered the bathroom, he found it astonishing that there was a dead body in his bathtub, even though he already knew it was there. It was real yet unreal at the same time. It was like a very weird space-time continuum that seemed to be happening to someone other than himself; he felt as though he was a third person, an impartial witness to the macabre scene.

But it soon became very real indeed as Tyler knelt on the floor and lowered his sharp knife towards the dead man in the tub.

Tyler knew that the chest cavity would be full of congealed and coagulated blood, so he wanted to avoid that area. Instead, he started at the left elbow. He made a slit in the skin, and was surprised when the cut did not spurt blood. Then he remembered that the stilled heart no longer pumped any blood through the veins of the dead man. There was only a pinkish-yellow underskin when the cut was widened, and some blood dripped, but none gushed.

He sawed through the fibrous ligaments of the elbow joint, annoyed at how resistant it proved to be, even with such a sharp knife. He rolled the joint open to cut the remaining tendon.

And then suddenly the lower arm was severed.

He held the arm aloft by its hand, and was disconcerted by how short the lower limb appeared. The stump at the elbow was ragged, torn…and dripping blood onto the bathroom floor.

He would need to be thorough when he cleaned this bathroom after he disposed of the body. He wanted no more mistakes on this night.

Suddenly Tyler heard a noise. Someone was knocking on his front door!

He froze for a moment, and then carefully placed the severed arm back into the bathtub, on top of its previous owner.

He glanced at his watch. The dial was covered in blood, and he used his other hand to wipe it away. The blood was thick and coagulated; it wasn't thin like fresh blood would be. It left a smear when wiped, but Tyler could make out the time.

11:10 PM.

Who in the world would be knocking on his door at this late hour? And who would venture out on such a stormy night?

Certainly he couldn't answer the door, not with blood up to his elbows. Should he ignore the knock, with the hopes that the unwanted visitor would think no one was home and go away?

But Tyler wanted to know who it was.

Grabbing a towel off the rack, Tyler wiped his hands the best he could. He threw the bloody towel on top of the closed toilet seat. He planned to disinfect the entire bathroom later, but a thought crossed his mind anyway: *Maybe I should try to limit the blood evidence in this bathroom as much as possible.*

There was already blood that dripped from the severed arm onto the floor. Maybe he should have thrown the towel into the bathtub on top of the dismembered dead man. Too late now.

He strode out of the bathroom and crossed the living room. He had no lights on in the living room, so he knew it would be okay to peek out a curtain. Slowly and carefully he pulled a corner of the curtain aside, and peered out the front window. Rain was running in rivulets down the windowpane, blurring the glass, so it was a moment before he comprehended what he saw outside the window.

Another eye was peering back in!

Startled at the face he saw in the window, Tyler stumbled backwards and sat down hard on the floor. Picking himself up, he realized that whoever was trying to look into his window had seen him, and knew he was inside. So, he had nothing to lose by confronting his unwelcome visitor with a question.

But he would not open the door.

"Who is it?" Tyler called through the closed door.

"Police!"

Oh my god! Tyler thought frantically. *They know! They had found out. And they were coming for him. In fact, they had already come.*

He made up his mind. No matter what, he wouldn't go back to prison.

Feeling like a cornered animal, he knew what he had to do.

The next day, all of the television news cameras were aimed at the Chief of Police as he stood at the podium.

"Tell us about the shoot-out!" one of the reporters yelled.

The Chief addressed the crowd, using the formal police-terminology-speak that was difficult for laypeople to follow. "The perpetrator shot a nine millimeter caliber gun at one of our officers through the door of the residence, wounding the officer in the shoulder. Backup was called and SWAT was initiated. But before negotiations could proceed, the perpetrator exited from the back door. When the perpetrator began shooting his weapon at the swat team, they immediately returned fire. The perpetrator is deceased."

"What did you find inside the residence?" another reporter shouted.

"We are withholding details at this time."

"Why did the police go to this man's house in the first place?" called still another reporter.

The Chief of Police hesitated a moment, then decided that this part of the events didn't need to be held close to the vest.

Appearing puzzled, he spoke in a more conversational, natural manner.

"Well, now, that's the thing," he said. "The officer was going to all of the homes on that street. He was giving warnings to all of the homeowners about an unrelated crime that had just occurred down the block. If the perp had not panicked, he might have never given himself away. Apparently it was a mistake on his part."

THE FAMOUS FILM STAR

I freelanced, which meant that I sold my celebrity photos to the highest bidder. Call me paparazzi if you want, but I called it lucrative.

And why was it so lucrative? Because I got exposés. I caught the stars in compromising situations. And I did it by stalking them.

I was very successful in my chosen profession, not just because I was clever, but also because I am female. For some reason, stars expect the paparazzi to be male. They let their guard down when they see a woman, so I got the goods.

And then there was Jeremy Hayes, the famous film star and Hollywood heartthrob. It was in the news that once a month he would disappear for a few days. Lots of photographers wanted to know why, but no one could get the goods. Did I mention that I am better than most of the paparazzi? I knew I could find out what Jeremy was up to if anyone could.

So I began to stalk him. I tailed his Lexus. I followed him to restaurants and bars, to clothing stores, and even to the set of his latest film. But nothing he did stood out as mysterious.

I decided to stalk him day and night, to hold a stake-out of his premises in my car. I would eat and sleep in my car. The only time I would leave Jeremy's house would be to relieve myself or to shower. It was a lot of work and stress but I knew that this would be "the big one."

I would park on the street outside his gate. Most Hollywood stars live behind tall fences, and Jeremy Hayes was no exception. His was an expensive home in Beverly Hills off of Highway 2, better known as Santa Monica Boulevard. Jeremy lived on North Rexford Drive, the same street where Boris Karloff had once resided. It was a neighborhood of stars and looked it.

A couple of times, I was rousted by the police as I was sitting in my car. But I was committing no crimes, none that they could see, anyway. I was simply parked on a public street. Besides, I had a press card, so overall I was left alone. No one knew that I had stuck a tracking device underneath the Lexus' car chassis one day when Jeremy had been inside a restaurant.

And then I got my break. It was a Thursday night at about 2AM. I was trying to keep from nodding off when I saw the gate open and the Lexus emerged, gleaming in the street lamps. Instantly I became alert and started my car, turning the GPS system on.

I followed the Lexus south to Wilshire Boulevard where we turned west. He got off Wilshire in Koreatown and stopped at a storage facility.

When he drove the Lexus inside, I knew I couldn't follow him because first, I would be spotted and second, I didn't know the gate code.

I waited on the street, and was rewarded when a blue Toyota drove out. *So that's how he doesn't get followed,* I thought. *He changes cars. I guess the GPS is useless for me now.*

I tailed the Toyota and Jeremy returned to Wilshire Boulevard, this time turning east to backtrack. We entered a neighborhood and I followed Jeremy to South Curson Avenue, right across from Hancock Park in Los Angeles. The homes here were by no means cheap; but they couldn't begin to compare to Beverly Hills prices.

My adrenaline raced. Jeremy Hayes had never been connected romantically to anyone. Was I about to find out why? Was there a secret woman, or even a secret man in his life? At only thirty years old, there had to be "a someone." If so, what about that someone could be so damaging to his career that Jeremy wouldn't want the world to know?

I aimed to find out.

I parked on the street, many cars away from the Toyota so as not to be seen. I exited my car with one of my cameras at my side. It was a Nikon Coolpix S9100, perfect for shooting photos in low light settings.

Covertly, I began taking pictures. I shot Jeremy as he exited the Toyota in front of a house and walked up to the door, which opened before he got there. As my camera clicked away, I realized that whoever lived in this house had been expecting Jeremy. Perhaps he had called ahead of his arrival.

The person who opened the front door was an older man who had graying hair and looked to be in his sixties. *So it's a man,* I thought.

Romantic partner? Drug dealer?

The door closed with Jeremy inside, and I realized that would be enough for one night. I got back into my car and drove home.

But now I had an address to research. I intended to find out who the older man was, and why a famous film star would be visiting him in the middle of the night.

<< — >>

As I expected, Jeremy Hayes had vanished again. And I was the only one who knew to where he had disappeared.

I researched the address, but for some reason, I was unable to locate the owner of the property, not through public inquiries and not through my private channels. That in itself was highly unusual.

So I decided to simply go to the house and knock on the front door. I was no stranger to a direct approach.

The morning was beautiful. April in Los Angeles is the perfect time of year; sunny but not yet seasonably hot, the air not exactly clean but not choked with smog either. The smog would envelope the city come July and August, trapped by the Santa Monica, San Jacinto, and San Gabriel mountain ranges.

The house was a modest one-story, with a stucco arch above the front porch. It was painted an unusual color, a beige-pink, and looked like it was supposed to be a Spanish style, but just missed the mark. It sure didn't look like the kind of place a famous Hollywood star would use for a tryst, but then again, I reminded myself that looks are often deceiving. After all, most Hollywood stars did not drive Toyotas either, but this one did.

I parked my car on the street and went up the walkway. It was about ten in the morning, and I figured they'd be up by now.

Knocking on the front door, I listened for any sounds inside. I could hear someone walking on what was probably a hardwood floor.

The door opened and I was face-to-face with the older man. "Can I help you?" he asked politely.

In anticipation, I stuck my foot in the door as I said, "I'd like to talk to Jeremy."

Sure enough, the door began to close, but my foot prevented the man's success. I pushed at the door. "I'll call the cops!" the man said.

"If you do," I threatened, "I'll plaster photos of this residence all over Hollywood. Now all I want to do is talk. If you let me in, I'll keep my mouth shut and my camera off."

I could feel the man's hesitation. "What do you want?"

"Just to talk. That's all. Here's my identification." I shoved my credentials at him.

I could hear the man sigh as he opened the door once again. "There is nothing here but I'll let you in anyway."

The living room was smaller than I expected, the walls painted cream. He gestured to an overstuffed chair and I sat down. He sat in an identical chair across from me.

"Listen," I said, "I know that Jeremy Hayes came here last night. I have proof. I just want to know why."

"Why can't you people leave him alone?"

"Jeremy Hayes is a public figure and his fans want to know all about him. I'm just the middle-man, or middle-woman, I should say."

Then I got to the point. "What's going on between you two?"

The man sat against the chair, as if a wind had blown him backwards. "Going on? I'm his father."

I wasn't expecting that. No wonder I couldn't determine who owned this house. Sometimes money could buy anonymity.

"I'm Donna; what's your name?"

"George."

"Why does Jeremy come here every month and stay for three days?" I asked.

"Who says he does?"

"I say."

"You have a problem with a son visiting his father?"

I smiled grimly. "That depends. Is he here now?"

"Yes, in the back bedroom. He's sleeping and I am not going to disturb him."

No amount of probing made George open up any further. No amount of pushing or cajoling had any effect. Eventually I decided to leave. For now.

After he saw me to the door, I got back into my car and started the engine. I knew that George was watching me from inside the house through the window. I drove away.

Around the block.

Then I parked my car once again and snuck back, on foot.

As did most homes in California, this one had a six-foot tall redwood fence around the back yard. When I first arrived, I had noticed a tree stump next to it. I knew I could climb into the back yard using that stump. I also knew there was no dog, because the home was very quiet.

A perfect house to spy upon and snoop into.

The fence was easy to climb. It was well maintained so it bore my weight well and gave me no splinters. Once on top of the fence, I leaped to the ground inside the back yard.

I quietly approached one of the two bedroom windows. I was happy to see that they weren't covered by blinds, only curtains. In both rooms, the curtains were slightly parted, allowing me to peek inside.

The first bedroom was apparently used as an office, having a computer desk and file cabinet.

The second bedroom contained a bed, but it was empty.

George had lied. Jeremy wasn't asleep in a back bedroom. So then, where was he? I knew he was somewhere in that house. He had to be.

I would come back that night, after dark. I was an expert at breaking into people's homes, even when they were there at the time. The trick was to disable the alarm, go in silently, and not wake the inhabitants. This time I wouldn't even have to drug a dog. I could do it. I knew I could, because I have done it many, many times and never woken up a single homeowner.

Illegal? Yes. Immoral? Yes.

But even if my methods were not above board, I had no guilt. I was the paparazzi, and I always got the goods, no matter what. I agreed with the old saying that the end justifies the means. I also liked the saying that it takes a thief to catch a thief. I was a thief of secrets and since no one was as skillful at as I was, no one could catch me.

<< — >>

Although the days in April were warm, the nights could get down to the low-60s. I wore a sweater over loose-fitting pants, everything black, of course. The pants were a cargo type with lots of pockets.

I parked my car three blocks away and walked to South Curson Avenue. The full moon enabled good visibility, so I had no trouble finding the stump at the redwood fence. Quietly I mounted the fence, held onto it on the other side, and let myself down gently. There would be no jumping over the fence tonight. Everything must be as silent as the grave.

Stealthily I crept through the backyard, staying close to the fence, using it as cover. I kept my mouth open so that I could hear well. I moved slowly, stopping every two steps to listen, and when I heard nothing, I continued on another two steps.

I had a tool for my profession in one of my pockets. Once I reached the sliding glass door on the back porch, I removed the tool from my pocket and slid it into the door frame. Sliding glass doors were never a problem for me to open, even when they were locked. This one didn't have a bar placed in its bottom track, the best kind. As anticipated, the door smoothly and silently opened a crack.

Again I hesitated; waiting, listening. I had already disabled the alarm. I knew I could continue inside. Still, I waited an extra minute or two just to be sure. Outside, I could still change my mind. Inside, I was committed.

It was now or never.

I slid the door open just enough to allow me to fit though. I pushed the drapery aside, entered the room, and stopped. I needed time for my eyes to adjust from the moonlight outside to the full darkness inside. And I needed to listen once again.

No sounds. So far, so good.

When my eyes adjusted, I could see that the room inside the door was a family room, complete with a brick fireplace. In the center of the room was an open doorway leading to the front of the house. To the left was the hallway leading to the bedrooms. To the right of the fireplace was an archway and I had no idea what was behind that arch.

Since I had already seen the front of the house, the logical place to start snooping would be the bedrooms. I crept down the hallway, hoping the doors were open. They were.

Silently peering into the first, I saw that the office was unoccupied.

No one had placed a cot there for any guests. That left the second bedroom.

I could hear soft snoring from the second room, and slowly brought my face forward through the door to see the person asleep on the bed. I saw silver hair on the pillow. Moonlight shined on it through the curtains. This was the father. I wasn't interested in George.

Only Jeremy.

Slowly I backtracked and made my way into the family room. What lay beyond the archway to the right of the fireplace? I needed to find out.

The archway was short, much shorter than the open space leading to the living room. I poked my head through, watching and listening. There was a closed wooden door inside the archway. Where did it lead? The basement?

Suddenly I heard something. I froze completely. No quick moves now; I depended on my own silence.

I opened my mouth again in order to hear better. It sounded like a dog was sniffing at the other side of the door. What? I had been so sure there had been no family dog. I became angry at myself. This was a situation where mistakes would be incredibly costly.

I immediately calmed myself. Emotions were deadly, so I needed to keep my cool.

I slowly and silently reached inside one of my pockets for mace. I retrieved it, held it in my hand, and listened at the cellar door.

There was definitely something on the other side, moving against the door. Too tall to be a dog. Jeremy?

Why would he be in the cellar? Perhaps it was a finished basement with another bedroom down there. But if that were the case, why would Jeremy be up at the door?

I realized that if Jeremy was at the cellar door, it was because he knew someone was on the other side of it. He knew someone was in the house. He was listening to me just like I was listening to him.

An impasse. No, that sort of thing was for quitters. I was no quitter. I would get the story no matter what.

I silently touched the doorknob, and tried to turn it. Locked. But the key was right there up on the wall, hanging on a hook.

All I had to do was to quickly open the door, snap a photo, and run like hell back outside. The flash would blind Jeremy and I could make good my escape. By the time George got out of the bedroom, I would already be over the fence and running away at full tilt boogie. With my camera.

I carried a tiny camera meant for nefarious jobs. I put the mace back in my pocket and took the camera out of yet another pocket in the cargo pants. I aimed it as I grabbed the key off the wall.

Holding the camera in one hand and the key in the other, I unlocked the cellar door.

I was about to drop the key on the floor to free up my hand so I could turn the knob when suddenly the door burst outwards at me, throwing me backwards off my feet. I crashed to the floor and the wind was knocked out of me. The camera fell from my grasp and bounced away.

Gasping for breath, I saw a thing towering over me. It was huge and dark and smelled like musk. It was an animal, hairy and roaring with rage. I could see fangs and suddenly the creature swiped at me with razor-sharp claws, ripping the black sweater from my body in one fell swoop.

I grabbed the can of mace from my pocket and tried to raise it but it was knocked from my hand, clattering away on the hardwood floor. Why had I ever thought such a small thing as mace could protect me?

The thing attacked me again. I tried to shove my forearm sideways, because I knew that a sharp elbow could be an effective weapon. But the creature seemed to be everywhere. I began to feel disoriented and didn't know where to aim.

Desperate for survival, I tried another tactic. I tried to kick the creature; but again, the animal was quick, too quick, and it was a whirlwind of weight, razor teeth and slashing claws. I was aware of intense, searing pain coming from seemingly everywhere on my body, even on my face. It felt like the thing was attacking me for an eternity, although what was left of my rational thoughts was sure it had only been for a few seconds.

Suddenly I heard an ear-shattering BOOM and the creature fell away from me.

I didn't feel like a thief of secrets. I didn't feel like the paparazzi who always got the goods. I felt like a frightened, panicked little girl, and I screamed.

"Shut up, it's over now," I heard George say. He flipped on a light switch.

Still on the floor, blinking from the sudden light, I sat up. There was Jeremy, lying face-up next to me, naked, with a gaping hole in his chest that was dark with blood. The wet, maroon fluid dripped down his sides to pool upon the hardwood floor.

"What?" I couldn't say anything else. Somehow, that single word spoke volumes.

"We agreed that if he ever tried to kill someone, I'd shoot him," George said.

"What?" I repeated.

"If you're such a hot-shot reporter, why didn't you ever figure out that his disappearances coincided with the cycles of the full moon? Legends are always based on facts. The bullet was silver."

It dawned on me what he was saying. "That's not possible," I said, and managed to get to my feet.

"That's my son I just killed," George said. "But you are just as responsible for his death as I am. Why couldn't you just leave him alone? It was only for three days a month. I hid him and locked him up during those times. For chrissakes, he volunteered to have me hide him. He didn't want to hurt anyone."

Tears coursed down the old man's cheeks as he stomped violently upon my camera, smashing it. "He was a good boy, and he was a famous film star. Maybe he was a monster sometimes, but now he is human. You can't prove otherwise. You have no photographs."

Then he turned to look directly at me. "Where will you go for three days every month?"

HORRORSCOPE

The first thing I do when I wake up in the morning is read my horoscope.

I do that even before I have a cup of coffee.

I read it in the newspaper. It's not my newspaper; it really belongs to my mother. In fact, everything in this house belongs to my mother. I live with her.

Yes, I know; I'm a forty-two year-old man, and I live with my mother. Some people think that's weird, but my mother needs me. Well, I sort of need her too, but I think she needs me more.

But anyway, I read my horoscope. I'm a Leo, and I'm really proud of my sign. I mean, it's symbolized by a lion, so it's royal and all that. King of the jungle. Plus I was born in summer, and everyone knows that summer is the best time of year.

A couple of years ago, I started reading books about astrology, and I learned how great the Leo sign really is. What I learned in those astrology books is that Leo is a special sign, so at that point, I started realizing that I'm special, too.

Soon I found out that reading about my birth sign was only the beginning for my understanding about my full potential. Yes, I am very special; I stand apart.

It isn't always easy to stand apart. Being better than other people has a price, and sometimes I don't exactly fit in. People think I'm weird. Oh, they don't always tell me to my face that I'm weird but I know they think it by the way they look at me.

That's okay. I'm aware that other people simply don't understand me. How can anyone understand something as unique as me? People are used to the norm, the commonplace... the average things in life. Average people are used to other average people. Anything that stands apart is considered weird, but weird just means different. And different means special.

So, I don't hold rudeness against anyone. I am mature enough to overlook it and to forgive average people for their inferiority.

Well, at least, most of the time I can overlook things...well, okay, maybe not all of the time. I admit that sometimes even I get upset at certain people. Like, I hate it when people don't appreciate my efforts to make them happy.

Sometimes I lose control when I am not appreciated.

Anyway, we're talking about my horoscope—let's get back to that. I told you I read it first thing every morning. It's important to me and I won't start my day without it, because it's all written in the stars, man. We don't have control of our lives, that's for the stars, but it's okay, because the stars give excellent advice. Horoscopes give guidance as to how we should go about our days. Without horoscopes, people would be lost and just flounder. Without horoscopes, nobody would get anything done. So everybody needs horoscopes, it's just that most people don't know how to read them correctly.

You see my point, right?

Of course you do.

The problem with my life is that I've always been underappreciated. I haven't been able to stay on one job very long because my bosses always hold me back. I mean, I'm certainly not going to start any job as a janitor. Half the time I know more about the job than the damn supervisor. But do I get any credit?

And anyway, I can't go out of the house on days when my horoscope tells me I'm about to have a bad day. You see the sense in that. And all of those jobs only give a guy a limited number of sick days. None of it's been my fault.

But you want to know about the women.

Where do you want me to start? Oh, at the beginning. You want me to start with what I think is the beginning.

Guess that means the hooker. I don't know the hooker's name. Guess it doesn't matter.

On the day I find the hooker, I have a good horoscope. It tells me I'm going to have a good day so I know I can leave the house. Let me look in my scrapbook…oh, here it is.

Okay. This day, my Leo horoscope says: *Outlook for the day: Good. You get cooperation and good fortune comes your way. A loved one will be agreeable now. Don't count on current romantic conditions to last very long because there could be a change of mind. Still, you have good probabilities for achieving objectives today.*

There, you see? On that day, my horoscope was predicting that I would meet a girl and she'd be initially agreeable to my advances, but that a little while later, she'd change her mind. So everything that happens is pre-ordained. I can't alter what is supposed to be. I just have to do what my horoscope says, and since my horoscope didn't specify what my objectives were that day, I figured that part was up to me.

Anyway, that day…when is it…oh I know, I'll look in my scrapbook again. Let's see; yes, here it is: it was March third. I'll tell you about it.

You know I don't drive because I'm supposed to take medication. So I always take the bus when I go downtown. I figured I'd go downtown looking for love, because my horoscope says someone would be agreeable to my advances. And since my horoscope says the love wouldn't be permanent, I figured the stars must be talking about a prostitute.

So you see, sometimes I have to interpret my horoscope. I mean, it's there in black and white, but the newspaper only has so much space in which to print the horoscopes every day, so they can't be including names and places and stuff. But I'm really in tune to the stars, so my horoscopes never need names and places, because I can figure out that part on my own.

On this particular morning, I decide to take twenty dollars from my mother's cookie jar; ha—real original place to hide money, isn't it? Anyway, I sure don't want to spend more than twenty dollars on a hooker, know what I mean?

I put a hammer underneath my coat. I figure the hammer would work just fine to knock someone out.

I get on the bus and ride downtown. I get off on Twenty-Third Street because everyone knows the cheaper hookers walk around on Twenty-Seventh. That means I only need to walk four blocks from the bus stop for me to reach the streetwalkers.

So I get to Twenty-Seventh and look around. It's about one o'clock in the afternoon so there aren't a lot of hookers around. They usually come out in full force after dark, but there're always a couple of them strolling the street no matter what time of day or night. It's a twenty-four hour deal. It's just that there's more to choose from at night.

So I see this girl, right? She's white, and I want someone from my own race. I'm not prejudiced or anything; it's just that I have to have one with red hair. A redhead is a must, and this hooker has red hair.

I have confidence. I know the hooker will be okay with me because my horoscope told me so. She'll say yes.

I walk up to her. She's wearing this really short pair of cutoffs, showing her butt cheeks in the back and all. She's got on high heels and some sort of sweater-top. She looks sort of skinny but I figure she's probably more concerned with finding drugs than with finding food most of the time.

"I got twenty," I say. I don't feel like negotiating. My horoscope promised she'd say yes. And she does.

"Where'd ya wanna go, big fella?" she asks me.

"Somewhere private," I tell her. She says she knows the place.

I follow her behind a building; there're dumpsters and other crap back there. But it's sort of an alley, and she's right, it doesn't seem like anyone could see us real well.

She takes off her sweater. No bra. I'm not excited; the girl is scrawny, but that's not why I'm so ho-hum about it.

"How're we gonna lie down?" I ask her. "This is nothing but an alley."

"For twenty, you don't get to lie down," she tells me. "You want a motel, you pay forty. For twenty, I'll lean against the wall. I'll face the wall and you can get me from behind. Not in the ass, though."

Perfect, I think. She's gonna turn around.

The minute she does, I grab her. I'm a big guy; you see my muscles? So I take out my hammer that I have under my jacket. Right there in the daylight.

But she starts to fight. I had forgotten that part about my horoscope. My horoscope warned me that the girl would change her mind. Stupid of me to forget! Anyway, she really fights hard. I'm surprised. She looks so scrawny.

Somehow she gets away. She starts screaming, so I turn and run. Nobody catches me. A few minutes later, I'm back on the bus headed to my mother's house. I wouldn't be surprised if at about the same time as I'm on the bus, that hooker is back on the Twenty-

117

Seventh Street stroll as though nothing happened. Just another day in the life of a cheap hooker.

But my horoscope is right, because it's still a good day. I learned something. I learned that I needed to be more prepared for the next time. And that hooker wouldn't have done me any good, anyway, even if I had bopped her over the head right there in that alley with my hammer. I need a girl I can bring home. What am I going to do, bring a hooker home on the bus?

No, I didn't kill anyone that day. What about the time I did commit murder, you ask? Listen, who's telling this story, anyway? I'll tell you about the murder in a minute.

I begin to search my horoscopes every day for guidance. I figure I want the next time to be just right.

Then, one day, there it is. I get all excited.

Wait, let me look in my scrapbook and I can read to you exactly what it says. Looks like March twenty-sixth. Anyway, here it is: *Outlook for the day: Excellent. This is a good day to follow up on new prospects while putting a high value on your skills and knowledge. A major decision you make now can lead to good results if you show courage and faith. In order to take advantage of what is offered, you must see things through to completion.*

Now, you can just bet that's a direct order from the stars telling me I need to act again. Can't you understand this? I keep telling you that all things we do are pre-ordained; it's in the stars.

So this time, I decide to stick around closer to my mother's house because I need to bring a girl home with me. I figure, maybe a nicer, inexperienced girl might be easier to grab than that stupid hooker. But no matter who it is, she has to be a redhead.

So I do what my horoscope says. I decide to have courage and faith, and to use my skills and knowledge. I gained knowledge after that hooker incident. I know what to do this time, I will take advantage of what is offered. I won't go seeking, instead, I will wait for a redhead to come to me.

I decide that since my horoscope says the outlook for the day is excellent, I can go out of the house. I can run some errands. I have courage, and I have faith that the stars will put a redhead in my path. I know that my destiny is about to be realized.

Anyway, I put the hammer under my jacket again because I'm sure the stars are going to provide someone for me. I go to the grocery store because I need a gallon of milk. I don't need a car for that, because it's only two blocks away from my mother's house and I can walk.

I go into the store, and sure enough, there's a redhead working there. She's a checker. She must be new because I've been to the grocery store lots of times and I've never seen her before. See what I mean about the stars? They have control of our lives. Everything is pre-ordained.

So I'm not surprised to walk into the store and what do you know, there's a redhead. Now, I will grant you that she's not very good-looking, sort of dumpy and all, but who cares, it's only the color of the hair that matters.

I decide to forget the milk and buy something simple just to get nearer to her. I pick up a diet soda and stand in her line. When I get near to her, I feel sort of tingly inside. I feel happy. I know I have courage and faith, and that this is the opportunity my horoscope promised. I know I must see things through to completion, which means that although I will leave this store now, I'll be waiting outside for this woman. Waiting just for her.

What do you mean, did I choose her at random? Aren't you listening? Nothing in this world is random, it's all in the stars. That woman was put in the grocery store for a reason. So to answer your question, no, I didn't choose her at random, the stars chose her for me. I only do what my horoscope tells me. You just don't listen, do you? No wonder I think you're inferior. It's because you are.

Oh is that right? Well fuck you, too.

Listen, asshole, you want me to go on with this story or not?

You know, the only reason I'm talking to you in the first place today is because today's horoscope told me to. Otherwise, I'd sure blow you off.

Well, I've got to remember to be patient with people like you. I'm special; I'm in tune to the stars. Most people are just average, so they don't have the ability to understand the stars. Only special people like me have the ability to read horoscopes correctly.

Okay, back to what I was saying. Where was I? Oh yeah.

Anyway, I wait until the store closes. I hang around, because I mean, what if the redhead only works part time? She'd leave early, before closing, and if I go back home, I'll miss her. Now, I know I look weird hanging out for a couple of hours in front of the grocery store, but I keep remembering that my horoscope says to have courage and faith, so I hang out in the parking lot…waiting.

It's a Ma and Pa store, so it closes at eight-thirty. It's only March, so it's dark already. Days are still sort of short. I'm glad it's dark; I know it will make things easier.

I see the woman come out of the store, and again I feel good, sort of tingly. Maybe it's anticipation. I don't know, but it's really cool how I feel. I feel excited, happy, powerful. I feel superior over this woman who is too dumb to realize that she shouldn't be walking all alone in a dark parking lot. But then I remember, this is all pre-ordained by the stars. Maybe the woman is smarter at other times. But tonight is not her night; this is *my* night.

I silently follow the woman, crouching among the parked cars. There're not many cars right now, but it's dark and the woman seems preoccupied anyway so she has no idea that I am stalking her. I am thinking to myself: *This is so easy. I am meant to do this.*

I sneak up behind her. I glance around quickly. All is quiet. There's no one around to interfere. This parking lot isn't very well lighted, and this store makes the employees park in the farthest parking spaces so that the customers can park close. All to my advantage.

I slide my hammer out from underneath my jacket. I feel the rough wooden handle in the palm of my hand. I grip it tightly but the hard wood does not give. I move the hammer and see the dim streetlight reflecting off the metal top. It looks very powerful in my hand; the hammer makes me *feel* powerful.

I know it's time and I can feel my heart pound. This is really happening! I am this woman's destiny, and this woman is my destiny. My heart soars.

I am right behind her. I watch as she fumbles in her purse for her car key. That gives me the right opportunity. With courage and faith, I lift my arm and swiftly bring the hammer down on the woman's head.

It's more than I could ever ask for. The woman drops silently to the ground, landing in a heap. She is sprawled on the black tar of the parking lot, motionless.

I feel exhilaration. I feel potent; almost omnipotent. It is glorious how I so efficiently fulfill the commands of the stars. I am special! Looking at the woman lying unconscious on the ground merely reminds me of my superiority: I am better than this average woman lying limp beneath me.

You keep interrupting me. You keep asking me about the murder. I'm not at the murder part of this story yet, okay?

What?

You want to know why I murdered? Listen, I told you I'm not at the murder part yet. So far I haven't killed anybody.

Hey, I'm going to tell this story either my way or no way. If you want to hear the rest, then you can just shut up and listen. You already read me my Miranda rights, so I know I don't have to talk to any cops, much less a rude one like you. Consider yourself lucky that I *am* talking.

Damn, you keep interrupting me, and now I forget where I was. Oh yeah, the redhead. I just bopped her one over the head.

Well, I need to take this girl home, see? So I figure, she has her car keys in her hand. Probably the stars planned that too. Anyway, I told you I don't drive because the DMV won't give me a driver's license, but that doesn't mean I *can't* drive.

So I pick up the redhead from the ground. I'm surprised at how heavy she is, but she's none too slim, you know? Dead weight and all that. Ha, that's funny; she feels like dead weight but she isn't dead. She's only unconscious.

I realize it's easier to drag her, so I do that until I have her at the passenger side of the car. I push her inside, and sort of prop her up. She looks like she could be sleeping. Works for me.

I go back around the car and get in the driver's side. All this time, I keep thinking, *Man oh man, my horoscope will never let me down. This is just so cool.*

I feel like I want to rejoice. It is like I am drunk with power and I know I can do anything, as long as the stars guide me.

I turn the car towards my mother's house and drive off. I am bringing home my prize.

I am so excited! Only two blocks away.

Finally I reach my mother's house and I park in the back. I am taking the girl inside the house, going in through the back way. Nobody will catch me, because my horoscope said there would be good results if I follow through to completion.

And now is the time for completion.

This woman I'm dragging into my house is supposed to be my sister. My sister was a redhead. Now you see why the hair color is so important?

What do you mean that you don't understand how a stranger can substitute for my sister? God you are so dense. Don't you get it? My sister was killed when she was little, run over by a car. I figure she'd be grown up by now if she were still alive.

My mother always wants my sister. My mother still cries over her. My mother tells me all the time that I'm second best. You know, how it should have been me who got run over by that car instead of my sister because I'm, well, damaged….and my sister was perfect.

My mother needs to quit thinking that I'm damaged. I'm really just different. And as you know, different means special. I told you that I am superior to the average people in this world. I'm different, not damaged.

But my mother always wants my sister. So I figure, what the hell, I'll bring my sister back. Maybe then my mother will like me, too. We could be a real family again.

So, this redhead is my gift to my mother. This is my sister.

There you go again, interrupting me. Don't worry, I'm getting to the murder part. Quit rushing me.

I figure if this redhead isn't quite right, and my mother doesn't think she's good enough to be my sister, then I'll just get rid of this redhead and find another one. I could try this or that one on for size as my sister. You know, life is really very simple if people are smart enough to put things in perspective. It doesn't have to be rocket science.

But because my horoscope is so positive for this day, I am pretty convinced that this is the right redhead to be my sister.

But something is wrong now. To this very moment, I still can't figure it out. I can't understand what is wrong. I keep looking at my scrapbook, and my horoscope doesn't change for that day. Horoscopes are always right. So what is wrong?

Do you think I lost that special ability to be able to really be in tune with the stars? Did I suddenly stop being able to read my horoscope correctly?

It's confusing and upsetting.

But now I'm getting to the murder part. You happy? It's what you've been waiting to hear.

My mother's reaction is what's wrong. Here I have her daughter in my arms. Alive. Here's the perfect sister that she's been wanting all these years. I have done the most wonderful thing in the world. I have brought my sister back from the dead.

Why is my mother screaming? What the hell?

Shut up! Shut the hell up!

Look at your daughter! Don't you want her back? What's the matter with you? I did this for you! Don't you appreciate it?

Oh man.

I let the girl go, and she falls to the floor. I am really confused now.

I decide that this must not be the right redhead. So I have to kill my sister. I reach into my jacket and pull out the hammer.

But then I realize that my sister is already dead. She was run over by a car, a lot of years ago.

How can I kill someone who is already dead?

Okay, here it is—what you've wanted to know. We're finally reached the murder part of my story.

I don't kill the redhead. But my mother is being so rude.

Now do you finally understand why I am justified in killing my mother?

THE BOOGEYMAN

The scent of pine cleaner was there; faint, but still detectible. Since the recent cleaning, the dust bunnies had not yet had time to gather again. The wooden floor was smooth and bare, except for an occasional sock or two.

There was no boogeyman under the bed.

At least, not now.

Kenny Willis took his head out from under the bed and then got off his knees to stand erect. He was not quite four feet tall, and he wore his blue jammies that had pictures of footballs all over. He would be going into third grade next fall, and he was proud of the fact that he was a big boy. But there were still some things that even a big kid couldn't take chances about.

So next he had to check the closet.

Carefully he felt the cold brass doorknob and gripped it tightly. Kenny pulled and the closet door slowly swung open. He held his breath for a moment as he peeked inside. The closet was almost worse than under the bed, because the hanging clothes resembled silhouettes of people. And it was dark, crowded, and hard to see past everything. A boogeyman could easily hide inside a closet.

So Kenny took extra time and special care to ensure that nothing was lurking inside the dark depths of his closet.

Finally satisfied that he was really alone in his room, Kenny was ready for bed. He turned out the lamp on his nightstand, wishing that the tiny night-light in the corner of the room illuminated the room more than its feeble glow managed to do. Even with that night-light, it just seemed so dark.

Sleep was long in coming. He had too many things to think about; yet the memories revolved around a focal point of which he was unsure. Every night, Kenny lay awake for a long while, trying to remember the part he had forgotten. It was like a blind spot; he could see everywhere except exactly where he wanted to see.

He only knew that one night a while back, something had happened to him. Something bad. But he couldn't pinpoint exactly what that something was.

Kenny remembered things after that bad event. He remembered his father shouting at his mother in the kitchen. He remembered his mother crying.

But most of all, the bad event taught him that there was a boogeyman in the world. The boogeyman had been trying to get him.

And that was all Kenny could remember. So he didn't know if the boogeyman was still after him or not. That was why he always checked his room before he turned out the light. He needed to always keep watch for the boogeyman. Just in case.

Finally Kenny drifted off to sleep, and dreamed the same dream he had so often these nights. He was back in the kitchen that awful time when his father was screaming at his mother. He could see his mother crying and cowering against the sink. Kenny was standing in the doorway of the kitchen, watching and feeling both fear and dread.

But the dream suddenly changed to something he hadn't done before. He could see himself running from the boogeyman. He was outside, and it was night. Kenny was running for the woods at the edge of his yard. He felt absolute terror, because somehow he knew, he just knew, that if the boogeyman caught him, he would die a horrible death. Kenny was running for his life.

And then there was red…lots of the color red…and then Kenny woke up. Every time he had this dream, this was the point where he woke up.

Then the night terrors came. He was all alone in his room, or was he? Had the boogeyman managed to sneak in while he was sleeping?

Too afraid to get up and turn on the light, Kenny lay immobile, sweating and shaking underneath the covers that were drawn up over his chin to his nose. He strained his ears to listen to any noise that could be something taking a breath, a footstep; any sound that could mean the presence of the boogeyman right there in his dark room.

He heard a creak as the house settled on its foundation. A branch scratched against his window in the night breeze. The air conditioning system kicked on. But he didn't hear the boogeyman.

And Kenny lay in his bed, his mind filled with fear and foreboding, until in the way that only children can do, he managed to drift back into sleep.

When the morning sun shined through his window, Kenny's first thought was that *oh no!* His mother forgot to wake him and now he'd be late for school. But then he remembered that it was summer vacation, so he relaxed. He got out of bed anyway because he smelled bacon frying.

His mom worked only part time so she was able to make breakfast in the morning. Later on in the day, she'd drop him off at the neighbor's house before going on to her job at a dentist's office. His mom didn't have to work on anything gross like people's mouths; she just kept the books and typed up the invoices.

His dad worked full time, so he was gone every weekday by the time Kenny woke up, even on school days.

Kenny left his bedroom without bothering to check under his bed or to look into his closet, because everyone knew that the boogeyman only came out at night. Mornings, especially sunny ones like this, were entirely safe.

When he climbed down the stairs and reached the kitchen, Kenny asked, "Is the bacon cooked the way I like it?"

His mother smiled. "Well good morning to you too, young man. Have I ever let you down about the bacon?"

Kenny liked the way his mother was always so cheerful in the morning. Most of the time his dad was cheerful too…except for that one night in the kitchen…but today was not the day to think about that time. And today was certainly not the time to think about the bad thing that happened. Not that he could remember exactly what the bad thing was, anyway.

No. Today was sunny, there was no boogeyman, and there was crisp bacon for breakfast. There was no bad thing today.

When the time arrived for Kenny to be dropped off at the neighbor's house, Kenny was still in a good mood. Not that he enjoyed being babysat by old Mrs. Taylor; she was a busybody who always seemed overly interested in any neighborhood gossip. Often Mrs. Taylor would press him for news about his family, and then she had the nerve to make him swear to never tell his mother that she asked so many questions.

"How are you today, little boy?" Mrs. Taylor asked after his mother had driven off. For one thing, Kenny certainly didn't consider himself a little boy. For another thing, he knew what the next question would be, and sure enough, Mrs. Taylor asked, "And

126

how are your parents doing? Are they getting along with each other these days?"

Kenny, of course, would answer the same way every time. "Good. Everybody's good."

But this time, Mrs. Taylor didn't follow the script. "What's your mom going to do about your father's brother?"

"What?" Kenny wasn't sure he had heard right. "What brother?"

"You know," Mrs. Taylor said. "Your uncle."

"I don't have an uncle."

Mrs. Taylor raised her eyebrows but said nothing more.

Later, when Kenny's mom came to pick him up, he was full of questions. As she began bustling around in the kitchen to prepare dinner, he asked, "Do I have an uncle?"

His mother stopped in her tracks. "I'm surprised that you're asking," she said slowly.

"Well, Mrs. Taylor says so."

"Oh, that old busybody," Mrs. Willis said. "God, I wish she'd butt out of everything. It's not enough that I pay her good money to watch you. She has to have a daily soap opera report, too."

Kenny figured he hadn't heard an answer to his question. "Well, do I have an uncle?"

His mother looked at him for a moment. "You really don't remember, do you?"

"Remember what?"

Mrs. Willis ignored that and said, "Yes, your father has a brother, so you have an uncle. But Uncle Johnny made some mistakes in his life. So he's been away paying for those mistakes."

"How much did his mistakes cost?"

His mother laughed. "Just a couple of years out of his life. That's what your dad and I were fighting about that night you saw him yelling at me in the kitchen. I don't want your father's brother anywhere near us. Hey, why don't you help me make these hamburgers? Go get the buns out of the freezer."

Kenny could tell that the subject of his uncle was closed.

He sat at the kitchen table, waiting for dinner. After a few minutes, his mother sat with him. "Let's wait until your father gets home before we start to eat," she said.

And so they waited. And waited.

After about a half an hour, Mrs. Willis rose from her chair and wordlessly began serving him his dinner. She sat across from him and ate silently.

Kenny's father didn't come home for dinner, nor was he home when Kenny got ready for bed. His mother came in Kenny's room to tuck him into bed, and she seemed tense and distracted. She turned off the lamp that was always perched on Kenny's bed stand, but left the little night light on in the corner.

Kenny didn't want her to leave. He knew that once he was alone in his bedroom again, the night terrors would begin, because the night-light was so tiny that it didn't produce enough light to do any good. But he felt this was something he couldn't share with his mother, especially since she seemed so worried about his dad. So Kenny let his mother leave the room, and he didn't cry out to her; he let her go.

As soon as his mother closed his bedroom door, Kenny was apprehensive. There was a tingling at the back of his mind...memories. He remembered lying on his bed once on a dark night when it wasn't summer. He knew it wasn't summer because he remembered having a lot of blankets under which to hide. Back then, he didn't have a night-light because those were the days before he needed one. Before that night, he used to be able to sleep without checking under the bed and checking the closet first.

Something was still tingling at the back of his mind...yes, it was a memory. Why had he not remembered this before? What triggered this now?

But that night...he remembered that there was something in his room that night; something that crept stealthily towards him. It was an evil that didn't want to alert Kenny; didn't want him to know that it was on its way toward his bed. It planned to sneak up on him in the darkness, to touch him; to do things to him that he didn't want done.

And Kenny remembered screaming as the evil thing touched him with a scaly, cold hand. And yet he knew he had been rescued that night. But by whom? His mother? His father? Who had rescued him, and from what? Kenny couldn't pull out anything else from his mind about that night, no matter how hard he tried.

And so Kenny reached to switch on the lamp at his bedside. Once the light was shining brightly, he began the ritual all over again. First he crawled out of bed and then got down on his knees; he leaned over and checked underneath his bed for the boogeyman. The scent of pine smelled fainter this time and the dust bunnies were increasing in number. But the floor under the bed contained no boogeyman.

Next, of course, was the closet. He hated checking the closet because that would be the most logical place for a boogeyman to hide. Odds were if there were a boogeyman in his bedroom, it'd be hiding in the closet.

He was always afraid to check the closet. Wouldn't it be horrible to open the door and meet the boogeyman face to face? Why, it would stop his heart.

But the only other alternative would be to not check the closet. If he didn't check the closet, then the result of that could be that the boogeyman might creep out at night to grab him while he slept.

Kenny stood up, and crept toward the closet. For seemingly the millionth time, he carefully felt the cold brass doorknob and gripped it tightly. Kenny pulled and the closet door slowly swung open. He held his breath for a moment as he peeked inside.

And then his insides turned to ice and he was unable to take a breath. He felt a warm stream of urine wet his blue football jammies, and he could hear a loud thumping in his ears that he didn't realize was his own heartbeat.

The boogeyman was crouched low in the corner of his closet.

The boogeyman had come for Kenny Willis.

And the boogeyman was red.

He turned to run. He tried to scream but he was so terrified that no noise came out of his mouth. In his complete terror, he stumbled and fell. Finally he opened his mouth and screamed as loud as he could. He was paralyzed with fear, lying on the floor, shrieking.

He could hear his mother thudding up the stairs, running. She threw his bedroom door open and ran to pick him up off the floor.

"My God, Kenny!" she cried. "What's wrong? What's the matter?"

She looked almost as frightened as he was.

"The boogeyman's here!" Kenny sobbed in her arms. "We gotta get out of here before he gets us!"

"The boogeyman? What boogeyman? Kenny, there's no such thing as a boogeyman. You've been dreaming."

"No!" Kenny sobbed. "It's true! He's in my closet!"

"Kenny, there is no boogeyman. Calm down."

"I told you! The boogeyman's in my closet!"

"I'll look in your closet and show you that there's nothing there."

Mrs. Willis got up and walked to the closet. Kenny had left the door slightly ajar. She took the doorknob in her hand and pulled it completely open.

The boogeyman was still there, crouched in the corner and drenched in blood.

Kenny shrieked at the top of his lungs. His mother had gone into the closet and was touching the boogeyman, shaking him.

Kenny heard her tell the boogeyman, "Wake up! Oh my God, wake up!"

But then his mother rushed out of the closet. She ran to pick Kenny up, leaving the closet door open.

She carried Kenny, as he continued to shriek with fright, out of the bedroom and down the stairs.

She put him on the downstairs living room couch. "Baby, it's okay," she told her son. "I need to phone an ambulance. I need to get some help. Please Kenny, listen to me. Stop crying. Nothing can hurt you while I'm here with you. Here, come into the kitchen with me so I can use the phone."

She grabbed her purse and rummaged through it, searching for her cell phone. Then she turned to the land line on the wall. She picked up the phone, but then put it back down. "Kenny," she said slowly, "we need to go next door to Mrs. Taylor's house and use her phone. Ours is broken."

Kenny had seen enough television to know what that meant. "Somebody cut our phone line, didn't they? What about your cell phone?"

Mrs. Willis said, "My cell phone seems to be missing. We're going next door to see Mrs. Taylor."

But then the lights went out.

"Mom, I can't see!" cried Kenny. "The boogeyman shut off the lights! He's going to get us!"

"Kenny, be quiet," his mom said and Kenny noticed that she sounded funny. He could tell from her tone that something else was wrong besides the cut phone line and missing cell phone. So he was right: the boogeyman was coming and she knew it just like he did.

"I hear something," his mother said.

"What?" he asked, but then suddenly he heard it too.

He could hear breathing and then footsteps. It was not his mother, who was standing still and quiet.

The boogeyman was in the kitchen.

He was coming to get them both.

Kenny couldn't see in the kitchen. It was as dark as a tomb. But he could hear that something grabbed his mother, yanking her from his side.

"Kenny!" his mother screamed. "Run! Go out the back door and run!"

"Mom!" he shrieked. He was rooted in place, frozen with fright.

He could hear a shuffling and some sort of struggle. But he still couldn't see anything in that dark kitchen. Then he heard his mother again, "Do it, Kenny! Run!"

Suddenly he heard a loud, ear-shattering BOOM. It was the loudest sound he had ever heard in his whole life. It was so loud that it almost deafened him.

The sound pushed him into action.

He turned around and raced for the kitchen door, fumbling as he unlocked it. When it finally opened, Kenny burst through it and took flight. He headed for the woods on the outside of his family's property.

It was just like that horrible dream he had so often. He was running for the woods. He was running for his life.

And the boogeyman was chasing him, in hot pursuit right behind him. Kenny could hear pounding feet and panting breath. The boogeyman was close behind; so close!

He leaned forward, his knees pumping, his breath wheezing, his lungs beginning to hurt. He was too afraid to look back to see who was chasing him. And he was afraid that he could lose ground if he hesitated and looked behind him. If only he could reach the tree line! In his dream, he had found safety in the trees. He could hide in the underbrush in the darkness of the night.

He made it!

Kenny reached the woods.

Instinctively he knew that his small size would be a benefit for hiding. He ducked into the dense underbrush, and started to run in a zigzag pattern, doing his best to draw himself in and somehow become even smaller than he already was.

Then, in the way that small boys do, he found a little dark hovel underneath a log. It was almost as good as hiding under a bed. Maybe better. He hoped it was better.

He crouched under the rough bark of the fallen tree, and tried to weld himself into the large hole in the ground that some animal had dug. Kenny tried to calm his rapid breathing and also his rapid heartbeat.

He shut his eyes as though that act would shut out the world. He strained his ears to listen. And he heard the boogeyman. Kenny could hear branches snapping and the limbs of bushes being shoved aside. But the sounds seemed random. Maybe the boogeyman couldn't tell where he was hiding.

Could it be that the boogeyman was not all-seeing and all-knowing?

Was that too much to hope for?

And then Kenny froze, because the boogeyman spoke.

"Kenny!" the voice called. "Kenny! Come out!"

Kenny froze in confusion, because the voice was that of his father.

"Kenny!" his father called again. "Where are you? Come out! I'm not going to hurt you."

What should he do? Kenny felt the panic of indecision. What should he do? Was the voice really that of his father, or was the boogeyman playing tricks on him? Could the boogeyman pretend it was his father?

"Kenny, I'm not playing games now. Come out, and that's an order!"

A lifetime of obeying his parents won control. Kenny's indecisiveness left him. His father was calling.

He would go to his father. It was simple; it was how life worked.

He crawled out from his little hidey-hole under the log. "Dad, I'm over here."

"Come here, Son."

And Kenny went to his father.

When he got close, Kenny saw that his father was covered in blood. Here was the red in the woods that he had seen in the dream. His father was covered with blood.

Whose blood?

Mr. Willis took his son's hand to lead him through the forest and back towards home. "Thank God you're safe."

"Dad, what happened?" Kenny asked as the two stepped carefully through the dense underbrush until they found the trail. "Why are you all bloody?"

"It doesn't matter," his father answered. "The police are at our house. Everything's all over now. It's all over."

"Dad," Kenny said, "I'm a big boy now. You can tell me the truth. What happened?"

Mr. Willis sighed as he walked next to his son. "My brother just got out of prison. He came here. He's crazy; he thinks I'm the reason he went to prison because I testified against him. You don't remember what he did to you one night last year, do you? No, I suppose you don't."

Kenny's father went on, "My brother came today to rob us and then steal our car. He beat me up. I'm sure he thought I was dead. I've got a pretty bad cut on my head and that's why there's blood all over my shirt. I must have been unconscious for quite a while. Anyway, my brother dumped me in your closet, thinking he had killed me. But he didn't."

"Is Mom okay? Was that my uncle in the kitchen who grabbed her?"

"Yes, Son," Mr. Willis said as the two continued to walk towards home. "I managed to get out of the closet. I think I have a broken arm because it hurts real bad and I can't move it. Plus I already told you that I must have been knocked out. But I woke up in time to stop my brother from hurting your mother. I came down the stairs just as my brother was trying to hit your mother. She's okay now, but my brother isn't quite okay, so that's why the cops are at our house."

"I thought you were the boogeyman in my closet," Kenny said.

"No, I'm no boogeyman. But your uncle is about as close to a boogeyman as anyone could be."

"So there really was a boogeyman."

"Yes, Son, I suppose in a way, there was. But the boogeyman is dead. I took off his head with my shotgun."

"But Dad," Kenny said, "nobody can ever kill a boogeyman. He'll be back."

URBAN LEGEND

"Jenna, don't you know that's just an urban legend?"

She looked at Darrell. "What's an urban legend?"

"Christ, where have you been all your life? You know, *urban legend*. The stuff that people make up and tell each other around campfires. After a while, some people start believing those stories. Like you."

She hated the way he talked to her like she was an idiot. Well, maybe in this one instance, she wasn't being super smart; she would give him that much. But an idiot?

She defended herself. "I'm just saying that I heard that if you stand in front of a mirror and say Bloody Mary three times, a ghost will appear." Then she hastily added, "I never said I believed it."

"Sheesh Jenna, that Bloody Mary one has been around for ages! What are you, a child? Check Snopes for crissakes."

She had enough. "You're nasty. I'm leaving."

Darrell called to her as she walked away, "Watch out for Bloody Mary, unless it's the kind you drink."

And then he laughed.

<< — >>

That night, just to spite Darrell, Jenna lit candles in her bedroom. She turned off the lights and walked over to her full-length floor mirror. She could hear the rain drumming upon the only window in the room.

The gloom of the candlelit room unnerved her. She felt uncomfortable as the flickering flames seemed to make the room come alive with shadowy movements.

Perfect environment for a ghost to appear, she thought.

She looked into the mirror. In the candlelight, her face had a reddish tint and her features seemed distorted. *Maybe I'm the Bloody Mary*, she thought.

It was time. She had to say the words.

She no longer trembled. She stared at the mirror in defiance, and loudly said, "Bloody Mary."

Jenna held her breath, still staring into the mirror. When nothing besides her own image appeared, she turned to look around the room. Nothing was there, either.

She tried again. "Bloody Mary, Bloody Mary, Bloody Mary."

She waited another minute or two. Then she gave up, deciding that Darrell was right: it was only an urban legend.

She turned on the lights and blew out the candles. Later, she slept well.

The next morning was Saturday, so Jenna decided to use her free time by googling the term "urban legends" and was surprised to find Bloody Mary at the top of the list. She read:

> *Bloody Mary is a folklore legend consisting of a ghost or spirit conjured to reveal the future. Bloody Mary allegedly appears in a mirror as a corpse, a witch or a ghost; sometimes covered in blood.*

Jenna wondered how a former queen of England could find her way all over the world to appear in mirrors when summoned. She chuckled to herself, yet she could feel goosebumps on her arms.

She closed her laptop and went into her bedroom, and stopped in her tracks.

Her stand-up floor mirror was cracked. It distorted her image, making her appear broken like a puzzle where pieces no longer properly fit. Even more disturbing, one crack stretched across her throat like her flesh was slashed with a razor.

She was frozen in place for a moment, then cautiously approached the mirror. She felt an overwhelming desire to touch it. Gently she fingered the broken glass, and suddenly saw blood on the mirror.

Jenna screamed and jumped back. Then she felt a sharp stab on one of her fingers and lifted her hand to study it. She quietly laughed in relief; one of her fingers had been slightly cut on the sharp, broken glass, leaving a spot of blood behind.

Getting a grip, she realized there was nothing supernatural here. She must have broken the glass the previous night when she acted so silly. Who knew...she had called Bloody Mary by candlelight, so her room had been dark. She couldn't remember looking at the mirror when the lights were turned back on.

But as she went about her business that Saturday, she couldn't stop thinking about Bloody Mary.

Her days began to bleed into one another and she lost track of time. She went to work like a robot and couldn't seem to focus. Her job performance began to suffer, and one day she was fired.

She couldn't bring herself to care. It was as though she was outside her own body, observing herself as a separate entity. She wondered if she was depressed, but decided she didn't think so, because she wasn't sad, just…different.

While her days had blended into each other before, now she was having trouble even distinguishing night from day. She spent a lot of time in her bed, in front of the mirror. She would lie there and stare at the cracked glass on the mirror.

She began to like her image, all distorted and broken. She often found herself standing in front of the floor mirror, staring at herself in pieces, and it made her relate to how she felt inside.

The mirror knew she was broken. It merely reflected the truth.

And one day after her bath, she saw the bathroom mirror fogged by steam. Jenna took a dry washcloth and wiped it. Suddenly she saw herself reflected as whole, unbroken and no longer distorted.

She stared at the mirror over her bathroom sink, fascinated. This mirror reflected a different truth.

Did she feel strong enough to try again, out in the world? Could she trust this new image of herself as a whole human being?

She went back into her bedroom, removed the towel from her body, and stood naked in front of the full-length floor mirror. Sure enough, it wasn't just her face that appeared broken; it was her entire body.

She was used to this reflection, so surely the mirror in the bathroom told a lie. This broken image in her bedroom was familiar; she was so accustomed to seeing it that now she accepted it as reality.

She felt that having two different versions of her was like having a multiple personality disorder, so she made her way into the kitchen, opened the junk drawer, and pulled out a hammer.

She took the hammer into the bathroom and slammed the tool against the mirror above the sink. It shattered instantly, and she felt elated. Things were normal again, but maybe not quite.

There was one more thing she needed to do.

She pulled a broken jag of glass off the bathroom mirror, and cut her hand again in the process. She held the shard, fingering it and turning it over and over, watching how her own blood from the cut reddened the glass with maroon, sticky and coppery wetness.

She took the precious sharp treasure and took it into her bedroom. Standing naked in front of the floor mirror, she got into position so that one of the cracks showed across her throat once again.

She could do this. She could use the reflection as her guideline, showing her where to slash.

She held the razor-sharp tip of the glass to her throat, watching her other self in the mirror carefully. She felt strong and empowered. Since she could not step through the mirror, she would become one with its image: the truth.

Her hand thrust the broken glass against her throat. The sudden pain was surprising. She began to gurgle as she realized that she must have cut her airway along with her artery.

She felt lightheaded, and threw down the dagger of glass. Still watching the floor mirror, Jenna put both hands to her throat to try to catch the spurting blood and rub it all over her naked body.

Her last thoughts as she sunk to the floor were: *I was right about Bloody Mary. It's me.*

UNDER THE HOUSE

Her father was yelling again.

Ten year old Kayla cringed, even though this time the screams were directed at her mother, and not at her. Kayla wished for the courage to rush in and save her mother. But she didn't, and despised herself for being the coward that she was.

Instead Kayla began to slink away, out of the house. Because her father's wrath was directed elsewhere, she figured that she would not be noticed as she made her getaway. If she could disappear, perhaps she could avoid her father's fury, which always ended in brutal beatings.

Once outside, Kayla noticed a hole in the clapboards that criss-crossed underneath the back porch. *Well, this is new,* she thought. The hole hadn't been there yesterday.

Could she hide in there? Doubtfully Kayla peered under the stairs. It seemed pretty dark under there.

And then suddenly Kayla heard her father's voice coming closer. No time to decide! She went through the hole in the clapboards and scooted under the house to hide.

The temperature was cooler down here. It smelled funny too…musty, moldy, like mushrooms. Kayla waited for her eyes to adjust to the darkness before she continued further into the underbelly of the house.

Since daylight was streaming in through the hole, she could see a few feet in front of her. The house was held up by wooden supports, surrounded by a brick foundation. The ground was earthen and dark. She saw some garbage, and she wondered, *How did that stuff get here, underneath the house?* There were a few opened cans and some rotting, discarded paper.

It was amazing how much she could hear down here. She could hear her mother and father talking very loudly, and walking about up above her in the house. In fact, this new hiding place would not only be a safety zone, but one in which she could probably eavesdrop as well.

Kayla was thinking that once she was under here, it did not seem as frightening as it had looked from the outside. Perhaps this would

138

indeed make a great hiding place for when...well, for when she had to hide.

And then things upstairs quieted down. Kayla realized that everything had become okay once again. Now there was no more need to hide, because up in the house, all the yelling had suddenly stopped. That gave Kayla the "all clear."

She scrambled back through the hole in the clapboards and stood in the open sunlight. It would be safe to go back into the house now, and check on her mother.

And when her father sobered up, life would become smoother, and her mother would smile once again. The seas of life would remain calm.

Until the next storm.

Groggily she was aware of a noise. It was dark, and when Kayla became fully awake, she realized that she was in her bed. She burrowed deeper into her blankets, and put her hands over her ears because she didn't want to hear the screams coming from the next room.

Despite covering her ears, Kayla heard her mother's voice. "Leave her alone!"

"I'll get that brat up out of bed!" yelled her father. "I'll teach her!"

She heard her mother scream, but Kayla knew that nothing could stop him. So it was to be Kayla this time who became the victim of his wrath, not her mother. Kayla knew her father would burst into her bedroom at any second. She had to get away!

And now she knew where she could go. She knew a place to hide.

Aren't you afraid of the dark? Kayla's inner voice whispered. *It will be dark under the house because it's night time now.*

But anything was better than sticking around here. She made her choice before she gave herself time to think about it. Her father was coming for her!

Kayla threw off the covers and jumped out of bed, landing nimbly on her feet. Rushing to the window, she lifted the sash. Thank god she lived in a one-story house.

Just as she was scrambling out the window, she could hear the door to her bedroom burst open behind her. As Kayla dropped to the outside ground, she could hear her father's voice become a roar of anger as he realized she was escaping. There would be hell to pay now.

Wearing only a cotton nightdress and underpants, Kayla felt the cool grass, slick with dew, under her bare feet. She couldn't take the time to be careful; *Please god, don't let me slip.* She didn't look behind; she couldn't risk any mistakes.

She ran for her life, turning the corner of the house to head for the backyard where she knew the hole in the clapboards waited for her. She leaned into the run, her knees pumping, her breath wheezing, her lungs beginning to hurt. If only she could get under the house in time!

And then she reached the hole under the porch. She took a deep breath and scooted inside. She tumbled across the hardpan dirt and rolled twice until she came to a stop. She tried to be quiet, tried to hold her breath, but her lungs were bursting and she had to breathe hard.

She could hear her father giving chase. Had he seen where she went? She ducked her head under her arm as she heard him run past the hole in the clapboards.

He hadn't seen! Could she dare to relax?

Kayla took her head out from underneath her arm. Better to not risk feeling smug; she had better make sure her father wouldn't find her. She had better go deeper underneath the house.

But it's dark, her inner voice whispered. *You never had a chance to explore here yet. You don't know what's down here.*

Again, Kayla felt faced with the idea that she had no choice. After all, which was she more afraid of? The unknown couldn't be as bad as the known. And her father's drunken rages were very well known to her.

So she scrambled deeper under the house into the bowels of the crawlspace.

The darkness enveloped her; it surrounded her in an almost surreal eclipse of light. Her sense of smell sharpened to compensate for her lack of sight. She could smell moldy, rich earth.

Too short a space to stand, Kayla felt her way over the ground as she crawled on her hands and knees. She could feel small pebbles,

140

and then she felt one of the discarded cans that she had noticed the last time she had been down here. She tossed the can aside, careful not to cut herself on the rusted metal.

Finally she figured she had crawled far enough to not be seen if her father wised up and peered through the hole in the clapboards.

She curled up into a ball and waited, listening intently for sounds coming from the house above her. She could hear the front door open and close. Her father must have made the entire round of the house, and when he didn't find her, he must have gone back inside. What was her mother doing? Kayla could hear nothing upstairs except the sounds made by her father.

Why was her mother so quiet? Even more odd, why wasn't her father yelling? It would be more normal for Kayla to hear him shouting abuses than to hear this silence.

There came a scraping noise that seemed to move across the floorboards. Kayla strained to listen, but she couldn't make sense of the sounds.

And then she heard the back door swing open.

Oh no! Was her father coming back outside to look for her once again?

Cringing in fright, Kayla scrambled sideways like a crab to travel deeper underneath the house. She couldn't see in the darkness, so she started with surprise when she hit a brick wall. She was cornered against the foundation that held up the house. There was nowhere else to go. So she crouched; waiting, fearing. She tried to make herself as small as humanly possible.

An ax! She could hear her father chopping at the clapboards. How had he known she was down here?

Kayla heard the boards being pulled away. He must have put down the ax because now she could hear that he was using his hands. She could see the light entering from the hole he was making. Even though it was night outside, it was still lighter out there than it was underneath the house.

And then something blocked the hole, but only for a moment. Light shined in again. And then her father blocked the hole. He was coming inside! He was pushing something in front of him.

Kayla braced herself. He had found her. Now he would grab her and drag her outside. And then he would take her into the house and beat her within an inch of her life. So she hadn't escaped after all; there was never any escape.

But just as she resigned herself to her fate, her father reversed direction and backed out of the hole. Kayla was stunned. What did that mean?

And then she realized that the hole in the clapboards was being blocked again. Except this time, her father was nailing the boards back into place.

He was closing the hole!

She was being buried alive!

Fear froze her; she remained immobile. She waited for her father to finish nailing the clapboards back into place. Under the house, it became dark as a tomb; as dark as death.

Still Kayla could not bring herself to move. She waited. And then she heard the back door slam, and she understood that her father had gone back inside the house.

Finally Kayla decided to take action. She thought she would crawl to the place where the hole was covered and test her father's handiwork.

Maybe he hadn't taken too much care with the patch job he had done to cover the hole. Maybe he hadn't nailed the boards down very securely.

Maybe Kayla could push the boards back out if she leaned hard on them, and if so, then she could set herself free.

Where she would go once she got out, she didn't know. But she would deal with that later. Now, she just needed to get out from under the house.

She began to creep back over the hardpan earth. She felt her way along, because it was too dark to see. She desperately hoped she remembered the direction of the way out. She had mental images of herself crawling through the bowels of the house for an eternity, hopelessly lost.

But then she could tell she was headed in the right direction, because the dirt began to feel warmer under her fingers. It would make sense that the sunlight had warmed the area closest to the back porch earlier in the day. It had not totally cooled down yet, even though Kayla figured it was probably around midnight now.

She moved forward an inch, touched the ground in front of her, and then moved forward another inch. It was a slow progress, but it was the only way.

And then her fingers felt an obstacle in her path. It seemed to be blocking her way. It must have been the thing that her father had pushed ahead of him when he had entered the crawlspace.

She desperately wished she could see.

Instead, her fingers nervously probed the object in front of her. It felt smooth and clammy; soft and moist. And warm. Repulsed, she quickly withdrew her fingers.

A horrible thought was dawning on her. She suddenly understood.

She had always been such a coward. She had never run for help, had never gone to a neighbor or a teacher. Her father always threatened her to not tell anyone, ever, about the abuse.

But why hadn't her mother done anything? Who was the adult and who was the child?

After Kayla crawled over her mother's prone body, she reached the clapboards. She pushed and pried at the repair job her father had done until a nail holding one of the boards popped free. Kayla knew the boards would come off to make another hole. And then Kayla could escape to a neighbor's house.

She didn't have to worry about what her father would do to her mother anymore if she told.

A CASE OF LYCANTHROPY

Her name was Susan. She was an ordinary person living an ordinary life.

Until the day the dog bit her.

Susan hadn't noticed the stray until it was too late. One day, while locking the door to the church where she volunteered, she saw movement out of the corner of her eye. A dark projectile launched itself out of the church parking lot, heading straight towards her.

The dog was so quick that it seemed like a blur. Susan felt rather than actually saw the dog bite her arm. Before she could react, the dog ran off, vanishing back into the bushes at the far end of the deserted blacktop.

It had all happened so fast.

Stunned, Susan stood still for a moment, staring stupidly at her arm where her sleeve was torn. She thought, *Rabies? What are the odds?*

Finally she reacted. Shaking, she pushed up the sleeve of her blouse to view the damage. She was surprised to see that it wasn't a very bad wound on her arm. Her skin was only slightly broken.

Still, there were a few drops of blood welling from the shallow bite mark.

The drops of blood made her again contemplate the idea of rabies, which led to the question, should she go to the doctor?

She decided she should take no chances. Walking away from the church, she got into her car. She drove, calling the doctor on her cell phone while she steered her car out of the parking lot. When she connected with the nurse, Susan was told that she better come into the office and get immunized against rabies. And so she did. Five times. It took five treatments to receive all of the immunizations.

So, that was that. Life went on.

Susan had short dark hair, worn in an unassuming style, bound by barrettes. She had no children. She was thirtyish, bookish, and married to a man named David who seemed to prefer long hours at his job instead of spending time with her.

Normally she went through her days as though sleepwalking…she did everything by routine, and one day in Susan's life was the same as the next. But after the day of the dog bite, Susan began to feel different.

Changes to her emotional well-being began slowly. She noticed people; she was becoming attracted to strangers. She would find herself staring at strangers in stores, on the street, even on television; scrutinizing these strangers closely for...she was not even sure what she was hoping to find. But she would stare so blatantly that people started frowning at her, turning away in irritation.

She was becoming aware of a budding sexuality. Something new, something different, something overpowering. She felt younger. She felt as though she were coming alive; for the first time in all of her life, she felt sensuous, womanly, and in sync with her body.

She was conscious of the feel of her breasts against the material of her bra; it made her feel bound, restrained. So she removed her bra, and went without, feeling reckless and brave.

She soon abandoned her underwear altogether, and pondered the new sensations this allowed. She reveled in her little secret, that she was exposed underneath her clothing. But even that became not enough. She wished others would guess her secret, so she began wearing more revealing clothes, as though to give them a hint.

Susan removed the barrettes from her hair, and no longer visited the hairdresser. She wanted to let her hair grow long. In the meantime, she wore it in a loose style. She would never look beautiful, but now she had reached an *almost*. She began wearing makeup, a little at first, and more as time went on.

Then came the day when it was not enough just to look passionate. She needed to act it out, she needed to *be* passionate.

It was a Tuesday night when Susan gave in to her passions. She paced her living room, alone as usual at eight o'clock. David hadn't come home from work yet. She was restless and irritable, and was aware of a tingling sensation under her skin, like the 'pins-and-needles' after an arm or leg goes to sleep; except she felt it everywhere. She wanted to get out of the house. She wanted an adventure.

She wanted to do something uncharacteristic, to do something devious and perhaps downright dangerous. She craved something negative, an underworld, something wicked. She wanted to shed her school-marm skin to reveal something sordid underneath.

Susan changed into a slinky black dress, grabbed her car keys, and walked out the door.

She drove to the south side of town. She purposely chose the worst neighborhood in which to find a bar. The multi-colored lights on the sign that said *Don's Drinks and Dancing* caught her attention.

Later, as she walked out of the bar with the stranger she had picked up, she strolled arm-in-arm with him across the street to the motel. Unembarrassed, Susan went into the lobby with the younger, dark-haired man. She was unconcerned that the motel clerk gave her a knowing look as he extracted the room fee out of her escort.

Susan and the dark-haired man found their room. They barely had time to shut the motel door when his mouth was on hers, and she tasted him. He pulled her against him; his hands were on her back, holding her fast to him. She responded in kind, pulling up his shirt, and her arms slipped over his skin, over the hard, muscled back that was slick with sweat. She felt feverish; on fire. Her heat came out of her in waves, and she imagined her hands searing into his back. She wanted to blister his flesh, to brand him with her passion and desire.

The dark-haired man pulled Susan to the bed, and they fell on top of it in a heap, entwined. They yanked at each other's clothes, peeling them off, almost tearing fabrics in their haste.

And then Susan bit him.

She broke the skin on his arm. The coppery taste of coins was on her tongue. His blood was hot and moist, and she wanted to drink it…to swallow it.

"You bit me!" the man cried, pulling himself off of her. "What are you, some kind of freak?"

He hopped off of the bed. "Damn it, you hurt me. Look at this, I'm bleeding!"

He stood there a moment, looking from his arm to her, as if deciding what to do next. Then he said, "Hell, I paid for this room, and I'm going to get my money's worth."

So he came back to the bed. He grabbed her hips and inserted himself between her legs. Pumping wildly, he was rough with his thrusts, mean, almost brutal. Susan became just as rough and violent, screaming "Wolf! Wolf!" until both of them were spent.

He rolled off of her, breathing hard. The bleeding on his arm had stopped. Calming down, he said, "You know, you're a real freak, yelling about a wolf and all. You into animals, baby? Yeah, you're

146

some kind of wild animal. Lord knows you bite like one. You hungry like a wolf?"

"Something like that," Susan said. Then she sat up in the bed. "I have to go."

"What's your rush?" the man asked her. "I mean, this room is paid for. We can do it again. Just don't bite me this time."

"No, I have to go. I'm married."

"Hell, so what. So am I."

She looked at him. "I'm leaving now."

When she got off the bed, he stepped in front of her to block her path.

"If you try to stop me from leaving, I'll kill you," Susan told him.

Something in her voice made him hesitate. She sounded level, matter-of-fact, her calm tone belying her words. Even though he was much bigger than she, it was something about her voice that made him step aside.

"All right, get out," he said. "Go bite your husband, you freak."

"Maybe I will," she said, as she got dressed.

<< — >>

Driving home, Susan remembered about the dog that bit her at the church, so many days ago. That had been the catalyst for everything that had followed.

She hadn't contracted rabies, but maybe she had gotten something else from that dog. As she drove, she looked at the night sky outside of her car window and saw that the moon was full.

She thought back to how strong her urge was to bite the man in the motel, and how satisfying the coppery, warm taste of his blood had seemed. It was something she had to do at the time; it was a need.

In her thoughts, she connected the dog bite to her own biting of the stranger in the motel. The word *werewolf* came to her mind.

She felt no panic at the idea that she could be a werewolf. That would explain many, many things. It made sense out of senseless behavior.

She decided she would accept her condition. After all, what else could she do about it at this point? Susan was neither afraid nor remorseful. It was neither good nor bad, it just *was*.

Arriving home, she drove her car into the garage, noticing that her husband's car was missing. Late again. He was late again at the office...or was he?

For the first time, Susan wondered about David.

After all, she had been unfaithful this very evening. Could David have been unfaithful as well? Of course he could.

She was willing to bet he wasn't working late at the office.

Suddenly she was willing to bet that he had been cheating on her for a long time, probably during their entire marriage.

She resented him; felt abandoned by him. She had quit college to marry him, to bear his children.

Now he rarely came home, paid no attention to her when he did, and of course there were no children. One of them was not able to reproduce, and David wouldn't agree to see the doctor to discover which of them was to blame.

And now Susan was thinking that David was cheating on her.

It was of no matter that she had just done the same to him. She knew her own cheating could be justified, because lust was the sort of thing to which werewolves were driven. Werewolves were of the underworld, and did wicked, decadent things. It was the nature of the beast.

But David was no werewolf, so he had no reason to cheat.

She thought more about David, and examined her feelings for him. What did she get out of this marriage? Not much. David ignored her, and the few times he did pay attention to her, it was merely to complain. He was too demanding, too critical. He made her feel bad; he caused her to feel stressed all the time. She would be so much better without him.

So the werewolf inside her would kill him. The stranger in the motel had been practice for the actual event. The stranger had been her first taste of blood, but wouldn't be her last.

She wanted to kill her husband, and she knew why. In the end, it really had nothing to do with her resentments towards David.

It was because tonight had a full moon; a killing moon.

Susan walked out of the garage and entered the house. She didn't bother to turn on any lights; her eyesight seemed to be keener, and objects were clear even in the dark. Her senses were heightened, and she could feel the blood coursing through her veins; she seemed to be focused on blood, all blood, even her own. The lust she was now feeling was not for sex, but for blood.

She went to the kitchen and took a large knife out of the drawer.

Then she crouched on the living room sofa in the dark, holding the kitchen knife. The blade gleamed, reflecting the bright moonlight that streamed in through the front window. As she waited, she moved the knife up and down, its sharp tip penetrating the sofa cushion again and again.

She was a hunter awaiting her prey.

She heard the key in the door, and readied herself for an attack.

The front door opened, and a shape entered the room. Susan could see David's hand groping for the light switch. The light came on, and he seemed momentarily blinded by the brightness as he stepped forward and shut the door behind him.

Seizing the advantage of David's momentary blindness, Susan leaped from the couch. She screamed with primal rage and lifted the gleaming knife high above her head. She used her forward momentum to add force to her thrust. She found her target, the knife plunging deep within David's throat.

He was unable to scream, or make any sound at all as he collapsed. Blood gushed from the carotid artery, spraying everywhere. Susan relished the fact that she was being rapidly covered in blood. She opened her mouth, tasting it. She held out her hands, reveling in the warm dark wetness of it. She began smearing David's blood all over her body.

The defense attorney asked for the credentials of the doctor who was sitting on the witness stand during the murder trial of Susan Hennings. The attorney, Craig Schafer, wanted to establish the validity of the doctor's statements to the jury.

"I am a psychiatrist at the Davis Medical Center located on University Avenue here in this city," Doctor Benson told the jury. He went on to describe his various medical degrees and his lengthy experience. Schaffer felt that the doctor was a very important witness for the defense.

"Doctor Benson," Schaffer asked, "is it true that the defendant, Susan Hennings, has been under your care in the psychiatric unit in Davis Hospital for the past six months?"

"It is true," answered Benson.

Schaffer concealed his anxiety. To prove not guilty by reason of insanity was a notoriously difficult verdict to achieve. When the M'Naughten Rule was adopted, it stated that a defendant is only legally insane if he or she cannot distinguish between right and wrong in regard to the crime that is charged. Any attempts by the accused to lie, to cover up the crime, or to flee the crime scene threw M'Naughten right out the window.

But Susan Hennings did none of those things. She had stayed in her living room, cutting up her husband with a kitchen knife. When she was found by a neighbor, she had been putting pieces of her husband into her mouth.

Schaffer jerked his thoughts back to the trial. He continued questioning the doctor. "To your knowledge, which is extensive in the psychiatric field, are you aware of the possibility that a person can believe that he or she has been changed into an animal?"

"I am aware of this."

"What is this belief called?" Scaffer asked.

"It is called Lycanthropy," Benson answered. "The word Lycanthropy is derived from the ancient Greek words *lykos*, meaning wolf, and *anthropos*, meaning human being. So you can see that the word Lycanthropy has been around for a very long time."

"Can you describe Lycanthropy?"

Benson began, "This condition is a valid mental illness—"

"Objection!" called the prosecutor. "Speculation as to validity."

"Sustained," agreed the judge.

Schaffer tried again from a different angle. "Doctor Benson, are you aware of any medical documentation of Lycanthropy as a mental illness?"

"Absolutely," Benson said. "Clinical Lycanthropy has been documented to be a mental illness in 1988, published in the *Psychological Journal*; and in 1989 by Denning and West, published in *Psychopathology*. Also in 1999 by Moselhy in *Psychopathology*. Also in…"

The doctor continued to give examples of documentation for ten whole minutes. There were a lot of examples for him to give.

"Very good. Thank you." Schaffer hoped the jury was impressed. "Doctor Benson, can you please describe the symptoms of Clinical Lycanthropy as a mental illness?"

"Certainly," Doctor Benson said. "Affected individuals have a delusional belief that they have transformed into an animal. It has been linked with the altered states of mind that accompany psychosis. These are delusions and hallucinations, because the transformation only seems to happen in the mind of the affected person. In other words, other people still see them as a person, but in their own mind, they have changed into an animal."

"What could cause this to happen to a person?" Schaffer asked.

Benson answered, "The condition seems to be an expression of psychosis."

"In other words, this could be an expression of a mental illness?"

"That's correct. It is an illness of the mind, a delusion, because in reality, no human being can change into an animal."

Schaffer relaxed. "No further questions."

"No questions," said the prosecutor. Schaffer felt exhilarated.

While Doctor Benson exited the witness stand, Schaffer sat at the table next to his client. Susan Hennings had sat immobile, expressionless, throughout the entire trial. "It's going well," he whispered to her. She gave no indication that she heard or even cared.

The trial continued to go well for the defense. Schaffer was confident when the jury exited the courtroom to deliberate.

Although no one could predict a jury's decision in advance, Schaffer felt if any trial could win by reason of insanity, it would be this one.

When the jury filed back into the courtroom, only three hours later, they looked at Susan. She did not return their gaze.

But Schaffer noticed. He held with the superstition that if the jury looked at the defendant, they were not planning to convict.

And this jury looked at Susan.

The judge asked the foreman if the jury had reached a verdict.

"We have, your Honor."

"Would you read the verdict?" asked the judge.

"For murder in the first degree, we the jury find the defendant not guilty by reason of insanity."

The courtroom clamored with commotion. This was big news! Reporters and other media people ran for the door to report the outcome of this trial to their newspapers and to their local television news stations.

Schaffer turned to his client and said, "This means a hospital for a while, but you can be out in about five years with good behavior."

He was stunned to see Susan's eyes glowing red.

THE FREEGANS

Jordan

One day, Jordan received two pink slips.

The first came in the mail, and it was a notice telling him that he was now the legal owner of his car, a Nissan that was more than a couple of years old with a lot of mileage. But it ran, and he could celebrate the end of car payments.

The other pink slip was an entirely different type, given to him at work. And that one meant he was officially laid off from his job.

It was very bizarre to be experiencing two such strong emotions in a single day. Jordan felt it was like that old joke: *There is good news and bad news, so which do you want to hear first?*

Most times finding a new job was not a concern for him, but it was a recession year, and companies weren't hiring. Instead, they were too busy laying off the workers they already had.

So the days turned into weeks with no luck. When March approached, Jordan was getting nervous because his savings was running out. When April approached, his savings was completely gone. When May approached, Jordan was wondering how he could pay the rent on his apartment.

The truth was, he couldn't.

Soon after, a sheet of paper was taped to the outside of his front door, embarrassing Jordan because the whole apartment complex could see it, and everyone knew what that sheet of paper meant.

It was an eviction notice.

And so the next step was living in the car that he now owned. And then came the day when he had no money for gas, so the car sat on the side of a residential street, hidden near an overgrown bush. But apparently Jordan hadn't hidden his "car-home" well enough, because one day he returned to find it gone. It had been towed, and Jordan certainly did not have the three-hundred-dollar towing fee to get the car back.

At least he still had a change of clothes in the backpack that he carried with him at all times, thank god.

And so Jordan wound up eating dollar hamburgers at McDonald's and trying to wash himself at the sinks of gas station restrooms. He washed his clothes whenever he had quarters to use in the Laundromat, but more often than not, he needed those quarters to buy his dollar hamburgers, so his clothes weren't as clean and fresh as they used to be.

His only income was "spanging," his word for asking people for spare change. It was a humiliating experience because more often than not, people would tell him off. He heard things like, "Get a job, you bum."

Once someone spit at him.

Jordan was beginning to look shaggy, and he felt dejected and depressed. Both of his parents had died in a car accident four years earlier, and he had no siblings. That meant that no one, anywhere, could help him.

He was desperate, and at that point, he figured he would try anything to survive.

And that was when Jordan met the Freegans.

Her name was Hailey and Jordan thought she was beautiful. He was standing near her on a street corner in the south part of town, and Jordan noticed her lip ring and her shirt that said *Dead Kennedys*, although he wasn't sure what that meant. Of course most of the Kennedys were dead, and he wondered why anyone would wear a shirt proclaiming that.

But at least Hailey had a sort of style, while Jordan felt shame about wearing clothes that he figured made him look like a bum. Yet Hailey didn't even seem to notice his lousy clothes. Jordan was taken with her; because she seemed so, well, different...kind of punk, kind of...who knew what.

Jordan found her exotic.

He watched Hailey as she raised her hand without thinking to brush the hair out of her eyes, before she seemed to realize it was too short to have gotten into her eyes in the first place. Her hair stood up in one inch bristles from her scalp, and was dyed very, very black.

Jordan didn't know what to say, because Hailey wasn't alone. A young man was standing at her side, but after a few minutes he realized the guy didn't act like he had any claim on Hailey, so Jordan relaxed. Maybe they were just friends.

The young man stepped forward and introduced himself as Blaine. He had longer hair than Hailey, but his was dyed red at the tips. He wore a tight black t-shirt that sported the words *Rikki and the Last Days of Earth*, and again Jordan had no idea of what that meant.

"Dude, you live on the streets?" Blaine asked.

Jordan felt his face flush with shame. "I, um, lost my job. And I sorta lost my car too."

"No problem," Blaine said.

Jordan was shocked. "What?"

"He means," Hailey said, "that you can join us."

"We're Freegans," Blaine said. "Rhymes with vegans."

"What's a Freegan?" Jordan asked.

"Come with us and we'll show you," Hailey said, and Jordan was mesmerized by her smile. He knew he would follow her anywhere.

So Jordan walked a couple of blocks with these unusual people. He was happy to be accepted by them, or by anyone, since he had not been able to accept himself lately because of his circumstances. Too often of late, people had given him looks of contempt as he wandered the streets.

But Hailey and Blaine didn't look at him with disgust or anything else negative. It gave him hope that perhaps he could be part of something once again and no longer a discard of society.

The neighborhood they took him to was shoddy and dilapidated; not so much gang-related as just simply old and neglected. Houses were small and most had chain link fences in front. Finally they came to a beige, A-frame house with no fence, and it was even tinier than its neighboring homes. Paint was chipping off the clapboards, and the porch posts were leaning precariously. There was a sagging couch and lots of plants in tiny pots on the porch. Jordan thought it looked like some sort of eclectic herb garden.

Hailey opened the front door, and it made a creaking noise as though it belonged in a haunted house. Inside, the main room was dimly lighted and a drum set took up most of the space. A bass and a six-string guitar were propped against a wall. Another sagging couch was propped against the other wall. The floor was abused hardwood, well-worn and bare of any rugs.

But what got Jordan's attention was a skeleton dangling off of some sort of stand. It was the size of a short adult. He realized he was staring.

"You like Bernard?" Hailey asked. "My mom gave me that. She's into practical jokes. Don't worry, Bernard is plastic, although he sure looks real, doesn't he? Sometimes we dress him up when we have parties."

"What kinds of parties have skeletons as the guest of honor?" Jordan asked.

Hailey laughed. "Here it's Halloween all year long. It's the coolest holiday there is."

"Hey man," Blaine said, changing the subject, "you hungry?"

"God yes," Jordan said.

They led him into the kitchen. It was in disarray and was certainly not spotless by any means. Still, Jordan wasn't exactly an advocate of clean living anymore.

"We call this house 'Off the Grid.' Lots of people live here," Blaine explained. "We gotta get organized, you know, delegate cleaning duties and all. Hailey, how many people are living here now?"

"Thomas and Eric have been here the longest, and Heather just moved in," she said to Blaine, "and then there's you and me, of course. Ryan told me he's moving out at the end of the month."

"That's just in the front house," Blaine said. "There's Alex and Sophie out back."

"Out back?" Jordan asked.

"Sure, there's a mother-in-law house out there; I think that's what they call it, anyway," Blaine said.

"More like a shed in the yard," Hailey said. "Don't worry, Jordan, we'll keep you in the front house. At least we have a bathroom in this one. Alex and Sophie have to come in here to use ours."

"Anyway, let's eat," Blaine said as he opened the refrigerator. "Here're some noodles with eggplant and soy sauce. It'll take just a moment to warm up on the stove. We don't have microwaves here."

Jordan felt his stomach grumble. He didn't care what it was; after months of dollar hamburgers, he knew he would eat anything.

"Not to change the subject, but I have to ask," he said, "why are you wearing a t-shirt about the Kennedys?"

Hailey looked down, as if to remember what she was wearing."You mean the *Dead Kennedys*?"

"Well, not all of them are dead," Jordan pointed out. "I mean, there're still a lot of JFK's nieces and nephews running around."

Hailey laughed out loud, and Jordan was smitten by her musical sound. "It's not *those* Kennedys, it's a band," she told him. "The *Dead Kennedys* are a punk band. They're awesome. I was so lucky to find this shirt."

"Where'd you find it?" Jordan asked.

She looked at him in surprise. "Why, in a dumpster, of course. It was too big, so I cut it and re-sewed it to fit me."

Blaine was busy stirring the noodles on the stove. "You know how we work here, right?"

"Not really," Jordan said.

"We make enough money to pay rent and utilities, and that's it," Blaine explained. "See the drums and guitars in the front room? Thomas and I do paying gigs at clubs, or sometimes just at parties. Hailey works part time as a waitress. We only work enough to pay rent and utilities. Everything else is free."

"Where does the food come from?" Jordan asked.

"We dumpster it," Hailey said.

Jordan stood still for a minute, but his eyes moved to stare at the noodles still heating on the stove.

Hailey answered his unspoken question. "Yes, that too."

Blaine jumped into the conversation. "It's just a different lifestyle, that's all. All of this is by choice. It frees us from the chains of working class oppression. This materialistic society seeks to suppress our creativity by forcing us to be robots stuffed into little office cubicles to earn money. But not Freegans! We are truly free because we live for free."

"Don't mind Blaine," Hailey said. "He gets, how shall I say, enthusiastic."

"All right," Jordan decided. "I'm starving."

Smiling, Blaine said, "And now it's hot and ready to eat."

Perhaps it was because Jordan had spent so many months eating dollar hamburgers that he was happy to eat something different. Or perhaps he was just ravenously hungry. Because once Jordan tasted it, he was surprised to find that it was actually pretty good. He wolfed his meal down, and even asked for seconds. And he never got sick from it.

Hailey

"Don't call me punk."

"What are you, then?" Jordan asked.

She raised her hand automatically, without thinking, to brush the hair out of her eyes once again before she remembered that she had cut it all off the night before. "I don't like labels, so don't categorize me. I'm an individual. I do things my way."

"You sound like Frank Sinatra."

"Who's Frank Sinatra?"

"He's some dead geezer who did everything his way," Jordan said.

"Never heard of him. Hey, are you going with me or not?"

"Hailey," Jordan told her, "I don't know about this dumpster diving business. I mean, what's it all about, anyway?"

Hailey put her hands on her slim hips. "You should learn how to dumpster dive if you want to live here, Jordan. I already told, you, all of us are Freegans."

"Isn't Freegan a label?"

Rolling her eyes, Hailey said, "It's not a label, it's a lifestyle. We live off the land, except we do it in the city. We use bicycles instead of cars so that we don't support Big Oil. We recycle everything; we get our clothes from thrift stores, or even better, from the dumpsters. You know, things that would otherwise needlessly get thrown away. And we eat for free. That's from the dumpsters as well."

"Jesus, Hailey, how do you know the stuff from dumpsters is fit to eat? I mean, maybe we just got lucky last night with the noodles, so we didn't get sick, but maybe next time..."

It wasn't the first time Hailey had been asked that question, and it never failed to annoy her. Of course, she would never let anyone eat anything bad. Didn't Jordan realize that? A lot of things out of dumpsters were in their original packaging. Food was generally still fresh up to a week after the expiration date.

158

Sometimes high-end stores threw away perfectly good food because of something minor, such as one cracked egg in a dozen or if the packaging was dented or torn.

More than that, Jordan would be able to judge the condition of the dumpstered food for himself once he saw it. So, she hated that question. It was a stupid question.

But she didn't let her annoyance show when she answered. After all, Jordan was still a novice. She simply told him, "We never go to private trash cans, or even to apartment dumpsters. We only choose dumpsters in the back of high-end stores."

"Aren't they all locked?" Jordan asked.

"Someone, I don't even know who any more, stole a key, and made copies for all of us. We can get into just about any dumpster now. The keys get passed around among us. We make copies of copies."

"All right," Jordan decided. "I'll try it."

When they went out the door, Hailey sniffed the air. It smelled fresh and there was no scent of rain. The sky was incredibly clear, and the moon was a tiny crescent. Millions of stars sparkled and shimmered. Hailey took another deep breath of the fragrant night air, and felt how wonderful it was to be alive in such a world.

The crickets hid in the cracks of the sidewalks, singing for mates. It might have made for a country sound, if it weren't for the traffic noise and the occasional ambulance sirens that reminded people of where they really were.

But Hailey loved the city. And she had city survival skills.

She led Jordan to an alley, and was like a cat as she gracefully strode through it. Then she said, "Tonight is Monday."

Jordan looked puzzled, so Hailey explained, "We don't want full dumpsters; we want freshly filled dumpsters. That only happens on Monday nights. Because on Monday days, most grocery store dumpsters get emptied of the weekend trash. So nothing has been in the dumpster longer than a few hours if we dive on Monday nights. Everything in the dumpsters is relatively fresh."

"Uh, sure, I guess." Jordan glanced at her sideways as he walked. "I don't know if I will ever get used to this Freegan business."

"It's just a different lifestyle, that's all."

Suddenly Hailey stopped. "Here, this is the back of a high-end store. Let's try here."

159

She stood in front of a large, green, metal dumpster. "I'll unlock it and put the top up. When I do, don't lean over the edge. You can get hurt that way."

"Safety first," Jordan said. "We don't want the dumpster to kill us...we'll let the food inside it kill us instead."

Hailey whirled around. "Look, you don't have to do this. You can go home. I can do it without you."

"Okay, okay, I'm sorry. I wanted to see what this is all about, so let's go for it," Jordan said with his hands up. The last thing he wanted to do was to lose the only people who were nice to him.

Hailey turned back to the dumpster. "The best way to go through a dumpster is to lower yourself into it. Most of the good stuff tends to settle at the bottom because it usually weighs more than papers and stuff. So, you can't just stand outside the dumpster and reach in. You have to go completely inside."

She climbed the dumpster and jumped in.

But suddenly the lid flipped back over with a loud *clang*. Hailey realized that she was shut inside with the top closed.

And it was dark inside the dumpster. Very dark.

"Jordan!" Hailey yelled, but even to herself, her voice sounded muffled because of the confined space. "Open the lid!"

She couldn't stand completely upright because the top of the dumpster was too low. She pushed against the lid, but it seemed to be jammed shut. It was too heavy for her to move.

She could hear the lid being bumped from the outside, so she figured Jordan was trying to help open the dumpster. But the lid remained closed. And the dumpster remained dark.

"I'll get help!" She heard Jordan's voice say.

"No!" Hailey cried. "Jordan, don't leave me!"

Only silence greeted her. Jordan must have left.

She knew that if the dumpster had locked itself when the lid closed, only she had the key. But she was sure that Jordan would go back to the house, get help, and get another key.

In the meantime, Hailey was alone. Alone in a dark, confined space.

And then she heard the noise.

She suddenly realized that she wasn't so alone after all.

Hailey tried to see in the darkness. There was no light of any kind; no moonlight peeking through any cracks in the dumpster lid. It was dark—as dark as a tomb; as dark as death.

She tried to listen intently. She could swear she had heard a sound, but when she strained her ears to listen again, there was nothing. She tried to breathe through an open mouth, in order to keep her ears focused. She strained to hear. What else was in the dumpster with her?

There! Hailey heard the slight sound again. She could hear a faint rustling, and the fine hairs on her arms prickled as goosebumps caused them to rise.

Then Hailey froze, because suddenly she knew. She was sure he knew what made the slight rustling sound.

Rats!

There were rats in the dumpster.

Hailey sucked in her breath. She pictured the rats coming at her in the darkness…getting closer, and crouching in their approach. Were the rats hungry? Hungry enough to bite a woman who was unable to defend herself because she was confined to such a small space?

Hailey stepped to the corner of the dumpster, feeling the sponginess of the debris beneath her feet. She wanted to get into a corner. That way, she would have her back to two walls, and perhaps find limited protection.

Aw crap! she thought, feeling a tickling at her ankle. It was too dark to see, but Hailey thought she could feel a rodent's whiskers sniffing her flesh.

She crouched in the corner of the dumpster, feeling the hard metal sides protecting her. But that still left her front exposed.

A moan escaped her, because once again, she felt a rat sniffing at her ankle. Hailey lifted a leg and swung as hard as she could against where she had felt the rat. She heard a startled squeal, and took satisfaction that she must have hit her target.

But she knew that her margin of safety wouldn't last because the rat would come back. Vermin never gave up. It would approach her again, and soon. She tried to keep her ears finely tuned to any sounds that would indicate the rat would try to stalk her again.

Minutes passed. Then she heard noises again. This time it sounded like more than one rat. She could hear their little claws scrabbling on the paper debris on the bottom of the dumpster. She could hear a faint rustling and an occasional squeak.

"Shoo!" Hailey shouted, and the rats quieted, but only for a minute. They seemed to sense that she could not defend herself. The rats were getting bolder.

Again she felt the whiskers against her legs. She tried to kick, but a rat unexpectedly latched onto the bare skin of her arm. Hailey began to scream.

Suddenly she was blinded by light. The lid of the dumpster swung open, and a flashlight was shining inside.

"Hailey!" Jordan called. "Are you okay?"

The rats scurried away, diving into the dumpster debris. The creatures scrambled to find dark places to hide, but not before Hailey could see their fat, stubby bodies and the long, scaly tails that trailed behind like whipcords. They scrambled all over each other in the rush to find concealment.

It was over in an instant. All of the rats were gone.

"I'm fine," Hailey said. She stood up straight, still in the dumpster. "Shut the flashlight off."

When Jordan turned off the flashlight, she could see that he had brought Blaine.

"Here," Jordan held out his hand, "let me help you out of there, Hailey."

She looked at him in amazement. "Why?"

"Don't you want to get out of that dumpster?" Jordan asked.

"Not until I go through it," she said. "There's a lot of good stuff in here."

"I'm going in, too," Blaine said, "because it's Monday night. There'll be lots of good stuff in this dumpster tonight."

GHOUL

"I'm being haunted."

Well, I'm a psychiatrist, and I thought I'd heard it all from my patients until that moment. I shifted in my leather chair, and noted Lisa's words on my pad of paper. I made a conscious effort not to show any reaction.

"What makes you think you're being haunted?" I asked, keeping my voice void of emotion.

I observed Lisa out of the corner of my eye as she sat in a leather armchair that matched my own. She certainly beautified my office. The sunlight streaming in through the only window reflected golden highlights upon her light brown hair, creating an almost halo-like effect. Lisa was dressed in jeans and a T-shirt, but it didn't matter, for she would be striking no matter what she chose to wear.

She shifted on her chair just as I had done, and I wondered briefly if she was mimicking my movements. "Doctor Keith, I have strange dreams," she told me. "I dream of being followed. You know, pursued."

I hesitated, and then told her in my best psychiatrist lingo, "Actually, this type of dream is not uncommon. Sometimes unresolved issues from a person's past can materialize in the subconscious as feelings of persecution. The dreamer is actually trying to escape the past. This cannot be interpreted as a haunting, although you probably feel distressed by the feelings these dreams are causing."

She looked up at me, meeting my eyes for the first time in this session. "No, Doctor Keith. This is not something from my past. I'm dreaming of my present."

"Go on," I said.

She cast her blue eyes downwards once again, and her fingers nervously plucked at the arm of the chair. My office was casual, and I had planned it that way. I felt the formality that usually went with psychiatry had no place here. Although framed credentials hung on the wall, everything else resembled a living room more than an office. Except that there was no couch.

"You were saying?" I gently prodded.

"A few weeks ago," she said, "I was dreaming the same dream over and over. Let me describe the dream: I hear strange sounds in the night. I open my front door and I see that my front yard has disappeared. Instead, there's a graveyard. The sounds are coming from somewhere in that graveyard. I follow the sounds until I reach an open grave. The grave is empty, but I know the sounds are coming from that hole in the ground."

Lisa stopped, and I waited. At last she continued, "In my dream, the headstone over the open grave has my name carved upon it."

She looked up and quickly sat forward. Her fingers grasped the arms of the chair and she said in a rush, "But I told you that the grave is empty! It's been dug up. There's a mound of dirt next to it; the casket is gone. What happened to my body? What happened to me?"

"Okay," I said, "take a deep breath."

She sat back, and then spoke again more slowly, "Lately the dreams are getting worse. They're changing. I'm being haunted. Except I am being haunted by myself. In my dreams, I see an image of myself everywhere. In dark corners. In other rooms. In alleyways. I always see myself out of the corner of my eye. I know this sounds weird, but in my dreams, I'm being followed by *myself*. My body came out of the grave! That's why it was missing. It came out of the grave, and now it is following me."

I waited, but Lisa was silent. I realized that it was my turn to speak. In most cases, the revelations of the patient were symptoms of the patient's problems, and were not to be taken literally. It was my job to interpret and then evaluate whatever I heard.

"Perhaps your feeling of being haunted by yourself simply means that you do not accept yourself," I tried, still spouting psycho-babble. "Perhaps you have feelings of isolation from the 'real world' and those feelings are manifesting themselves into an alter ego. That would explain why, in your dreams, you are experiencing another version of yourself. Remember, dreams are products of your subconscious, not products of reality."

"Then I want to be hypnotized," she said. "You said I have an alter-ego. That means I have a split personality. I've heard good things about hypnosis. Maybe the answer is in my subconscious, like you just said; another personality."

I said quickly, "I'm not talking about another personality. An alter-ego does not mean multiple personality. Multiple personality disorders are so extremely rare that I'd be willing to bet I won't see a real case in my entire career."

"Okay, but what about my hypnosis idea?" she asked. "Would you do it?"

"What are you hoping to find? Your Id?"

"What's an Id?"

"Well," I explained, glad to have yet another opportunity to show off my expertise, "the Id is an unconscious energy source derived from one's instincts, not from one's intellect. It takes one to a primal level. It makes one want immediate gratification of biological drives, such as sex, thirst and hunger."

Lisa shook her head, and I felt vaguely disappointed that I had somehow failed to impress her. "No," she said, "my problem is not my body…it's my ghost, I suppose I should call it. Not my Id. Listen, Doctor Keith, I want to stop the haunting. I want a confrontation with the ghost of myself that came out of the open grave. I want to know how the ghost can be me when I'm me. And I'm no ghost; I'm alive."

"First, you've got to stop treating this like it is real," I told her. "Dreams are not reality."

"Maybe not," Lisa said. "But suddenly it's not just limited to dreams."

"What do you mean?"

"Lately I've been seeing myself even when I'm awake," she said. "I told you that I see my own ghost lurking in dark places; I see it out of the corner of my eye, but when I turn around, it vanishes before I can get a good look. All this is now happening when I'm awake. And sometimes, when I look in a mirror, I see it for a split second standing behind me. It always vanishes before I can really look. I'm telling you, I'm freaked out. I need to stop haunting myself. Help me, Doctor Keith."

"Well, I want you to understand what hypnosis is," I said, once again trying to impress her with my knowledge. "Monotonous visual stimuli can put people in a trance-like state. Take the examples of people staring at televisions or the familiar 'highway hypnosis,' you know, when people drive on long stretches of boring roads without breaks. People go into a trance-like state."

165

I stopped, and then added, "Actually, the word trance can be misleading, because hypnosis is not technically a sleep or a stupor. It is a breakdown of the ego, making some people susceptible to suggestions."

"So how will you do it?" she asked.

"You've heard of the hypnotist dangling a watch in front of the patient. That's a monotonous visual stimulus. I use a device similar to the musical timer that keeps the beat, except mine doesn't make any noise. It's just a mechanized stick that moves back and forth."

"Let's do it."

"You'll have to sign a consent form," I warned her. "I assume no liability for anything."

"Let's do it," she repeated.

Suddenly I realized what she meant. "You mean right now, during this session?"

"There's still over a half hour left in my session," she pointed out. "And there's no time like the present."

I don't consider myself a spontaneous person, so I don't know what made me agree. But I did agree. I had her sign the form as I gathered my materials together. I set the stage, and then began to hypnotize my patient.

Lisa went under very quickly. Soon she was in a hypnotic state, still seated on the leather chair, with her eyes closed and a dreamy expression on her beautiful face.

I brought her back to her original dream; the first one she had weeks ago. I asked her to describe where she was and what she was doing.

"I'm in my nightgown," she said. "I feel the coarseness of the material, because the night seems to be cold, so I'm wearing flannel. For some reason, I'm in my parent's house; it's a big house, one of those Southern mansions. But I haven't lived here for over a year. I know I moved into an apartment. Yet here I am, somehow back in my parents' house in the middle of the night. I hear a noise, and I'm wondering, *Where are my parents?* Nobody seems to be home."

"What happens next?" I asked.

"I'm at the top of the stairs," she said. "I can feel the smooth wood of the railing with my left hand. It's dark, but there's a night light at the bottom of the stairs. I can see well enough so that I know I won't have a misstep. Plus, I know this house. I've been up and

166

down these stairs so many times. But something feels different right now about the house. Wait—I know what it is. Somebody must have turned the heat off. It's cold in the house, very cold; that's what's different. I pull my nightgown closer around me and I can feel how scratchy it is. And I'm thinking, *I'm all alone. I hear a bad noise and I'm all alone.*"

"What's the bad noise?" I asked. "What does it sound like?"

"It sounds like moaning, except it is, well, sort of moaning mixed with sounds of the wind. I think the wind is blowing. I can hear branches of the old tree scraping against a window. Yes, that means it's windy outside.

"I'm starting down the stairs now. I can feel the wooden steps because I'm barefoot. I'm scared. I don't want to find out what the sounds are. I don't want to know. But I can't help myself. Something makes me keep walking down the stairs. I feel a sense of dread, of impending doom. But I am compelled to find the sounds. Something is waiting for me…something wants me. Something is out there. I need to find whatever is out there.

"I'm at the bottom step. Now I'm passing the night-light plugged into the wall socket. I feel glad that I'm not in complete darkness. There's some comfort in having a light.

"I'm reaching for the doorknob. I feel the smooth metal in my hand. I'm turning the doorknob, and I hear the creak as the front door opens. I look out. Where is the front yard? Oh my god, there's a cemetery outside! No, it's more like a graveyard, like those types they used to have in churchyards, small and run down. The tombstones loom out of the ground, and some are leaning over, and others are pitted and chipped. This must be a very old graveyard.

"I leave the security of the night-light to step outside. I'm afraid of the dark, but I can't seem to help myself. I go outside. A rickety picket fence surrounds the graveyard. One of the pickets is loose and it bangs in the wind, startling me, making my heart race.

"And now I hear the moaning again. Wait, it's a word; it's my name! Someone is calling my name, but it sounds scary, all weird, like someone is in pain."

She became silent, striking a pose as though she were listening.

"What's happening now?" I asked, coaxing her.

167

"I see someone standing over an open grave. He is pointing at the headstone. Oh my god, the headstone has my name carved into it! The date of my death is this year."

Aha, I thought, *this is something new, something only revealed by hypnosis. Lisa never mentioned anyone else being in her dream before other than herself.*

"Is this person standing over your grave a man or a woman? What does he or she look like?" I asked.

"He is a black man, dressed funny, like he's from Haiti or somewhere, like he's a bush person. He has paint on his face. Yes, he looks like someone about to perform a Voodoo ritual. I want to look around to see if there's a bloody chicken or something.

"The man is speaking. *Mark of Guede, Loa of the Dead, curse this woman,* the man is telling me. Oh no! He's pointing to my empty grave. What does he mean? Is this weird man putting a curse on me?"

At that, Lisa became agitated, thrashing about in her chair. I made the decision to take her out of hypnosis and therefore take her back to the present. Besides, we were running out of time, and I get paid by the session. It wouldn't be in my best interests for any overruns.

"You will immediately awaken," I commanded.

She stopped thrashing and opened her beautiful eyes. "Did I go under?"

"Yes you did."

"What did I say?"

"Not much more than you already know," I lied. I wanted to do some research on whatever a *Mark of Guede* was before I discussed it with Lisa. I didn't want to upset my patient more than she already was.

"Lisa," I then said, "your time is up. Go ahead and make another appointment with Jenilee. She's my secretary. Make the appointment for next week, and we'll go into what you said during this session at that time."

"Now you're leaving me dangling," she said.

"Don't worry," I assured her, "everything is fine. I'll see you next week. In the meantime, I'm going to prescribe sleeping pills for you so you don't dream. Sleeping pills help you sleep, but they suppress REM sleep, so no dreams."

"Okay," she said as she rose to leave my office.

Later, I began typing on my computer. I wanted to know if there really were things called *Guede* or *Loa*, or if those things were simply figments of an imaginative dream.

I got a hit on an Internet search engine. I hesitated, but then I opened the file and began to read.

> *Mark of Guede: The target of this power becomes marked for death. Guede is the Loa of the Dead and is usually the one whom Voodoo priests or priestesses address when they wish to curse someone. The Loa is the Lord of the Cemetery and has the power to command disciples to open the Gateway to Hell. When the Gateway has been opened, the person targeted for the curse begins to attract malicious spirits that follow the cursed person and torments him or her.*

Well, that's interesting, I thought. And disturbing.

I wondered if Lisa had knowledge of Voodoo, or even practiced it, because that would explain why this sort of thing had entered her subconscious, surfacing to appear in her dreams. I jotted down a note in her file as a reminder for me to ask her.

But when I left my office for the day, I put Lisa's problems out of my mind. That is, until I received a frantic phone call at my home that same night.

"Doctor Keith, you have to help me," Lisa pleaded, her voice soft.

I was greatly annoyed. "How did you get my home phone number?"

"I have a friend who works for the local phone company. I can't give you his name or he'll get in trouble."

"You bet he'd get in trouble," I growled. "Lisa, you can't call me at my home."

"Doctor Keith, this is an emergency," she said, and I wondered why she was speaking so quietly.

I took the bait. I'll admit I was curious about this very unusual patient of mine. "What's the emergency?"

"She's here," Lisa whispered.

"Who? Who's there?"

"My ghost."

"Lisa. . ."

"I mean it, Doctor Keith. My ghost is in my apartment right now."

"You can't be asking me to come to your apartment."

"Please come," she whispered. "I need you. I can't call the cops. They'd never believe me. So, I don't know who else to call. You're the only one who understands."

"Lisa," I said, "I cannot get emotionally involved with any of my patients. We need to keep this on a professional level."

"Please," she pleaded.

Against my better judgment, I let my barrier down. I know it sounds crazy to have an attraction for a patient because it could land me in big trouble. I knew it was mostly because she was so incredibly beautiful that I went against all the rules. I'm a psychiatrist, but I'm also a man. A very human man. And I'm single.

I thought, *Lord help me*, because I was looking at professional suicide. This could ruin me, yet I did it anyway. The danger and the inappropriateness simply made it more exciting. *Perhaps I need my own psychiatrist,* I thought ruefully.

"Tell me your address," I said, ignoring my inner voice of reason. "Your file is in my office. I keep no patient information at my home."

"Then you'll come?"

"I'll be right over."

I got into my car and drove to Lisa's apartment. She lived smack in the middle of New Orleans, whereas I lived on the outskirts of the city. I looked for her name on the outside of the gated building and found it. I buzzed the button.

I began to fret, because Lisa didn't buzz back to unlock the gate. I pushed the button again. And again I received no response.

Greatly disturbed, I went to the apartment that had the word *Manager* posted above the front door. This apartment openly faced the street, so there was no gate and no buzzer.

I knocked on the door, and within a few seconds, the door swung open. A bedraggled, dark-haired woman of about thirty stood on the threshold. "Whaddya need?" she asked.

I explained who I was, showing identification. "I'm requesting that you unlock the door to Lisa McDurmont's apartment. I'm responding to her phone call about a psychiatric episode that she had been experiencing. I have a bad feeling about this. We need to check on my patient."

"Dontcha need a warrant?" the manager asked.

"This is not a legal affair, and no one is in trouble," I explained. "It's a medical emergency."

The manager unlocked the gate, and I followed her to Apartment 17. I stood impatiently behind her as she unlocked Lisa's door. We then stepped inside together.

My patient was lying on the floor in a face down position, her limbs outstretched. The manager gasped as I kneeled beside Lisa's body and felt for a pulse. There was none.

Lisa was dead.

She was not yet cold, so I knew she must have been dead for only a short time. And after all, I had just spoken to her twenty minutes before. "Call 911," I instructed the manager.

Within minutes the paramedics arrived, but it was of no use. Two cops from the New Orleans Police Department arrived and questioned me extensively, and then one said, "Probably an overdose, although we can't be sure until the toxicology reports come back and the autopsy is performed. You said you prescribed sleeping pills? Let me check in her bathroom. Maybe the bottle's still there."

He left the living room, but immediately returned. "The pill bottle's there, all right, but it's full. If there was an overdose, it wasn't from your prescription."

Then the cop looked at me with a strange expression on his face. "Doc, maybe you'd better come and take a look at the bathroom mirror."

Curious, I walked down the hall and stepped inside the bathroom.

On the mirror, written in large letters with red lipstick, was a single word.

I realized that the cop was standing directly behind me. "Doc," he asked, "what does it mean?"

"I have no idea," I told him as I stared into the mirror at the red word *Ghoul*.

During the next few days, I found myself so busy that I never seemed to have the time to dwell on Lisa's death. I was drawn back to the case when I received word on the toxicology report. It came back negative.

The autopsy revealed a coronary occlusion. I was stunned. How on earth could a young woman like Lisa have a heart attack?

Fear, I thought. Intense, sudden fright could indeed cause the heart to stop. It was rare, but it was possible. In layman's terms, it was called *being scared to death*.

By what had Lisa been so frightened?

Ghoul, my mind whispered.

On Monday morning I went to my bathroom mirror to shave. I had just stepped out of the shower, so I wore nothing but a towel. I lathered my face, a routine thing that I did every morning. I raised my razor to my face.

I saw movement behind me.

Quickly I turned around, my heart racing. But there was nothing. There was no one else in my bathroom.

I stood there for a minute, immobile. Then I turned back around to finish shaving.

You're letting this get to you, I thought. *You're playing into a patient's fantasies. Stop it right now.*

But why did Lisa write the word *Ghoul* on her bathroom mirror with red lipstick? Did Lisa even do it, or did someone else write the word?

Once dressed, I got into my car and began to drive downtown. I saw movement out of the corner of my eye. From where?

I looked into my rear-view mirror and realized, *Mother of God, someone is in my back seat!* Why hadn't I looked in the back before I climbed into my car?

Panicked, I pulled the car over, amazed that I didn't suddenly feel a gun at the back of my neck. I put the car in park and jerked my upper body around so that I could peer into the back seat.

Nothing. There was no one there.

I was stunned. My vehicle shook every time a car sped by. But I felt immobile, helpless with fear, and I remained parked on the shoulder of the road.

Again I thought of Lisa. But this time, I thought of her because I felt very sure that it was Lisa I had seen in my rear view mirror.

I felt a tingling sensation in my scalp, as though all my hair was standing upright in their follicles. I decided that this would not be a good day to go to work. I put the car in drive and returned to the causeway traffic. But this time, instead of heading towards New Orleans, I took the first off ramp to turn around to go back home.

At home, still shaking, I called my secretary, Jenilee, to tell her I would not be coming into the office. Then I decided to consult my reference books.

I searched my many bookcases until I found what I was looking for. The book was titled *Psychology of Less Common Religions*. I understood that Voodoo was considered a religion by many of its participants. Certainly it was less prevalent then, let's say, Catholicism or even Buddhism or Muslim. Maybe I'd find information about Voodoo from this book.

I did. I found a section on Voodoo and read:

> *With Voodoo, it is possible to create a ghoul, which is a reanimated human corpse similar to a juju zombie. A ghoul is created by means of Black Magic—usually evil Voodoo. Ghouls are among the lowest forms of the undead, lower than zombies, reanimated to serve their Loa in some way—by providing effective slave labor, protection, or solving vendettas by extracting revenge.*
>
> *Creating the undead through evil Voodoo is really a form of possession of a body. There*

173

is a small window of opportunity—the victim cannot be dead longer than seven days if the spells are to work. The method of creating ghouls can be performed by retrieving hair from the dead victim in conjunction with Voodoo dolls, rituals, and spells.

There have been some rare occasions of ghouls temporarily retaining part of their mental faculties. For reasons beyond explanation, a ghoul's mortal persona is able to assume partial control over the ghoul's bodily actions. This rare occurrence has only been observed when a ghoul encounters situations that contain heavy emotional connections to his or her life when he or she was living. But ghouls are unable to resist the commands of the Loa for long.

I closed the book. So ghouls were supposed to be on an even lower playing field than zombies. I hadn't realized that there was an assumed hierarchy among the so-called undead. That was enough to absorb for one day.

I didn't feel well, so I decided to lie down, even though it was still morning. I undressed down to my underwear and got back into bed.

I began to dream.

I dreamed I was back in my office, and Lisa was my patient. I realized that this would be my opportunity to ask why she was haunting me.

"What are you?" I asked.

"I am the walking dead."

Ever the psychiatrist, I said, "Tell me about it."

"Did you know that Voodoo is alive and well in New Orleans? That's why I'm no longer alive and well."

"I'm aware of Voodoo," I told her, trying to maintain control of the direction of this conversation. "You say you're the walking dead. You are a ghoul? Are you haunting me?"

"You already know the answer to that," she said.

174

"Humor me," I said, "and pretend I know nothing. Tell me everything."

"I'll tell you what I am allowed to tell. I dabbled in Voodoo. Before I knew it, I got in over my head. By the time I came to you, I was desperate to find conventional ways out of my situation. I didn't tell you that I practiced Voodoo, because you would have scoffed. I had hoped that Voodoo was all a myth, that science could overcome superstition, and that's why I came to you. I had hoped that my practicing Voodoo was all a harmless game. But here I am among the undead. Voodoo is real; it is very real indeed, and it is certainly not harmless for a blundering novice like me."

"That doesn't explain why you were targeted to be haunted, and certainly doesn't explain why you were reanimated after death," I said.

"The attraction for me to Voodoo was the power it promised. Imagine," she said, "having the power over life and death. But I made a lot of mistakes, and one of those mistakes was a big one."

"What was the mistake?" I asked, encouraging her to continue.

"I hexed a lover who jilted me. Not the worst spell; not like wanting him dead or anything, just a spell to mess up his life for a while. Actually, I really never expected the Voodoo to work. But suddenly, the guy lost his job, his car broke down, and he was evicted from his apartment. Then when he got his car fixed, he got into a horrible accident and was confined to a wheelchair. So the curse worked," she told me. "Actually, this was the guy who introduced me to the Loa. The Loa was the one who cursed me and made me a ghoul."

"So that explains you. What about me?" I asked. "Why are you haunting me?"

"That I cannot tell you. The Loa commands my silence."

"There is still some of Lisa in you," I said. "That Lisa has compassion. Stop the haunting. And tell me why you're doing it at all."

"I can't tell you," she said. "But you can find out why yourself. Find the Loa. Once you know the Lord of the Cemetery, you will be able to protect yourself."

"How can I find the Loa?"

"Find Papa Legba."

"Who?"

"Papa Legba," she repeated. "I can't tell you any more about him. I am not allowed."

"Why does the Loa want me dead?"

"Because of something you did against the Loa," Lisa said. "If you can figure out what you did, then you will know who the Loa is."

Then she said the most chilling words I have ever heard in my life: "Ghouls recoup vendettas and extract revenge. I am the ghoul that will kill you."

With those horrible words echoing in my head, I woke up from my dream. Yet, I knew with my entire being that it had not been a dream.

My conversation with a ghoul had indeed taken place.

I felt a great sense of dread. I needed to find out about Papa Legba. At least that would be someplace to start. I got out of bed and threw on a pair of pants. Then I went back to the bookcase that held the book titled *Psychology of Less Common Religions*.

I opened it once again to the section about Voodoo. I learned that Papa Legba was near the top of the temple of Voodoo, a demon. Legba was a protector, and he was the master of the crossroads between life and death, earth and Hell.

I read all I could about Legba. And that gave me an idea.

I knew that on this night, there would be a full moon. I would call Papa Legba at midnight.

I would summon a demon up from Hell.

The night was clear. I drove away from the city of New Orleans, heading north on the Lake Pontchartrain Causeway. At the north shore, I headed east until I came to an unmarked parish road that turned into the pine woods.

The full moon's light shimmered on the narrow sandy road in front of me, and I was amazed at how the moonlight created such visibility, even though it was filtered by the trees. I slowed my car to about twenty miles per hour, and the trees' under-story seemed to close in upon the road. I swerved to avoid a large snake, and soon after, three deer leaped across the sandy road in front of me.

I parked my car on the shoulder of the one-lane, narrow road and got out. The air was heavy with southern humidity. The dampness caused dew to sparkle on the roadside weeds, crickets chirped merrily away, and a screech owl shrilled as it hunted in the darkness. The sounds of toads and frogs calling from ponds and small swamps to either side of the road created a musical opus.

I reached into the back seat of my car and extracted a live chicken from its cage by grasping its feet and holding it upside down. With the other hand, I grabbed a hatchet that I sharpened just hours before. I stepped away from the car.

And there it was, right in front of me: the crossroad.

It was at the X-sign that signaled a railroad track crossing the tree-lined sandy road. I laid the struggling chicken upon the road next to the railroad crossing X-sign and quickly chopped off its head with the hatchet.

The chicken's body convulsed violently despite the loss of its head, twisting and squirming in my grasp as blood spurted from its neck artery and darkened the road directly underneath the X-sign.

I felt shame and remorse for my actions. I had nothing against chickens. Still, live chickens were plentiful in a Voodoo-rich city like New Orleans, because that was the animal of choice for small Voodoo rituals. I knew that larger animals such as goats, sheep, or dogs were sometimes used for larger ceremonies, but tonight I hoped a chicken would do.

I held the chicken down until all movement ceased. Then I went back to my car to retrieve an open coffee can. I turned back to the dead chicken and shook the coffee can so that the grounds created an axially symmetric pattern drawn on the road. I was drawing Voodoo symbols with the coffee grounds, directly on top of the chicken's blood, which had been splashed upon the ground.

I carefully placed the empty can away from the mystic symbols that appeared so dark upon the earth. The full moon cast its glow upon the scene, reflecting the macabre stage that displayed the construction of a Voodoo spell.

I began to chant. *L'envoi morts, the sending of the dead. Open the gate between the human world and the spirit world. Papa Legba, come to me and show your presence.*

I didn't know if I should feel silly because it might be all a fake superstition, or apprehension because it just might possibly be a reality, but either way, I was determined to continue. Although it was night, the air was warm, and sweat trickled down my forehead, stinging my eyes. I blinked and wiped my eyes with my sleeve, but I did not stop the chanting.

L'envoi morts, the sending of the dead. Open the gate between the human world and the spirit world. Papa Legba, come to me and show your presence.

And then I felt something.

Oh my god, could it be real?

It was like a mild electric current passing through me. I felt the hair on my arms stand up in their follicles. My scalp tingled. I stopped sweating; instead, suddenly I felt very cold.

I knew that the spell was working.

Papa Legba was coming.

And then, with that certainty, I became deathly afraid, and I trembled violently. But I knew I had to continue. It was too late to stop; I couldn't turn and run. I knew in my heart that this thing I was doing was my only chance to save my own life. If the demon from Hell was real, then so was the ghoul. This was my only weapon against a ghoul.

So I stood there in the moonlight, bracing myself to meet face-to-face with a demon that held the key to the gateway of hell.

A fine mist seemed to congeal next to the X-sign, on top of the railroad tracks. The mist swirled until it began to form a shape. Then the shape became solid and I was able to view a demon in the moonlight.

It was more frightening than I ever could have imagined. The skin was reptilian, dark and shiny, with scales. It was about six feet tall, and although the arms and torso were that of a man, the legs were that of a hairless goat. The creature had exposed male genitals, large and dangling.

The head was not human. It was an oblong shape, bare of hair, and the ears were long and slanted. Two small goat horns protruded from above the ears.

But it was the face that horrified me the most.

The face was human yet not human. The nose was long and pointed, just like the chin. Unlike the scaly body, the face and neck were smoother, dark and somewhat leathery. But the eyes—my god, the eyes! They were large and long and were slanted upwards at the corners, and they glowed red.

"Who is this that disturbs my peace?" the demon hissed.

I shuddered under his scrutiny. "Papa Legba, I have a request."

"I asked you who you are," the demon demanded.

I took a deep breath and tried to stand taller. "I am Keith Couvillion, and I am being haunted by a ghoul. I summoned you because I have a request."

"So I heard. State your request."

"I need to know the identity of the Loa who reanimated Lisa McDurmont."

"And you expect me to give you the name of the Loa?"

"Yes." Then I added, sounding foolish, "Please."

The demon shifted his stance on the railroad tracks, and his eyes glowed an even deeper, bloody red. "Would you scorn your Christian God?"

I was taken aback. "What?"

"I think my question was clear."

I hesitated, then said, "No."

"Then I will not give you the identity of the Loa," the demon said.

I was frightened beyond my wits. I in no way wanted to anger a demon from Hell. I was afraid about what could result as a repercussion from his wrath. But to renounce God? If this demon really came from Hell, didn't that mean there was also a Heaven? Was God in that Heaven, watching me now, waiting for my decision?

I had to say something. "I cannot renounce my God. But I will keep an open mind to anything else you might command of me, other than committing my soul to you," I tried, and then cringed. I was so scared that I couldn't think. If Papa Legba accepted what I said, what would he command of me?

"Are you worthy?"

His question startled me. I had no idea if I were worthy or not. I couldn't even imagine what he meant by worthy. Worthy of what? To do what? But I took a chance and said yes.

"Then you will participate in a Voodoo ceremony," the demon commanded. "You will go to Lacombe Bayou at midnight on Saturday night. The information you seek will be found there."

"Thank you," I said, breathing out with a sigh. I didn't know if I was thanking him for the information or for not killing me.

Then suddenly the demon spoke again.

"By summoning me, your soul is at risk," he said. "Now that I am aware of you, Hell is aware of you as well."

Then the mist began to swirl around him once again. The demon began to fade from my view.

"Wait!" I cried. "I told you I will not scorn my God! How can my soul be at risk? Wait! Come back! You must tell me!"

But the demon was gone. He had simply vanished, gone back to manning the gateway to Hell.

I stood there for a moment, blinking in disbelief. Had I really been standing at a railroad crossing, talking to a demon? Apparently I had. But if I believed in God, how could my soul possibly be at risk? Didn't I tell the demon that I would not renounce my God?

Or did Papa Legba mean that I could wind up just like Lisa, a juju zombie, a ghoul?

My knees threatened to buckle underneath me. Somehow I felt that I had narrowly escaped death, narrowly avoided being smote down by a demon from Hell. I trembled, more with relief that I was still alive than from fear. My mouth was bone dry and tasted of pennies. Sweat began to bead on my forehead once again.

I looked sadly at the chicken's head, severed from its body at my hands. I kicked the Voodoo symbols that I had drawn with the coffee grinds, smearing and spreading them into an undecipherable mess. I tried to erase the evidence of my macabre deed. I picked up both the chicken's body and the head, and threw them into the weeds. I knew animal scavengers would dispose of the remains.

I got back into my car and started to drive home, feeling incredibly drained and tired.

The next day I called my secretary and told her to cancel and reschedule my appointments for the rest of the week because I was sick. Actually, I was sick. My nerves jangled and my stomach felt acidic. I had heartburn and I couldn't seem to eat much.

"All week?" Jenilee asked.

"Just do what I say." I snapped. "Is it so difficult to understand English?"

"I only understand nice English," she snapped back.

"I don't believe you need to know the details."

"What if someone goes and commits suicide or something, because you are sick and they feel all alone and so they get desperate?"

I took a deep breath to try to stop myself from screaming at her. "I seriously doubt that any of my patients will jump off bridges this week. Now, do as I say and cancel those appointments. And, if you think you can handle talking to those poor desperate patients, try to reschedule them so that they don't feel so all alone."

"You can't ignore people who need you," Jenilee said. "Bad things could happen if you do. Bad things!"

"If you keep arguing with me," I warned, "I'll have to fire you."

There was silence on the phone. I reached my breaking point.

"So do what I said!" I yelled.

"Okay, okay, Doctor Keith," Jenilee said. "I'll reschedule all of your appointments right away."

"See that you do," I told her and hung up the phone.

Afterwards, I wondered why I had been so harsh, and rude Jenilee. Yet it just seemed that she grated on me, and goaded me into anger. After all, who was the boss and who was the secretary here? I never hid my ill temperament towards her very well and in this particular incident I had been too upset and nervous to keep from losing my temper. Still, I knew it was no excuse for my behavior, because after all, I was a professional and was supposed to behave like a professional.

I told myself I would apologize and to Jenilee just as soon as things calmed down in my life.

And then I would fire her.

And so the week passed at an excruciatingly slow pace. Finally it was Saturday night, and when the clock struck eleven, I got in my car and drove to the Lacombe Bayou swamp.

I drove until I came to another sandy road to nowhere that wound through the pines, dense kudzu, and under story brush until it paralleled the levee bordering Lacombe Bayou. What looked like an ill-kept farm road went over the levee, and ended on the other side.

I parked the car and walked slowly into the swamp along a narrow trail that seemed better suited to deer and hogs than to people. I was glad that I had brought a decent flashlight to help me see the various snakes so active at night this time of year.

Grasses grew on slight elevations, and an occasional hummock supported the growth of low bushes. The trail wound along on what passed here for higher ground, and to either side I could see the shine of water in the flashlight and dim moonlight. The water was shallow; less than a foot deep.

I walked further and entered a more elevated part of the swamp where the soil supported the growth of increasingly dense forest, the tree branches festooned with Spanish moss that hung in eerie-looking clumps. The air was warm and heavy with moisture. The moon was only a tiny crescent, so I was completely dependent upon the light of my flashlight for visibility.

Suddenly I realized I could hear the sound of drums. As I walked further, I began to hear some sort of singsong chanting, and I realized I was hearing another language, possibly Haitian Creole.

I followed the sounds to a clearing in the swamp. The Voodoo practitioners had found raised ground, because they were all on the dry earth. Obviously they must have, at one time or another, cleared the trees and the underbrush from their Voodoo 'temple.' It looked like a place that had been well tended.

There were about twenty participants, a mixed group of whites and blacks. A half dozen of them beat on drums of various sizes. The drumming was rhythmic; and each musician played their instruments at different tones and pitches, yet it all seemed to somehow merge into a very exiting sound.

The ratio of men to women seemed about equal. The black women wore colorful dresses accompanied by likewise colorful turbans on their heads. The white women wore similar dresses but had nothing on their heads to cover their hair, which swung side-to-side with the rhythm of their dancing.

The men, both black and white, were shirtless despite the fact that it was still only spring; but that night, the air was warm and humid.

A man spied me and began to walk towards me, beckoning me to step forward. Here appeared to be the black man Lisa described from her dream. His hair was wild, in semi-long dreadlocks. His nostrils were flared with excitement and his chin jutted firmly outward. He was dressed as a bush person. But odder still was the paint smeared in patterns upon his face.

"My name is Macumba, the bokor. I know who you are, Keith Couvillion," the man told me, speaking loudly to be heard over the drumbeats, "and I know why you have come."

I stepped into the flickering light of the fire. "Why have I come?" I asked the bush man, to see what he would say.

"You have come to be mounted," he told me in his deep voice.

I hesitated. "What are you talking about?"

"Mounting is possession," he said.

A chill ran down my spine. "No thanks."

"It's a temporary thing," the odd man assured me. "You will gain the knowledge you seek."

"How do I know it's temporary?" I asked.

"You don't." At that, he laughed, and beckoned me to join the circle of dancers, all illuminated by the fire.

I thought to myself, *What have I got to lose if I participate in this Voodoo ceremony? I just might die here, but I will die for sure at Lisa's hands when she comes after me. And she will.*

I didn't underestimate the power of Voodoo. After all, I had seen with my own eyes what its magic had done to Lisa. More importantly, I had been commanded to attend this ceremony by a demon from Hell. Papa Legba had told me he was aware of me; so I had no doubt he knew where I was at this very moment.

I realized the dancers were circling a goat that was unhappily tethered next to the campfire. The dancers moved slowly and seemed to be dazed; I briefly wondered if they were drugged. The goat bleated pitifully, but no one paid attention. I knew what would be the goat's plight.

Macumba led me to the dancers. With a wave of his hand, the dancers moved away from the goat. The drummers continued the rhythmic beat. Macumba stepped back, then leaned over to pick up a sack from the ground. Just as I had done on a previous night, Macumba began pouring the sack's contents onto the ground, creating mystic symbols. Only he wasn't using coffee grounds; the powder appeared to be cornmeal. I knew that Voodoo symbols could only be drawn with coffee grounds, cornmeal, or flour, all substances that could be consumed.

"Cut the goat," Macumba commanded, and a woman stepped out from the dancing circle. She picked up something from the ground that gleamed in the firelight. I realized it was a very large knife, almost the size of a machete.

A man stepped out of the circle of dancers and picked up some sort of urn or clay vessel. He too approached the goat.

Suddenly the drums were silent and the dancers stopped moving. All were stock still; watching.

Both the man and the woman approached the goat. The animal must have sensed impending doom, for it tried to struggle, but the tether was very short. There was no escape for the goat.

The man kneeled, but the woman made a single swiping motion with her arm, and the knife deeply slit the throat of the animal. Choking and squirming, the more the goat struggled, the faster the blood spurted from its neck artery. Then I realized what the man was doing. He was capturing the blood, filling up his urn.

Then the goat fell to the ground, and the woman dropped the knife. The man stood up and held the blood-filled urn to Macumba.

Macumba turned to me and held up the urn. "You must drink."

My stomach fluttered, but I was committed to participate. I took the urn and raised it to my lips. It smelled like raw meat. When I drank, I was surprised at how warm the blood was, and how the taste was so coppery. I closed my eyes and gulped two large swallows.

My reflexes kicked in, and I couldn't help but heave. I lowered the urn, kept my eyes closed, and took some very deep breaths.

My stomach settled. It would keep the blood down.

The drumming began again and the dancers picked up the beat. Macumba reached for my hand as he began dancing, and I found myself joining in. Macumba continued to hold my hand, and he and I danced side-by-side to the rhythmic beating of the six drums. I began feeling lightheaded; dazed, and it was as though I was looking at myself from afar. I felt drugged and wondered if the goat had been drugged, with an unknown substance circulating in its bloodstream. Or perhaps there had already been a drug placed in the bottom of the urn, and it had merged with the goat's blood.

I can barely remember what happened next. I fell to the ground, but felt no pain. My mind was no longer my own. I felt bewildered, but then my mind cleared. Except I was no longer alone within myself.

And then I knew. I knew the identity of the Loa.

It was my secretary. It was Jenilee.

<< — >>

I woke up, groggy and confused. I thought, *Where am I?*

I sat up, blinking my eyes. It was daylight, and from the position of the sun, I figured it was around noon. Again, I wondered, *Where am I?*

Then I remembered. I had participated in a Voodoo ritual just hours before. I looked around. There were no signs of any ritual. Had it happened at all? Had it really happened?

But then I noticed a scorched patch on the ground. And when I looked to where the goat's blood was spilled, I observed that the ground had been cleaned with what appeared to be broom marks. There were no symbols made of cornmeal; the mystic marks must have been also cleaned up somehow.

Then it hit me. Jenilee was the Loa. Why? What had I done to her? Why did she want me cursed?

I honestly didn't know. I needed to confront her to find out.

Damn, I should have fired her months ago.

I stood up, shaky at first, so I didn't move until my nerves calmed down somewhat. Then I walked back through the swamp until I reached my car. Getting in, I turned the car around, barely making the turn on that narrow road, and drove back towards my office.

I was driving on the compacted sand through the tree-filtered sunlight, when suddenly there was a movement on the road right in front of me. For a split second, I thought it was a deer, but then I realized it was a person. I hit the brakes.

Lisa had run across the road.

She was following me.

I sat in my car for a few minutes, trying to collect my wits. I wiped my forehead with my sleeve. When my heart began beating normally once again, I put the car into drive and resumed my trip

185

back to my office. I needed to confront Jenilee if I wanted to end this ordeal.

I presumed it was Sunday, so my secretary would not be at work until the following day. But I knew I had an employee file on Jenilee; I would look up her address and pay her a personal visit at her home.

As I drove, my mind was asking a question over and over, *Why?*

Why would Jenilee want me cursed? What had I done to her?

I tried to think about it. Could it be because I had so often been curt and rude to her?

Nonsense. If people killed people just because they were rude, then people would be killing other people on the streets every day.

But…weren't they? It seemed like there were a lot of murders in New Orleans.

My thoughts drifted to Voodoo. What was the connection between Jenilee and Voodoo?

Voodoo presented equal opportunities for men and women, African-Americans and Caucasians; all could participate. The misconception was that Haitian blacks are the only ones who practiced Voodoo. But in New Orleans, a *houngan* or *mambo* could be your next-door neighbor. None of the stereotypes applied when it came to Voodoo.

I realized that Jenilee must be pretty immersed in Voodoo to have become a powerful Loa. I would have to be very careful as to how I approached her.

Once I reached my office, I found the employee file on Jenilee. I jotted down her address and then left to drive to her house. It wasn't far.

My nerves jangled as I drove. I was so afraid I would see Lisa lurking in my back seat. I was even more afraid to confront a Loa. Oh god, if I had only known earlier, who and what she was, I could have…what? What could I have done?

I found her house, a small cottage, and knocked on the door. Jenilee opened the door. She looked at me, then took a step backwards.

"Doctor Keith," she said, "Come on in."

I entered her small living room.

Then I turned around to look closely at her. I wanted to gauge her demeanor; to decide if she could pose any threat to me. She shifted her gaze away from me under my scrutiny, and her face flushed. The submissive way she did not make eye contact gave me the confidence to proceed.

I got straight to the point as I sat on a wicker rocking chair. "I need to talk to you about Voodoo."

Any submissiveness instantly disappeared. "Okay, Doctor Keith. But guess what? I know that you know about me. I know that you've been mounted."

It seemed that there were no secrets in Voodoo.

Jenilee met my gaze. I saw her pupils dilate with hatred.

I felt a stab of fear. Had I misjudged her a moment ago? Was I not so domineering in this situation after all? What happened to my psychiatric skills? Could I have been too hasty in my confidence to enter her house, to be alone with a Voodoo Loa?

I needed Jenilee to sit down. By standing above me, she held the assertive position. "Please sit down," I told her. "It hurts my neck to look up at you."

She sat, so I plunged ahead, trying to regain dominance. It was vital that I showed no weakness. I wanted to put her on the defensive, so I made myself sound accusatory. "You are the Loa. You! But there is no reason to target me."

"First," she told me, "you'd better get your facts straight. I am not a Loa. You misunderstood. What I have done is taken vows, and I'm now married to my special spirit. That gives me the power of a Loa. The Loa is not human, but a spirit. I have the spirit and the power of a Loa."

"I am not seeing the difference," I said, "but please continue."

Jenilee was having none of it. "We're not in the office now, Doc. We're in my home. So knock off the condescending bit. I am trying to explain Voodoo, and you are being your usual all-important, asshole self. But you need to know the facts from the very beginning. You need to know who and what you are dealing with. So, I will go on with your lesson."

She continued, "A lot of the Voodoo spirits are associated with Catholic saints. Erzulie is associated with the Virgin Mary; and Ougon with Saint Jacques, just to name two. Papa Legba is associated with Saint Peter, because in Catholicism, Saint Peter is the gatekeeper. Of course, there is a difference between the two.

187

Peter is the gatekeeper of Heaven, and as you know, Legba is the gatekeeper of Hell."

She took a breath, and then said, "Ougon is the strong, dominant, and prophetic warrior spirit. He is my Loa. By accepting Ougon's spirit, I accept the power he gives."

"Can I speak now?" I asked.

Jenilee made a face. "No one ever seemed to be able to stop you before, you asshole, so go ahead."

"What do you perceive I have done to you that is so bad, you feel you need to have me cursed? I know you sent a ghoul after me."

"Yes, I did."

"So tell me why. What do you think I have done to you?"

"It wasn't me you ruined," Jenilee said, "it was my boyfriend."

"Who is your boyfriend?"

"You mean, who *was* my boyfriend," she spat.

"Okay, who was your boyfriend?"

"Ron Hanson. I loved Ron more than I loved life itself," she said. "We were going to be married. But he had some problems. I tried to get you to accept Ron as your patient. But you wanted him to go somewhere else, because you said Ron was too close to me and I was your employee. But employee? Ha! You always treated me like a slave. Just like the French treated the Africans in 1500. That's how you treat me every day. And when I asked you for a raise last year, you turned me down. See, slaves don't get paid very well."

"Wait a minute," I said. "Please stay on one track. You are talking about two separate issues."

I felt that the hostility Jenilee displayed was pushing her into a manic state. I tried to bring her back into the present, to discover the real reason for her rage. I wanted to calm her. "Are you talking about your boyfriend or your employment with me? Because, like I said, they are two separate issues. Let's keep them separate."

"Oh, I have lots of issues with you. But let's get back to Ron."

"You feel that Ron is relevant to all of this? Is he the center?"

"Ron was the center of my life. You wouldn't take Ron as your patient. I begged you. I really begged you. I knew Ron was in crisis. You see, I met Ron when he was in the same mental institution as I was."

"You were in a mental institution." I repeated what she said slowly to keep my shock from showing. Hadn't I done a background check before hiring her?

I was trying to buy myself time to think, and then it dawned on me that of course it would make sense that Jenilee had previous episodes of mania. I was not surprised that her previous episodes may have been severe enough for her to be institutionalized. This sort of thing didn't happen overnight, so I must have missed it.

I knew I was dealing with a very mentally disturbed person. Certainly she was paranoid. Did she have a dissociative disorder? I was tempted to try to diagnose her on the spot, but then I realized that what I really needed to do was to keep her calm.

I would have plenty of time to diagnose her later.

If I lived long enough.

Going into my psychiatrist mode once again, I prompted, "Why don't you tell me about yourself? I'm a good listener. When were you institutionalized?"

She ignored my question. "I'd only been out of the hospital a couple of days when I started applying for jobs," she told me. "You hired me. You were too busy to really look at me."

"Jenilee, I can help you," I tried.

"No Doctor Keith," she said. "Don't try your psycho-babble on me."

"What happened to Ron?" I asked, hoping to bring her back to her story.

"He killed himself. Shot himself in the head. Want to see the mess? It's in the other room. I cleaned it, all right, but you can still tell that someone lost his brains all over the wall if you look real close. Speaking of looking, I was the one who found his body."

"That must have been very traumatic for you," I said. And then a new thought hit me. "But what does this have to do with Lisa? Why did you do what you did to her? She has nothing to do with me."

"Maybe Lisa had nothing to do with you," Jenilee said. "But Lisa was not blameless either! It was her Voodoo spell that caused my boyfriend's accident. She needed to pay for that. So, I made her pay."

"So that's the connection between you and Lisa," I said. "The connection was Ron."

"Oh!" Jenilee cried. "Don't think I didn't know all about Lisa and Ron. Lisa wanted my boyfriend! Ron was too good for Lisa, but when he rejected her, she cast a spell on him. Well, I sure turned the tables on Lisa, didn't I? She should not have dabbled in Voodoo against a master, which is what I am."

She stood up and reached for a jar on the coffee table. "And now it's your turn. You're the last one I need to punish."

Suddenly Jenilee snaked out her hand and slapped something wet onto my bare arm. I recoiled instinctively, touching the sticky spot on my arm above the elbow. I had thought the jar on the coffee table was a candle. For a moment I couldn't comprehend whatever else it could be.

I stood up. I could smell a medicine-like scent, pungent and sour. "What did you put on my arm?"

She laughed. "It is tcha-tcha."

Slowly Jenilee replaced the jar on the coffee table.

"What the hell is tcha-tcha?" I felt sweat break out on my forehead, forming into droplets that trickled down my face.

"Notice there is none on me, only on you."

"I asked, what is it?" I seemed to be having trouble focusing, or was it the sweat in my eyes that caused the blurring of my vision?

"It's a member of the legume family, *Albizia lebbeck*. It has pharmacological activity due to a group of glycosides known as saponins. The symptoms of tcha-tcha poisoning include nausea, vomiting, excessive secretion in the respiratory passages, and pulmonary edema. Why, Doctor Keith, you could drown in your own fluids."

Now I was truly frightened. The room seemed to get brighter as I felt a panic that was suffocating to me. Or was it the tcha-tcha causing me to have trouble breathing? Which were the real symptoms of the poison and which were psychosomatic? What good was being a psychiatrist if I couldn't even tell the difference about myself?

Badly shaken, I began to walk towards the front door. But I saw movement out of the corner of my eye. I turned towards the movement so I could see it.

Something was coming down the hall into the living room.

I knew it was Lisa, but she looked like something I could describe only as a creature. The creature was formed like the human

190

Lisa was but seemed smaller and withered now. Parts of the skull showed through the hair and the bone gleamed, reflecting the room's light. What was left of the hair clung to the disintegrated scalp in patches.

I couldn't see the face very clearly because it was shadowed in the hallway; still, from what I could make out, the skin appeared as though it were sliding down towards the chin. One opaque eye still remained, deep within the socket, but the other had sunk down into the skull, leaving a black cavity in its wake. The lips were receded back from the mouth, accentuating the teeth and making the Lisa-Ghoul look as though she were snarling.

I couldn't catch my breath. I was too frightened to move, rooted in place, frozen with horror and fear.

Was the Lisa-Ghoul coming for me or for Jenilee?

I didn't want to find out.

Adrenalin hit me, and I jerked into action, running to the front door. I grabbed the doorknob and tried to open it. I shook and shook the doorknob before I realized that the door was locked.

"Dead bolts can lock from both the inside and outside," Jenilee said. "I have the key, not you, Doc."

I couldn't believe how calm Jenilee sounded. Didn't she see the hideous ghoul coming?

And that's when I realized why Jenilee was so calm. The ghoul was coming for me, not for her.

"Jenilee, think about what you're doing," I pleaded. "This is murder. You'll get life in prison."

"Who's going to find out?" Jenilee scoffed. "And anyway, life without Ron is no life at all."

The ghoul was coming closer.

Was there nothing I could do?

I turned to face the ghoul. I still felt the stinging sweat in my eyes and now I felt nausea in the pit of my stomach. Was it fear making me feel so sick or was the poison of tcha-tcha snaking through my system?

"Lisa," I tried to talk directly to the ghoul, to look at her, to view the hideous being she had become. "Sometimes zombies retain some of the mental faculties they had when they were alive. Lisa, I know you're in there. Your mortal persona is able to assume control over the ghoul's bodily actions. Lisa, help me! Please, for God's sakes, don't hurt me! I'm begging you! You know inside that this is wrong. Don't do this."

The ghoul hesitated. I felt hope. Could she have heard me? Could what I said be true, that there was really some part of Lisa left in this horrible ghoul-thing?

Or was everything I read about Voodoo zombies wrong? So much depended upon everything I read being right! My very life depended on it!

"Please Lisa," I heard myself babbling, "you were, are, a good person. You would never have hurt anyone when you were alive. Don't hurt me. You can resist Jenilee's power. Stop now!"

"Kill him!" Jenilee screamed.

But Lisa didn't move.

And then came my salvation.

"Go, Doctor Keith," the ghoul that was Lisa said. Her voice was rasping and hollow.

And then I saw that Lisa held a key in her bony hand. She threw it on the floor.

"Thank you Lisa," I breathed as I scooped up the key to the front door.

"No!" screamed Jenilee. "I have power over you! Kill him!"

"I am stopping you," Lisa rasped at Jenilee. "Your boyfriend killed himself not because Doctor Keith rejected him. He killed himself because of what I did to him. Yes, it was my fault. But you have already punished me. So I need to stop you."

Lisa stepped forward and continued, "Ghouls extract revenge. You should have known that before you unleashed me. Now I'm going to take my own revenge out on you for making me a ghoul."

I unlocked the front door with Lisa's key. I took a second to look back. Lisa was approaching Jenilee, the ghoul's arms held out as if she were going to grab her.

Jenilee tried to run towards me. Quickly I went outside and slammed the front door behind me. I put the key in the lock and locked the door. I could hear Jenilee screaming as she pounded on her own front door.

I hesitated for a moment. What was I doing?

If I left now, Jenilee would be killed. Did I want that?

Run! my inner voice shrieked.

I inserted the key back into the lock. I didn't know what I was intending to do. Here I was, about to go back and face the spirit of the Loa that I had been running from all this time. But I couldn't have Jenilee's death on my conscience.

"Come on!" I cried when I opened the door. "Jenilee, I'll take you out of here!"

Jenilee burst out the door and ran to my car. I quickly peeked inside her living room. Suddenly shock paralyzed me.

Lisa began to fully decompose, right in front of my eyes. It was as though what had begun was suddenly accelerating at a wild pace.

The skin peeled from her bony fingers, exposing the knuckles, and her yellowed, hawk-like fingernails extended out. Her remaining eye sunk into her head and her lips receded. Her hair fell out in clumps.

And suddenly her whole body caved inwards, underneath her clothes. It was an implosion into itself, and the torn burial gown shook with movement.

Then Lisa's degenerating body fell to the floor, and yet it was still not done. The decomposition accelerated. Finally, the clothes covered only bones that rapidly disintegrated. They became ragged and frayed, then also began to disintegrate.

Finally there was nothing left on the floor except ashes; the memory of what Lisa was.

It had all happened within a matter of minutes. I studied the dust on the floor with great sadness. I hoped that Lisa had finally gone back to the grave from which she had risen. I understood that if a ghoul resisted the Loa, then it would be the only thing that could break the reanimation spell. It was the only thing that could bring her eternal rest.

Suddenly I shook myself into action. What was I standing there for? I had a medical emergency! I had been poisoned. I needed help, *now*.

I ran outside, slamming the door behind me. "Let's go!" I shouted to Jenilee. "Get in the car!"

She just stood there, by the passenger door, appearing dazed.

I shoved her roughly onto the seat. She didn't resist. I realized that she was bordering upon catatonia.

My very life depended on getting to the hospital immediately, while I could still function well enough to drive. Frightened, wiping sweat from my eyes and trying not to vomit onto my own lap, I pushed the gas pedal down hard. I weaved in and out of traffic, hoping a cop would red light me so I could get his assistance. None did.

As I drove to the hospital emergency room, Jenilee sat silently at my side. I was quiet too, wondering how long it would be before the tcha-tcha took complete affect and I would die. Already the skin on my arm was burning and I was shaking badly.

Finally I reached the hospital's emergency room. I left her in my car, ran inside the hospital, and yelled that there was a mental patient outside in the parking lot. I told the hospital staff that I was a psychiatrist and that the medical team should take Jenilee to the psyche ward.

Then I ran to the admittance desk. "I've been poisoned!" I screamed at the nurse.

She sat straight in her chair. "We need you to wait in the lobby until it is your turn to be evaluated for your medical emergency."

But that is when my world went black. They told me later that I had passed out right then and there.

I spent two weeks in the hospital, recovering from the tcha-tcha poisoning. The hospital treated me with charcoal, hydration and muscle relaxers. My limbs had stiffened up the first week and although most of the stiffness went away, I would need physical therapy for a couple of months to regain flexibility.

Jenilee was committed to another mental institution. I am hoping she will get the help she needs. I cannot help her; it would be unethical for me to be her therapist. I would be biased against her.

But today I am fully recovered. At least, physically I have recovered.

Emotionally I am not quite the same. Now I know how it feels to be mentally unbalanced.

I still see things behind me when I look into mirrors. And I swear I still see people in the back seat of my car when I drive down expressways. Of course, when I turn around to face my tormenters, nothing is ever there.

So, I still have emotional trauma, even to this day, which is why I am seeing my own doctor. Imagine a psychiatrist going to a psychiatrist, but that is exactly what I am doing. I acknowledge that some things in life are just too much to deal with alone.

Even for me, the man who was once so exalted inside my own mind. Me, who once believed I was better than anyone else.

Me, who was once such a sanctimonious asshole. I take comfort in the fact that I am trying my best to become a better person. And I really *am* trying very hard.

But there is one thing that gives me more problems with sleeping at night than anything else.

And that is...I remember the demon, Papa Legba.

I remember that Papa Legba had told me he is aware of me.

And I remember he said Hell is aware of me too.

THE HOLE

Laura glanced out the window and saw the black dog digging in her back yard. She cried out and dropped the drinking glass into the sink. She raced to the door, threw it open and yelled at the dog to *scat*.

She felt vindicated when the dog panicked at the sound of her voice and ran away. She spent a lot of time and effort to create a beautiful garden in her yard, so how dare someone's stray dog try to ruin it?

Might as well find out how much damage there is, she thought as she walked to the area where the dog had been. She hadn't wanted to put up a wooden fence to protect her yard, opting instead for a row of shrubs bordering her garden. Now she realized that shrubs gave only the illusion of privacy; obviously they were no deterrent to dogs.

Dismayed by the sight of dug-up flowers scattered on the ground, Laura surveyed the hole. It was pretty deep. She was surprised to see something on the bottom reflecting the sunlight.

Was that what had so attracted the dog? She stood, studying it. Apparently it was just a portion of something larger. The bulk of the shiny thing was still buried and so she had no idea what it could be.

Mad at herself now more than at the dog, Laura knew she had to finish what the dog began. There was no way she was going to throw the dirt back into the hole without knowing exactly what was down there.

She had the skin-prickling sensation of being watched. Shading the sun out of her eyes with her hand, she surveyed the bushes and saw movement. The leaves parted and there stood the stray dog, his black body smooth and sleek, his mouth panting, his eyes locked on hers.

"Shoo!" Laura cried, and this time the dog didn't bolt away, but instead sulked slowly back into the shrub-line. She had the feeling that the dog hadn't left completely, but was waiting in the shadows…for what? For her to reveal to them both what was buried in the hole?

A cloud passed over the sun, creating a moment of gloom in the yard. *Goose walked over my grave,* Laura thought. *Nonsense, what superstition!*

She shrugged off the bad feelings and went to the shed to retrieve her shovel. When she returned to the yard, she was infuriated to see that the dog was back, digging in the hole again.

"Get out of here!" she screamed, and the dog once more melted into the cover of the bushes. She was sure it would wait there. In fact, she could feel its presence, lurking somewhere in the dense foliage at that very moment.

Sighing, Laura gripped the shovel and tentatively touched the blade against the shiny thing at the bottom of the hole. It didn't yield. She tapped the shiny thing, and it sounded like it was metal. She lifted the shovel and peered intently at the thing. It looked to be a sort of a grayish hue, almost silver-blue.

She began digging. She knew it would be a mess no matter what, so she simply chucked the dirt into a pile on the ground, damaging more of her flowers.

The more she dug, the larger the shiny thing seemed to be. Sweat trickled down her face, and she rubbed her skin with a dirty hand, leaving brown streaks that she didn't know she created around her eyes. She worked mechanically.

The sun began to set and she still hadn't figured out what lay in the hole. It was long and the top of the object was rounded. She dug enough to discover that the object seemed to be some sort of box…a really big box with metal latches.

Laura remembered her grandmother's funeral. The family had opted to purchase one of the cheaper caskets, a metal one that was a grayish hue, almost silver-blue…

She heard a sound behind her. She had forgotten about the dog. Surely it was gone by now, wasn't it?

She straightened up, and groaned at the stiffness in her back, surprised that it was getting dark. She peered nervously into the bushes. She heard a soft growl and felt an irrational stab of fear. "What do you want?" she cried, and realized it was a stupid reaction; it was just a stray dog, for crissakes.

She wanted to be in control. "Get out of my yard!" she yelled. She heard movement and knew the dog had backed off, but hadn't left completely. To hell with the dog.

The sun was gone, and darkness crept in. The trees seemed to be ever so slightly moving and rustling in the cool, soft breeze. The moon broke through the clouds, casting an eerie glow upon the lawn.

She continued her quest until the top of the casket was completely revealed. She stopped to study it in the light of the full moon, wanting to get a flashlight, but knowing she could not leave her find to the dog for even a minute.

How could she open it? If she jumped into the hole on top of the coffin, she could unlatch it but not lift the top with her weight on it. Well, one thing at a time. She climbed down into the large hole and got on her knees on top of the cold, metal casket. She fumbled with the first latch until she heard a click. She crawled on her knees, feeling her way, until she reached the second latch and undid that one too.

The hole was about four feet deep from the top of the coffin, so it was difficult to climb back out but she managed. Once she got out and stood on the ground, she wondered, *Now what?*

She had to find something with a hook to lift the lid of the casket. Which meant, of course, leaving the hole to the dog.

It's too deep for the dog to reach inside, she reasoned. *I will get the hook, and a flashlight too.*

She turned around and ran back to the shed. She could hear movement behind her as she ran, and knew the dog was heading back to the hole. She had to be quick.

She grabbed a "big reach" extension pole from the shed, took a flashlight from a shelf, and then rushed back into the yard.

As she expected, the dog was at the hole, except this time it wasn't digging, but sniffing. The dog seemed bigger in the darkness, its black body looming over the hole like a horizontal headstone, as though it belonged there.

"Get out!" she cried. This time the dog simply lifted its head and growled, standing its ground, its lips drawn back, its teeth glinting in the moonlight.

Laura hesitated, then gripped the extension pole tightly. With the hook on the end, it would make a good weapon. She dropped the flashlight on the ground and swung the pole through the air as a warning gesture.

The dog backed away. "That's right!" Laura screamed. "Go back to hell where you came from!"

It shrank into the bushes once again, and Laura bent to grab the flashlight. Turning it on, she walked to the grave and shined the light inside. Was it her imagination, or did the coffin lid already seem to be slightly open?

She dropped the flashlight again so she could grab the pole. She lowered the hook, and tried stabbing the underside of the lid. Finally the hook connected and stayed secure, grasping the coffin lid, and Laura knew that this would be it. She pulled the pole, and the lid creaked, sounding rusted.

Feeling a wave of adrenaline, she let go of the pole and picked up the flashlight so she could see her treasure. She moved to the very brink of the grave and stared at what lay within. Her eyes felt as though they were burning; she couldn't even blink. Her lungs felt full, and it was difficult to force more air inside.

A fine mist seemed to congeal from inside the coffin. The mist swirled until it began to form a shape. Then the shape became solid and Laura was able to view a demon in the moonlight.

It was more frightening than she ever could have imagined. The skin was the color of the mud from which it came and the creature undulated with shuddering movements. As it raised itself from inside the coffin, it was so tall that it loomed out of the hole. The arms and torso were that of a man, but underneath it had the appearance of a snake; slithering from its single tail.

The creature spoke, "Get away."

Laura stood her ground, staring at the monster in the coffin, immersed in her insanity. "You can't have what's in the grave. I found it. It's mine."

The demon tilted its scaled face, and its reptilian eyes reflected the moon. "You claim this?"

She lost any grip on reality that she may have had a week ago, a day ago, an hour ago. The hole was on her land. She had fought the dog for this. She had dug all day, giving it her all. She worked for it. She deserved it.

"It's mine," she repeated.

"Then it's between you and Lucifer," the demon said, and dissolved back into a mist that swirled and dissipated into the night air.

She heard a growl as the large black dog crept out of the bushes. There would be no scaring it away this time.

SPIDERS

Jason sighed. "Yes, I know that the silk from spiders is an extremely strong material. But it's simply too hard to extract. And besides, we couldn't extract enough from each spider to be cost effective."

Lee smiled.

"What?" Jason asked.

"Let me show you my lab."

"I don't have time."

"Make the time."

Intrigued, Jason said, "This had better be worth it." He stood up to follow Lee out of the restaurant.

"We'll take my car," Lee offered.

Lee unlocked the metal door, and Jason thought that it sounded like a haunted house movie as it creaked open. He peered inside, but it was too dark to see.

Lee relocked the front door from the inside, and then flipped the light switch.

"Wow," Jason said. "Don't you ever clean this place?"

"Too busy," Lee said.

The basement room had cement-block walls, and a lot of glass aquariums stacked against those walls. There were no windows. The linoleum on the floor was worn and stained. There was a desk in the middle of the room, and although the desk was old, it held a state-of-the-art computer on top. There seemed to be dust everywhere.

There were also spider webs in every corner of the room at the ceiling.

"So," Jason observed, "the only visitors to your lab are spiders? Certainly you can't entertain humans in this mess."

"I don't clean those webs because they don't bother me," Lee said. "Those belong to wild spiders that find their way in here. They're not the spiders I'm interested in."

"I don't have a lot of time," Jason said. "Show me why we came here."

Lee again smiled that weird grin. He took out his key ring again and said, "There's a back room."

Jason hesitated. "Listen, I don't want to see any mad scientist experiment."

"I may be a scientist, but I'm not mad. If you like what you see, and I know you will, then I want to offer a partnership deal to you. If you invest, then I will produce a product that will be a sensation around the world."

Jason pretended boredom, but in reality he was intrigued. He certainly had the money to invest, but it seemed that everyone was always hitting him up for money. A wealthy man, Jason knew that restraint was why he made money on good investments and didn't lose it on bad investments. But the only way to make money was to fully investigate potential offers.

If Lee really discovered an efficient way to extract spider silk, then this lab visit could prove very lucrative. Especially for the military. Imagine what they could do with a lightweight, flexible material that was stronger than steel. Why, a government contract…

He was jerked out of his musings when Lee put the key into the back room door. It, too, creaked open as though it belonged in a ghost-infested mansion.

"Jesus, why don't you get some WD-40?"

Lee seemed annoyed. "Listen Jason, I am not a patient man who listens to meaningless comments. Here I am about to show you the eighth wonder of the world, and you are talking about WD-40, which incidentally has already been invented. I am going to show you something new."

With that, Lee reached inside the back room and flipped on the light switch.

It looked like a pet store. There were cages and very large aquariums, all stacked upon each other. Jason could smell sawdust and could see glimpses of steam, which told him that this room held some sort of humidifier.

Jason heard a rustling sound. "What's that noise?"

"We disturbed the spiders by turning on the light. Don't worry, they'll settle down in a minute."

Jason felt the hairs on his arms stand up in their follicles. Slowly he asked, "Your spiders are big enough to sound like that when they move?"

Lee turned to flash that weird grin again. "How do you think it can be cost-effective to extract silk from spiders? Make them bigger, of course." He stepped over to a glass aquarium. "Take a look at this guy."

Jason fought a sick feeling in the pit of his stomach, but he was unable to suppress his curiosity. He followed Lee and peered into the large glass container.

Red eyes glowed back at him. Jason was shocked to see the size of this arachnid; probably twelve inches across. Even weirder was its coloration. The rotund abdomen was almost flesh-like, its head a silver-gray, and its long spindly legs a shade of amber. He jerked back when the creature moved quickly to the glass, seemingly just as interested in Jason as he was in it.

"Can he see me?" Jason asked.

Lee snorted. "Of course he can. Spiders have very good vision with their eight eyes."

Suddenly there came a deep rustling sound, louder than anything preceding it. Jason looked at Lee and felt fear when he saw that the other man's face had blanched white.

"We've got to get out of here," Lee said.

Jason was too panicked to argue. He didn't know what was going on, but he knew that if Lee was scared, then something was wrong, very wrong. He jumped towards the door leading out of the back room.

He was running when he heard a scream behind him. He turned his head and saw that something was loose...something really huge had somehow gotten out of its cage. It knocked Lee to the floor.

Jason started crying when he realized that he was too frightened to try to help. He always made his fortune off of other people's ideas. His biggest secret was that he was hollow inside...he never cared about any science that helped people; only the science that helped himself. He was a selfish man, and now he knew he was also a coward.

He found the front door and jiggled the handle. He realized, *Oh my god, it's locked. Lee locked it from the inside to keep the world away from his secret spiders.*

He was openly sobbing now. It was the basement, and there were no windows. There was no escape.

Would that giant spider be satisfied with Lee or would it want a second victim? He couldn't take that chance. Maybe there was another set of keys in the old desk.

Jason ran to the desk and flung open the drawers. His fingers frantically searched the contents, grabbing papers and throwing them onto the floor.

No keys.

He started moaning as tears gushed down his cheeks. He was trembling so badly that he didn't notice the warm stream of urine trickling down the front of his pants.

And then he heard it coming into the front room.

"Oh God, please let me live! I swear I will be a better man, I swear it! *Oh please, oh please!*"

He didn't want to look but was unable to shut his eyes as the thing advanced. It crawled across the old, stained linoleum. It loomed upwards of five feet in height. Its bloated, round abdomen was flesh-colored, but covered with black hairs. Worst of all was the head. It had pincers around the mouth and its red eyes almost glowed, and were so numerous that they covered most of the face.

Its many long legs were jointed, with claws at the tips of the front two. The claws were aimed at Jason.

He ran back to the front door, clawing at the handle with the delusional hope that somehow, the lock would malfunction and the door would open.

The spider kept advancing, finally reaching him. It ignored Jason's screams and knocked him down onto the floor.

It bit him, and Jason instantly lost feeling in his arms and legs. His mind continued to remain intact; he retained the ability to think clearly. He waited for the poison to kill him. After a minute, he understood that he was not going to die after all; he was only paralyzed.

The spider had already fed on Lee. It dawned on Jason that it wanted to hold him for when it got hungry later. It wanted to keep him alive as fresh meat.

And as the creature spun its web around him, Jason realized that Lee had been right: a spider's silk was really strong.

A TEENAGE GHOST STORY

Chapter One

"Are you afraid of graveyards?"

She wasn't expecting that question. Come to think of it, it wasn't a question anyone would expect. She didn't know what to say.

Brian looked at her. "I'm serious."

"Why are we stopping?" Cat peered out the car window and felt nervous. She and Brian went to the same high school, and both had stayed after school for different reasons. Cat stayed late for drama class and Brian stayed late for football practice. Brian was sixteen and a junior in high school, one grade ahead of her. He was cute and popular. And not many guys in her own grade had a car.

She was thrilled when Brian Castleman had asked to drive her home from school; enough so that she agreed when he suggested they go for a ride instead of going straight home. She had a huge crush on Brian.

Now, as she glanced nervously at her surroundings, she was wishing she had walked home. If she had, she'd be home by now, not out here…across the street from a graveyard.

"Cat," Brian said, pushing his brown hair away from his dark eyes with a quick stroke of his hand. "Listen to me. My gas gauge is broken. I thought I had enough, but...well, I guess I just ran out of gas. It sure doesn't look like there's a single gas station close to here, so where does that leave us?"

"You don't have a cell phone?" Her given name was Catherine, but most people weren't even aware of that. Everyone called her Cat—Cat Daniels. She had long, golden hair that seemed to reflect the sunlight when it shined. But now the sun was going down, creating dim shadows.

"The battery's dead on my cell. So that's why I asked, are you afraid of graveyards? There's a store on the other side of this cemetery." Brian pointed out the car window.

Cat stared at him. "Do you mean we have to walk *through* the graveyard?"

He gripped her arm with to get her attention. "Let's face it, my car isn't going anywhere. I know the other side of this cemetery is in the wrong direction from home, but there's a convenience store past the creek. It's one of the few stores left in the world that actually has a pay phone in front. We can call our parents from their pay phone to come and get us. It beats walking home."

And then she knew she was put on the spot, because Brian added, "Are you brave enough?"

It was a dare, and she was well aware of it. How could she back down? If she did, she'd never have another chance with Brian. And besides, what would he tell everyone at school tomorrow? That she was just a baby tenth-grader?

Called Creekside Cemetery, it was set apart from the suburb on the outskirts of town where people traveled less frequently, so there was little hope of anyone passing by to help. The road didn't have any markers; for that matter, it didn't even have a proper name. The street was simply called Road 18. The absence of houses surrounding the graveyard only made it seem more foreboding.

"Well, if we're going to do it, then let's do it," Cat said. Suddenly, from nowhere, she felt a strong sensation of curiosity about the people buried in the cemetery. At one time, these people felt love, felt pain, and felt hope. She tried to imagine that the tombstones jutting out of the ground were representing real people who once lived in this town.

Brian stepped out of the car and slammed the door. Cat got out on her own side. He met her at the back of the car by the trunk. Standing apart from each other, they both hesitated, once again gazing at Creekside Cemetery.

The setting sun created shadows cast by the twisted and bent trees which were few in number but seemed oppressive in the graveyard. Limbs and branches stretched out as if they were fingers upon a hand wasted away by time. In the corners of the graveyard, bushes were overgrown from decades of neglect.

Brian sighed and started walking across the street. Cat followed.

She knew Brian intended to get this whole business finished quickly by walking through the cemetery as fast as he could possibly manage. Still, she barely noticed that Brian appeared annoyed when she stopped to examine one of the tombstones they passed.

205

"Look at this," Cat said. "Here's a person who died in 1897. Wow, that was forever ago, like, two centuries."

The grave maker was on what looked like a raised bed, the dirt held in place by a border of cement.

"No big deal," Brian said, sounding impatient. "All of these graves are old. Nobody has been buried in this graveyard since 1935."

Her initial fear of the cemetery was forgotten in her amazement of the dates on the headstones. "These graves were living people once. They all lived in a time when life wasn't as easy as it is now. I kind of admire people who were forced to struggle just to survive."

"Yeah, well, this is Rivertown. Sacramento is just down the freeway at the bottom of these hills. You have to remember that the pioneers came to places around Sacramento looking for gold in the 1800s. People didn't live very long way back then. They probably had a lot of mining accidents, you know, things like that. Not to mention tuberculosis and the rest of the diseases around in those days. C'mon, let's get going—it's getting pretty dark."

"Just a minute." Cat walked to the next gravesite. She touched one of the headstones, feeling its rough surface. No marble or anything fancy here; instead, it appeared to be granite or some other type of local stone.

She read the headstone: "Peter Haas, aged fifty-one years, four months, and seven days. He died in 1922. Weird that they put how many months and days old he was. I guess every day mattered a lot." Cat felt mesmerized by the grave. She saw it was a family plot, because next to Peter, Louise Haas was buried. The date of her death was 1926.

Suddenly Brian burst out, "Okay, I've had it! You can go ahead and admire these dead skeletons all by yourself. I'm getting out of here!"

He stomped off. Surprised, she watched him go. For some reason, she didn't follow him as he walked away.

Suddenly she heard the sound.

Looking up, she listened carefully. It sounded as though someone were crying. A man…it sounded like a man was crying.

Where was it coming from?

Cat's eyes searched the graveyard. The sun was now completely set, and visibility was getting poor. But then she spotted a figure dressed in...what was it? Some sort of black robe? A man was standing apart from the headstones, his head in his hands in a gesture of sorrow.

A realization dawned upon her. The man looked like a priest...a Catholic priest.

He was standing behind another family plot. Cat approached slowly, and got close enough to read the name *Foster* inscribed on a very large headstone. It was odd, because the priest was not standing inside the Foster plot, but instead was standing in the weeds behind it.

Was he crying over someone he knew personally? Was he experiencing a deep sorrow over the loss of someone he had loved? She felt embarrassed to be a witness to this scene. It seemed somehow wrong to be watching someone who was obviously going through a very private, emotional experience.

Suddenly she remembered the words that Brian had spoken just a few moments earlier: *"Nobody has been buried in this graveyard since 1935."*

It made no sense. This was a young priest, perhaps between twenty-five to thirty years old. That meant he was too young to have had a close relationship with anyone buried in this cemetery. Why would he be mourning someone who was buried before 1935?

Almost before she realized what she was doing, Cat found herself walking over to the priest, carefully picking her path through two family plots. It struck her that something about his religious robes was strange, somehow different. She couldn't decide why.

When the priest saw her approach, he looked up. She came close enough to see him well, even in the fading light. He had dark hair that formed soft curls, framing his face. He had deep brown eyes surrounded by long, black lashes, wet from tears. His face held almost perfect features, as though chiseled by an artist.

"I hope I'm not bothering you," Cat began, feeling awkward and clumsy. "Maybe I can help. But if you want me to go away, I will."

"No, please don't go." The priest wiped his eyes on his sleeve. "You must forgive me. I am Father Santiago."

"Did you lose someone?" she asked gently.

"When someone has not been found, that someone is lost. This one," Father Santiago paused and pointed to the ground, "is lost."

Cat was confused. She felt the priest was talking in riddles. There was no headstone where Father Santiago pointed, only overgrown weeds. "But there is no grave here."

"This is a very old cemetery," he said. "Not all is as it seems."

She looked down, trying to see whatever Father Santiago saw, but there were only autumn leaves that had fallen from the gnarled trees onto the moist ground. She felt a chill from a cool October breeze, and pulled her jacket closer against her shoulders.

She looked back up.

Father Santiago was gone.

How could he have possibly moved so fast? And where could he have gone? Was he hiding behind a tombstone? What kind of priest would play a hide-and-seek game?

Suddenly Cat was scared. "Father Santiago!" she called. There was no answer. *Oh no*, was she all alone?

Maybe she could catch up with Brian. "Brian? Brian! Wait up!" She scanned the graveyard, searching for the bright red San Francisco 49ers jacket that Brian was wearing.

But she was alone. Alone in the dark…in a cemetery.

She became terrified. The sun was gone, and complete darkness had set. The moon broke through the clouds at that moment, casting an eerie glow on the headstones. The trees seemed to be ever so slightly moving and rustling in the cool, soft breeze. The moon vanished and reappeared as clouds crept across its surface, creating shadows that danced in the night.

She began walking quickly in the direction where she had seen Brian leave. The darkness had become dense, so she started to jog. Bushes and briars appeared threatening as if they were hiding evil spectators to the scene within their midst. The ground was cool and moist; the fallen leaves slippery. Headstones reflected the moonlight, looming out of the ground, some in tilted directions as if drunken monoliths.

The night creatures were awakening; an owl screeched. A mouse scurried by, close to her feet. Cat was startled, her heart pumping. She began to run, hoping to catch up with Brian.

"Brian!" she called.

A small animal fled out of a bush at the sound of her voice. Cat slowed for a second in fright, but whatever it was went too fast to her to see it in the darkness, so she sped up again. She was truly frightened now. "Brian!" she screamed, louder this time.

"Cat! Where are you?" Brian's voice came from the area by the creek that bordered the far side of the cemetery. He had been on the other side of the creek, but was now coming across the bridge back towards her. Relieved, Cat cried, "Over here!" And she started to run in the direction of Brian's voice.

She found Brian next to Shallow Creek, the one that gave the cemetery its name. This time of year they could have walked across it, as it was almost a dry bed, but because of the darkness, they chose to take the small wooden bridge as they headed to the convenience store.

"How come you ditched me?" Cat asked.

"I'm not going to hang around some stupid cemetery reading gravestones," Brian retorted. "It's dark, and I don't want to leave my car parked way out on Road 18 for very long. That'd be like an invitation for someone to steal it."

She didn't feel it was necessary to explain to Brian that in order for someone to steal the car, the thief would need to have a gas can handy. Instead, she walked beside Brian to the end of Creekside Cemetery, and neither one spoke. She thought that maybe Brian would take her hand and hold it as they walked, but he kept his hands in the pockets of his jacket. It would be nice if he took the initiative to comfort her, but instead Brian continued to ignore her until they reached the convenience store with the pay phone in front.

"You call your parents, and I'll call mine," Brian said. "You go first."

She called home, and her father answered. Her father sounded upset that she was in her predicament, but promised to come and get her right away.

While Cat and Brian stood outside under the lights of the convenience store, she asked, "Did you see the priest?"

Brian was looking away, seemingly interested in the parking lot. *Anything but me*, Cat thought.

"What priest?" Brian asked absently.

"The one in the graveyard."

Brian finally looked at her, but he had a strange expression on his face. "Listen, Cat," he told her, "I don't think there was anybody in that place but you and me. I think you got scared or something and you probably imagined it. That's what you get for reading those old tombstones. I mean, come on, a priest just wandering around an old, has-been cemetery?"

She didn't answer, so they stood in silence for awhile. Soon a familiar Toyota pulled into the parking lot with her father at the wheel. "I'd like to see you tomorrow," Cat told Brian pointedly before she got into the front passenger seat.

Brian had begun staring at the parking lot again. He said vacantly, "Sure, maybe I'll see you around, kid."

Kid! I'm fifteen years old, thought Cat as she and her father drove off, *only one year younger than Brian, but he called me a kid. Well, I'm probably too sensitive. It must be just the way Brian talks. After all, he has to like me or else he wouldn't have asked me to go for a drive with him today.*

Chapter Two

"Cat's got a boyfriend!"

She turned around to see her ten-year-old brother in the back seat. "Did you have to bring him?" she complained to her father.

"Brett is your brother and he has just as much right to be in this car as you do," Mr. Daniels said. "Don't change the subject—why did you take off after school without letting us know?"

"I couldn't let you know where I was because Brian's cell phone battery died," she explained.

"Then you shouldn't have gone with him. This is not going to happen again. You need to let us know where you are." Mr. Daniels looked more exasperated than angry. "After you eat dinner, you can just go to your room and think about this little episode."

Fair enough, Cat thought. *I got off easy this time.*

After dinner, she went to her room to accept her punishment. Her room was small. She had a single twin bed that usually went without being made. Her closet had white sliding doors that she considered boring, so she put up posters of rock bands. She had an old-fashioned CD player on a small bookcase in the corner from which rock music sounded most of the time. The volume was kept low enough to keep her parents from entering her room and complaining.

After her homework was done, she lay back on her bed and thought about Brian. He was a football player and had all the popularity that went with it. Brian always had girls talking to him at school. She had been trying to get his attention for a month now by figuring out his school schedule and by just "happening to be" in the places where she knew he'd be.

She really thought she'd had a chance with Brian today. Cat went over every minute of the drive after school in her mind and critiqued her own behavior. Was it her fault that the afternoon didn't go well? Would Brian ever give her another chance?

If only we hadn't wound up at that creepy graveyard! she thought. *Everything was going great until then.*

The graveyard. Creekside Cemetery.

It should be named Creepside Cemetery, Cat thought, then shivered.

And what about the priest? Father Santiago, wasn't that his name? Why hadn't Brian seen him?

Oh, I don't want to think about it anymore. With that, she went to bed and drifted off to a restless sleep.

As do all people who dream, Cat slipped into the far corners of the mind. She entered the vast corridors that remain unexplored while in waking hours. During her dream, she ventured between the borders of what was real and what wasn't.

She dreamed she was in a room with wooden walls painted white. Was she in someone's kitchen? Candlelight was the only illumination. Eerily the candles flickered, creating dancing shadows.

She felt fear imminent, surrounding her, so near that she imagined she could feel its icy fingers closing around her shoulders. She knew someone else was in the room; she could sense the presence of another.

Father Santiago stepped out of the darkness, his handsome face concerned and intent. He stood not speaking for a moment, and Cat squirmed under his scrutiny.

"You are the one," the priest finally said.

"What are you talking about?"

"You are the one who must discover the truth," Father Santiago continued. "I can come to you no more. I am now ready to enter the light. Directing you to this soul in need has removed the last elements of burden and I have been purified."

"I still don't know what you mean!"

211

The tears that Cat saw earlier on his face returned. "I was the confessor. I was appalled—horrified," he told her. "I tried to help but I couldn't, because I was prevented by fate from doing so."

Father Santiago covered his face with his hands. "A soul needs to be released from torment. You must pay attention to the efforts made to direct you."

Then the priest took his hands away from his face and looked directly at her. "Through this contact with you, I am now able to give the assistance I was unable to give before. I cannot recount what was said during the confession since the sacred confidentiality cannot be broken. Because I cannot tell you, it means you must find out the truth on your own. In the cemetery, I pointed to where you can begin. Go back there, and learn who lies underground."

Cat awoke to her mother's voice. "Time to get up for school!"

Groggy, she wondered how it could be morning already. Suddenly the haunting dream came back to her in vivid clarity. It felt like it had actually happened because it seemed so real. Her forehead felt wet and she realized she must have been sweating in her sleep. Fear still gnawed at the pit of her stomach when she remembered the dream.

Father Santiago's voice echoed in her mind: *A soul needs to be released from torment. Go back there, and learn who lies underground.*

Cat knew it was going to be one of those types of dreams that can't be pushed out of a person's thoughts so easily. She tried to remember the room in her dream. It looked like a kitchen, but none that she had ever been in before. In fact, it looked old-fashioned, like something straight out of a museum.

Realizing that she was daydreaming when she should be getting ready for school, she got out of bed.

She dressed for school. Rivertown High School was close enough for Cat to walk every day, but it still was a long walk.

Her best friend Tara Whitfield lived only three houses away. Tara lived in the direction of the school, so they always met in front of Tara's house to walk together. It was only the argument that Cat would not be walking alone that allowed her parents to decide that she didn't have to ride the bus. She felt her parents were overprotective. Really, her parents always acted like they believed someone would kidnap her right off the sidewalk if she were alone.

"You are not going to believe what happened yesterday!" Cat exclaimed when she met Tara on the sidewalk. "Brian asked me to go for a ride with him after school!"

"Ohmygosh!" Tara gushed, all in one word. "I was sick yesterday and absent from school. See what I missed! Did he tell you he likes you?"

"Not exactly." Cat told her friend the events of the previous day. When she finished, she said, "I'd sure like to know who that Father Santiago is. I had a bad dream about him last night."

"I'm not surprised that you had a bad dream," Tara said. "Especially after walking through a cemetery at night. But you came *that close* to getting Brian Castleman to say he likes you! I'd say he'd be worth dreaming about instead of some priest."

"No, I mean it," said Cat. "I guess I could check with the Catholic Church and see if I could find Father Santiago there and then talk to him. It has to be Saint John's—that's the only Catholic Church in Rivertown. At the cemetery, Father Santiago wanted to tell me something. But then he just took off. Really strange. Anyway, I'd like to find out whatever he wanted to tell me. Otherwise, I might have another bad dream. I'd rather hear what Father Santiago *really* wanted to tell me instead of imagining him telling me the kinds of scary stuff he did in the dream."

"I'm not much help because I'm Presbyterian," Tara said. "But I'd like to go with you. Why don't we go to the church right after school? Today is Friday, so there won't be any homework. Where's Saint John's again?"

"On Cardoza Street," Cat answered. "Okay, but I'd better call my parents from school before we go. My dad is kind of mad at me for taking off yesterday and not letting him know where I was. He always thinks that Jack the Ripper is hiding around every corner."

"You can tell your parents," Tara spoke with a faraway look in her eyes. "Mine don't care where I go."

Cat looked at her friend with sympathy. At first it seemed cool that Tara had so much freedom, but after awhile, she realized it could get lonely having parents who were so distracted with other things that they ignored their only child.

"I care about you," Cat told Tara, and smiled. They were the very best of friends, and each one knew it. The two girls looked very different from each other. Cat had long, straight blonde hair, while

Tara's was shoulder-length, dark and wavy. Cat's eyes were green to Tara's brown, and Cat was taller by about two inches. Both were blossoming into pretty girls.

When they got to school, they each went their separate ways to their lockers. Cat emptied her book bag at her locker, which was next to Ashley Long's.

She groaned inwardly. Ashley was at her locker. She was so annoying because she acted like she was always better than Cat, or anybody else, for that matter. Ashley was a cheerleader, and wanted everybody to appreciate that fact. Cat admitted to herself that Ashley was beautiful, but her hair was dyed fake-blond and her make-up was overdone.

Cat turned as someone called hello. It was Brian!

He waved as he walked by, smiling his handsome grin. Cat's heart skipped a beat and her pulse raced. Dizzy for a minute, she called back to Brian, "Great to see you here!"

As Brian hurried by, the absurdity of her remark hit Cat. *Great to see you here? It's Friday and this is school—where else would he be? Stupid, stupid! Every time I see him I act stupid!*

She turned back around, and Ashley was almost in her face.

"I believe Brian Castleman was saying hello to me, not you," Ashley said.

"Oh, I don't think so," Cat said, inwardly wondering—*Is she right? Was he saying hi to Ashley, and not to me?* "Brian and I hung out last night."

"Come on—you and Brian?" Ashley looked at Cat closely, examining her.

"That's right. We went for a drive after school. We really had a good time. Gotta go!"

As Cat ran off, she couldn't help but glance over her shoulder, just in time to catch Ashley still standing there staring, hands on her hips. But inside she wondered, *Did Brian say hello to me or to Ashley? Oh no, did I make a fool of myself again?*

Sighing, hating her uncertainty, she went to class.

Later in the day, she had third period English with Tara. As the two friends walked into the classroom, Tara asked, "Still on for after school?"

"Sure."

At three-thirty they met at Cat's locker. Both girls were relieved to notice that Ashley Long was nowhere in sight.

The October air was so brisk that it bordered on cold. The nights came faster this time of year, so the teens walked quickly to make sure they would be home before dark. Cardoza was the busiest street in the small community of Rivertown, tree-lined and wide.

The wind gusted in starts and stops, carrying crisp golden leaves into tiny whirlwinds. Houses were cheerfully decorated with Halloween pumpkins, all grinning silent, gap-toothed smiles.

The girls took large steps, ignoring the cars that rushed by. When they came to the church, they went up stairs leading to the main doors.

The doors in front of the church were double, massive, and made of heavy wood. Cat opened one of the doors and peered inside. Rows and rows of pews stood as if they were silent sentries. A magnificent, life-sized crucifix of Jesus Christ reared over the pulpit. The ceiling was very high, and from the walls, colors reflected off the stained glass windows onto the altar.

And the church was empty.

"What do we do now?" asked Tara. "How are we going to find somebody?"

"Well, they probably only come into this part of the church for services or for mass," Cat said. "I'll bet there's an office somewhere."

The girls walked over the lawn and across a parking lot until they came to a building that resembled an office. A sign identified the office as "Parish Rectory." Not feeling sure of themselves, they went to the front door and reached for the knob to open it. This time the door was locked.

"Well?" Tara looked at Cat.

"Well, we knock."

A smiling priest answered. He had dark hair and olive skin, and looked very pleasant. "Hi girls, what can I do for you today? Would you like to come in?"

Cat felt irrationally nervous. Tara nudged her, as if silently saying, *You got us into this, so you get us out.*

"I, um. . ." Cat began, sounding just as foolish as she felt. "It's just that I was wondering, I mean, do you have a priest here?"

"We have two priests here, after all, this is where priests usually like to hang out. In case you haven't noticed, I'm one of them." He smiled even wider as Cat's face burned red in embarrassment.

He introduced himself as Father Guzman. "Come in, come in."

The girls were led through an entryway into an office. It held a desk, a phone, a file cabinet, and a computer just like any other office.

"Now how can I help you girls?" Father Guzman asked. "You aren't wearing uniforms, so you must not go to school here."

Cat stammered, "I was wondering if Father Santiago works here. Or worships here. Or does what priests do here."

Father Guzman had a warm, understanding smile, and Cat began feeling better. "No, there isn't a Father Santiago in this parish," he said, "at least, not now. We had a Father Santiago back in the 1930s; in fact, it was Father Santiago who founded this parish in 1932. Of course, that's not the original church next door. That church was built in 1957. In the thirties, there was a depression going on in this country, so there was no money to build churches. You've probably learned about the Great Depression at school. You think what happened in 2008 was bad. Trust me, the Great Depression of the 1930s was much worse."

"Well, the Father Santiago who founded your parish would be long dead by now," Cat said. "The one I'm looking for is between twenty-five and thirty years old and is very much alive."

"There's nobody by that name here. Wait a minute."

Father Guzman walked over to the file cabinet and began rummaging around in one of the drawers. He came back holding a photograph. "Here's a picture of Father Santiago."

Cat peered at the photograph. There he was—Father Santiago, his dark hair framing his exquisitely handsome face.

"Yes!" Cat exclaimed. "That's him! That's Father Santiago! I met him last night."

"My dear, that's impossible," Father Guzman told her, "because this photo was taken in 1932. Can't you see how old it is? This photo is brown with age. You see, Father Santiago died in an accident in 1935, practically a whole century ago."

"But I saw him in the cemetery!" Cat blurted.

"What cemetery?" asked Father Guzman.

"Creekside Cemetery."

"Oh no, you must be mistaken," the priest said. "I'm sure you saw somebody, but it wasn't Father Santiago."

Doubts zipped through Cat's mind. Could she have imagined seeing a priest at the cemetery, just as Brian had said? Why did she have all these doubts about so many things lately? She had been feeling unsure of herself in seemingly every situation during the last few weeks. What happened to all the self-confidence that she used to feel?

Father Guzman was talking. Cat tore herself away from her musings and listened when he asked, "What were you doing in Creekside Cemetery?"

"Oh," Cat stammered, "I was in a car that ran out of gas, so I had to walk through it."

"You girls stay out of that cemetery." Father Guzman shook his finger in Cat's face. "I've heard stories."

"What do you mean, stories?" asked Cat.

"I'm not one to spread gossip, and I'm sure that's all those stories are," said Father Guzman. "Still, I don't think you girls should be hanging around cemeteries."

"I wasn't hanging around a cemetery, I was in a car that ran out of gas," Cat said. She felt a sudden pressing need to get out into the fresh air. "Anyway, thank you for seeing us. I guess we'll go now."

On the way home, Cat and Tara talked about Father Santiago.

"Are you sure the priest you saw in the cemetery is the same one in the picture?" Tara asked.

"It *had* to be him," Cat said firmly. "They're the same guy. I know this doesn't make much sense, but I'm telling you that priest in the photograph is the one I talked to last night."

The two girls walked in silence for a few minutes as they both digested this dilemma, and its implications.

Tara finally spoke. "Do you believe in ghosts?"

"Ghosts! What do you mean, ghosts?"

"Well, didn't you say that Father Santiago had a message for you? I think ghosts do that kind of thing, you know, come back to earth to deliver messages. All the scary books I read say so. What if Father Santiago is a ghost?" Tara stopped walking and looked at Cat.

Cat stopped walking too. "How could a priest become a ghost? Of all people, priests should go straight to Heaven."

They began walking again.

"Well," Tara said, "what about your dream? Didn't you say that Father Santiago couldn't come to you anymore; that he was now ready to enter the light? That sounds like he went to Heaven after he talked to you. Maybe he had to deliver a message first before he could rest."

"Tara Whitfield, what are you saying?" Cat wasn't sure she wanted to know.

"Just think about it for a minute," Tara said. "In your dream, Father Santiago told you there is a soul in torment. He said to go back to Creekside Cemetery and learn who is buried where he showed you. Maybe there really is someone buried there."

"Why wouldn't there be a headstone if someone was buried there? Or some other kind of marker on the grave? That's if we're assuming there is even a grave there at all."

"I don't know. It's like some sort of mystery. Listen," Tara said, "can you show me where Father Santiago was pointing? I want to see it."

"You mean go back to Creekside Cemetery?" Cat asked in surprise. "I don't think I want to do that, especially if I was talking to a ghost in that cemetery last night."

"We won't go at night. We'll go in daylight. Nothing can happen in the daylight, all the scary books I read say so. How about tomorrow morning? Tomorrow is Saturday. Let's do it!"

Tara sounded brave. Cat thought, *She's brave because we're on Cardoza Street, not in Creekside Cemetery. She might not be so brave if we were actually in the cemetery right now.*

She walked in silence for a few moments, considering it. Then she shrugged her shoulders. "Oh, all right, why not? I'll swing by your house at about eleven tomorrow morning to pick you up."

When she got home, her brother was waiting for her. Brett was the typical ten-year-old, full of energy. He had sandy light brown hair, and the same green eyes as his sister. He was watching television in the living room when Cat walked in the front door, but quickly bounced out of his chair.

"Hey," he demanded, barely giving Cat time to get into the room. "Where were you? Does Dad know you didn't come home right after school?" Both of their parents worked.

218

Cat walked by Brett, lightly pushing him out of her way. "For your information, I called him from school. So he knows. Anyway, why do you care?"

Brett made a face. "Just for that, I won't tell you about your phone call! And it was from a boy!"

She stopped dead in her tracks. *Could it have been Brian? Could it be possible? Could he have called me?*

"Ha!" Brett sang, dancing out of her reach just in case she decided to make a lunge for him. "Cat doesn't know who called! Cat doesn't know who called!"

"You'd better tell me!" She was furious, and tried to grab him. Again Brett danced out of her reach, laughing and infuriating her further.

Then Cat tried a different tactic. "Oh, I don't care," she lied. "I don't like anybody right now anyway." She walked into the kitchen, hoping she appeared calmer than she felt.

"I'll tell you if you'll give me a dollar," Brett tried, following her into the kitchen.

Cat whirled, too furious to pretend any longer. "If you don't tell me right now, you little shit, Dad's going to know about this tonight!"

She caught Brett off guard, and grabbed the sleeve of his sweater, pulling it out of shape. She shook him, stretching the sweater to its limit without tearing it.

"Okay! Okay!" Brett howled, "It was somebody named Brian. I took his phone number—it's written on the pad in the kitchen. Leave me alone!"

"I'm going to call Brian right now, so take off."

Brett didn't have to be told twice. He dashed out of the kitchen without looking back.

Nervously Cat dialed the telephone number Brett had written on the note pad, and her cell phone felt cold to her ear. It rang once with no pick up, and Cat's hands began to tremble.

The phone rang twice, and her palms began to sweat.

It rang again and she began panicking, thinking she should hang up. She was just about to put the phone back when it was answered.

Cat thought, *It's Brian! What do I say?*

"Hi, Brian!" She tried to steady her voice so she wouldn't let on about how nervous she was. *What if I make a mistake? What if I say something stupid again?* "I heard you called, so I'm calling you back."

"Oh yeah," Brian sounded disinterested, and his voice was muffled, as though he were eating something. "You left a book in my car."

"Oh, so *that's* where my English book went." She was secretly delighted that she had left something in Brian's car. It gave him a reason to call her. It made it possible to talk to him.

"Yeah, well, I'd like to get rid of it, so I'll bring it to school on Monday. See you then. Bye."

He hung up.

Cat stood there for a minute, holding her cell phone at arm's length, looking at it in surprise. He hadn't even given her a chance to say goodbye.

She was thinking she should feel elated that she had talked to Brian on the phone, but she didn't. Instead she felt empty, tired…and very, very disappointed.

Chapter Three

Saturday morning was bleak. Dark, threatening clouds loomed in the west. The wind was mild, but an occasional gust suggested a pending storm. The air was unseasonably warm for October, a drastic change from the previous week, but it was humid and thick with moisture.

Cat met Tara in front of her house. "Are you still sure we should do this?"

"I saw the weatherman on TV last night, and he said it's not supposed to rain until around five o'clock today," Tara answered.

"That's not what I meant, but okay, let's go. Do you have your sandwich?"

The girls had agreed to bring their lunch along. They were wearing light jackets, and both had backpacks.

The walk to Creekside Cemetery was a long one. Gradually the scenery changed from suburban housing to green, empty lots. The empty lots soon changed into fields overrun with weeds. As they continued, there were fewer and fewer cars passing them by.

The farther the two walked, the more the sidewalk was becoming less manicured, with uneven concrete slabs that alternatively sank and protruded. Grass pushed through the cracks. In the fields, wild trees grew at odd angles, limbs untamed from lack of pruning. Small creatures scurried among the weeds; occasionally the girls could hear the rustling of the animals that were frightened as the girls walked by.

The sky continued to darken as black clouds approached. A rumbling sounded in the distance, reverberating softly across the land. The dark clouds created an eerie effect, because even though it was day, a sense of half-light dominated the surroundings.

When the girls reached Road 18, they stopped.

"Boy, there's nobody around here at all," Tara said. "If we yelled, no one could hear us."

"What's that supposed to mean?"

"Nothing," Tara said. She took a step, then stopped again. "Well, I guess I mean if we got in trouble, there'd be nobody around to help us."

"Tara, don't you start getting all scared on me. This was *your* idea. Now that we're here, I want to see the place again. Maybe if I see the cemetery today, I'll be able to figure out if I imagined Father Santiago or not."

The entrance to Creekside Cemetery was simply a gravel road among the weeds with an old, cast-iron arbor above it. There was no fence of any kind; probably because a fence would require maintenance. Since no one had been buried at Creekside since the 1930s, maintenance was kept to a minimum. The cemetery was overgrown with weeds that were only periodically mowed.

The two girls paused briefly at the entrance, then Cat pushed ahead and Tara followed. "This is what I was telling you," Cat said when they reached the first headstone. "Look at the dates on these tombstones; it feels like these people lived centuries ago. It even lists how many months and days old the person was."

"Peter Haas," Tara read out loud. "Aged fifty-one years, four months, seven days. I see what you mean. Where my grandfather is buried, the dead people just have dates on the tombstones when they were born and when they died. No age is mentioned. This graveyard is different."

"Most of these people were born in the 1800s. Can you imagine that long ago? Life must have been different way back then.

Probably really hard, too. You know, I'd like to know more about these people."

"History is not my favorite subject," Tara wrinkled her nose.

"That's because we always have to read about it in books," Cat said. "This would be real history. I wonder how I could find out more about these people? I know, I'll call the Rivertown Chamber of Commerce and find out who maintains this cemetery. Somebody is weed-wacking the grass, even if they aren't doing it very often. Maybe that somebody will have some information about who was buried here."

"Well, in the meantime, let's go where you saw Father Santiago," Tara said. "Maybe we can figure something out about it. You know what? I feel like a detective. This is sort of fun, but I have to admit, I'm a little scared because this place sure is spooky. Even in the daytime."

At that moment, thunder rumbled again, coming closer. A breeze picked up, rustling the shrubbery and causing fall leaves to take flight from the trees. A light sprinkle began, and the girls ducked under a large, malformed tree. Shrugging, Cat pulled a sandwich out of her backpack.

"Imagine, a picnic in a graveyard! In a *haunted* graveyard." Tara said as she also grabbed a sandwich. "I don't think this rain will last very long."

"Yes, after all," Cat said, "you told me the weatherman said it wouldn't rain until five o'clock and here it is only two. And quit saying this cemetery is haunted."

As they ate, both girls became silent as they took in their surroundings.

Creekside Cemetery was divided into two halves by a short, unused gravel road. The road ended at the creek, and the low bridge was visible from where the girls sat. The cemetery was small, only containing about thirty family plots. Some of the headstones were tall and carved, but most were toppled over or in pieces, having been the victims of vandalism over the years.

Four huge trees lined the gravel road, their misshapen branches visible because they had already dropped most of their leaves. Overgrown shrubs and bushes on the outskirts made fence-like borders. The cemetery was alive with animal sounds; insects buzzed, an unseen bird shrilled from one of the many shrubs, and a crow cawed raucously.

The rain subsided just as quickly as Tara had predicted. Cat suggested they get on with the reason they came. They headed slowly down the gravel road in the direction of the creek. It had rained for such a short period that the stones were barely wet.

"Caw, caw," screamed the crow loudly as it suddenly swooped down from a tree. Both girls jumped. The crow flew to a dark gray tombstone that was large and rounded. Ominously the big black bird sat on top of the marker as it intently studied the girls.

"They say that crows were used by witches to watch people the witches didn't like," Tara whispered. "They say that the witches used magic so they could see the same things the crows could see."

"Tara, that's not funny," Cat cried. "Besides, who are 'they'?"

"You know," Tara said, "*They*. People. Old stories."

"That's all witches are…old stories."

"Well, all the scary books I read say so."

The crow flew away, and Cat breathed a sigh of relief.

Cat led Tara to the Foster family plot. "Father Santiago was on the other side of this Foster plot. See, here's the Foster name on the cement. That's how I know exactly which gravesite the Father was standing behind."

The Foster family plot was a large raised bed with a seven-inch high cement border, like most of the other gravesites. Inside no grass was planted, instead, there was only brown, hardened dirt.

"I'm not going to walk across any dead people," Tara said.

"No, of course not. We can walk between the gravesites."

The girls walked on the ancient, cracked pavement between two family plots. Behind the Foster gravesite was nothing but weeds, all brown, dried, and grown to at least six inches tall since they were last mowed.

"There's nothing here," Tara commented.

"Well, this *has* to be the place. Let's go back and read the Foster tombstones. Maybe that will give us a clue."

Tara said, "You can read those tombstones—I'll stay here."

Cat stepped away from the weeds back onto the dirt of the raised family plot. The Foster gravesite was wide but only contained one large headstone.

"Wow, you're not going to believe this!" she exclaimed. "There are two names on this big tombstone, James and Edith Foster. But listen to this—both James and Edith died on the same date. The tombstone says, 'Joined in life through marriage, joined in death through tragedy. James R. Foster, died November 1, 1935—Edith S. Foster, died November 1, 1935.'"

Tara apparently forgot that she didn't want to walk on the grave. She came up beside her friend to read the headstone's inscription. "Death through tragedy," Tara read aloud. "Wow, do you think it was an accident? Why would both Fosters die on the same date?"

"I don't know, but I'd sure like to find out," Cat said.

Tara suddenly realized that she was standing on the graves and let out a small shriek. She leaped back on to the old pavement next to the gravesite.

Cat joined Tara on the cracked sidewalk, then walked back to where she had seen Father Santiago standing. She studied the ground behind the Foster plot carefully. It was frustrating, because nothing seemed out of the ordinary. It just looked like dirt and weeds.

"I wish I knew what I was supposed to be looking for," Cat wondered aloud.

Suddenly, she felt dizzy. The trees and the headstones began to spin. She felt herself falling. She could feel herself hit the ground, yet she felt no pain. The tombstones of the graveyard began to disappear into a mist, and instead the insides of a house seemed to emerge into her vision.

She found herself in a room with wooden walls painted white. Was she in someone's kitchen? Candlelight was the only illumination. Eerily the candles flickered, creating dancing shadows upon the walls.

I know this place, Cat thought. *I've been here before in a dream.*

She touched a crude, hand-made table in the center of the room. She pulled out a wooden chair, and it scraped the plank floor as it slid. Sitting on the chair, she saw an old-fashioned stove that looked like it belonged in a museum. *So this is a kitchen,* she thought.

She turned her head at the sound of a door opening. A tall man with a dark beard walked into the room. He wore funny-looking brown pants, a white shirt, and suspenders. She looked at her own legs, and was surprised to see herself wearing a floral-print dress that covered her knees instead of the jeans she had put on in the morning.

"Jessie, you shouldn't have come here," the man wearing the suspenders said. "They'll find you."

"I didn't do it," Cat heard herself say.

"I know you didn't, but everybody in this town thinks you did," the man said. "The sheriff wants you real bad. But I think if your uncle finds you first, you won't even get a trial. Come on, I'll help you hide. You've got to get away, because your uncle's been by here looking for you, and he'll be back."

"I don't know where to go," she heard herself speak again.

"I know a place," said the man with the beard. "I've always loved you, Jessie, and I'll never turn my back on you."

"Cat!" She heard a voice from far away. "Cat, wake up!"

Groggily, she opened her eyes. She was unsure of her surroundings, and tied to control the nausea that threatened. Then the spinning stopped and the lightheadedness faded. Her stomach settled and she knew she was no longer in danger of getting sick.

"Why am I on the ground?" she asked. She was lying in the weeds, behind the Foster gravesite.

"I don't know!" Tara shrieked, sounding hysterical. "I think you fainted! Ohmygosh, I've never seen anyone faint before! Are you okay? Can you get up?"

"Yes, I think I'm okay." She got to her feet. "But I don't think I fainted. I think I had some sort of spell, like I was in a time-warp or something."

"What?" Tara cried.

"It's this place, this graveyard. Maybe you're right, maybe it's haunted! I swear I was in somebody's kitchen, and it seemed so real. I just want to go home now."

"Okay, let's go. That is, if you're sure you're all right."

"Yes, let's just go home." Cat stood still for a minute, to steady her legs. When she was certain she felt fairly normal, the girls picked up their backpacks and walked down the old gravel lane to Road 18.

"It's like I had some sort of vision. It seemed so real. Between Father Santiago and these other people in a kitchen, I think you're right—now I really believe that somebody is trying to tell us something. We have *got* to find out what it is."

Chapter Four

225

Sunday was a gray day, and it rained incessantly. Cat spent the remainder of the weekend recovering from Saturday's stressful ordeal. She stayed in her room, listened to music, and read a book.

Tara phoned once to talk about the upcoming Halloween dance planned by their school.

No mention was made of the fainting spell, or time warp, or whatever it was that she had experienced at the cemetery. It became uncomfortable because the girls were almost trying too hard to avoid the subject. She was listless, and wasn't in the mood to discuss the dance, so their conversation was short.

By the time Monday morning arrived, the rain had stopped. She felt better.

She looked forward to her day at school because she knew she would be seeing Brian. Today Brian would talk to her! He had to, because he still had her English book.

She happily began to plan how she could turn that situation to her advantage. She just *knew* she could get Brian's attention today. She would have to be witty and attractive. Cat didn't wear much make-up, usually only a light lipstick. But today was special, so she applied mascara on her lashes. She spent so much time practicing her smile in front of the mirror that she was almost late to meet Tara.

Five minutes before class began, she searched for Brian but couldn't find him. She tried looking for him again at lunchtime, and found him standing in line in the cafeteria.

She approached him and said, "I figured you'd be looking for me to give me back my English book."

She tried out the smile she had practiced.

"Oh, yeah." Brian was looking at the lunch menu, trying to make up his mind. "Well, I don't have any books with me right now. I'll meet you after school at your locker and give it to you then."

"Okay, see you then," Cat said as she walked away.

She was thrilled. Brian wanted to meet her after school! Maybe he would give her another ride home in his car. If so, she hoped that Brian had recently filled his gas tank.

The rest of the afternoon inched forward, so slow that she thought the day would never end. When the last bell rang, she raced to her locker and waited.

A boy she'd never seen before approached her. "Hello Cat," he said.

"Hi. Do I know you?"

"I'm Randy Harris," he told her. "I saw you in the office last week—I think you called your dad. I'm new here, that's why I was in the office. I was registering in this school."

She looked at the new boy, appraising him. He was cute enough, with large brown eyes that were flecked with gold and an easy smile, but his clothes were old and out of style. His sneakers were worn, and one actually had a hole in the toe. He didn't look as if he had any idea of what other kids thought was cool.

The new boy seemed nervous under her scrutiny. "I noticed you, so I asked who you were. I mean," he went on. "I wasn't trying to spy on you or anything."

Ashley Long came to her locker, standing next to her as she worked her combination. Randy seemed to take that as his cue to leave. "I'll see you around," he said to Cat.

When he left, Cat felt relieved. After all, she was expecting Brian, and she didn't want him to see her talking to someone like Randy. She braced herself for some sort of comment from Ashley. Ashley always had something to say about everything.

Sure enough, Ashley said, "Lucky you! Maybe you'll get a date for the Halloween dance after all."

"Who do you mean?"

"Well, that new tenth-grader. What's his name? Randy something-or-other? He looks just your type."

She was dumbfounded. She knew Ashley could be snide, but she wasn't expecting anything like this. The new boy—Cat's "type?" Why, he was so obviously out of style that he had to be some sort of nerd. And his clothes looked so old.

"I have other plans for the dance." She slammed her locker shut. "In fact, Brian is going to meet me here any minute now."

Ashley began to laugh. "Dream on, girl! Brian is meeting *me* after school. You'd better stick to guys like that Randy. And just so you don't get your hopes up, Brian asked *me* to go to the dance with him!"

Cat felt as though someone had punched her in the stomach. Her face drained of color, and she felt she had to gasp for air. Ashley saw the reaction to her news and smirked in satisfaction.

Cat took a deep breath, and thought quickly. She had to intercept Brian before he came to her locker. She just had to talk to him without Ashley around.

Ashley had to be lying!

Running across the quad, Cat spied the bright red San Francisco 49ers football jacket that Brian always wore. He was walking towards her.

"Brian!" she called.

He waved, his face expressionless. He stood, waiting for her to approach.

"I have your English book," he told her when she was in front of him. "Here you go."

Numbly she took the book from Brian's outstretched hand. She just *had* to know at any cost.

In desperation, she blurted out, "Are you taking Ashley Long to the Halloween dance?"

Startled, Brian looked closely at her. "What's it to you?"

"I thought you and I were going out," she answered lamely.

"You and me? You're kidding, right?" Brian started to laugh, then saw that Cat was serious so he stopped. "Listen, I've liked Ashley for a long time. Then I thought, since you had a locker right next to Ashley, maybe she told you if she liked me or not. I always see you two talking at your lockers. So when I noticed that you could use a ride the other day, I thought I could give you a ride and ask you if she likes me at the same time. But you talked so much in my car that you never gave me a chance! Sheesh. Now I don't need you to tell me anyway, because Ashley said yesterday she'll be my girl. Sorry if you misunderstood the car ride, but I never figured you'd think I'd like you as a girlfriend."

Her face drained of color for the second time that day. She didn't say another word to Brian; instead, she just turned and fled. She knocked into two people who gave her dirty looks, but she didn't care.

She didn't know where she was running, but she just had to get away. She felt weak, shaky, and nauseous. She felt almost as bad as she had when she fainted on Saturday. Tears began to stream down her cheeks.

Suddenly she stopped short. She thought, *Where am I going?*

The mascara that she had put on so painstakingly that morning was now stinging her eyes. She felt as though her heart would break from sadness, and that her face would burn up from shame. How could she ever face Brian Castleman again, much less Ashley Long? Both of them must think her a complete fool. And she felt they would both be right.

She began looking for Tara, avoiding eye-contact with the other kids who were still mingling around. The students were clearing out, and many were already on their way home.

Tara was waiting by Cat's locker, and one look at her stopped any questions Tara may have had.

"Let's get out of here," Tara said, "and you can tell me what's wrong on the way home."

Gratefully she followed her friend. She didn't say a word until they were two blocks from the school. Then Cat blurted out everything that had happened.

"Look," Tara comforted, "remember last September when I liked Ritchey Lopez, and I found out he didn't like me? I felt really bad, you know? But I think that kind of thing happens to a lot of people, not just you and me. When Ritchey dumped me, you listened to me when I felt bad, and that helped me feel better."

"I feel better after talking to you, too." said Cat.

Tara continued, "The people who listen to Ashley Long are the people who act just like her. They are nobody who matter. Besides, Ashley and Brian are both in eleventh grade. Nobody in eleventh grade cares about us tenth-graders. So don't worry, they won't be talking about you because no one will want to hear about any tenth-graders. Lots of times you think people are talking about you but really they're not. People want to talk about themselves. You'd be surprised at how quickly people forget things. It's like, to them, life goes on."

Cat saw the logic in that. How lucky she was to have a friend like Tara! Tara always helped when things went wrong. Everyone needed a best friend.

"What you need is something to get your mind off of Brian Castleman," Tara said. "I have an idea. How about us investigating Creekside Cemetery? Why don't we find out who is buried behind the Foster graves?"

"You mean *if* anyone is buried behind the Foster graves," Cat corrected. "There's no tombstone or any other kind of marker. We don't know for sure if there's anybody there. It might be just dirt behind the Foster family plot."

They went past Tara's house, but Tara kept walking. "Why don't I come over to your house?" Tara offered. "We can make some phone calls. That's how we'll start. But Cat, first you need to wash your face. You have mascara smeared all over. You look like a raccoon."

Chapter Five

Finding information about Creekside Cemetery wasn't as easy as Cat would have thought. The girls began by calling the Rivertown Chamber of Commerce, who referred them to the County Supervisor's Office, who in turn referred them to the County Board of Cemetery Management. Finally they were able to find someone who could help.

"I'd like to know where I can find more information about Creekside Cemetery," Cat spoke into the telephone.

"What sort of information did you have in mind?" asked the woman from the County, who identified herself as Mrs. Dunisch.

"Actually," Cat explained, "I was hoping to find out more about the people buried there. Like, maybe about the Fosters. That's the name of a family buried in one of the gravesites—Foster."

"Well, that figures," said Mrs. Dunisch.

"What do you mean?"

"It figures that if you'd want to know about anyone buried at Creekside Cemetery, it would be the Foster family. The Foster killings were big news around here at that time," Mrs. Dunisch said. "They were murdered by their own daughter and it made headlines in the local newspaper."

She was shocked. "They were?"

"What?" Tara cried, trying to get her ear close to the phone. "Tell me!"

"Sssh!" Cat hushed Tara. "I'll tell you in a minute."

"What did you say?" Mrs. Dunisch asked.

"Nothing. What do you mean, the Fosters were murdered by their own daughter?"

"Wow!" Tara exclaimed.

"Oh Tara, be quiet! I'm trying to listen." Cat had her hand over the mouthpiece this time.

"Well," continued the woman on the phone, "the story goes that the Fosters were very rich, and had only one child. During the depression of the 1930s, with the stock market crash and the economy taking a nosedive, everybody lost most of their money. But the Fosters still had a lot of valuable property, paintings, jewels, and so on—and their house was paid for. Even though the Fosters didn't have a lot of money in the bank any more, rumors went around that they had a lot of cash hidden somewhere in their house. So—the daughter murdered her own parents for the property they still owned. Maybe she even knew where the money was hidden. The 1930s were desperate times, and I guess the daughter had no desire to be poor."

"Is the daughter dead? Where is she buried? I only saw two Foster graves," Cat said.

"Oh, you were at the cemetery?" Mrs. Dunisch asked. "I don't know what happened to the daughter. I don't even know what her name was. All I know is that she's not buried at Creekside Cemetery."

"How can I find out more about the Fosters?"

"I suppose the County Library will have microfilm of old newspapers."

"What's microfilm?"

"You know—photographs of newspapers on tiny film. You run the microfilm through a machine that magnifies the film so you can read it. Oh, one more thing. A man named John Gatland is what you'd call an expert on Creekside Cemetery. I think his whole family tree is buried there. And John is the one who takes care of the cemetery. I'll give you his phone number. I'll bet he could tell you a lot of that cemetery's history."

"Thanks," she told Mrs. Dunisch as she wrote down the phone number, "you've been a lot of help."

When she hung up, Cat turned to Tara, who was waiting impatiently for news.

"Wow!" Tara cried. "I just knew there was something weird about all of this. This proves that Father Santiago was a ghost. This proves that the cemetery is haunted."

"Wait a minute," Cat said. "If Creekside Cemetery is haunted, why wouldn't it be haunted by the Foster family? Why on earth would it be haunted by a priest?"

"I know why!" Tara went on breathlessly. "Father Santiago said there is a soul in torment. Maybe he meant one of the Fosters."

"Tara, when I thought I saw Father Santiago, he was standing *behind* the Foster gravesite, not on top of it," Cat pointed out. "And it still doesn't explain why a priest would be haunting the cemetery. I wonder if Father Santiago has a connection to the Fosters or if it's just a coincidence that he was standing behind the Foster family plot. And I also wonder...if someone is buried behind the Foster graves, maybe it's that man or that woman from the kitchen in my dream. You know, that kitchen looked like something that must have existed a long time ago."

"You mean, when you fainted at the cemetery, you think that one of the people you saw in your hallucination might be the one buried behind the Foster graves?"

"Hallucination! Tara, I swear I was in some sort of time warp. I'll bet there really *is* someone buried behind the Foster graves. That's an old cemetery. Maybe the grave marker got lost over the years. You saw how there was all that vandalism at Creekside Cemetery, so maybe somebody destroyed the marker. Anyway, it's something to think about."

"We need to find out more about this." Tara said. "Let's go to the County Library tomorrow after school."

"School, great," moaned Cat. "I hope Ashley Long leaves me alone."

"Don't worry, I'll be there," Tara said. "That's the thing about people like Ashley Long—they only pick on you when you're alone."

"No, don't worry about me," Cat said. "I have to face her sooner or later. It might as well be sooner so I can get it over with."

Tara smiled."That's the spirit. You know what? No one has asked me to go to the Halloween dance. It's this Friday night, remember?"

"Yeah, but nobody has asked me to go, either. And next Saturday is Halloween. Do you want to come over my house and help give out candy to the trick-or-treaters?"

"Or you could come over to mine," Tara suggested. "Nobody will be home at my house, as usual. We can watch scary movies on Halloween night. Scary movies for a scary night."

"Sure, why not? I'll come over your house. But about the dance, are you going?"

"Only if you are," said Tara. "You know, there're always boys who go without dates. Why don't we go, and we'll dance a lot— you'll see. There'll be lots of single guys at the dance."

"Yeah, I guess so, After all, I have a new shirt. I got it when I was hoping Brian would ask me to go with him."

"Forget about Brian," Tara said sternly.

But that night when she was alone in her room, Cat couldn't seem to forget about Brian. She felt that her heart ached. She allowed herself one more cry into her pillow over the whole situation—Brian's rejection of her, Ashley's mean comments, and dateless for the dance on top of it all.

She drifted off into sleep, and if she had dreams, she didn't remember any of them. Morning came before she was ready. When her mother woke her for school, she buried her face deeper into the pillow. It took her a few moments to remember what she had to confront on this day, then she turned over in the bed to face the wall.

"Get up or you'll be late for school!" her mother called again.

Cat groaned aloud, but managed to get out of bed. *Well*, she thought, *I might as well see Brian and Ashley and get it over with.*

She met Tara at the usual place on the way to school. "Any dreams last night?" Tara asked.

"Don't you mean hallucinations?"

"Well, *excuse me!*"

"I'm sorry—no dreams last night," Cat explained. "Listen, I don't mean to be crabby. I'm just worried about what to say to Brian and Ashley today, and I'm taking it out on you."

"Don't worry about me. I told you I'd be there if you need me," Tara said. "But about what to say, just don't say anything. Like I said before, sometimes we think people are talking about us, when really they aren't talking about us at all—in fact, they aren't even *thinking* about us. People are self-centered; they spend their time thinking about themselves. I'll bet what happened isn't as big of a deal to Brian and Ashley as it is to you."

"What if they *are* talking about me? What if it *is* a big deal to them?"

"I think that we're supposed to go through these kinds of things—you know, to learn from them."

"What am I supposed to learn?" Cat asked.

"Well, maybe it's to show us that what seems really bad one day can seem better after enough time goes by," Tara said. "Like with Ritchey Lopez—when he dumped me, I felt really bad, remember? But now enough time has gone by that I don't care about Ritchey anymore."

"But time takes too long."

"I know how you feel. Listen Cat, it just happens. To everyone, I think, at one time or another. You just have to keep on going and believe it will get better. Because it really does get better."

"So how should I handle Brian and Ashley today?"

"Just hang in there," Tara said. "They'll forget about all of this soon. Hold your head up in the meantime. Keep your dignity; that is important. Don't let them know it gets to you, and they won't get satisfaction. Start by pretending it doesn't bother you, then after a while, it really won't bother you."

"Thanks. You really are the very best friend anyone could have."

They separated, and Cat went apprehensively to her locker. She began entering her combination on the lock when Ashley Long approached.

"Well, well, look who's here," Ashley taunted. "Are you still hoping that Brian will meet you here at your locker and whisk you away to the dance?"

Cat turned to face her. "Listen Ashley. I know that Brian likes you and not me, and I'm okay with that now. I hope you and Brian have fun at the dance. I really mean it."

Ashley appeared speechless, with a surprised look on her face. Cat laughed inwardly as she realized that Ashley didn't seem to know how to respond to the unexpected nicety. After all, Ashley was the type of mean person who only understood other mean people.

"Gotta go," Cat said. "See you later."

She rushed off, but couldn't resist one peek over her shoulder. Ashley was still standing at the lockers and staring after her, hands on her hips.

Cat felt exhilarated. It was true. Sometimes people were mean, and sometimes they were petty, but if you held your head up high, things would get better.

One down, she thought. *Next, I'll face Brian if I run into him today.*

She went to her morning classes, and at lunch, she went to the school library. Cat decided she wanted to learn more about the Great Depression of the 1930s. What could possibly be so bad that it could drive a daughter to kill her own parents?

As she sat at one of the school library's computers, she googled *Great Depression*. She was surprised at how many matches there were. She clicked on the first listing, and was annoyed that the file seemed to take a long time to open. When it finally did, the words *File Not Found* appeared on the screen.

Sighing, Cat went back and tried the next listing. That file opened immediately.

She read the following:

> *The Great Depression of the 1930s was the longest economic downturn in the United States' history, beginning with a financial collapse in 1929, and lasting until the start of World War II. Before the Great Depression, people bought stock in the stock market on credit, intending to pay off their loans with the money that they thought they would make. But then inflation made prices go higher, and the cost for stocks rose far beyond what they were worth.*

She read more. The article continued:

> *It is commonly thought that the Great Depression was caused entirely by the stock market crash in October 1929, but other things also played important roles. Before the Great Depression began, the United States was the world's chief*

creditor, lending money to foreign countries that could not repay the loans. And it was not just the government who gave credit. Stores gave credit, too. People in America bought a lot of things on credit, and when they could not repay the stores, many of the stores went bankrupt and had to fire their employees. That made even more people who became poor and couldn't pay their bills.

She frowned. This was mildly interesting, but not exactly what she was looking to learn. She wanted to learn about the *people*. How did the Great Depression affect the people? What drove the Foster daughter to commit a horrible crime during that desperate time? She typed *Great Depression, People.*

There were not as many matches in this search as in the last. She opened the first file and read its contents.

During the worst of the Great Depression, around 15 million Americans lost their jobs. Discouragement and despair were everywhere because banks went out of business and didn't give people their money back. So people lost their life's savings. Americans found themselves out on the street, homeless because they couldn't pay their rent. Charities created soup-lines to try to feed the hungry, but were often overwhelmed by the sheer numbers of the newly poor.

Wow, Cat thought, *I'm glad I didn't live then.* She read further:

Children were also hard-hit during the Great Depression. There were children who found themselves no longer able to attend school, and some dropped out to help seek food for their families by taking jobs if they could find them, or by begging if they could not. Many people lived only to survive the day, with no plans for the next.

She tried to imagine herself in that situation, so desperate that she had to beg for food for her little brother. Brett might be a pain in the neck sometimes, but she wouldn't want him to starve.

Still, she decided that she could never murder anyone, not even during the Great Depression. There had to be something more that would drive the Foster daughter to murder her parents. There *had* to be something that she was missing. What was she overlooking?

Suddenly she realized that someone was sitting at the computer terminal next to her own. She looked up, and was startled to realize it was Randy Harris, the new boy in school.

Quickly she looked him over, once again noticing the ragged jeans and old shoes. Didn't he realize that the "grunge" look had gone out of style decades ago?

Maybe I shouldn't be so quick to judge, she thought. *After reading all that about the Great Depression, maybe I should be thinking that it might not be Randy's fault that he seems so poor.*

"Hi," she said.

Randy seemed surprised that she was the first to speak. He smiled and said, "I didn't know if you wanted to talk to me or not. I'm glad you do. Your name is Cat. Do you remember mine?"

She looked closely at him. His large brown eyes were flecked with gold. His skin was smooth, and his hair was almost the same golden-brown as his eyes. "Of course I remember your name. You're Randy, the new guy."

"That's right!" Randy spoke too loud for the library, and in embarrassment, he changed to a near-whisper. "Are you here to do your homework early?"

"Not exactly." She didn't want to explain her real reason, so she quickly turned the focus back to him. "What about you?"

"I'm trying to look up my family history on the Internet, you know—my family tree," Randy said. "My grandmother was born in Rivertown, but we don't know too much about her. My mom wanted to move back here because she keeps talking about trying to find

237

'her roots.' That's how she puts it, crazy as it sounds. Not that I'm saying she's crazy," he added hastily.

She laughed softly. "No, of course not."

"Well, I don't have a lot of friends yet, since I've only been here a couple of days. There's nobody to hang out with at lunchtime. I thought I'd kind of help my mom out, you know, look up some information for her on the Internet. We don't have a computer at home."

The librarian glanced their way. Cat said, "We have to talk quieter, or else we'll be kicked out."

"Okay, sorry." Randy smiled, and she realized he was really cute.

"Hey listen, I'm glad I have a chance to talk to you," Randy continued. "I wanted to ask you about the Halloween dance the other day at your locker, but then that other girl came, and well, you know. Do you have a date already for the dance Friday night?"

"I…" Cat stammered. *What should I do?* Her mind raced. *What should I say?*

"I can't go with you because I already promised that I'd go with my friend Tara. She wouldn't be able to go if I didn't go with her, because she told me she wouldn't go alone. But can I see you there? Maybe we can dance some dances together."

Randy smiled. "I'll be there."

The bell rang, and Cat realized she had better run or she would be late for her next class. "Don't you have to go to class?" she asked him.

"My next period is study hall. It's held here, so all's I have to do is to wait for the rest of the class to come in."

She logged off the computer, said a hurried goodbye to Randy, and raced to leave the school library to go back to the open quad. She found herself thinking of him. He really *was* cute.

She burst through the library door, and crashed smack into Brian Castleman. Upon impact, her books flew out of her hands and landed on the campus sidewalk.

"Oh no!" Cat cried involuntarily, and quickly bent to retrieve her books. Brian did the same thing. They bumped heads, and Brian straightened up, but she still stooped, picking up her books from the ground.

When she stood up, she apologized to Brian.

He looked disgusted. "You know what? You're really stupid."

Cat was astonished. "What!"

"You can't do anything right," Brian complained. "First you go around thinking I would like you for a girlfriend, then you practically run me over."

She became furious. Who was this guy to be so mean? And why blame her when it was obviously an accident? She suddenly couldn't imagine why she had ever thought she liked Brian.

"I can't believe you can be such an ass," she said. "It never occurs to you that other people besides you have feelings. Okay, I misunderstood when I thought that you and I could go out, but that's all it was, a misunderstanding. It should be no big deal, because you've told me how you feel so now it's all straightened out. It's over! And I already apologized for running into you. What right do you have to call me stupid? You don't know what you're talking about because you talk before you think." Cat paused, and looked Brian squarely in the eye. "I've got to go now, because I'm already late for class."

With that, she turned around and quickly walked away, but couldn't resist peeking over her shoulder. Just like Ashley, Brian stood there staring after her. His hands were not on his hips, but she noticed that his mouth was open as he watched her leave.

Chapter Six

When they met by her locker after school, Cat told Tara all about her day and the confrontations she had with Ashley and Brian. Both girls were in good moods as they walked to the County Library.

The autumn air was cool, and the wind blew multicolored leaves in spurts, sometimes creating tiny twisters of leaves. Jack-o-lanterns silently laughed from their perches on the porches of the homes the girls passed. Straw-stuffed scarecrows and cheerful pumpkin-colored garbage bags filled with leaves decorated the lawns.

"What do you think of that new guy, Randy Harris?" asked Cat, trying to keep her voice sounding uncaring as they walked.

"Cute—but did you see the way he dresses?"

"Sometimes things happen that are nobody's fault. Maybe his family doesn't have a lot of money."

Tara looked closely at Cat. "Why do you ask? You don't like him, do you?"

"I don't know yet. He seems nice. And you're right, Randy is really cute. It wouldn't be his fault if he doesn't have any money. It's probably not his parents' fault, either."

"I guess so. Besides, after Brian, Randy looks better all the time."

Both girls laughed.

"You know," Cat said, "I've been reading about the 1930s Great Depression. I've been thinking that people shouldn't judge other people by how much money they have."

"It works for me," Tara said. "But I don't know about the rest of the world."

The library was only four blocks from Rivertown High School, so the girls reached it quickly. The building was only one level, situated next to a small parking lot. They entered, and were immediately greeted with a musty smell coupled with the scent of furniture polish. The lighting was bright, and from the doorway the girls could see the entire room. Three people were browsing among the books around the library. The librarian's desk was placed in front of rows and rows of books that were on shelves from the left side to the center of the room. Towards the right wall, three display cases contained gold panning artifacts, and the walls were dotted with old, black and white photographs of gold miners. Some photos showed men panning in the river, while others showed hydraulic mining machines. The library was a repository of gold rush artifacts.

Cat strode to the reception desk, and Tara followed. A man was examining books. His nameplate said he was Russell Pabalan. He looked up when the girls approached. "Can I help you?"

"Yes, does this library have a microfilm machine?" Cat asked.

"Certainly," Mr. Pabalan answered. "Right behind my desk."

"Um…" Cat thought a minute. "What we're looking for are old newspaper articles. Do you have them here?"

"We have the local newspaper, *The Rivertown Register.*"

"Great! That's the paper we want, anyway. We're looking for 1935. Do you have newspapers that old?"

"Sure do." Mr. Pabalan was obviously very proud of his library. "We have *The Register* starting from 1882 and continuing up until last month." He rose from his chair and walked behind his desk. The girls followed him. "They're in these two file cabinets here."

Cat was confused. "How can all those newspapers fit in only two file cabinets? Is microfilm that small?"

"It's pretty small. There are three months of newspapers on every spool of film. And each spool has its own box. The film is filed in boxes by the months and then by the year. Here, I'll show you." He pulled open a drawer from the cabinet and started thumbing through five-inch boxes.

"Here's 1935." He pointed inside the file drawer. "Which month do you want first?"

"How do we start?" Tara looked at Cat.

"Well," Cat said, "the news we want to know about happened on November first. We'll start with November."

"Then you want this one. This box has September through December of 1935." Mr. Pabalan closed the cabinet drawer. "We have what you need here because this library is very thorough about tracking the history of this town. We get money from the Historical Society for that purpose."

Mr. Pabalan pointed to a machine that in some ways resembled a computer monitor, except it was larger, completely square, and the screen was dark and flat. He continued, "Here, take out the spool of film and put in on this spindle. That loads the film onto the machine. There, see? You move this lever for forward and this lever for backward. The machine magnifies the words so you can read it. You can print what's on the screen, but if you do, it'll cost you twenty-five cents for every print you make. You'll get the hang of it. What are you girls doing? A school project?

"Something like that," Cat was evasive, and everyone stood there awkwardly as the librarian waited for an explanation that was not coming. After a few seconds he said, "Well, I guess I'll leave you girls alone to do your work," and went back to his desk.

"Do you think we have to look at all of the newspapers?" Tara wondered.

"The lady from the County said the Foster murder made the headlines in the local paper. That means we only need to look at the front pages. We can go through the papers far more quickly that way, if we only look at the headlines."

They scrolled to November 1, 1935.

"Wow, there weren't very many pictures in the newspapers in those days," Tara observed.

They scanned the headlines: *Large Earthquake Hits Montana. New Deal Spokesman Says Businesses Must Cooperate to Create More Jobs. State Investigates Gasoline Tax Fraud. Clark Gable Separates from Wife Rhea Lucas Gable.*

"Where's the story about the Foster murders?"Tara asked. "And who the heck is Clark Gable?"

"Never heard of him. And listen, maybe the police didn't find the bodies of the Fosters in time for the news to be printed in this edition of the paper," Cat said. "Let's try November second."

And there it was: *Two Persons Found Dead in Home.*

Cat read aloud:

> *A husband and wife were found dead yesterday in the bedroom of their exclusive family home located on Oakwood Drive in Rivertown. The coroner estimates the time of death to have been between midnight and four AM on Friday, November first. No signs of a break-in were observed, although the police report states that extensive damage was done to the interior of the home. The names of the victims are being withheld until notification of next-of-kin. More information will be reported when details are released by the police.*

"That's got to be the Fosters," Tara said. "Let's try November third."

The only headlines on the next day's front page were: *Graft Probe Holds Up Gas Tax Money. Child is Severely Burned as Kettle Overturns. Sacramento Solons Ball Club Aided by Branch Rickey of St. Louis.*

"No good," Tara said. "On to November fourth."

They advanced the film. "Here it is!" Cat exclaimed. "It says, *Two Persons Found Dead Saturday Are Victims of Murder.*"

She read:

The husband and wife found dead on Saturday morning, November first, are identified as Mr. James R. Foster and his wife Edith. The police stated that the Fosters were victims of murder. James Foster was the co-owner of the Foster Accounting Firm of Sacramento. Police are interviewing suspects but refuse to reveal the identities of the persons being questioned in this case.

"Let's keep looking," Tara said.

The next entry about the crime was on November 8. Large headlines read: *Brother of Murdered Man Blames Daughter of Deceased in Crime*.

Cat read:

Henry Foster, brother of murdered victim, James R. Foster, brought forth evidence yesterday which points to Jessica Foster as being responsible for the crimes. Jessica Foster, daughter of the dead couple and niece of Henry, is being charged with murdering her father, James, and her mother, Edith, both found Saturday morning in their home. Warrants are being issued for the arrest of Jessica Foster, who disappeared after being questioned last Tuesday. Police say that Miss Foster was last seen at Saint John's Catholic Church in Rivertown. Father Alberto Santiago, priest of that church, admits Miss Foster came to confession, but refuses to say anything about what Miss Foster told him. Father Santiago states that he does not know where Miss Foster went after she left the church.

"That's the woman from my dream—her name was Jessie!" Cat said. "Jessie is a nickname for Jessica. And she talked to Father Santiago before she disappeared."

"Wow! Jessica Foster and Father Santiago knew each other. There's a connection!"

The girls continued to scan the newspapers, searching the headlines. "Stop!" Tara cried. "Go back to that last page."

Cat moved the lever backwards. They were in December now. On December 3, the headlines said: *Local Priest Killed in Single-Car Accident.*

Cat read:

> *Father Alberto Santiago, founder of the Saint John's Catholic Church here in Rivertown, was found dead in his car early this morning on Folsom Boulevard. The police report states that Father Santiago lost control of the vehicle and hit a tree. Mechanical problems may have been at fault.*

"I think we need to talk to Father Guzman again." Cat looked at Tara. "Maybe he can tell us more about the connection between Father Santiago and Jessica Foster. Also, remember when he told us that he's heard gossip about Creekside Cemetery? I wonder if he would tell us more about that, too. I'll bet the gossip has something to do with the Foster murders. After all, the Fosters are buried at Creekside."

"It's too late to go to the church today."

"Yeah, and I have to stay after school on Thursday. So, we'll have to go tomorrow. Can you make it?"

"Sure, no problem," Tara said. "We'll walk to Saint John's church straight from school like we did last time."

They thanked Mr. Pabalan, left the library, and walked home. It was barely six o'clock and already the sun was setting.

The crisp autumn wind stung their cheeks, and the girls were glad they had jackets. The air smelled slightly of burning wood as smoke rose from many of the chimneys in the neighborhood. When they reached Cat's house, she invited Tara inside.

"I just thought of something," Cat said. "We haven't called Robert Gatland yet."

"Who?" Tara asked, puzzled.

"You know, the guy who takes care of Creekside Cemetery. The one that the lady from the County said knows all about the cemetery."

"Oh yeah."

They went inside and Cat used her cell phone. She typed the number that Mrs. Dunisch had given her.

"Hello?" said a deep voice on the phone.

"Hi, are you Robert Gatland?" Cat asked.

"Only if you're not a bill collector," the man guffawed. "Yeah, I'm Robert Gatland. But I'd prefer it if you'd call me Bob. Who is this?"

"My name is Cat Daniels, and I was told by a woman from the County Board of Cemetery Management that you are sort of an expert on Creekside Cemetery. Could you tell us some things about that cemetery? By 'us,' I mean me and my friend Tara Whitfield."

"Why sure," Bob said jovially. "What kind of information did you have in mind?"

"Do you have a, well, like a map of who is buried there?"

"I can do better than that," Bob said. "If you've got the time, I can walk you through the place and point out who is buried where."

Cat held her breath and thought furiously for a moment. That would mean she would have to go back to Creekside Cemetery. Was she willing to do that?

I came this far, so I can't quit now, she thought.

She made up her mind. "Yes, Tara and I have the time. When would you like us to meet you there?"

"Well, how about this Saturday?" Bob asked.

Cat felt a jolt pass through her. "Um…" she stammered. "Do you know that this Saturday is Halloween?"

"That's right," Bob said. "I always like to keep an eye on the cemetery on Halloween, so I was going to head out there on Saturday anyway. You're not superstitious, are you? Don't tell me you believe in ghosts?"

"Just a minute," She told him. She turned to Tara. "He wants to meet us at the cemetery to give us a tour on *Halloween*!"

245

Tara's face turned white, but she quickly recovered. "I guess it depends on the time. It goes without saying that I'm not going there at night."

"How about at twelve noon?" Cat asked Bob, taking her hand away from the phone.

"Sounds great. I guess I won't have to ask you what you look like," Bob said. "You shouldn't be that hard to find, because hopefully we'll be the only three at the cemetery."

"Why do you say 'hopefully?'" she asked. "Why would there be anyone else out there besides us?"

"Well, sometimes Halloween brings out the vandals to the cemetery. That's why I want to check on the place. But there won't be any vandals out there at noontime. Those people wait until dark so they won't get caught. And at noontime, I think you'll be safe from the other ones who come out after dark too."

"Who are the other ones?" Cat asked.

"Why, the Halloween ghosts, of course!" Bob chuckled. "Seriously, if you girls want a tour, I'll see you at Creekside Cemetery at twelve o'clock. Talk to you then!"

She ended the call, and Tara asked, "Are you sure you want to go back to Creekside Cemetery?"

"No, I'm not sure I want to go back, but I think I *have* to go back. We can't quit now. Something important happened in 1935, and I want to know what it was."

"Yeah, and I think some ghosts want us to find out what happened, too," Tara added.

"I never believed in ghosts before, but now I don't know what to believe."

"I'm positive that there are ghosts in the world," Tara said. "All the scary books I read say so."

"Well, I don't think that is exactly a concrete reference."

That night, Cat was up later than usual, working on her homework. When she was finished, she went to bed and quickly fell into a deep sleep.

She dreamed she was in the kitchen again. A strong feeling of déjà vu passed through her. Candles on the table provided the only illumination as they flickered eerily, creating dancing shadows upon the walls.

She touched a crude, hand-made table in the center of the room. She could feel the ridges from the grain in the wood. She sat on a rough wooden chair, and smelled the coffee that was brewing on the stove.

I must be having a dream, she thought. *But I can see, hear, touch, and smell. This seems so real.*

She turned her head at the sound of a door opening. The tall man with the dark beard walked into the room, exactly as he had before. He still wore the funny-looking brown pants, the white shirt, and the suspenders. She looked at her own legs, and realized she was again wearing the floral-print dress, just like she wore in her other dream.

It's happening again, Cat thought, *I'm dreaming about 1935. But this time I'm going to ask this guy some questions.*

"Jessie, you shouldn't have come here," the man said. "Your uncle is looking for you."

"I'm not Jessie," she told the man.

He stood by the sink, watching her.

"Why do you keep calling me Jessie?" she asked.

"My time does not change," he answered. "My time will always be 1935. Jessie exists in my time."

"You don't make sense. So, you realize that it is no longer 1935? I think that you know I am not Jessie, but you keep talking to me like I am. Why do you do this?"

"My time does not advance," the man repeated and shrugged his shoulders.

"Okay, let's try this in a different way. Is there something you want to tell me? Is that why I keep dreaming about you?" It was weird to talk about dreaming while she was in the middle of a dream.

"The Fosters are victims of another's greed and desperation," the man answered. It was eerie how he spoke of people long dead in the present tense. "But Jessie, you are also a victim."

"What do you mean that Jessie is a victim? Are you saying that Jessie is dead? Was she murdered, too?"

"The truth will be found out very soon," the man told her. "Look for the number eight. All other numbers are false."

"What numbers?"

"You will be given the numbers. Remember, only the number eight is real. Tell the sheriff about the numbers. But when you get the numbers, don't tell anyone else, or you will be in great danger."

"I don't understand," Cat said.

The man looked at her, a puzzled look on his face. "You're not Jessie."

"I've been trying to tell you that!"

"Find Jessie," the man instructed. "In fact, you already know where she is."

He turned to walk away.

"Wait!" she cried and he stopped. "Who are you?"

He smiled. "You'll find me at Creekside Cemetery."

Then he walked out of the room.

Cat awoke with a start and sat upright in her bed, feeling her heart pound against her chest. Sweat trickled down her temples.

I think I'm being haunted.

Chapter Seven

It was Wednesday afternoon. The girls met at Cat's locker after school to walk to St. John's church. Once again the weather was cold, and the air was moist. They had exchanged their light jackets for coats, and kept them buttoned as they walked down Cardoza Street.

When they reached the church, this time they knew to go straight to the Parish Rectory instead of the Cathedral. The girls walked over the lawn and across the parking lot until they came to the same building they had visited last time. Again Cat knocked on the door.

It was answered by a woman. "Can I help you?" she asked.

"Can we see Father Guzman?"

"Do you have an appointment?"

"Appointment?" Cat was surprised. "To see a priest?"

"Why of course," the lady explained. "Appointments are necessary because priests often counsel their parishioners about spiritual matters. It wouldn't do for someone to drop in while Father Guzman was with someone else. So, do you have an appointment?"

"No, but we were hoping he had some time to see us."

"I'll check and see if he's busy."

Cat felt relieved. The girls were led through the entryway into the office. "Have a seat," the woman instructed.

In a few minutes, Father Guzman came in and sat at his desk, facing Cat and Tara. "Hello girls! I remember you. Cat and Tara, right? I see you've met my secretary. Now, what can I do for you today?"

She looked at Tara, then said, "I don't know how to begin."

"Begin at the beginning." Father Guzman smiled his warm smile, and Cat relaxed.

"It's about Father Santiago," Cat started. "Tara and I went to the County Library and read some newspapers from 1935. We were hoping you could tell us some more about what happened."

Father Guzman's smile disappeared. "Girls, why are you so interested in something that happened so long ago?"

Cat glanced at Tara again, but neither one answered.

"Look," the priest said, "I'll consider telling you more about what happened in 1935 if you tell me why you want to know so badly."

"Cat sees ghosts!" Tara blurted.

"What?" Father Guzman exclaimed.

"Tara!" Cat cried.

Everybody was upset, so Father Guzman took control. "Okay," he said, "let's all calm down and discuss this rationally. What is Tara talking about? Cat, I thought I told you the other day that you were mistaken when you said you saw Father Santiago at Creekside Cemetery."

"It was him," Cat said. "At the cemetery, Father Santiago told me that there was a soul in torment. He was pointing to the ground behind the Foster graves. Then I had a dream about Father Santiago. In my dream, he told me that he had listened to a confession. He told me that he tried to help, but fate stopped him."

Father Guzman looked grim. "It was only a dream. You said so yourself."

"It was more than just a dream. I think he was trying to tell me something about Jessica Foster. I know she went to confession right before she disappeared. I think Jessica Foster is buried behind her parents at Creekside Cemetery!"

Father Guzman appeared stunned. "That's impossible! Jessica Foster disappeared. In 1935, they had police manhunts looking for her. If Jessica Foster is buried someplace, it is not anywhere in this county. She and her baby were declared legally dead after they were missing for seven years."

It was Cat's turn to be stunned. "Jessica Foster had a baby?"

"Who was the father?" Tara wanted to know.

Father Guzman hesitated. "Well," he finally said, "I might as well tell you girls, because I get the feeling you are becoming obsessed with what happened to the Foster family. I suppose after all these years, it wouldn't hurt anybody now to go ahead and tell you the story."

Cat and Tara both held their breath. Were they finally going to find out what the 'ghosts' wanted them to know?

They leaned forward in their seats to listen.

Father Guzman said, "You have to remember it was 1935, and the Great Depression was in full swing. You think the Great Recession we had in 2009 was bad. But it didn't come even near to how bad things got in 1935."

He took a breath, then continued, "Henry and James Foster were brothers, and owned a rather large accounting firm in Sacramento. Rumor had it that some of the bookkeeping at the Foster Accounting Firm was not completely honest. Nobody has ever proven this, though. And eventually that didn't matter anyway, because the Foster brothers lost everything when the banks closed."

He paused again, then went on, "Henry was the spendthrift brother, while James saved everything. Stories were spread that there was a large amount of cash hidden somewhere in James' house the night he and his wife were murdered. Certainly the fact that the inside of the house was vandalized that night indicates that the murderer was looking for the money."

"How was the house vandalized?" Tara asked.

"Well," Father Guzman told them, "it looked like it was searched by someone in a hurry. No one knows if the murderer found any money. Anyway, a couple of days later, Henry had proof that the murderer was his brother's daughter, Jessica Foster."

"What was the proof?" Cat asked.

"A diary kept by Jessica made direct references to the murder. Also, the murder weapon was found at Jessica's home. It was a huge kitchen knife."

"Hold it—are you trying to tell me that one young woman could overpower both of her parents and kill them with a knife?" Cat asked.

"On the surface, it does sound unreasonable, doesn't it? However, Edith Foster was disabled with severe arthritis. And maybe Jessica attacked James from behind and killed him first."

"What about Jessica's baby?" Tara asked.

"Jessica Foster had been seeing Mark Stratton for over a year. James and Edith Foster didn't like him. They felt he wasn't good enough for their daughter, and he was dirt poor to boot. They told Jessica that they would disinherit her if she married Mark."

"What does disinherit mean?" Tara asked.

"It means that the Fosters would not leave anything in their will for Jessica when they died if she married Mark Stratton," the priest told them. "Remember, even though the Foster Accounting Firm lost everything, James still had property, art, and jewelry. Some people say he had hidden cash in the house. In any case, Jessica married Mark in a secret ceremony."

"And the wedding was performed by Father Santiago," Cat guessed.

"That's what the church records say," Father Guzman agreed. "Now, this is the part that I have no way to prove as fact. But—the story goes that Jessica was visibly pregnant at the time her parents were killed."

"I'll bet Jessica and her parents got into a big fight about her pregnancy," Cat guessed again. "Her uncle probably told the police about it. The newspaper said he had evidence. Maybe her Uncle Henry even knew about the marriage."

Father Guzman looked at Cat. "You have a detective's mind, do you realize that?"

Then he continued his narrative. "There was indeed a fight between Jessica and her parents, and the police used that, plus the threat of being disinherited from the will, as motives for the murders. I suppose Uncle Henry was more than happy to help convict Jessica Foster. You see, after Jessica, Henry Foster was the only living relative, and he stood to inherit his brother's property if Jessica was sent to jail. Since Jessica disappeared, Henry was unable to inherit anything until Jessica could be declared legally dead. Still, the court put Henry in charge of the estate of James and Edith Foster, so Henry could spend the money and live in the house James left when he died."

"But you still haven't told us about the baby," Tara reminded him.

"There's nothing to tell. Nobody knows if the baby was ever born, or if it died along with Jessica. Nobody even knows if Jessica did die at the time; although if she didn't, she's absolutely dead after all these years, no matter what happened to her in 1935."

"What happened to Mark Stratton?" Cat asked.

"He died in an accident around Christmas of that year."

Cat and Tara exchanged glances.

"Is it my imagination," Cat said, "or does it seem like there were an awful lot of bad things happening to people who knew Henry Foster?"

"It would seem so. However, you have to remember that the legal system may not have been as thorough in 1935 as it is nowadays. For example, their science was not as good as it is today. They didn't have evidence like DNA and other crime solving tools back then. No computers, either. Maybe Henry Foster was involved in some terrible things. Probably some questions were not asked that should have been. It doesn't matter now anyway, after seventy years."

"Maybe it does matter, even after seventy years," Cat said. "Maybe the wrong person was accused of murdering James and Edith Foster."

"Or maybe Jessica Foster *did* do it," Father Guzman argued. "I keep telling you that after all these years, it no longer matters."

"Tell us about Father Santiago," Tara said.

"Records indicate that he was killed in a car accident. But the story goes that he was returning to the church from Mark Stratton's house."

"Another connection to the mystery!" Cat cried.

"Well, official church records say that the night he crashed into the tree, Father Santiago was robbed. Not by gunpoint or anything, but after he died. He was missing his wallet and some other personal items when they found him dead in his car."

"Maybe he had some evidence from Mark Stratton's house," Cat said. "Maybe somebody knew he had it. Maybe Father Santiago's accident was not really an accident! Maybe somebody wanted something he had. Maybe they took it, too."

"That's just a guess," Father Guzman cautioned. "After all, it would seem more likely that somebody just stumbled across his wrecked car and decided, since he was already dead, to simply take his wallet. Remember, there was a depression going on in 1935 and those were desperate times. Well girls, that's all I know about the Foster story."

"You've told us a lot," Cat said.

"Now you tell me about these 'ghosts' you've been seeing," the priest prompted.

"I swear I saw Father Santiago in Creekside Cemetery one night," Cat told him. "He was trying to show me that someone is buried behind the Foster family plot. I now believe it's Jessica Foster who's buried there."

Tara spoke to Father Guzman. "The last time we were here, you told us that you've heard stories about Creekside Cemetery, but you didn't want to spread gossip. Can't you tell us what those stories are?"

"The stories I've heard about Creekside Cemetery are the same stories that people tell about every cemetery," Father Guzman said. "All right, I admit I've heard here and there that people keep seeing ghosts in that cemetery. And yes, I have heard that the ghosts are usually seen around the Foster graves. But girls, over the years, Creekside Cemetery has become a frequent spot for late-night beer drinkers and for vandals. I don't consider these types of people to be reliable sources of information."

"I'm not a beer drinker or a vandal," Cat said. "How do you explain the ghost *I* saw?"

"You think you saw a priest," Father Guzman said. "But priests dedicate their lives to the Lord, and God in His righteousness would not abandon priests in death just like He wouldn't abandon priests in life. Although the Catholic Church acknowledges spiritual presences such as angels, it would seem that a ghost would be a lost soul who would be unable to find its way to God. Perhaps a ghost would be one that was not baptized into the Lord's flock during life. A priest would certainly not be among those poor souls. That's assuming ghosts even exist at all, which I doubt."

Cat shook her head again. "He did go to God. Father Santiago said in my dream that he couldn't show himself to me anymore. He said something about directing me to a soul in need and that because he'd told me, he'd removed a burden. He said he was ready to enter the light. But I believe Father Santiago had a message for someone first. I think that someone just happened to be me."

"Don't get carried away with your imagination," Father Guzman warned. "If you want to keep learning about Jessica Foster, that's one thing. But don't go conjuring up ghosts in the process. Don't get involved in things that you don't understand."

"There's a lot I don't understand about these ghosts, that's for sure," Cat told him. "But I believe this—someone is trying to tell me something."

"Maybe you're thinking that natural things are supernatural things. In any case, there's something you might want to see." Father Guzman stood up. He went to the file cabinet where he had originally found the old photograph of Father Santiago the last time the girls had come by. He opened the drawer and rummaged around inside.

"Here it is," the priest said. He took a thin brown book out of the cabinet and slammed the drawer shut. "This was filed away with Father Santiago's church papers because frankly, I don't think anyone knew what to do with it. It was found in this office, right after Father Santiago died."

He handed Cat and Tara the small, thin brown book. It was about seven inches long and about five inches across. She took the book and opened it. It contained lined, yellowed pages that smelled musty. There was encrypted writing on the pages, scrawled with an old-fashioned fountain pen.

"Looks like a bunch of numbers. What is it?" Tara said as she peered at the book over her friend's shoulder.

Cat's face lost color and she didn't answer. Her hands shook slightly.

"I believe it is a ledger of some sort," Father Guzman said. "But nobody knows for sure."

"Can we borrow it?" Cat asked. "If it belonged to Father Santiago, maybe it will give us some sort of clue."

"I suppose you can. But bring it back in about a week. I don't think it has any value, but after all, it was part of Father Santiago's personal effects and so I'd like to keep that book in his file."

"Thanks," Tara said.

"I think we'd better leave now." Cat stood up. "It's getting late."

Tara looked at Cat in surprise, but stood up also.

"What are you girls going to do next?" asked Father Guzman as he walked them to the door of the Rectory.

"Oh, we'll just keep trying to find out more information," Cat said evasively. She couldn't imagine what Father Guzman would say if he knew that she and Tara planned to go to Creekside Cemetery on Halloween, of all days. The girls smiled innocently and said good-bye to him as they walked back outside.

The sun was setting, and Cat knew it was getting late and that she'd better head home. But instead she sat down on a bus-stop bench at the corner of Cardoza and Milborne Streets.

"How come you wanted to leave like that?" Tara wanted to know.

"I've just *got* to look at this book," Cat said. "I need to see it right away."

"And if the bus comes?" Tara asked.

"If it does, then we just won't get on it."

"What's the rush about the book?" Tara asked.

"I had a dream about the number eight," Cat told her. "I need to see if there is the number eight somewhere in this book. A man in my dream told me that the number eight is the only number that's real. Maybe he was talking about this book."

Tara sat down next to Cat, and they looked at the book together. "Well, there's lots of eights," Tara observed.

Cat stared at the book in dismay. It was true—there was a lot of every number. There were some letters, too. It looked like some sort of pocket-sized accounting general ledger book, perhaps a method to track inventory for a business.

"Maybe it's in code," Tara suggested.

The bus approached from down the street. The girls stood up and waved at the bus to go forward so it wouldn't stop for them. As the bus lumbered by, Cat and Tara began walking home.

"I know," Cat said. "I'll show this book to my mom. She knows all about accounting stuff. Maybe she can figure out how to read this."

But when she got home, Cat remembered that her mother had left the night before on a business trip, and wouldn't be back until late Friday night. Her father was gone too, working late again, which meant he wouldn't be back in time for dinner. Sighing, Cat saw the note on the refrigerator from her dad asking her to get dinner together for herself and for Brett.

She reached into the cupboard for a can of chili. Brett came into the kitchen and made a face when he saw what she was choosing for dinner.

"I'm not eating that," he said.

"You'll eat what I give you," Cat told him.

"Ha, who do you think you are, Mom?" Brett laughed. "Just try and make me eat chili."

"Fine, you can starve for all I care."

"Look," Brett said, "if you make macaroni and cheese instead of chili, I'll share a candy bar with you afterwards."

"Can't. Chocolate is bad for my skin,"

"If you make macaroni and cheese, I'll tell you a secret!"

"What secret?" She was interested, despite herself.

"There's a new boy who moved into an apartment on Claybourne Street. His name's Randy Harris," Brett said. "He likes you!"

"That's not a secret." Cat got a can opener out of the kitchen drawer. "Besides, how would *you* know?"

"Randy Harris has a brother, Travis, who's in my class," Brett answered. "Travis told me when he found out that you're my sister."

"So what?"

"I know something about Randy's mom!"

"What?" Cat held the can opener up, as if saying, *this had better be good or else you get chili for sure.*

"Randy's mother is a psycho," Brett said.

"What!" she cried. A fleeting memory passed through her—she thought of her conversation at the school library with Randy. He had told her: *Of course I'm not saying my mom is crazy.*

She looked at Brett. "Are you saying that Randy's mom is crazy?"

"Crazy?" Brett was puzzled. "Who said anything about crazy? I said she can read minds."

"Oh!" Cat laughed. "You mean Randy's mom is a psychic, not a psycho."

"Yeah," agreed Brett, "that's what I said—a psychic."

"No, you said...oh, never mind." Cat shook her head. "Tell me more."

"First you gotta promise me that you'll put that can of chili back and make macaroni and cheese instead."

"Well, okay, but you had better tell me *everything* you know." She put the can of chili back in the cupboard.

Brett sat at the kitchen table and watched as Cat poured water into a pan and added the macaroni. "Travis says his mom has a second sight," he said. "Travis says his mom knows things before they happen."

"All moms are like that," Cat said. "Take our mom—she always seems to know what I'm up to. I swear I can't get away with anything."

"No, not like regular moms," Brett continued. "When she was young, Travis' mom used to charge people money to read their fortunes."

"Get out of here," Cat scoffed.

"It's true," Brett swore. "Travis said so. He told me that his mom used to work at a carnival before she was married."

"Well, a lot of people are fortune tellers," Cat said, "and most of them are fake. Maybe she did work in a carnival once. Big deal, that doesn't mean she really is psychic. So what does the dad do, swing on the flying trapeze? Or is he a lion trainer?"

"That's a circus, not a carnival," Brett was annoyed that what he considered to be big news was met with scorn by his sister. "Anyway, the dad left the family right after the kids were born. They don't even know where he is. I guess Randy and Travis don't have a dad anymore."

"Everyone has a dad," Cat told him. "It's just that not all of the dads live with the families. What does Travis' mother do now? When she's not telling fortunes, that is."

"After she got married, Travis' mom worked at a grocery store, but then she got into a car accident. She's okay now, but she can't work in the grocery store anymore because she has to be in a wheelchair."

"That's why he seems so poor," Cat said thoughtfully.

"What?"

"Oh, I just figure that if Randy's mother isn't working, then that's why she can't buy any clothes for her kids."

"His mother is going to some sort of school now," Brett continued. "Travis says she'll be able to go back to work after she learns how to do a different job."

"It must be hard for her to raise two boys all by herself. Especially since she's in-between jobs."

She stirred the macaroni, which was beginning to boil. "You know what, Brett? You might not be so bad for a little brother after all. At least now I understand some more things about Randy Harris."

Chapter Eight

On Friday, the Halloween dance was part of everybody's conversation at Rivertown High School. Some kids planned to go as couples, but just as many planned to go alone or in groups. Cat invited Tara over to her house to get dressed for the dance, and when it was time, her father drove the girls to the school.

The night was clear with no wind as Cat's father dropped the girls off on the sidewalk in front of the school. Streetlights overlooked the parking lot, and the school office loomed dark and deserted. How different the school looked at night!

Activity bustled from seemingly all directions as parents dropped off their children in a parade of cars passing through the parking lot. Cat and Tara hung around the parking lot for a few minutes to talk and gossip with their friends and acquaintances. While walking to the gymnasium where the dance was to be held, the girls couldn't suppress giggles as their anticipation increased. What boys would ask them to dance? What boys would *they* ask to dance?

When they reached the gym, the school's principal, Mr. Jackson, stood in front. "Students," he told the kids, "You will see a number on your ticket. Will numbers one through fifty form a straight line? We need to check your tickets and your student identification card at the door."

"We bought our tickets together so our numbers should be almost the same. What number are you?" Cat asked. "I'm sixty-four."

"I'm sixty-five."

"Let's sit on the picnic table over here. You look great," Cat told Tara.

Tara was wearing a new pair of jeans, and had on a shiny, slinky silver top. Her dark, wavy hair had been brushed until it gleamed.

"You do, too," Tara responded.

Cat was wearing a short skirt with a funky new shirt. She wore light make-up, and her long blonde hair was pulled away from her face and pinned back, making her large, green eyes even more noticeable.

The girls looked at how the other kids were dressed. A few of the bolder ones wore Halloween costumes, but most wore regular clothes. Some kids were dressed a little nicer than they would ordinarily dress.

"Will numbers fifty-one through one hundred make a straight line?" Mr. Jackson called.

"That's us!" Cat cried excitedly. She couldn't wait to get inside.

As they got in line, a boy named David stood behind them. "Hey Tara. Hey Cat. S'up?"

The line moved quickly. Cat glanced around, hoping to locate Randy Harris, but he was nowhere to be seen.

Inside, everyone took off his or her shoes to protect the wooden floor. The well-lighted gym had doors going to the girl's locker room off to the left, and the boy's locker room to the right. There was a stage against the back wall, but the curtains were closed so no one could see into it. In front of the stage, set up on the floor, was a disc jockey mini-station.

They looked at the decorations. A mirrored disco ball was rotating on the ceiling. Black and orange balloons were taped to all four walls of the gym. Some of the older kids were clowning around and pulling the decorations down. Cat heard the sound of popping balloons as three of the kids began stomping on them.

"Stop that, or we'll end this dance right now, even before it begins!" yelled Mr. Jackson. Everybody straightened up, and from then on, the balloons were safe.

By the stage, next to the deejay, teachers were serving soft drinks. There were chairs set out against the walls and people had already started to sit down. Others stood in groups, talking and laughing.

Suddenly the lights in the gym were turned off, and that meant that the dance had officially begun. The deejay had more energy than even the balloon-poppers, and he danced in place to the loud music he played. Colored lights shone from a spotlight on the console, aimed at the disco ball, which was still revolving on the ceiling. The colored lights reflected off the mirrored surface of the ball to create a sort of strobe-light effect in the room.

The song playing was one that played on the radio a lot. Kids were already starting to head for the dance floor. A boy tapped Tara on the shoulder and asked her to dance. He had to shout to be heard above the music, but Tara understood and went with him. She got onto the floor, and moved her hips and her shoulders in rhythm to the music.

Cat stood alone, feeling awkward. But soon a boy approached her. It was David, who had been standing in line behind them while they were outside. He asked her if she felt like dancing, also yelling above the loud music. Cat didn't waste energy trying to yell, so she just smiled and nodded, and she and David went to the dance floor.

It was so much fun. Secretly, Cat watched the other dancers out of the corners of her eyes and imitated the ones whom she thought danced well. She swiveled her hips and made sure her hair swayed with her movements. Her feet moved to the beat and her elbows were bent. Her hands moved ever so slightly back and forth, keeping time.

The song ended quicker than it seemed that it should, and Cat met Tara against the gym wall. She felt energized by the dancing and was ready to do it again. The deejay played a heavy metal song, and Tara cried, "Come on, let's join the 'mosh pit!"

They joined a group of kids who were bouncing, jumping, and intensely swinging their heads. The kids were dancing with complete adrenaline, as they hopped up and down and bumped into others.

Mr. Jackson stopped the song. "Students!" he yelled. "You've got to settle down! We'll have none of that! Somebody could get hurt."

The deejay put on a slow song, and everybody stopped the rowdiness. The rest of the dance went along without anyone getting into any more trouble.

David came back to Cat and Tara, and this time he asked Tara to dance. As Tara went onto the dance floor, Cat couldn't help feeling a little jealous, despite the fact that Tara was her best friend. *How come she always gets asked to dance more than I do? Here I am just standing alone again. Maybe I should ask a boy to dance.*

She stood all by herself, feeling self-conscious. But then she felt a tapping on her shoulder, and when she turned around, she was looking into the cute brown eyes of Randy Harris.

"I saw you dancing," he told her. He had to shout to be heard. "I was hoping I'd get a turn with you."

"I didn't think you were coming." At that instant, she realized how glad she was to see him, and how much she had been hoping he would be there.

"I was a little late," he yelled. "I had to walk to the school."

"You walked in the dark? You know, I can hardly hear you over the music," Cat yelled back.

Randy grabbed her hand. "Let's dance!"

As he led her to the dance floor, he still had hold of her hand. They bumped into another couple, and wouldn't you know it—it was Brian Castleman and Ashley Long.

"Ha!" cried Ashley. "Two losers together."

As Ashley twirled around to begin dancing with Brian, she stumbled and started to fall. Brian caught Ashley right before she hit the floor, but the people around them laughed.

Cat didn't laugh. She no longer cared what Ashley and Brian thought or what they did. It just simply ceased to matter to her.

She felt a renewed confidence in herself, and didn't mind that she was dancing with someone who wore out-dated clothes. Randy was cute, he was nice, and the way he looked at her gave her a happy feeling.

As far as Cat was concerned, there was nothing wrong with Randy; instead, there was everything right with him. She felt she had her own mind and nobody should make up her mind for her. Certainly Randy treated her better than Brian ever had. She smiled at the thought, and suddenly realized that she had her sense of values back on track.

David seemed to like Tara. They danced most of the dances together. Cat was happy to be with Randy, and she knew the feeling was mutual. They danced together for the rest of the evening.

What a workout! By eight-thirty, all the kids seemed to be sweating. Still, the dancing continued at a frenzied pace. Cat saw the teachers shake their heads in envy, as though they were remembering what it was like when they were that young and had so much energy.

But the clock soon said ten, and the dance was over just as quickly as it had begun, it seemed. The deejay had played the last song; a slow one to calm the kids in preparation for the mass exit, and Cat danced with Randy while Tara danced with David.

Outside the gym, David told Tara goodbye. He asked for her phone number, and she gave it to him.

Cat asked Randy if he'd like her number. He reddened, and told her that his family didn't have a land-line, much less any cell phones.

Cat was amazed. She thought that in this day and age, *everyone* had a telephone. She asked Randy how he was getting home, since he had walked to the dance.

"Walking," he said matter-of-factly. "Normally my mom would drive me, but my brother is sick tonight, so she stayed home with him."

"Why don't you catch a ride home with my dad?" she asked. "I'm positive he won't mind."

Cat, Tara, and Randy strolled in the moonlight to the school's parking lot. Again the parade of parents drove through the parking lot, only this time the cars were congested, and went at a snail's pace. Cat spotted her dad's white Toyota among the numerous cars. "Over there," she pointed.

As all three kids clambered into the Toyota, she asked her dad to take Randy home. When they finally navigated out of the crowded school parking lot, Mr. Daniels asked Randy where he lived.

"On Claybourne Street," he replied.

Cat was sitting in the front seat, and noticed that her father's mouth tightened into a frown. She wondered why, but decided not to ask. She turned to Randy and Tara in the back seat. "I had the best time tonight," she told them.

"Me too," chimed Tara, then she joked, "I think I'm in love with David."

"Love must be going around," Randy said, and winked at Cat.

As Randy gave Mr. Daniels directions to his apartment, Cat thought that she was beginning to understand why her father had frowned when he learned of the address. The neighborhood was a little scary, all dark because most streetlights were not working properly. The apartments on Claybourne Street were old and seemed to be maintained poorly. Children's toys and old barbecue grills were scattered around the doorways of the apartments.

"I'll see you Monday," Randy said as he got out of the car.

When Randy was gone, Cat's father drove away. "Is that the kind of kids you hang out with?" he asked his daughter.

"What do you mean?"

"Well, he sure comes from a rough neighborhood."

"So?"

"I don't know if I want you to associate with that type of boy," Mr. Daniels said. "What kind of grades does he get?"

"I have no idea," she answered. "Look Dad, Randy's mom is in-between jobs right now. I don't think we should think any less of Randy just because his family doesn't have as much money as ours does. That's not fair."

"Fair or not," Mr. Daniels said, "this is the 'real world.' I'm concerned about who you associate with. I don't want you hanging around kids that are no good."

"Wait a minute!" Cat cried. "How did we go from being poor to being no good?"

"People who have what it takes to make it in life are the ones who do," Mr. Daniels told her. "There's no reason why anyone should be poor unless they simply have no gumption."

"That's not always true. I've been reading about the Great Depression in the 1930s. A lot of people were poor then, and it was nobody's fault. Even today, sometimes things go wrong. Sometimes fate gets out of people's control. Remember the recession of 2009."

"I don't want you going to his part of town," Mr. Daniels warned.

"Okay, but maybe Randy can come over to our house some time," Cat said. "And listen, Randy's mom is disabled. She's in a wheelchair now because she got into a car accident. That goes along with the idea that sometimes people have no control over fate. *But—* now she's going to school to learn a new job. Randy's mom wants to take control of her life, and she wants to change her situation. I'd say that is *plenty* of gumption."

Her dad grunted in reply as he drove to Tara's house to drop her off.

At around nine o'clock the following morning, the smell of frying bacon awoke Cat. Her stomach growled, commanding her to get up and find out who was cooking breakfast. Then she realized, *of course—Mom came home last night.*

Excitedly she grabbed the little brown ledger book that Father Guzman had given her. Maybe her mom could figure it out. She hurriedly put on her robe and went barefoot into the kitchen.

"Happy Halloween!" her mom said by way of a greeting. "How many eggs?"

"Three." Cat sat at the kitchen table. "That's right, today is Halloween, isn't it? Mom—"

"Three eggs?" Mrs. Daniels interrupted. "You must really be hungry after all that dancing last night."

"Mom," she began again, "I have a book I'd like you to look at." She held up the little brown ledger book.

"Where did you get that? It looks really old."

"It is. This is a ledger book from the 1930s. I got it on loan from a priest, if you can believe that. Could you take a look at it? I was hoping you could tell me what it says."

"Right after breakfast."

Brett was already at the table. He was wolfing down his eggs.

"You're disgusting," Cat told him.

"What's your problem?" Brett said, then opened his mouth, which was full of egg. Cat groaned.

When breakfast was over, she got dressed hurriedly. She grabbed the book and gave it to her mother. Mrs. Daniels took the book with her into the living room. Sitting on the couch, Mrs. Daniels opened the ledger book and began to read.

"Well," she said, "this is a ledger of accounts payable and accounts receivable. That means it is a record of money owed to others and also of money received from others. On the surface, everything looks like normal business transactions. But..." she stopped talking.

"But what?" Cat held her breath.

"But something is wrong here." Cat's mother was turning the pages. "There are some numbers that don't balance. Let me put it this way: a normal accounting ledger has two sides, a plus and a minus. They are supposed to agree. But every so often, this ledger gets out of balance on the plus side. Then there are special notations that look like bank deposit entries. I can't say for sure, but this book looks like a record of illegal activities. It looks like someone was keeping track of fraudulent transactions."

"What are fraudulent transactions?"

"It means a situation where a business is doing things to cheat clients and then covering up their tracks. Why on earth would a priest have a fraudulent ledger book?"

"I think it's evidence of a crime," Cat said.

"Whatever crime, it must have happened a long, long time ago. Just look at how yellowed these pages are. It was written with a type of pen that nobody ever sees anymore. And this book even smells old."

"I told you the book is from the 1930s," Cat said. "Are you sure it shows illegal activity? And...does the number eight mean anything special in this book?"

Mrs. Daniels looked at her daughter in surprise. "You told me you didn't know what this book meant. Then how did you know the number eight was different?"

"I just had a feeling." She wouldn't look her mother in the eyes. She realized her mother knew she was hiding something, but for some reason Mrs. Daniels didn't pursue it.

"You could describe it as a number eight, but it's really an infinity sign," Mrs. Daniels spoke thoughtfully. "The infinity sign looks like the number eight turned sideways."

"What do you mean by an infinity sign?" Cat looked at it, and realized that it did indeed look like the number eight lying on its side.

"It's a symbol that means forever," her mother answered.

"What about it?"

"Every time there was a bank deposit, it was followed by the infinity sign, you know, the number eight on its side. I think that was a code so that the owner of this ledger book could quickly look down the page and see how much money he or she had. And since each illegal amount has that sign, he or she could figure out how much stolen cash there was in a hurry."

"How illegal does it look?"

"What do you mean?"

"I mean," Cat continued, "the entries in this book. Are they it just a little illegal or are they *really* bad?"

"By 1930s standards, this book looks *really* bad," Mrs. Daniels said. "This looks so bad, that although the amount of money stolen wouldn't seem like a whole lot now, back in those days, someone was getting *very* rich. And doing it *very* illegally."

"Do you think it's bad enough that someone would kill to keep this evidence from being found out?"

"So that's why this book is evidence," Mrs. Daniels said. "Well, let's look at the facts. Fact one, this book is proof of highly illegal activity. Fact two, a person who would get involved with such illegal activity must not have been a very good type of person. Probably that person would not want to go to jail. Fact three, the 1930s was the time of the Great Depression. Maybe the owner of this book was someone who didn't want to be poor. Desperation can make people who aren't very decent to begin with even worse. I'd say that yes, murder could be a possibility to keep this ledger hidden. I wonder why the owner of the ledger didn't just get rid of it if he or she felt it could put them in jail?"

Cat was amazed at how suddenly, the pieces of the puzzle seemed to fall into place. "I think the ledger's owner was a man named Henry Foster. I think another man, named Mark Stratton, stole the ledger book from Henry and gave it to a priest. I think the priest was going to turn it into the sheriff but before he could, the priest was killed in a car accident."

"These things happened in the 1930s?" Cat's mother asked.

"1935 to be exact."

"So—what happened to Henry Foster? He can't be still alive. That's seventy years ago."

"I don't know, but I intend to find out." Cat took the book back from her mother and put it in her backpack. She got up to leave the living room, but then hesitated. "Mom, how do we know that something like the Great Depression won't happen again?"

Cat's mother smiled. "There've been a lot of lessons learned from the Great Depression. Changes have been put into place. Nowadays, the government watches the money of this country. In 1933, there was an agency formed called the Federal Deposit Insurance Corporation. They guarantee that if a bank goes out of business, the customers of that bank will get their money back. These days, the government insures the banks so that the money is paid to customers no matter what. So, today no one in America could lose any money that they put into a bank, even if the bank itself develops problems."

Mrs. Daniels continued, "Also, in 1935, Unemployment Insurance was started. That means, if people lose their job through no fault of their own, they still get a paycheck for awhile while they look for another job. Unemployment Insurance would pay for it. Let's see, what else is there? Oh yes, the Securities and Exchange Commission. That commission was formed to be the 'watchdog' of the stock market, and they can halt trading if the market falls too far. They started in the 1930s, too. So you see, there are a lot more laws and agencies around these days to try to prevent a repeat of the Great Depression here in the United States. A lot has changed for the better since the 1930s. I think that is why President Obama was able to stop the country from sliding into another Great Depression in 2009."

Cat was relieved. "I wouldn't want to have to beg food to feed Brett."

"What in the world are you talking about?" her mother laughed.

"Forget it. I'm going over to Tara's house." She slung her backpack over her shoulder. It was off to Creekside Cemetery again, but she most certainly was not going to admit that to her mother.

"Be back around four o'clock," Mrs. Daniels told her. "We're going to eat dinner by five because we want to be finished before the trick-o'-treaters start coming around."

Chapter Nine

As the girls began the long walk to Creekside Cemetery, Cat was nervous. Again the sky was overcast, and black clouds advanced from the west. *Why do our trips to the cemetery always coincide with an approaching storm?* Cat wondered. It was as if an ominous force sensed where they were headed and was determined to make its disapproval known.

Neither girl spoke much during the walk. The farther away from the populated areas they traveled, the quieter they became. By the time they reached the cracked and uneven concrete slabs that began at the outskirts of town, both girls were completely silent, lost in their own thoughts. They stepped carefully, as the sidewalk alternatively rose and sank, with grass pushing through the cracks. In the fields, weeds grew with wild abandon. Cat looked at the limbs on the feral trees—how their twisted branches resembled fingers beckoning them forward.

"Everything seems spooky out here," Tara commented.

"It's just that everything is so wild," Cat reassured Tara. "Things seem to have a life of their own out here."

Tara didn't seem reassured. "I have a bad feeling about today."

"Let's get it over with. We've come this far. We'll talk to Mr. Gatland, and then we'll leave. We won't stay very long."

The girls reached Road 18. They saw a rusty old pickup truck parked in front of the old, cast-iron arbor that was the entrance to Creekside Cemetery. "That means Mr. Gatland must already be here," Cat observed.

Everything seemed quiet—too quiet. The sense of stillness was overpowering. Where were the birds? Where were the insects, or the squirrels? There was simply no sound, no motion, as if all the creatures were silently hiding; watching and waiting.

They came to the entrance of the graveyard. A slight wind picked up. The intense stillness was finally broken, and movement began again, as though the world was releasing the breath it held. A creaking noise sounded, as two twisted limbs of an old, gnarled tree rubbed together in the soft breeze. The weeds fluttered with a sighing sound. The ground rustled with small creatures that fled into their holes and other hiding spots, seeking shelter in dark places.

They entered the cemetery, and the uneven gravel road crunched beneath their feet. The girls carefully picked their way through prickly weeds with cheerful yellow flowers that belied the thorns hiding underneath. Passing by a centuries-old oak, they reached the first family plot, and noticed the moss and lichens on the cement border. The entire cemetery was bent with age, as gravity pulled tree limbs towards the earth, and many headstones lay prone on the ground, victims of time and vandalism.

Creekside Cemetery felt even more sinister than the last time they were here—almost scary. They were watchful, eyeing all directions as they continued. They had seen the pickup truck parked in front of the cemetery on Road 18, and they figured the truck belonged to Mr. Gatland. So where was he?

A man suddenly appeared from behind a tree, and the girls were startled. He was tall, gaunt, and wore jeans and a plaid lumberjack shirt. He had dark brown hair and had the beginnings of a beard; the stubble on his chin was flecked with gray.

"Hey there!" he called. "Are you Cat and Tara? Of course you are," he continued before the girls could answer. "Did I scare you?"

"No," Tara lied, "not at all."

"We knew you were here because we saw your truck," Cat added. "Are you Mr. Gatland?"

"Call me Bob," he said, and strode up to them. "Are you sure I didn't scare you?" he asked hopefully.

"Well," Tara admitted, "maybe we were a little scared, because you just jumped out from nowhere. And, this *is* Halloween, and this *is* a graveyard."

"That's right," Bob guffawed. "Say, girls, do you want a tour of Creekside Cemetery? Unfortunately there's been some more vandalism lately. I have to keep a special eye on the Foster graves. They were sort of famous back in the 1930s, so vandals target them the most."

"We've heard the stories," Cat said. "The newspapers claimed their daughter murdered them."

"Ain't no 'claimed' about it," Bob said. "The daughter *did* do it."

Cat asked, trying to sound casual. "Can you show us where other people are buried? Do you know, for instance, if there's anyone buried behind the Foster graves? And do you know where Mark Stratton is buried?"

"Now, how in the world do you know about Mark Stratton?"

"Oh," Cat quickly thought up a story. She didn't want Bob to know how much she and Tara knew about the history of Jessica Foster and Mark Stratton. "We had local history as a class project last week. You know, we learned about some of the people who lived in Rivertown a long time ago. The Foster murders are sort of a legend, and we were told that Mark Stratton was their son-in-law."

Bob turned his intense stare on Cat. "Mark Stratton never married anybody. And I never heard of a school teaching kids about murder cases."

"Well, at our school, they did," Tara spoke up. Bob turned to look at Tara.

Cat wondered silently, *Does Mr. Gatland really believe that Mark and Jessica never married, or is he deliberately lying?* Time seemed to slow to a crawl as Bob and Tara stared intently at each other. Cat had a fleeting thought: *This man could be dangerous.*

Then suddenly, Bob's face lit up in a grin and his whole appearance changed. "Okay, girls," he said cheerfully, "I'll give you murder stories. What better way to spend Halloween, right? But first I want to show you where all my relatives are buried."

He led the girls through the small cemetery, pointing out headstones, and identifying his cousins and grandparents that lay underground.

Eventually Bob made his way back to the Foster gravesite, and the girls followed on the ancient, cracked pavement in front of the large, raised bed. They looked at the seven-inch high cement border, where inside no grass was planted. There it was—the large tombstone that contained both Foster names.

"Can you tell us the story about the Fosters?" Cat asked. She wanted to hear Bob's version.

Bob began. "The tombstone says, *Joined in life through marriage, joined in death through tragedy. James R. Foster, died November 1, 1935. Edith S. Foster, died November 1, 1935.*"

He told the story. "The Fosters had a daughter named Jessie. She was pregnant and wouldn't tell anybody who the father was. So James and Edith told Jessie she would get no money from them. Well, Jessie didn't take to that one bit. Story goes, in the dead of night over eighty-five years ago, Jessie crept into her parents' house, sneaked into their bedroom under the cloak of darkness, and then *wham!* She murdered her own parents with a kitchen knife. Tonight is the anniversary of the Fosters' death—right after midnight tonight."

Completely unnerved, Cat dropped her backpack onto the ground. The little brown ledger book dropped out and rolled almost to Bob's feet.

"What's that?" he cried.

Cat lunged for the book, grabbing it before Bob could reach for it. She shoved it back into her backpack.

"What's that?" Bob repeated. "It looked like a ledger book."

"It's nothing," Cat told him.

"Let me see it!" Bob demanded. Cat could tell by his reaction that Bob already knew what the little ledger book contained.

"I told you it's nothing!" Cat cried.

"That book doesn't belong to you," Bob told her sternly. "Give it to me and I'll return it to its rightful owner."

"Who is its rightful owner? Do you mean Henry Foster? Is he still alive?" Cat was prepared to fight for the book if she had to.

But suddenly she was distracted by something she saw over Bob's shoulder; something that caught her eye. Bob was facing her and had his back to the Foster gravesite, so he didn't see what was behind him. But she could sense Tara stiffening, so she knew Tara saw it, too.

There was a shimmering light floating over the weeds behind the Foster gravesite. It was translucent and sparkled as though it was sprinkled with morning dew. It got stronger until it formed the shape of a person, but still it lacked any details, as though it was unfinished. The form seemed delicate and moved like waves in the ocean.

Both Cat and Tara continued to stare, their mouths open in surprise. Their hearts pounded in their chests as fear pumped through their veins, but the girls didn't run. It was as though they were so frightened, they were frozen in place.

Cat felt horribly afraid, but she couldn't stop herself from staring at what was floating above the ground. It moved and drifted in and out of sight, sometimes appearing easier to see, and other times almost disappearing.

The nearly transparent shape hovered in place, undulating as it shimmered. It resembled lace, having some substance, but thin enough to be able to see through it. It was a specter, a phantom; an elusive apparition that seemed like an impossibility, but it was there all the same.

Was it a ghost? Was she really seeing an actual ghost? Goosebumps raised the hair upright upon her arms, and she remained rooted in place, unable to move. She stared breathlessly at the ghost in the cemetery. She was too afraid to run, but she couldn't look away, either, even though she wanted to close her eyes.

Ohmygosh, Cat thought in alarm, *I really think I'm seeing a dead person come back to haunt Creekside Cemetery.*

Then suddenly, the ghost faded into a mist and then it simply disappeared from sight.

Bob, seeing the girls' expressions, turned around, but he was too late to witness anything. "What?" he asked in puzzlement.

"I think we just saw a ghost," Tara said, her voice cracking.

"You girls have had too much Halloween."

Cat realized she had been holding her breath, and she let it loose. "Let's go look at where it was!"

The girls rushed to the area behind the Foster gravesites, and Bob followed. There was a circular area on the ground where the weeds were strangely absent. Scratched on the surface of the earth, as though written in the dirt with a big, pointed stick, were the words, *She's here.*

"Ohmygosh!" Tara cried.

"It must mean Jessie!" Cat exclaimed. "Jessie is buried here!"

In a sudden rage, Bob jumped on the letters and furiously kicked his feet, stomping and scuffing up the dirt until the writing was completely covered with earth, sticks, and weeds. "Vandals!" he shouted. "It was just vandals!"

Cat and Tara both dropped their backpacks. "Don't!" they cried in unison.

Bob stopped. "Listen to me, don't you go getting any ideas about Jessica Foster being buried here. She isn't," he hissed at them. "She knew she would be caught for murdering her parents and so she ran away. Okay, there's someone buried here in this spot. But it ain't Jessica Foster."

Cat asked, "Then who *is* buried here?"

"Mark Stratton. Mark Stratton was buried here in December of 1935. He was killed in a fall. Seems he fell on some farm machinery. He was very, very poor when he died, so there's never been a tombstone here. Oh, there might have been a wooden cross at one time, but was over eighty-five years ago."

"Mark is buried here," Cat said softly in wonderment. She stood staring at the ground in fascination. She could still picture the ghost in her mind, hovering and shimmering. Now that it was gone, Cat no longer felt any fear.

Had the ghost been trying to communicate? Did it leave the words on the ground? Did the ghost write *She's here*? What was the ghost trying to tell them? If Mark Stratton was buried underneath this piece of ground, why wouldn't the ghost have written *He's here?*

"Cat, I want to leave this place," Tara said. "I admit it. I'm scared."

Cat was also upset. It was one thing to dream about ghosts, but to actually see one in real life was an entirely different matter. "Yeah," she agreed, "I'd like to leave too."

"Here, don't forget your backpacks," Bob had one of them in his hands. He had picked it up off the ground. "Do you need a ride?"

"No, we don't live very far," Tara said. Neither girl felt safe with Bob, and they sure didn't want to get into a car with him. "Thanks for the tour."

Cat picked up the other backpack, and the girls walked back to the graveyard's gravel road.

When they reached the centuries-old oak tree that stood sentry at the cast-iron arbor, Cat ducked behind it. She opened her backpack and searched inside.

"What are you doing?" Tara asked.

"The ledger," Cat said frantically. "I want to make sure it's still in here. Yes, here it is." She sighed in relief as her fingers touched the ledger book.

"It was *my* backpack that Bob had in his hands," Tara commented.

"Your backpack looks just like mine. Maybe just to be safe, you'd better take a look inside yours to see if anything's missing. I think Mr. Gatland wanted this ledger book. I have a feeling he knows what it is. I wouldn't put it past him to try to steal it."

Tara rummaged around in her backpack. "Oh no," she said, "I can't find my address book."

"Are you sure?"

"Positive." Tara stopped searching and looked at Cat. "And you know what? My address book looked just like your little ledger book."

"Do you think Bob took it, thinking it was this ledger book?"

"At this point, I don't care," Tara said. "I'm sure not going back to ask him for that address book. I just want to get out of Creekside Cemetery. I never want to see this haunted place ever again. And I never want to see Bob Gatland again, either."

The girls walked past the cast-iron arbor towards Road 18, gravel crunching under their feet. All the way home, they discussed the ghostly visitation, and also the odd behavior of Mr. Gatland.

Chapter Ten

That night, Cat ate her dinner quickly. She wanted to get to Tara's house before the little kids began the trick-o'-treating. When she first felt she was too old to trick-o'-treat, she missed the fun. She missed joining the neighborhood kids when they held out bags for candy as they went from house to house. But soon she found out that it was also fun to answer the door and give the candy out. It was interesting to see all the different costumes, from store-bought garments to creative homemade ensembles. She could always tell what Saturday morning cartoon was popular by the costumes the little kids wore on Halloween night.

"Can I spend the night at Tara's?" she asked her parents at dinner. Her father cleared his throat. He was the more cautious parent of the two.

"Where will her mom and dad be?" he asked.

"Well," Cat began, for it was well known that Tara's parents went out frequently, "they're going to a party, but they told Tara that they would be home by one AM."

"That's a long time for two young girls to be alone at night," Mr. Daniels said.

Cat turned to her mother. "Mom, would you tell Dad that I am fifteen years old, and that means I am old enough to take care of myself for a few hours?"

"Halloween is a bad night to be alone," she replied.

"Listen," Cat pleaded. "Tara only lives three houses away. I could call you if I get scared, and you could be there in two seconds. And if I don't spend the night, Tara would be all by herself, and that's even worse."

"Tara is not our child, and you are," Mr. Daniels said. "But I suppose, if it is okay with your mother, then it's okay with me for you to spend the night with Tara."

"Mom?" Cat asked, but she already knew she had won.

"Make sure you take clean pajamas," Mrs. Daniels told her. "And don't forget your toothbrush."

Cat started walking to Tara's house at five-thirty. Thunder rumbled, and Cat noticed that the impending storm, which seemed so distant earlier in the day, had now moved much closer. The air

274

smelled like rain. She hoped the rain wouldn't start until all the neighborhood children had a chance to trick-o'-treat.

By the time she got there, Tara's parents had already left, so the girls were alone. Tara showed her a huge bowl of candy for the trick-o'-treaters they anticipated would be arriving soon. Laughing, both girls helped themselves to the candy.

"We deserve Halloween treats too," Tara smiled. "After all, we have to keep our energy levels up so we can keep answering the door."

No sooner had she spoken then the doorbell rang. Cat swung open the door and Tara grabbed the candy bowl. Their first trick-o'-treaters were the littlest children, being carefully guarded by watchful parents.

"How sweet!" Tara exclaimed as they observed their visitors. Two children were on the porch, both about four years old. The boy was dressed as a Dalmatian puppy, and the girl was dressed as a princess, complete with a crown.

"Trick-o'-treat!" the children cried.

Tara distributed the treats.

And it continued as such for the next hour. After that, older kids rang the doorbell. Most of the older ones were dressed as hobos and gypsies. As the night continued, eventually the oldest kids came around. Some of the oldest kids didn't wear costumes at all.

Finally, at around nine o'clock, kids stopped coming. By this time, Cat and Tara were relieved to be finished, because although at first it had been a lot of fun to see all the different costumes; after awhile, it became almost like work to keep answering the door time after time.

The girls left the living room to go to the family room, which was located at the rear of the house.

"I rented some movies," Tara said as she started the Blu-ray player.

"Any scary ones?"

"Of course."

Lightning flashed, visible through the sliding glass back door, and rain came pelting down on the back porch. Tara lived in a two-story house, with the stairs off to the side of the family room. The kitchen was next to the stairs, separated from the family room by a counter and bar stools. On the opposite side of the room, a brick wall contained a fireplace that went mostly unused.

The girls turned off the family room light to create a spooky atmosphere, but left the kitchen light on 'just in case.' After all, they'd had a frightening encounter at Creekside Cemetery earlier in the day, and neither girl had completely recovered from that experience. Still, it seemed appropriate to darken the room and watch scary movies to get the most out of a stormy Halloween night.

They ate popcorn and watched the movies. Tara lay on the couch, and Cat stretched out on the floor carpet. The movie they watched was not as exciting as the cover promised, so soon the girls fell asleep. They slept quietly, taking in breaths slowly and deeply.

Lightning lit up the family room, and, still lying on the floor, Cat turned over to face the couch. She was disturbed by the thunder that followed. The thunder subsided, but it had woken her. She was dimly aware that the movie had ended.

Tara's house was silent, except for a faint dripping from the kitchen faucet. Rain still fell outside, and sounded loud as it dripped on the metal drain spouts. Sometimes the corners of the house would creak as the wood settled in the damp weather.

Cat was in-between sleep and wakefulness, drifting, when a sound caught her attention. This sound was different from the sounds of the rain falling outside.

She sat up and noticed that the kitchen light had gone out. Tara's house was very, very dark.

Suddenly scared, Cat shook Tara, who stirred on the couch. "Why is the kitchen light off?"

"I don't know." Tara was groggy with sleep. "Maybe the bulb burned out."

Lightning flashed, and Cat saw the back porch illuminated through the sliding glass doors. She could swear she saw movement on the back porch. Was it a dog?

The thunder followed, and she strained to see out the door, but it was so dark that she couldn't see anything.

She shook Tara again and pointed to the back door. "I saw something out there."

"There's nothing now," Tara told her and rolled over on the couch.

But Cat wasn't so calm. She was so sure she had seen something. What she had seen, she didn't know, but she had seen *something*.

She kept staring in the darkness, her eyes glued on the glass of the back door.

Then lightning stuck again, illuminating the back yard.

There! Cat saw something again. It was a person! There was a person in Tara's back yard! He was right outside the sliding glass door!

Her heart felt as though it skipped a beat as she saw a dark shape in that brief instant the lightning had lit up the sky. There was a man out on the back porch. Was he trying to look inside?

"Tara!" Cat whispered in terror, "I did see someone! There's a man on your porch!"

Instantly awake, Tara gasped in fright. She sat bolt upright on the couch. Thunder sounded, and the girls could no longer see outside.

"Ohmygosh, are you sure there's somebody out there?" Tara cried.

"Don't let him hear you," Cat whispered frantically. "The phone. Where's your cell phone? I forgot mine."

"I don't know. But there's a land line in the kitchen, you know that."

For a moment, Cat felt almost too terrified to move. But both girls got up, huddled together, and made their way through the darkness into the kitchen as the storm got worse, and began to rage outside. Rain slammed against the windows.

Tara grabbed the phone. She dropped it. "It's dead!"

"Are you sure?" Cat picked the phone cradle off the floor to listen for the dial tone. There was no sound on the phone.

Cat started shaking. She began thinking frantically: *Will the man try to break into the house? Will he come after us? What can we do? Where can we run?* "You need to find your cell phone!"

Tara started to cry. "I haven't been able to find it for two days now."

"Do you have another land line?" Cat asked frantically.

"In my parents' bedroom upstairs."

The girls raced for the staircase, and pounded up the stairs, staying close to each other. They flipped on the upstairs hall light switch.

Nothing.

There was no light. The whole house was dark. Very dark.

"This way." Tara led the way down the hallway into the last room on the right. Both girls burst into the bedroom, and Tara grabbed the cradle of the phone that was sitting on the table by the bed.

Nothing. There was no dial tone on this phone, either.

Lightning flashed, and thunder soon followed. The storm seemed to reach its peak, as rain pelted the roof furiously.

"Do you think the storm knocked out the electricity?" Tara asked desperately.

"I don't think the storm would wipe out *both* the lights and the phone."

"What are you saying?"

"Maybe that man outside cut the wires. Maybe he wants to rob the house. Maybe he doesn't think anyone is home."

"If he didn't think anyone was home, he wouldn't have bothered to cut the wires." Tara said.

"Tara," a new thought hit Cat, "did we lock the back door? Did we remember to lock the sliding glass door?"

Tara was still sobbing quietly. "I don't know."

Suddenly they both heard the sound. It was a banging noise, as though someone had tripped over a barstool in the dark kitchen downstairs.

"The man!" Cat was horrified, and so very, very afraid. "He's in the house. He broke in. He's inside the house!"

"What are we going to do?" Tara wailed, no longer quiet.

"Can we lock this bedroom door?"

"No, none of the bedrooms have locks."

"There's a big tree outside this window. Can we climb down it?"

They could hear the intruder coming up the stairs. He seemed to be groping in the darkness, the steps creaking under his weight.

"Can we climb the tree?" Cat repeated frantically.

"I don't know."

"We have to try," Cat said desperately.

They flung open the window and pushed out the screen, and it fell down to the ground, so far below. Rain spewed in, pounding against their faces and splashing into the room. The wind blew furiously, and a branch of the old oak tree banged against the house. How could they climb down that wet, slippery old tree?

Suddenly, the girls heard the bedroom door crash open with a loud boom as it hit the wall with the force of the intruder's push. That meant the man was in the bedroom! He was coming after them.

"Where's the ledger?" the intruder screamed, and Cat's heart raced. She glanced back into the room to see a dark shape approach. She could hear him shout above the noise of the storm. "Give me the ledger book!"

She realized it was now or never.

She pushed Tara out the window and then she went out the window herself, grabbing a large limb that almost touched the windowsill. She gripped the rough tree tightly as the storm tried its best to blow her off. Rain hit her like sharp needles, making the tree's bark slick and difficult to hold. She was horribly afraid, but she was more afraid of the intruder than of a potential fall.

The girls began to climb down the old oak tree, carefully finding branches to grip with their hands and notches upon which their feet could step. Carefully, carefully—and the storm raged around them. They moved slowly, one inch here and one inch there. They found themselves closer to the ground every moment…closer and closer to safety. If they could only reach the ground before the stranger came after them!

Please, oh please, Cat thought.

Suddenly she saw Tara leap the remaining distance to the ground, and she followed her friend. They had made it!

The girls slid when they hit the slick mud on the ground. Both of them were freezing and soaked in their wet pajamas, their hair in dripping ribbons as it hung around their faces. They hugged each other for a quick moment, then both ran toward Cat's house. They ran as fast as they could, splashing in the mud, running for their lives.

They ran together towards Cat's house.

They made it! They would be safe now.

<< — >>

The girls did not witness the scene unfolding in the upstairs bedroom of Tara's house. The intruder ran to the window, but he was too late to catch the girls. He pounded the windowsill in frustration, cursing his mistake. Surely the girls would go to the police.

He had to find the ledger before the police came.

He thought to himself that he would tear the house apart to find it, just as his grandfather had torn apart the Foster house so many years before. In 1935, the police had assumed his grandfather was looking for hidden money, when instead James Foster's household had been ransacked in search of the ledger book.

The intruder's grandfather was Henry Foster.

The intruder knew that all those years ago, Mark Stratton had stolen the ledger book, and intended to use it against his grandfather. He wondered in frustration: *Where had the ledger been all these years? Where has it been since 1935? Who had Mark Stratton given it to—was it true that he had given it to that priest, Father Santiago?*

But Father Santiago did not have it with him the night Henry Foster had killed the priest by running his car off the road. So who had the ledger book all these years?

The intruder turned away from the windowsill. He suddenly stopped, not believing his eyes.

A shape formed in the darkness, and the intruder suppressed a scream.

It looked like a ghost, appearing in the bedroom.

The specter glowed in illuminated brightness. It gained in intensity until it formed the shape of a person, but still it lacked any details, as though it was unfinished. The form seemed delicate and moved like waves in the ocean.

The intruder had no way of knowing that this was the same ghost the girls had witnessed earlier in the day at Creekside Cemetery.

"The end is near," the intruder heard a voice, seemingly coming from nowhere except in his own mind. But the intruder knew it was the ghost who was speaking. "The truth will be known."

The intruder felt a sharp pain in his left arm, and then his chest seemed to experience a great weight as though it were crushed underneath a huge rock. He felt cold and clammy, nauseous, and couldn't catch his breath.

The intruder lost consciousness and slowly dropped to the floor.

Only then did the ghost disappear.

Chapter Eleven

Two hysterical girls pounded the front door at Cat's house after midnight. Since they were wearing only rain-soaked pajamas, neither one had a key. "Open up!" they screamed. "Let us in!"

The porch light turned on, and the door swung open. The girls ran, crying and shaking, to the security of Cat's parents. Now that they knew they were finally safe, both girls sobbed with relief.

The police were summoned, and arrived quickly. Cat and Tara changed into clean, dry pajamas and robes. They calmed down remarkably, considering the circumstances, and were able to tell the sheriff's deputies all that had happened at Tara's house.

Brett came into the living room, having been awakened by all of the excitement, and he stood in the corner of the room, staring with his eyes open wide. Cat figured that Brett was thinking along the lines of what a great story this would be to tell all of his friends at school. She knew that Brett wouldn't want to miss a second of this.

One deputy stayed at Cat's house, and the other called for police back-up. When the back-up deputies arrived, they left for Tara's house. Time seemed to move at a snail's pace as the girls waited for news of what the police would find there.

About an hour later, a plain-clothes detective came to the door. He spoke quietly to Mr. and Mrs. Daniels, then came inside.

Cat and Tara sat on the couch next to each other. They looked up expectantly as the detective stood in front of them. Brett squirmed in anticipation.

"Tara, your parents are coming for you," the policeman began. "My name is Detective Lewis, and I'm from Homicide. I might as well be the one to tell you girls, because you'll hear about this on the news soon enough. There's a dead man at the Whitfield residence."

Cat and Tara gasped, and Brett yelled, "Wow!"

Detective Lewis went on, "Although I was called out to investigate, the coroner thinks the cause of death was a heart attack. Nothing is for certain, of course, until the autopsy."

"Who was he?" Cat asked. "Who's the dead man?"

"The dead man is identified as Donald Foster," answered Detective Lewis.

Cat's heart raced. Could Donald Foster be somehow related to Henry Foster?

The policeman told them, "We picked up another man who was waiting in a car outside of the Whitfield residence."

"Who is the other man?" Tara asked.

"His name is Robert Gatland," the policeman answered.

"Mr. Gatland!" Cat shrieked.

"Do you know him?" The policeman appeared very interested.

"No, not really," Cat said. "But we met him at Creekside Cemetery yesterday."

"What!" Mr. Daniels cried. "What on earth were you doing at a cemetery yesterday?"

"Can't we talk about that later?" Cat begged her dad. Then she turned back to Detective Lewis. "Why would Mr. Gatland be hanging around Donald Foster?"

"Mr. Gatland is, or should I say was, Mister Foster's cousin," the detective answered. "Mr. Gatland has confessed to some very interesting things. It seems Donald Foster was after a ledger book that exposes some criminal activities that happened back in the 1930s, if you can believe that."

Cat asked, "Why would a ledger from the 1930s be important to anybody now?"

"It seems that Mr. Gatland has answered that question," Detective Lewis said. "A lot of money was made illegally by the Foster Accounting Firm, which was half-owned by Donald Foster's grandfather, whose name was Henry Foster."

"We know a lot about Henry Foster," Tara said. "We went to the library and looked up some old newspapers on the microfilm machine."

"What else?" Mr. Daniels asked. "What else are you girls going to surprise me with tonight?"

"Dad, please—can't we talk about this later?"

"Maybe you could come down to the police station tomorrow and share some of the things you girls have learned about Henry Foster," Detective Lewis suggested. "Any facts you could give us would be a lot of help, and you'd save us time."

The detective went on, "In the meantime, I'll tell you this: back in the 1930s, a man named James Foster knew that his brother Henry was breaking the law. Mr. Gatland says that Henry Foster murdered

James Foster and his wife in order to keep them silent. Henry Foster vandalized his brother's house, looking for the ledger book on the night of the murder, but didn't find it."

Cat and Tara looked at each other. "We have it," they admitted.

"You do!" Mr. Daniels exclaimed. He had been standing, sometimes pacing the floor, but upon receiving this bit of news, he threw up his arms and sat down.

"The ledger is upstairs in my backpack," Cat told Detective Lewis.

"I hope you intend to turn it over as evidence."

"Sure, if it's okay with Father Guzman," she said. "It really belongs to him." Everyone looked at her in puzzlement, but she was too tired to explain.

"Can I see it?" Detective Lewis asked.

Cat went to her bedroom to retrieve the ledger book. When she returned, she handed it to Detective Lewis. He took it, opened it, and thumbed through it. "Ah," he commented, "here's a reference to bank account set up for James Foster's daughter. It's on page eight."

"The number eight," Cat murmured quietly.

"Anyway," continued Detective Lewis, "then Henry Foster managed to blame the murders on James Foster's daughter, whose name was Jessica. She ran away, with the help of her husband Mark Stratton."

"Mark Stratton—that's who I saw in my dreams," Cat said. "And the ghost must have been Mark, too."

"What?" Detective Lewis asked.

"Never mind," she said. "Go on with what you were saying."

"At the time of his death, James Foster had property, jewels, and art that should have been inherited by Jessica. And there was Jessica's bank account, which appeared legitimate. But Henry Foster managed to successfully blame the murders on Jessica. So she no longer qualified under the law to inherit. That meant Henry got it all, because other than Jessica, he was the only living relative of the Fosters. That is, until Jessica's baby was born."

"The baby!" Tara cried. "Who was the baby?"

"Well," said the policeman, "we're still tracking it down. But police reports state there has been a claim made on the Foster inheritance, a claim made by someone who says she is Jessica

Foster's granddaughter. That claim was made a few weeks ago in the county courthouse by a woman named Helen Harris."

"Helen Harris!" Brett suddenly yelled from the corner where he had been standing and listening. "That's Travis' and Randy's mom."

"What!" Cat cried.

"Yes, it is!" Brett shouted. He turned to the detective. "Doesn't Helen Harris live on Claybourne Street?"

"I believe so."

Cat remembered running into Randy at the school library. He had been looking up his family history on the Internet. He had said it was to help his mother research her family tree.

So there it was: Helen Harris was Jessica's granddaughter. That made Randy Jessica's great-grandson. Now she knew what Randy had been looking for. Randy had been looking for information about Jessica Foster, just as she herself had been doing. Had it really been only a week ago? So much had happened lately that October had seemed to last a year, not just thirty-one days as the calendar said.

"Detective Lewis," Tara asked, "How did Mr. Gatland and Mr. Foster know where I live?"

He looked at her silently for a moment. Then he reached into his pocket, and produced another little brown book. "I believe this belongs to you."

"My address book," Tara said. "So Mr. Gatland *did* steal it from my backpack yesterday."

Cat interrupted. "I still don't understand why the Foster Accounting Firm ledger book is so important today, over eighty-five years later. Why did Donald Foster and Robert Gatland want it so badly that they would break into Tara's house for it?"

"Because the money that was stolen was invested," Detective Lewis told them. "Over the years, it grew to be quite a lot of money. Donald Foster and Robert Gatland were living off that money. Living well, in fact. If it could be proved that the money was made illegally, then the money would become tied up in a court of law, and probably taken away from Foster and Gatland. But the money listed on page eight in the ledger is legitimate. That's the money invested for Jessica, and it's still good, no matter what."

Cat wanted to know one more thing. "What happened to Jessica Foster? Where is she?"

Detective Lewis grimaced. "Well, as far as we know from Robert Gatland, Mark Stratton was killed in December of 1935, and buried in Creekside Cemetery. Helen Harris says that Jessica's baby, Rebecca Stratton, was born in January of 1936, and given up for adoption. I guess Jessica was trying to protect her baby, because she knew that Henry Foster was still hunting her down, and Jessica figured she could only run so long."

He stopped and asked for a glass of water. Mr. Daniels retrieved a glass from the kitchen, and Mrs. Daniels poured him lemonade instead.

"Anyway," he went on, "Henry Foster caught up with Jessica, all right—just a few weeks later. Henry Foster found Jessica Foster and killed her. Robert Gatland told us that her body is buried in Creekside Cemetery, on top of that of Mark Stratton."

"What!" Cat and Tara cried in unison.

"Who would look there?" Detective Lewis said. "Everyone knew that Mark's body was buried there. Who would look for Jessica in Mark's grave? And—a freshly dug grave looks freshly dug for at least a month or two. Who would know that the grave had been opened up and then closed again in the middle of the night? What better place to hide a body then on top of another body in a new grave?"

Chapter Twelve

It was the Saturday after Halloween, on November seventh. Mr. and Mrs. Daniels sat in the front seat of their Toyota, and Cat and Brett rode in the back. They were on their way to a place that Cat thought, just a week ago, she would never see again.

The Daniels family was driving to Creekside Cemetery.

When they turned into Road 18, the family noticed that other cars were already there, parked in front of the old, cast-iron arbor that led to the cemetery. Mr. Daniels parked on the shoulder of the road behind a line of cars.

"Are you sure you're up to this?" her father asked.

"Yes," she answered. "I think I need to see the whole thing through, and this is the end, so I want to be here."

They got out of the car, and walked toward the group of people who were standing behind the Foster family plot. One of the group left the gravesite and approached to meet the Daniels family halfway. It was Randy Harris.

Randy said hello to Brett, then to Mr. and Mrs. Daniels, and hugged Cat. "I'm glad you could come for this."

Cat repeated what she had said to her father, "I want to see it through. This is the end, so I want to be here."

"Come on then," Randy said, "I'd like you to meet my mother and my brother." He led her to the plot behind the Foster gravesite, where the group of people were standing.

Randy introduced her and her parents to a woman sitting in a wheelchair. "This is my mother, Helen Harris."

Mrs. Harris shook hands with Cat's family, but when she turned to Cat, a surprised expression crossed her face. She studied Cat closely, then smiled, and shook her hand also.

"Thanks to your bravery," Mrs. Harris told Cat, "the Jessica Foster inheritance is going to come through for my family. Disabled people can do almost everything that other people can, and my dream was to work with animals. I was attending vocational school to become a veterinary assistant, because I didn't have the money for college where I could get a degree in veterinary medicine. But now that I have the money for college, I can become a real veterinarian. And there will be college money for Randy and Travis, too. Plus—I want to give you and Tara Whitfield a reward."

Her smile grew larger. "More importantly, now Jessica Foster has been proven innocent. She and Mark Stratton can rest in peace together—finally, after all these years."

Detective Lewis stood respectfully, as Father Guzman said prayers and read a service over the shared grave of Mark and Jessica. Cat read the inscription on the new headstone: *Mark Stratton and Jessica Foster Stratton, together in eternal peace.*

Cat knew the haunting would stop now. In her heart, she felt sure of it.

The service ended, and she turned to leave with her parents. But Helen Harris called her back. Cat told her family that she'd meet them at the car, then walked to where Mrs. Harris waited for her.

Everyone else began walking to the row of cars on Road 18 except for Mrs. Harris and Cat. Soon Cat was alone at the gravesite with Randy's mom.

"You wanted to speak to me?"

"Yes. Cat, I need to tell you that you have a very special gift. I can see an aura about you."

"What do you mean?"

"You have a gift of second sight. You have a sense of another dimension. I'm saying that you are 'sensitive' to communication attempts from the afterlife."

"Please go on," Cat said slowly. She thought she had an idea of where Helen Harris was going with this.

"I think you have the ability to 'tune in' to spiritual presences. I can tell by your aura."

"You're saying that I can see ghosts."

"Sometimes you can," Mrs. Harris said. "I was born with the aura, too. All my life I would get feelings, like I could know some things before they happened. And once I communicated with what you would call a ghost."

Mrs. Harris sighed, then continued, "For a while I even worked in a carnival, but I decided that was not using my gift for what it was intended, so I quit. Now I live in quiet harmony with my aura, but I am always watching others. Anyway, I have only seen the aura in one or two other people beside myself during my entire lifetime. There are not many people in this world that have the aura. But you, Cat, are indeed one of them."

Cat was quiet for a moment. Then she asked, "What should I do?"

"Just continue with your life," Mrs. Harris said. "Be a normal teenager. But you have already let your gift help two unfortunate souls. If another need ever arises, you will know what to do, and you will be ready."

She stood quietly besides Mrs. Harris, who sat in her wheelchair and looked thoughtful. They stayed in front of the Stratton gravesite for another moment, staring at the new headstone in silence.

Then they both turned away. Mrs. Harris rolled her mechanized wheelchair towards Road 18, and Cat walked beside her.

Cat wanted to join the others, waiting at their cars. She wanted to join the living, outside of Creekside Cemetery.

.

MORE FROM
JEANI RECTOR

PESTILENCE
A MEDIEVAL TALE OF PLAGUE

JEANI RECTOR

PESTILENCE: A MEDIEVAL TALE OF PLAGUE

"A very well-researched book full of facts about that time, how people lived, and the disease itself, yet it tells the story at an exciting pace." – Larry Green, *Death Head Grin Magazine*

Today there are many end-of-the-world tales, but the bubonic plague pandemic in the 14th Century is the original apocalypse story.

**Not a short story collection. This is a full-length novel of historical fiction.
Available on in both Paperback and Kindle.**

JEANI RECTOR

ACCUSED

A TALE OF THE SALEM WITCH TRIALS

ACCUSED: A TALE OF THE SALEM WITCH TRIALS

"An exciting and unflinching trip into a dark period of American history. I was really there with Ruth, trying to make sense of it all as the madness builds." – Jeffrey L. Shipley, Editor of *Tales of Blood and Roses*

What if you lived in 1692 Salem, and were accused of witchcraft?

Not a short story collection. This is a full-length novel of historical fiction.
Available on Amazon in both paperback and Kindle.

The Horror Zine Books also offers

A Feast of Frights from The Horror Zine

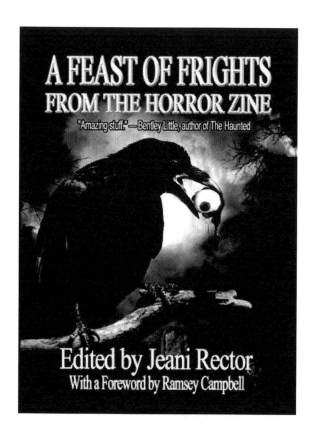

A FEAST OF FRIGHTS FROM THE HORROR ZINE

From the pages of The Horror Zine—the critically acclaimed online horror magazine—comes A FEAST OF FRIGHTS FROM THE HORROR ZINE. Featuring dark fantasy, mystery, pure suspense and classic horror, this book from The Horror Zine is relentless in its approach to basic fears and has twisted, unexpected endings. Come and find out what terrifying things can creep out of The Horror Zine to make your skin crawl.

A FEAST OF FRIGHTS FROM THE HORROR ZINE contains fiction from such renowned masters of the macabre as Simon Clark, Graham Masterton, Joe R. Lansdale, Scott Nicholson, Cheryl Kaye Tardif, Joe McKinney, Susie Moloney, Tom Piccirilli, Ed Gorman, Trevor Denyer, and Jeff Strand. This book has amazing articles from John Gilmore, Deborah LeBlanc, Earl Hamner, Kasey Lansdale and Tim Lebbon, and a Foreword from horror great Ramsey Campbell. Here you will also find other deliciously dark delights from morbidly creative people who have not yet made the big time…but will soon. Each tale and poem, every article and artful rendering is a dark delicacy of its own, making this a true Feast of Frights!

"I have seen the future of horror—and so has Jeani Rector. In fact, she's publishing it. The Horror Zine books are not only fantastic reads, but they provide a valuable public service, exposing the world to up-and-coming talent in fiction, poetry, and art. Amazing stuff."

— Bentley Little, author of *The Haunted*

ABOUT JEANI RECTOR

While most people go to Disneyland while in Southern California, Jeani Rector went to the Fangoria Weekend of Horror there instead. She grew up watching the Bob Wilkins Creature Feature on television and lived in a house that had the walls covered with framed Universal Monsters posters. It is all in good fun and actually, most people who know Jeani personally are of the opinion that she is a very normal person. She just writes abnormal stories. Doesn't everybody?

Jeani Rector is the founder and editor of The Horror Zine and has had her stories featured in magazines such as *Aphelion, Midnight Street, Strange Weird and Wonderful, Dark River Press, Macabre Cadaver, Blood Moon Rising, Hellfire Crossroads, Ax Wound, Horrormasters, Morbid Outlook, Horror in Words, Black Petals, 63Channels, Death Head Grin, Hackwriters, Bewildering Stories, Ultraverse*, and others.

Made in the USA
Lexington, KY
05 July 2019